nickelodeon

BIG NATE

DESTINED FOR AWESOMENESS

Inspired by the comics and
book series by Lincoln Peirce

Based on the episodes written by
Mitch Watson, Elliott Owen, and Sarah Allan

Andrews McMeel
PUBLISHING®

Andrews McMeel Publishing
a division of Andrews McMeel Universal
1130 Walnut Street, Kansas City, Missouri 64106

www.andrewsmcmeel.com

Book design, layout, and lettering by The Story Division
www.thestorydivision.com

Editor: Lucas Wetzel
Art Director and Cover Design: Spencer Williams
Designer: Niko Dalcin
Production Editor: Dave Shaw
Copy Editor: Amy Strassner
Production Manager: Chuck Harper

Special thanks to:
Jeff Whitman, Alexandra Maurer, and Jarrin Jacobs at Nickelodeon
Steffie Davis, Steve Osgoode, and Niko Dalcin at The Story Division
And special thanks to Lincoln Peirce for editorial guidance throughout this project.

22 23 24 25 26 SDB 10 9 8 7 6 5 4 3 2 1

ISBN (paperback): 978-1-5248-7560-2
ISBN (hardcover): 978-1-5248-7806-1

Library of Congress Control Number: 2022935046

Made by:
King Yip (Dongguan) Printing & Packaging Factory Ltd.
Address and location of production:
Daning Administrative District, Humen Town
Dongguan Guangdong, China 523930
1st Printing — 5/16/22

CONTENTS

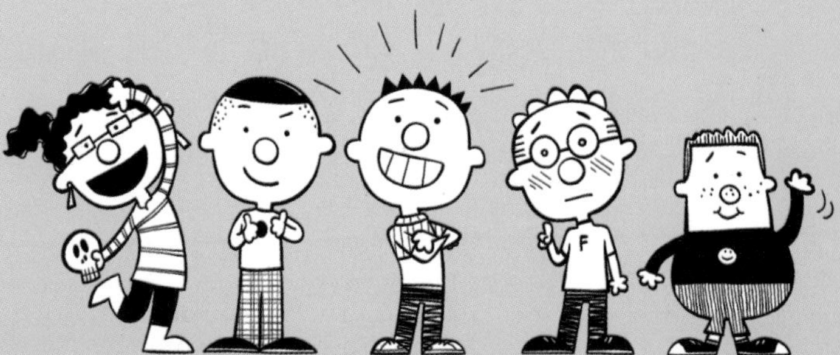
F

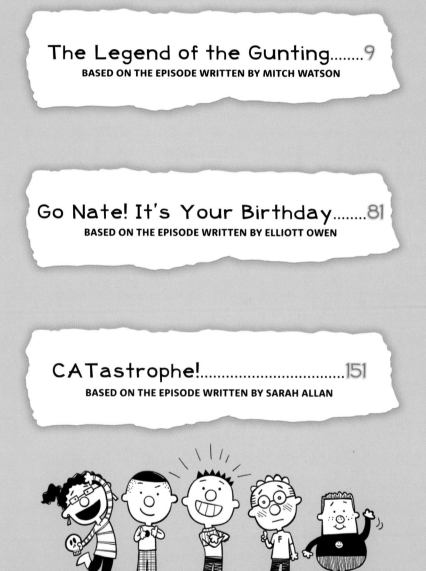

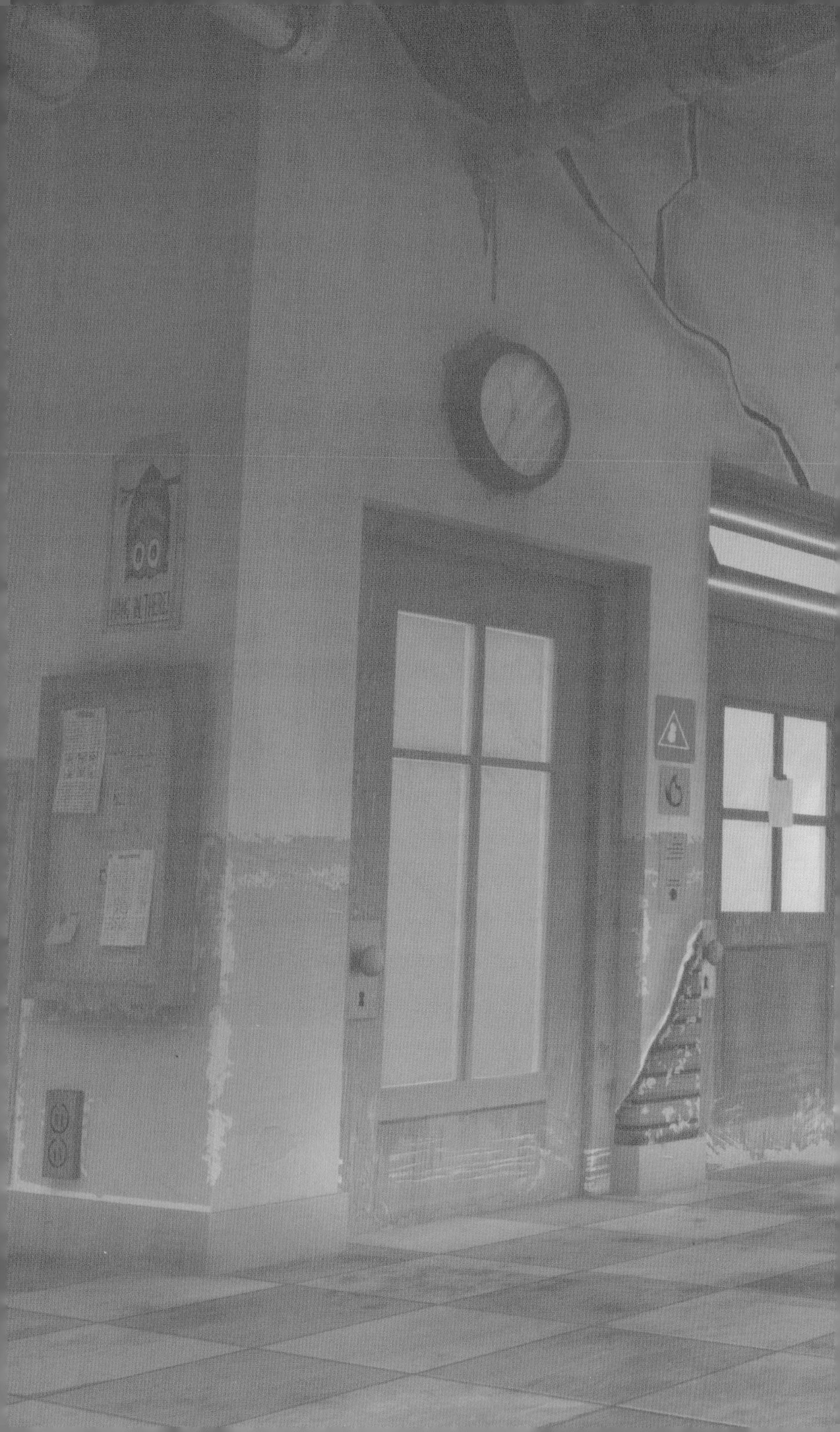

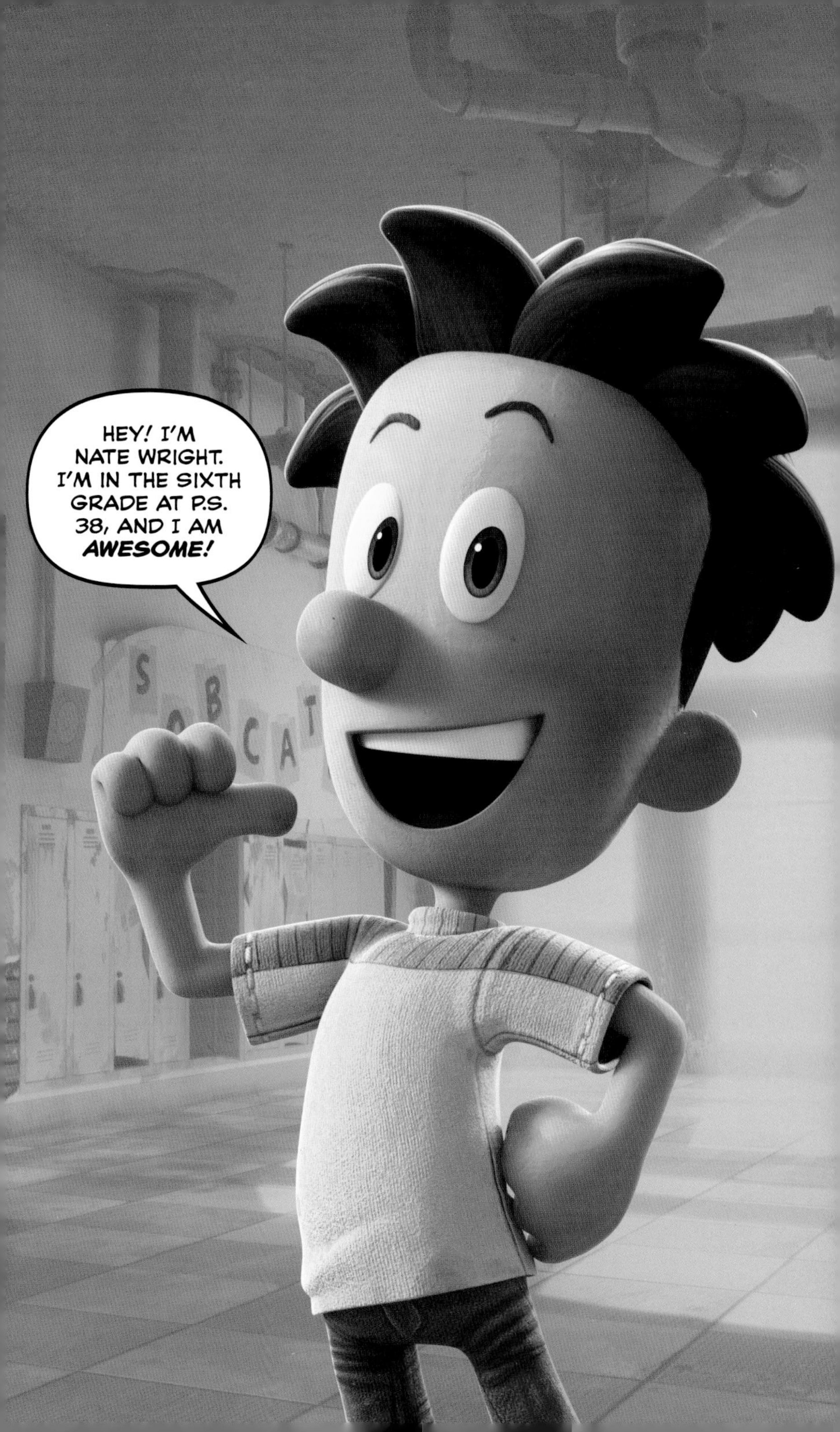
HEY! I'M NATE WRIGHT. I'M IN THE SIXTH GRADE AT P.S. 38, AND I AM ***AWESOME!***

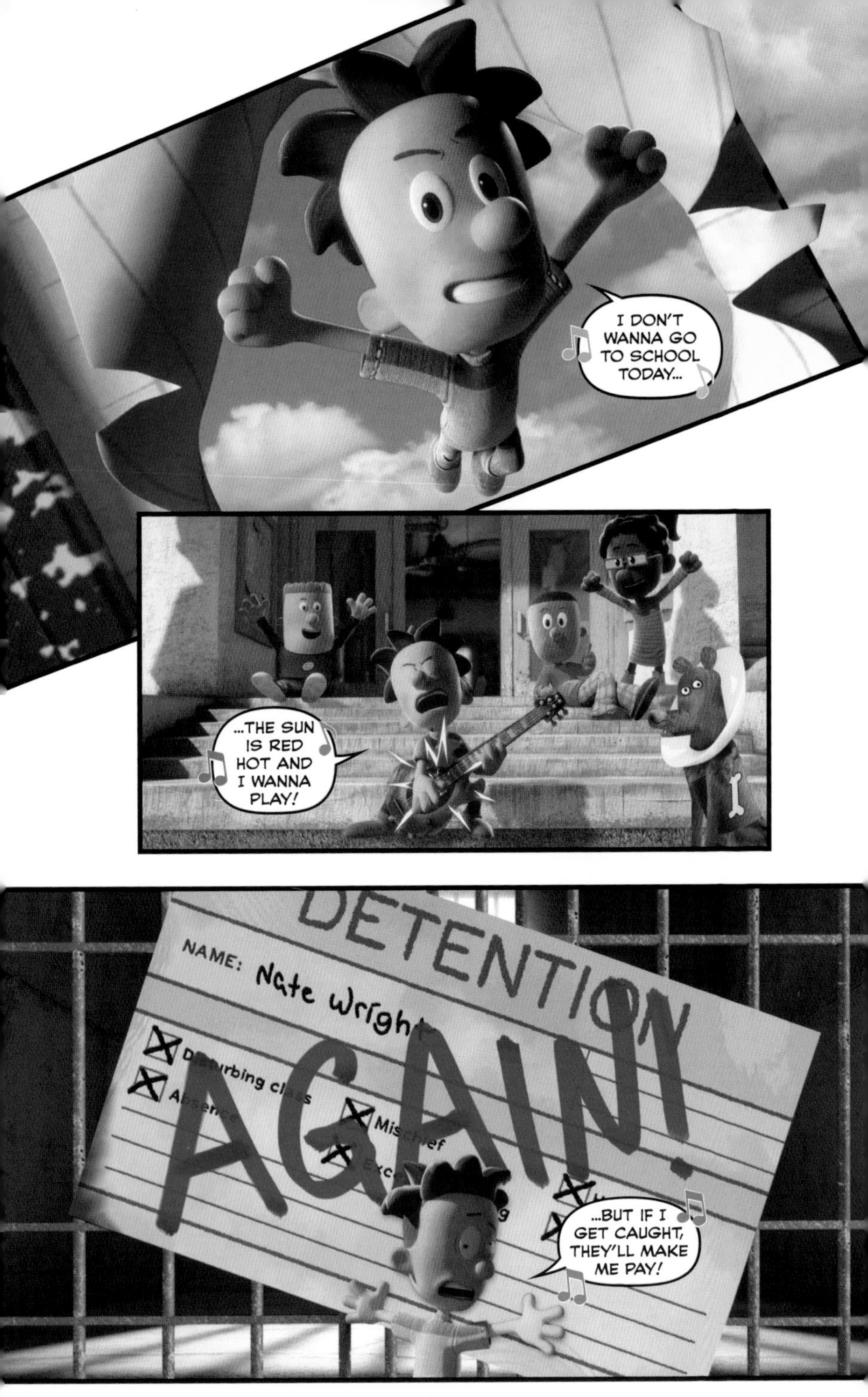
I DON'T WANNA GO TO SCHOOL TODAY...
...THE SUN IS RED HOT AND I WANNA PLAY!
DETENTION
NAME: Nate Wright
Mischief
AGAIN!
...BUT IF I GET CAUGHT, THEY'LL MAKE ME PAY!

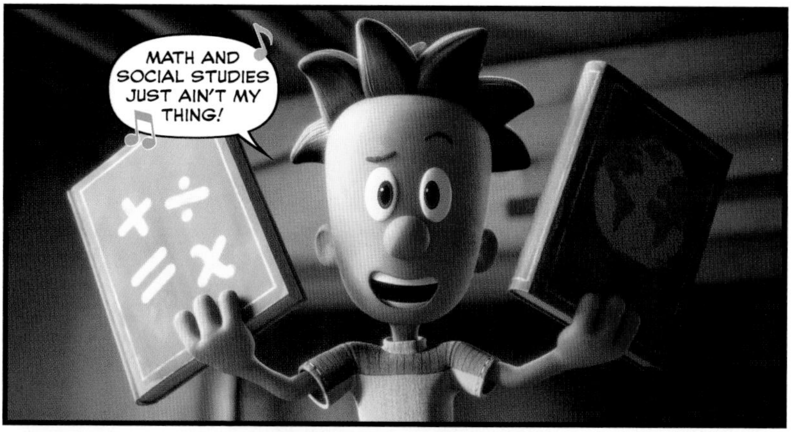
MATH AND SOCIAL STUDIES JUST AIN'T MY THING!

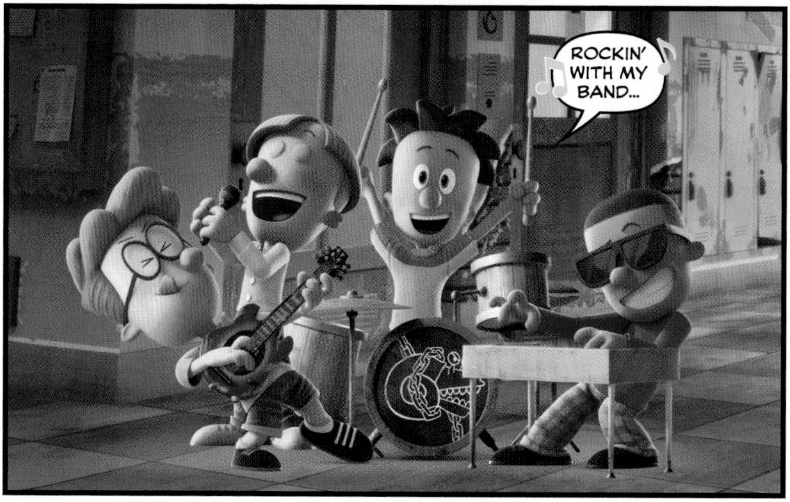
ROCKIN' WITH MY BAND...

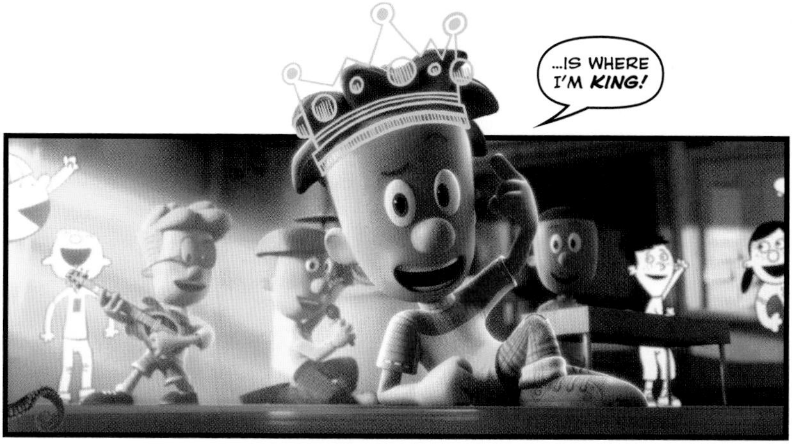
...IS WHERE I'M ***KING!***

TROUBLE IS ALWAYS FUN WHEN I'M AROUND... JUST ASK MY FRIENDS!

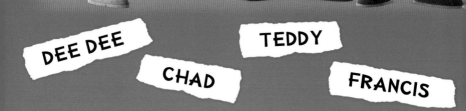

DEE DEE

CHAD

TEDDY

FRANCIS

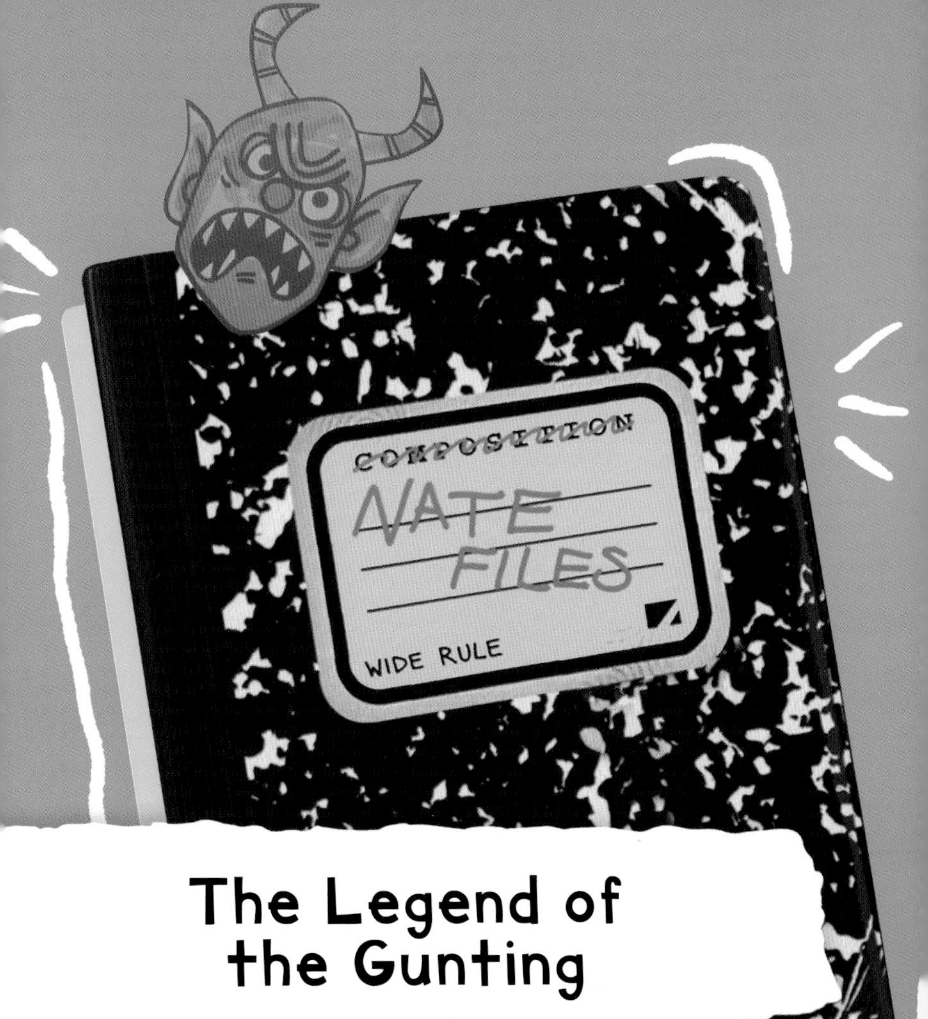
COMPOSITION
NATE
FILES
WIDE RULE

The Legend of the Gunting

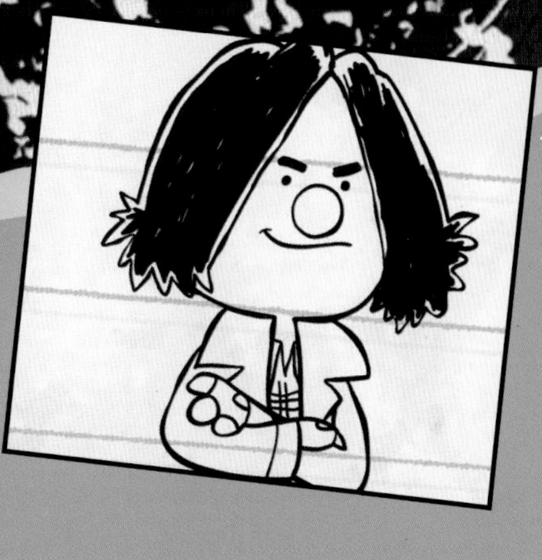

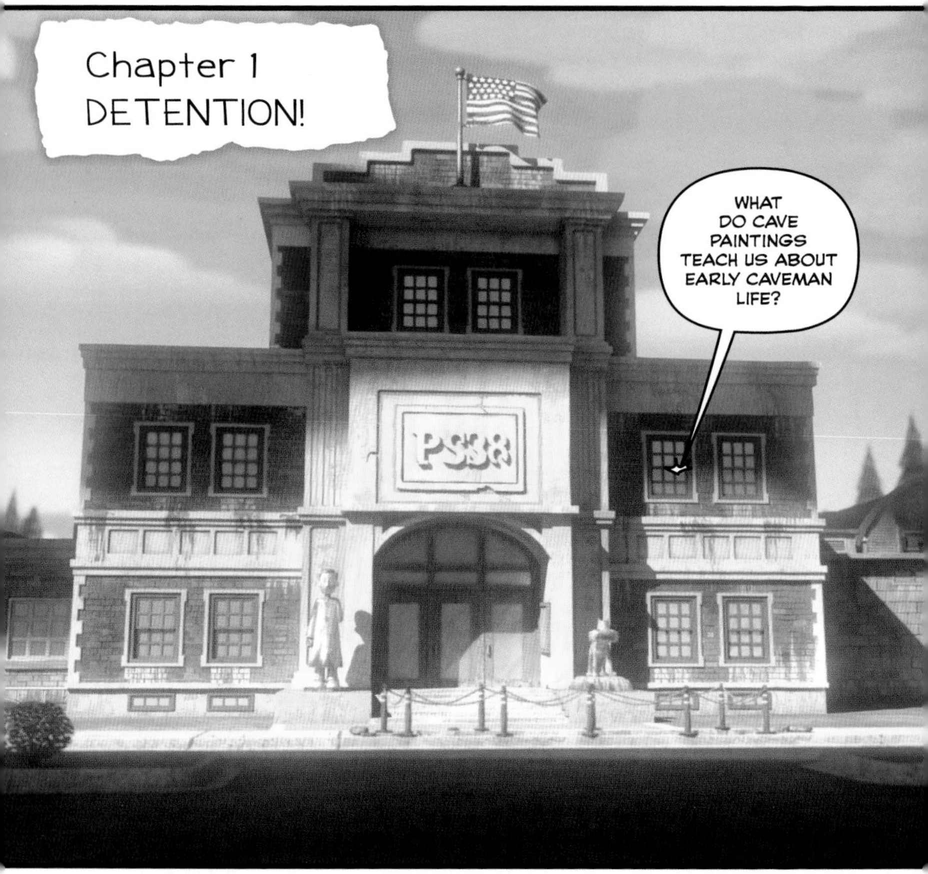
Chapter 1
DETENTION!
PS38
WHAT DO CAVE PAINTINGS TEACH US ABOUT EARLY CAVEMAN LIFE?

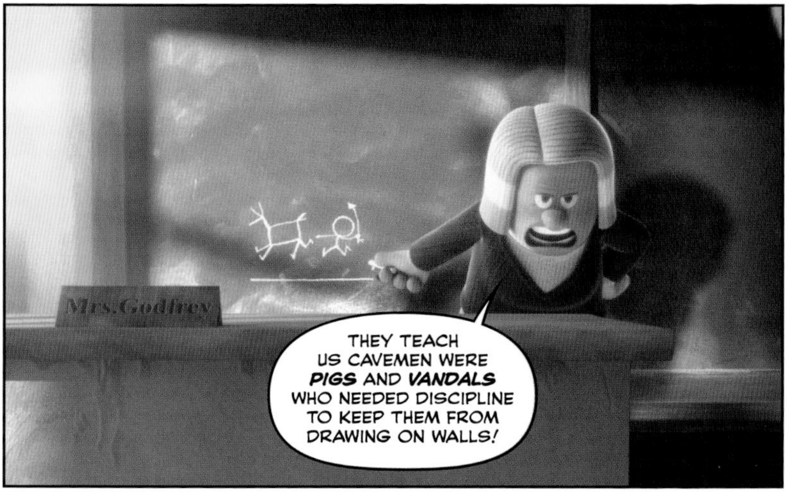
Mrs.Godfrey
THEY TEACH US CAVEMEN WERE ***PIGS*** AND ***VANDALS*** WHO NEEDED DISCIPLINE TO KEEP THEM FROM DRAWING ON WALLS!

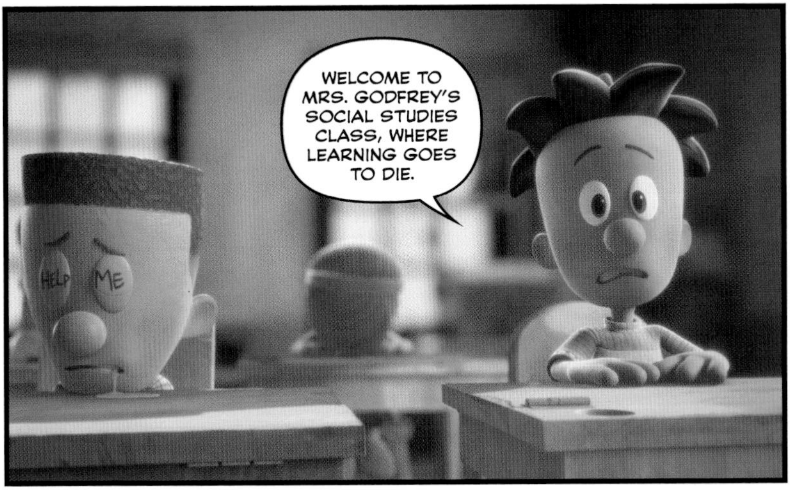
WELCOME TO MRS. GODFREY'S SOCIAL STUDIES CLASS, WHERE LEARNING GOES TO DIE.
HELP ME

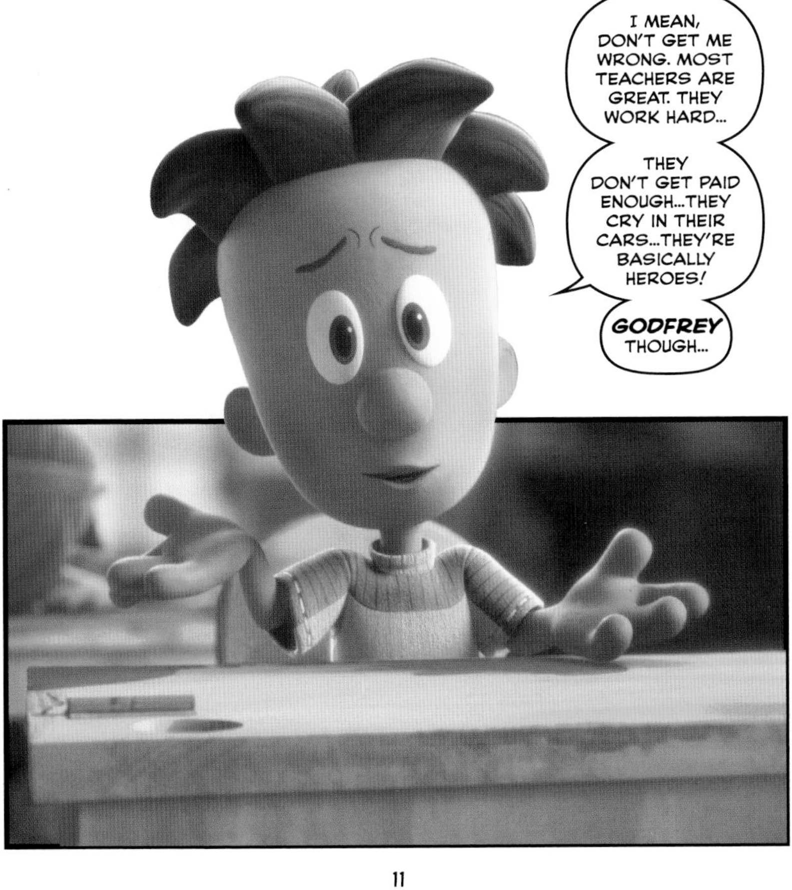
I MEAN, DON'T GET ME WRONG. MOST TEACHERS ARE GREAT. THEY WORK HARD...
THEY DON'T GET PAID ENOUGH...THEY CRY IN THEIR CARS...THEY'RE BASICALLY HEROES!
GODFREY THOUGH...

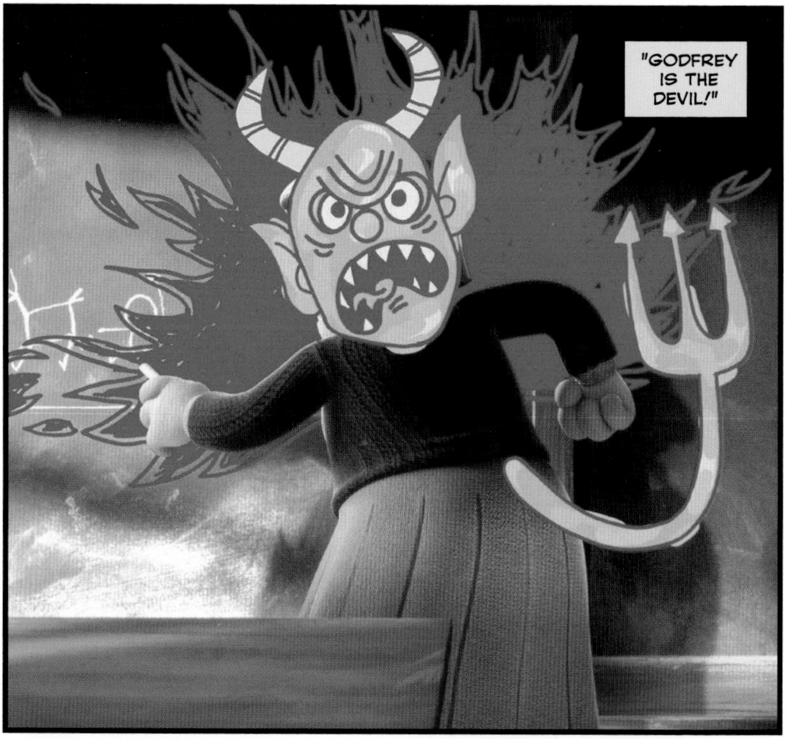
"GODFREY IS THE DEVIL!"

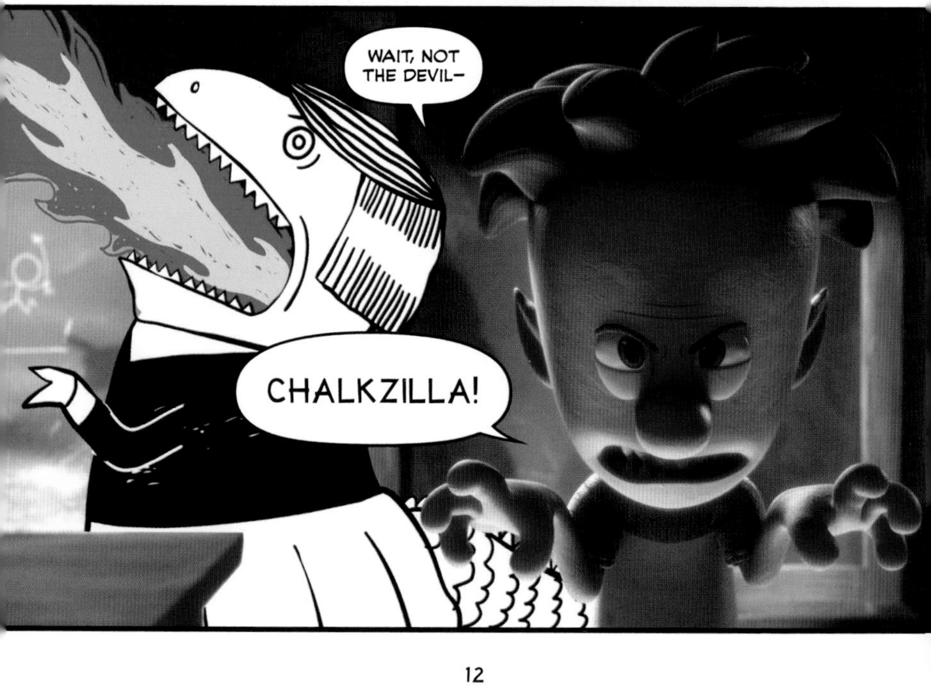
WAIT, NOT THE DEVIL–
CHALKZILLA!

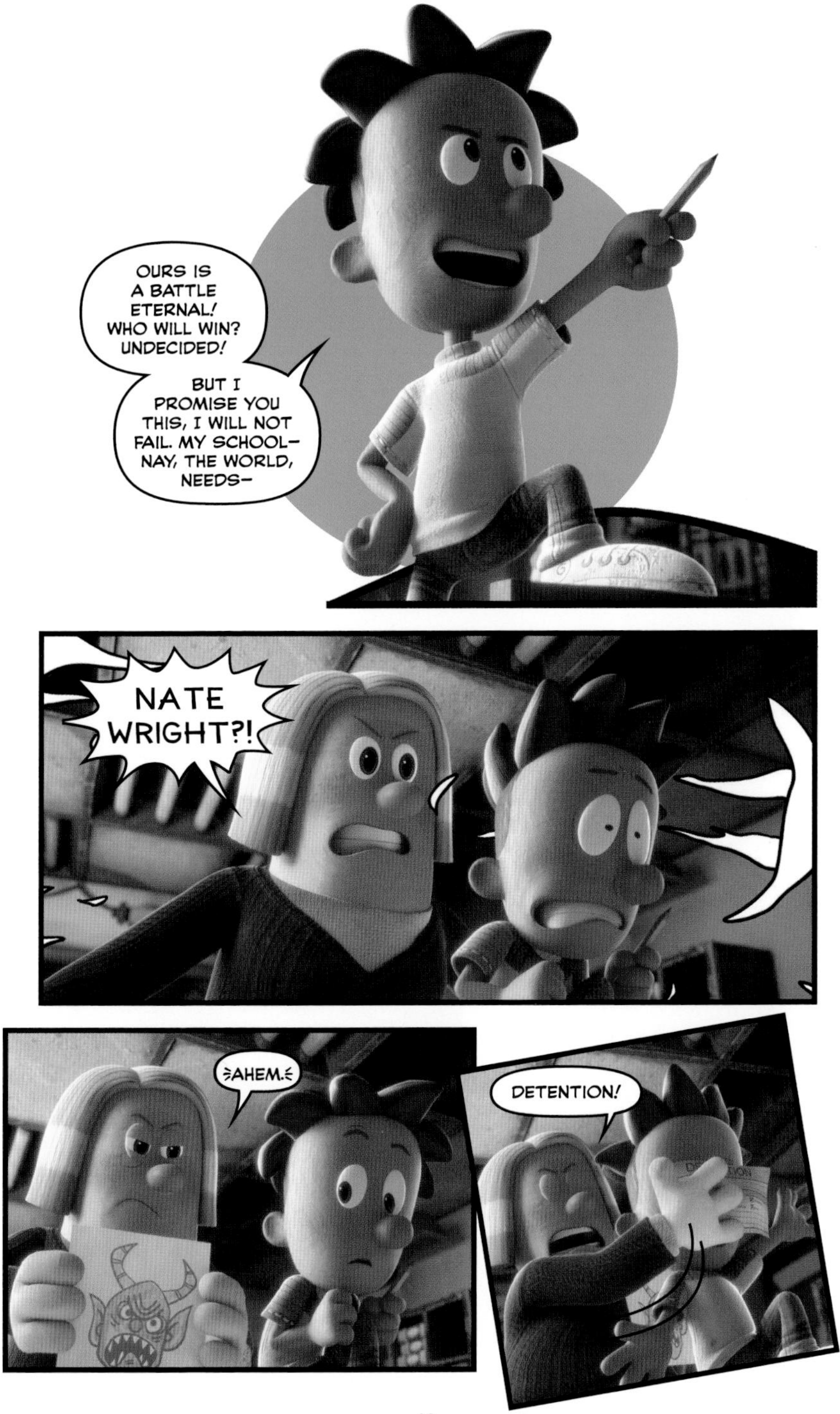
OURS IS A BATTLE ETERNAL! WHO WILL WIN? UNDECIDED!
BUT I PROMISE YOU THIS, I WILL NOT FAIL. MY SCHOOL-NAY, THE WORLD, NEEDS-
NATE WRIGHT?!
AHEM.
DETENTION!

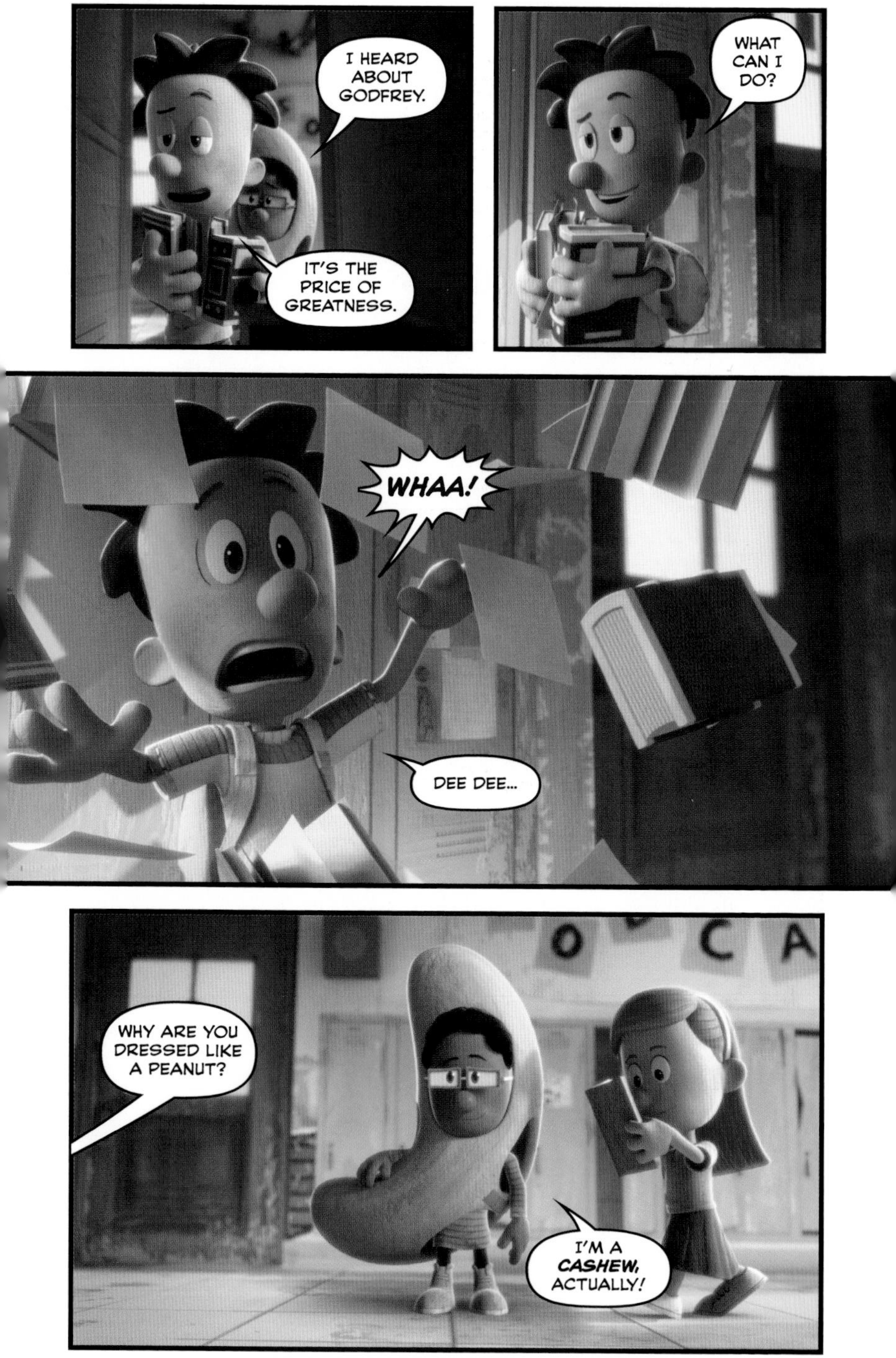
I HEARD ABOUT GODFREY.
IT'S THE PRICE OF GREATNESS.
WHAT CAN I DO?
WHAA!
DEE DEE...
WHY ARE YOU DRESSED LIKE A PEANUT?
I'M A *CASHEW,* ACTUALLY!

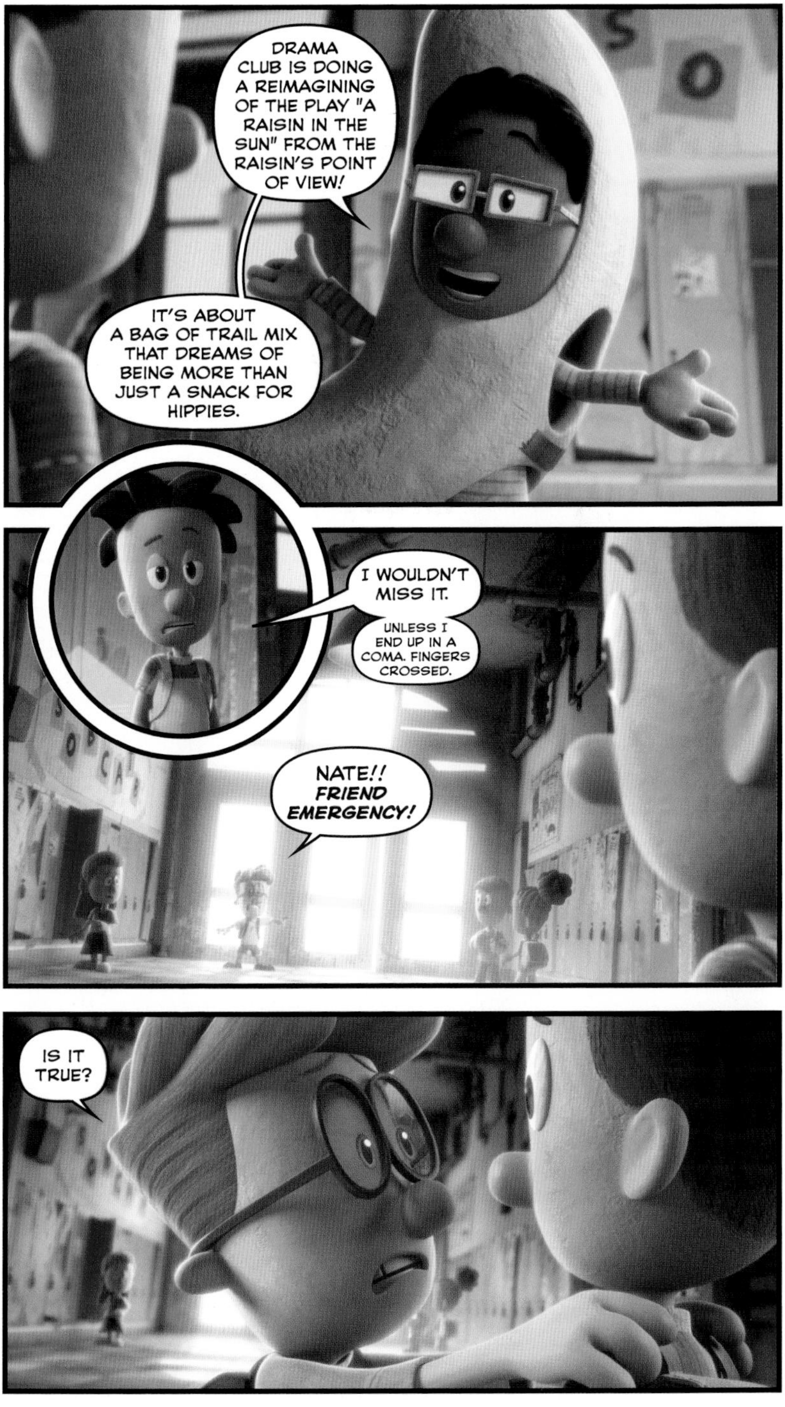
DRAMA CLUB IS DOING A REIMAGINING OF THE PLAY "A RAISIN IN THE SUN" FROM THE RAISIN'S POINT OF VIEW!
IT'S ABOUT A BAG OF TRAIL MIX THAT DREAMS OF BEING MORE THAN JUST A SNACK FOR HIPPIES.
I WOULDN'T MISS IT.
UNLESS I END UP IN A COMA. FINGERS CROSSED.
NATE!! ***FRIEND EMERGENCY!***
IS IT TRUE?

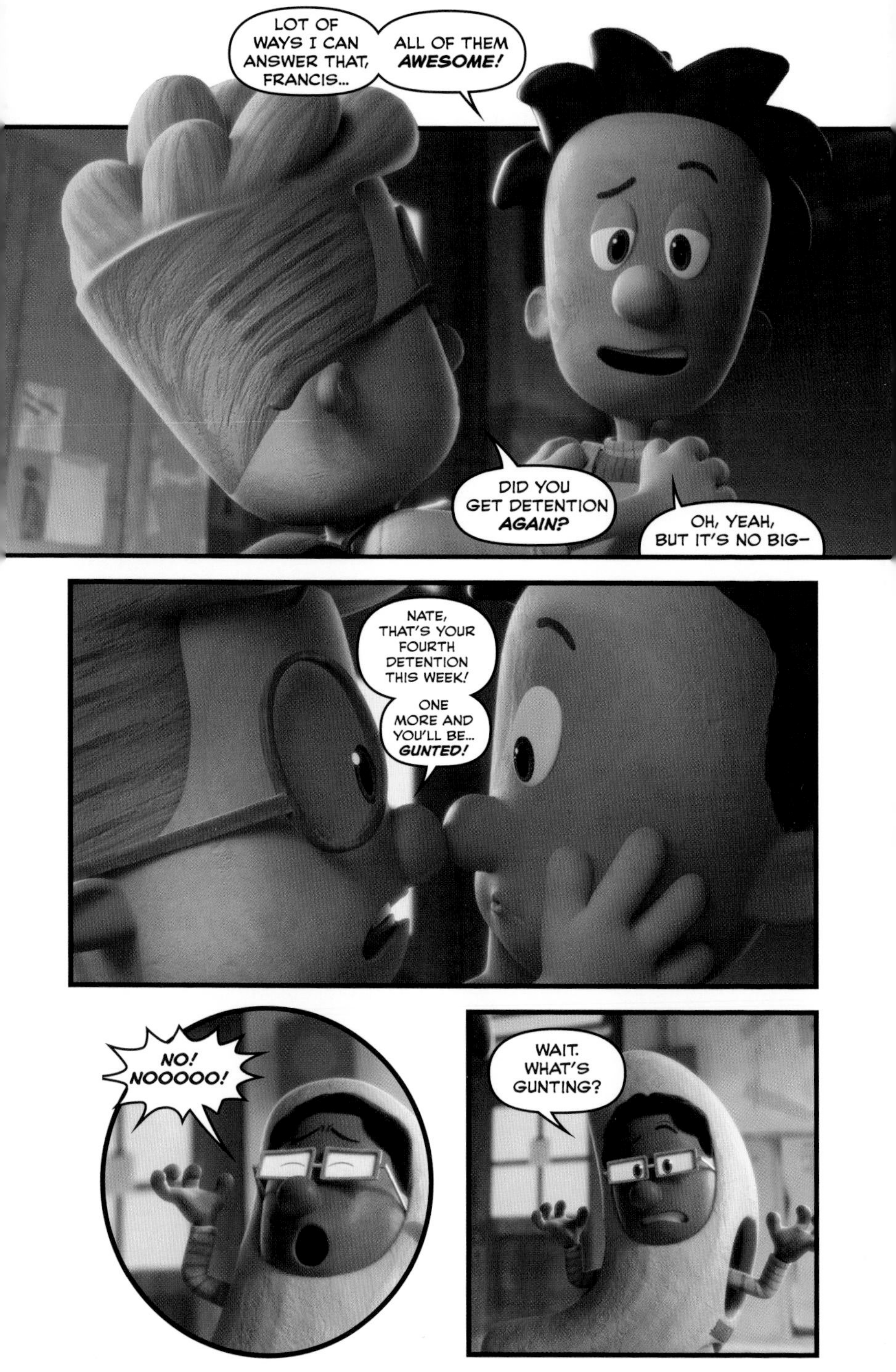
LOT OF WAYS I CAN ANSWER THAT, FRANCIS...
ALL OF THEM *AWESOME!*
DID YOU GET DETENTION *AGAIN?*
OH, YEAH, BUT IT'S NO BIG–
NATE, THAT'S YOUR FOURTH DETENTION THIS WEEK!
ONE MORE AND YOU'LL BE... *GUNTED!*
NO! NOOOOO!
WAIT. WHAT'S GUNTING?

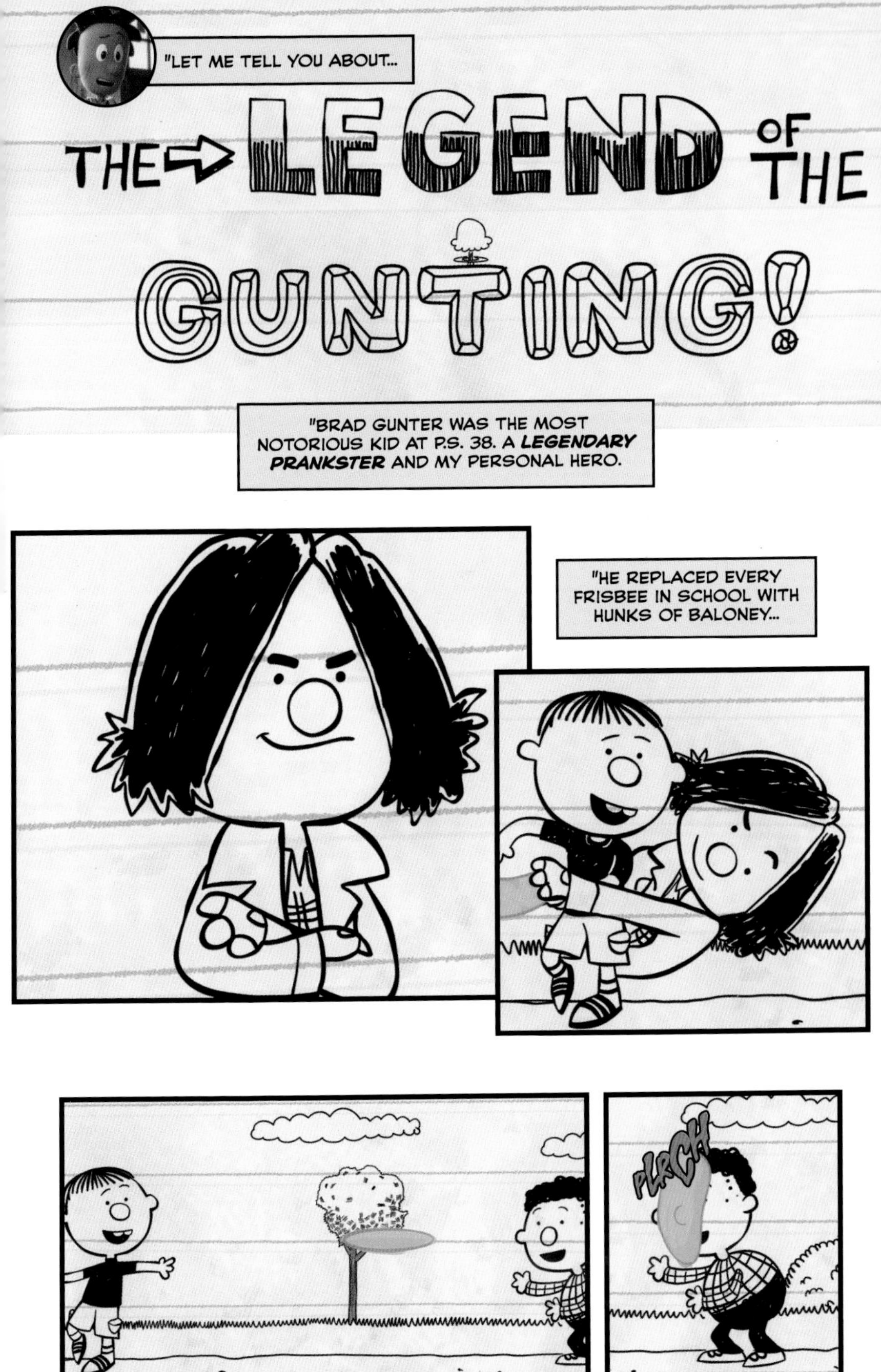
"LET ME TELL YOU ABOUT...
THE LEGEND OF THE GUNTING!
"BRAD GUNTER WAS THE MOST NOTORIOUS KID AT P.S. 38. A *LEGENDARY PRANKSTER* AND MY PERSONAL HERO.
"HE REPLACED EVERY FRISBEE IN SCHOOL WITH HUNKS OF BALONEY...
PLRCH

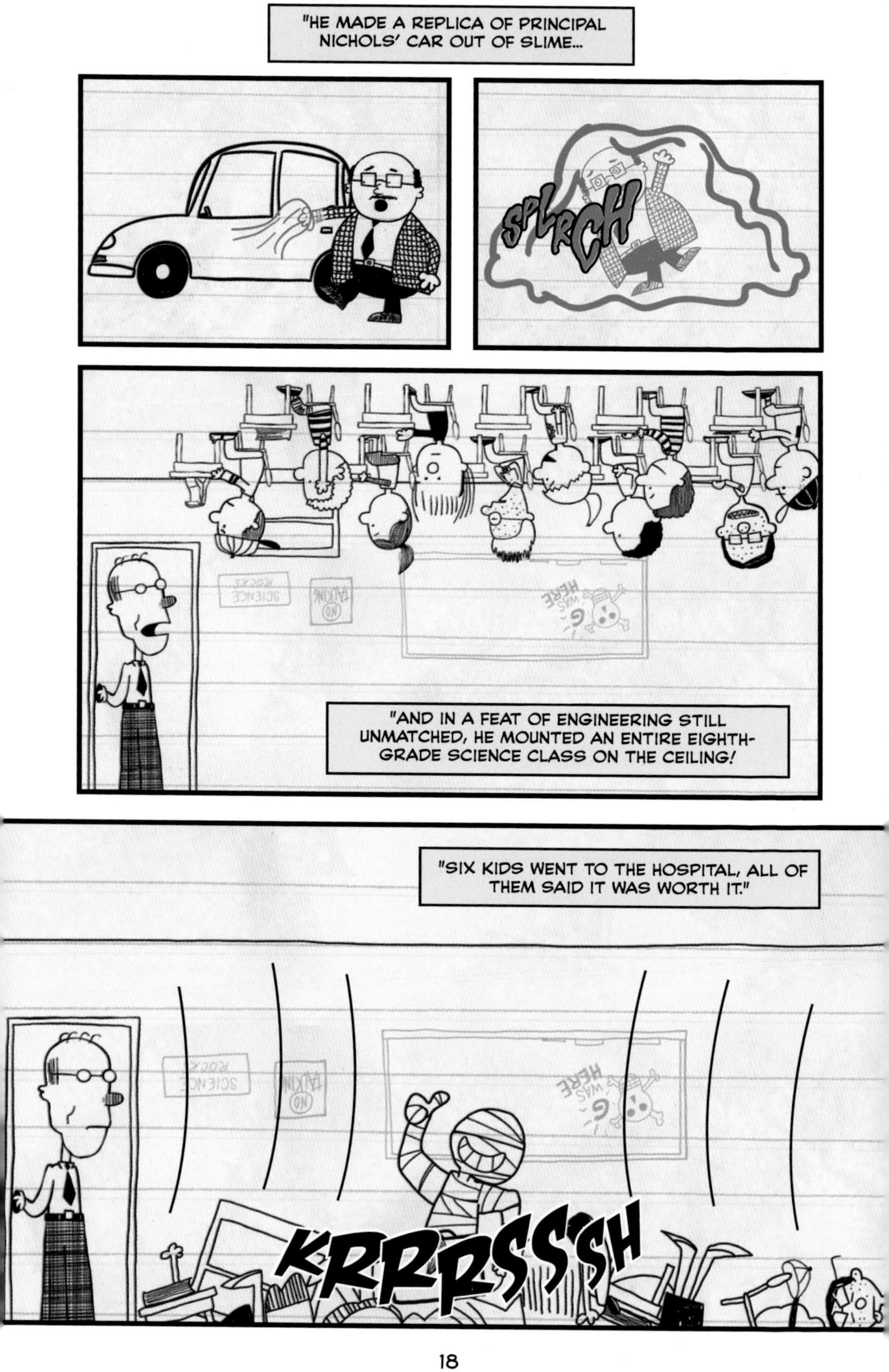
"HE MADE A REPLICA OF PRINCIPAL NICHOLS' CAR OUT OF SLIME...
SPLRCH
"AND IN A FEAT OF ENGINEERING STILL UNMATCHED, HE MOUNTED AN ENTIRE EIGHTH-GRADE SCIENCE CLASS ON THE CEILING!
"SIX KIDS WENT TO THE HOSPITAL, ALL OF THEM SAID IT WAS WORTH IT."
KRRRSSSH

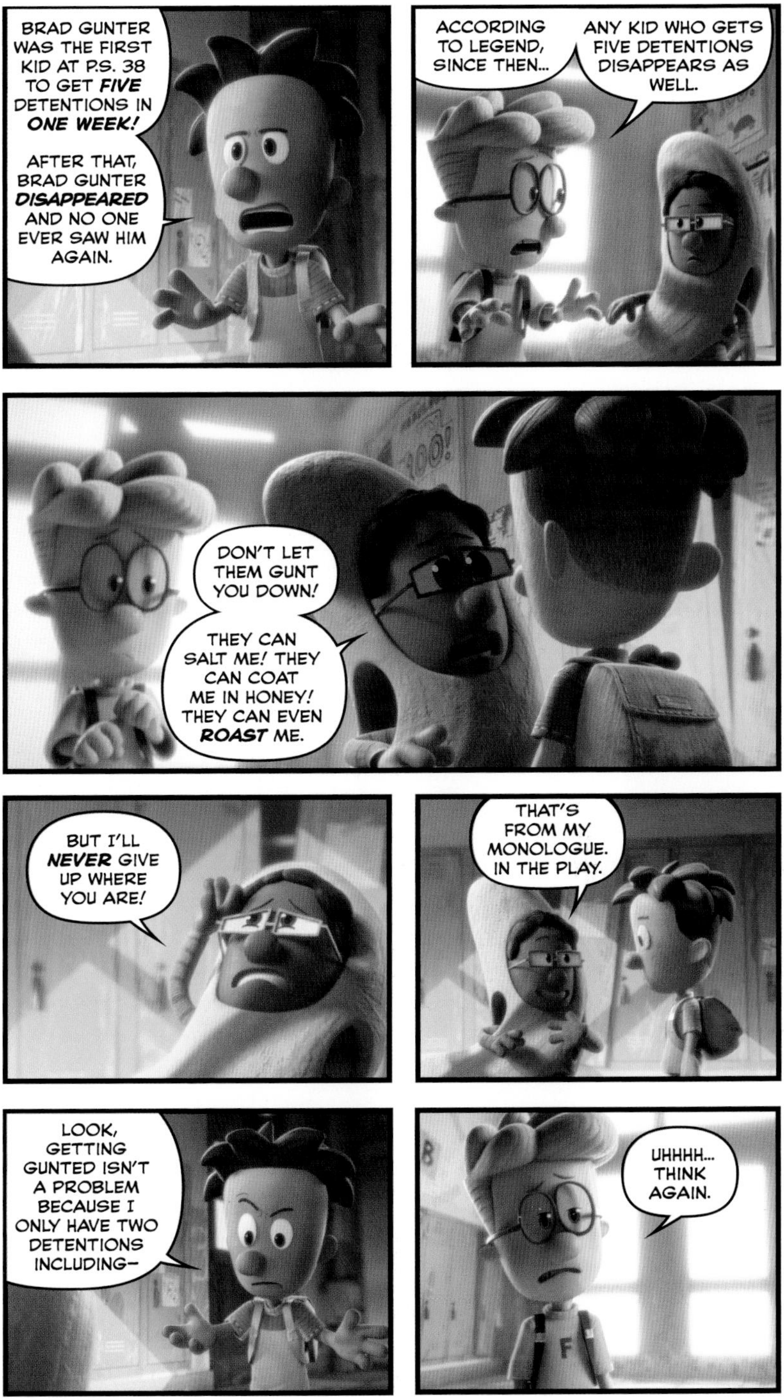
BRAD GUNTER WAS THE FIRST KID AT P.S. 38 TO GET ***FIVE*** DETENTIONS IN ***ONE WEEK!***
AFTER THAT, BRAD GUNTER ***DISAPPEARED*** AND NO ONE EVER SAW HIM AGAIN.
ACCORDING TO LEGEND, SINCE THEN...
ANY KID WHO GETS FIVE DETENTIONS DISAPPEARS AS WELL.
DON'T LET THEM GUNT YOU DOWN!
THEY CAN SALT ME! THEY CAN COAT ME IN HONEY! THEY CAN EVEN ***ROAST*** ME.
BUT I'LL ***NEVER*** GIVE UP WHERE YOU ARE!
THAT'S FROM MY MONOLOGUE. IN THE PLAY.
LOOK, GETTING GUNTED ISN'T A PROBLEM BECAUSE I ONLY HAVE TWO DETENTIONS INCLUDING—
UHHHH... THINK AGAIN.

DETENTION 1

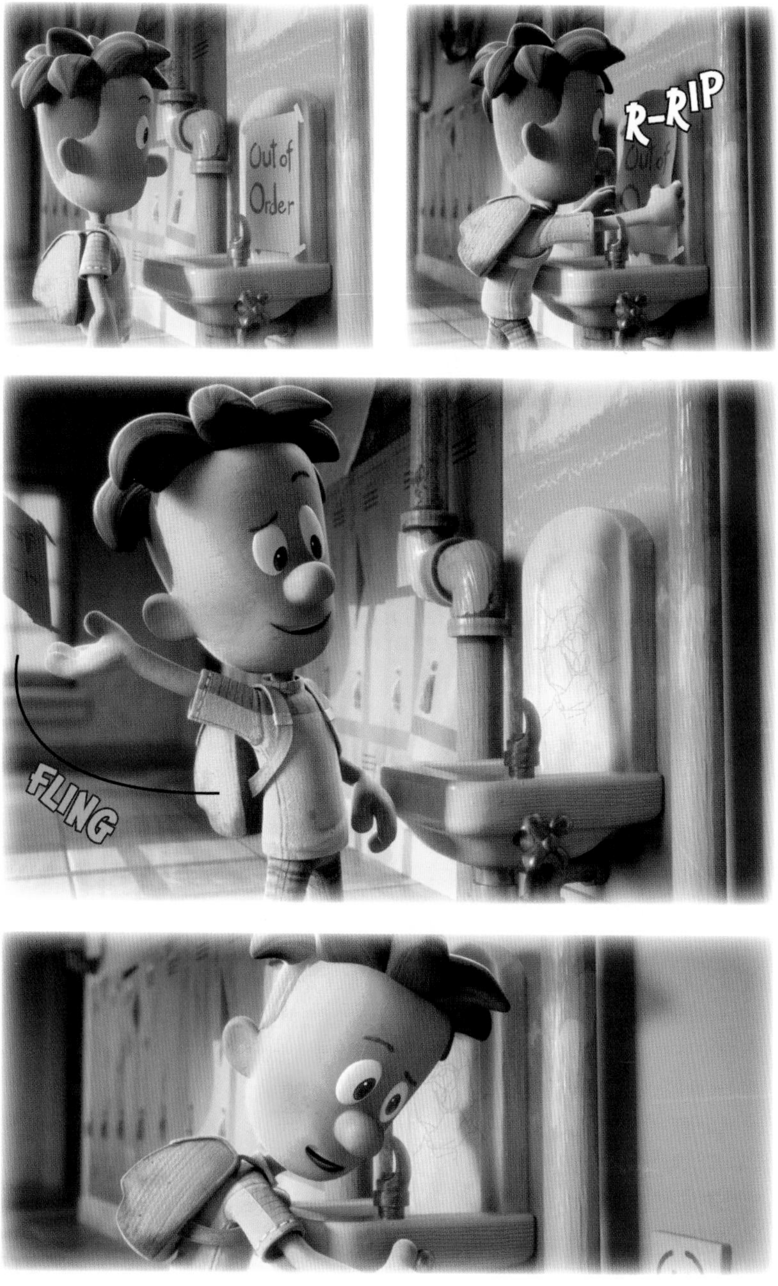
Out of Order
R-RIP
FLING

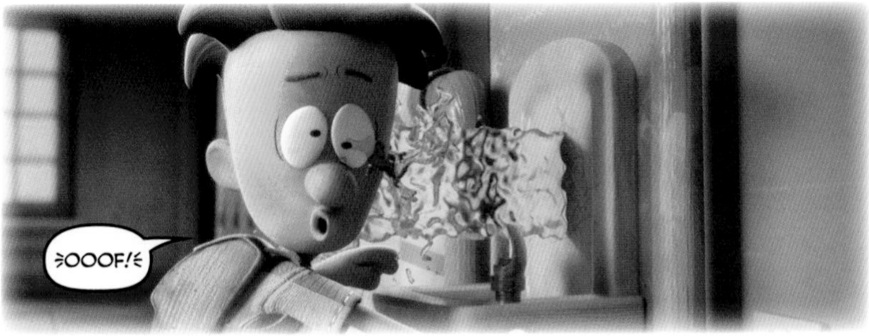
OOOF!

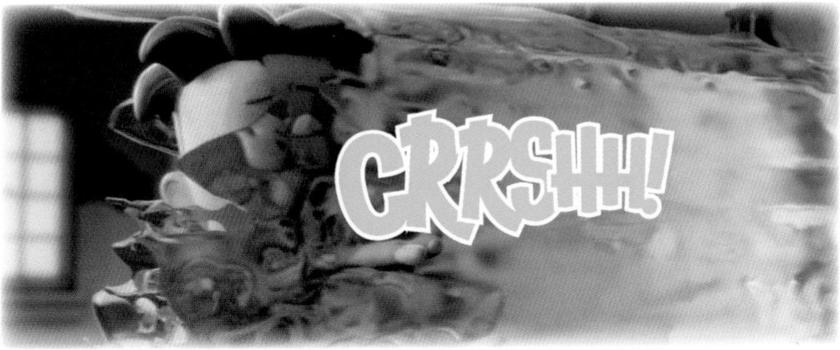
CRRSHH!

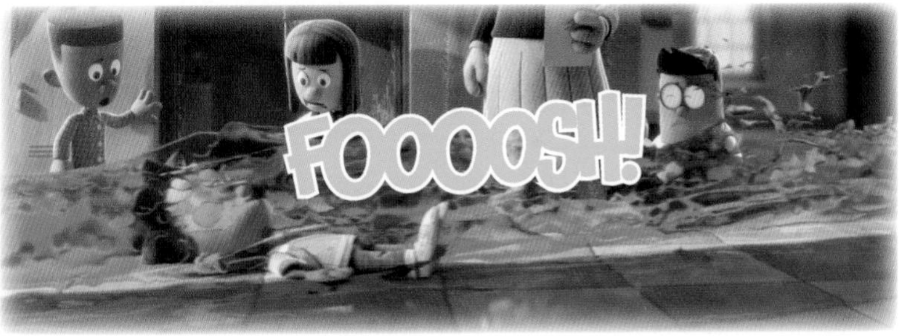
FOOOOSH!

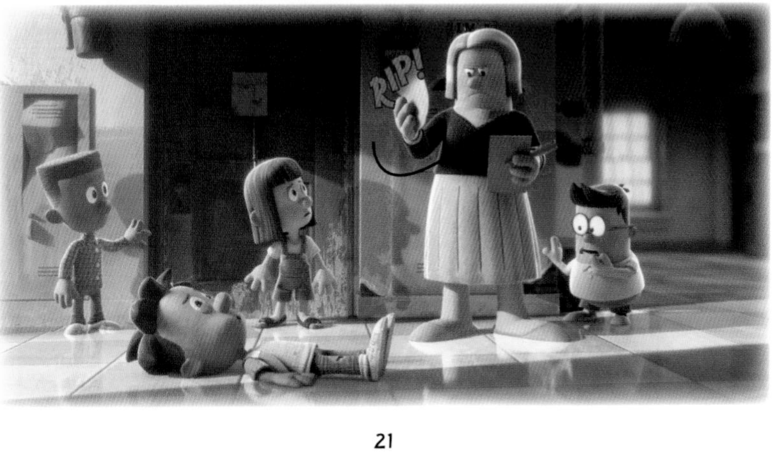
RIP!

DETENTION 2

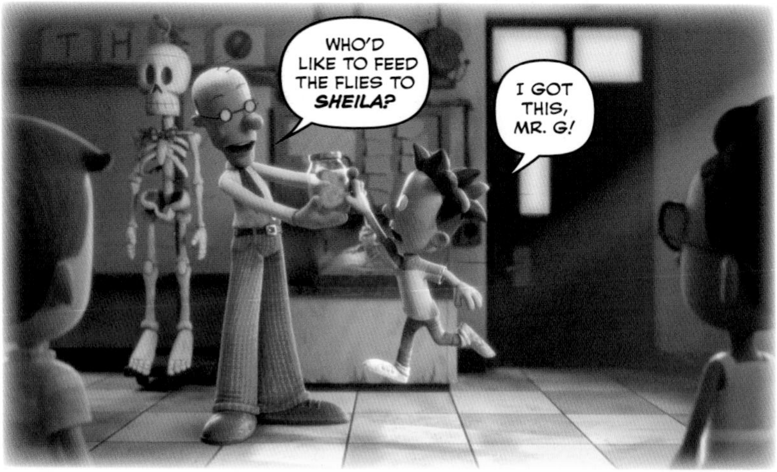
WHO'D LIKE TO FEED THE FLIES TO *SHEILA?*
I GOT THIS, MR. G!

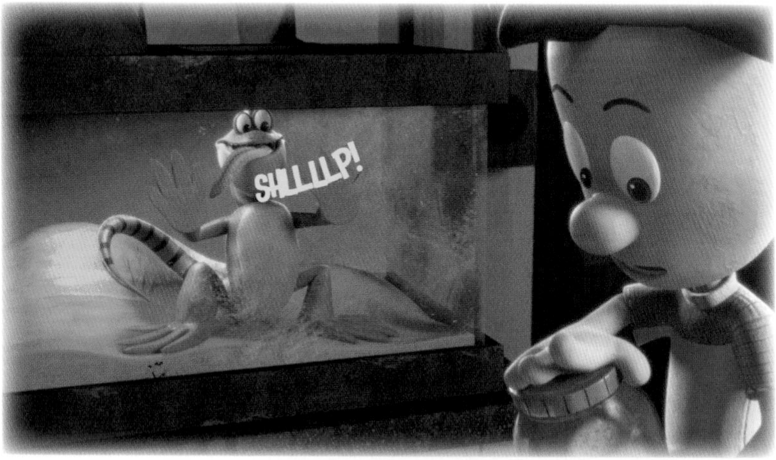
SHLLLLP!

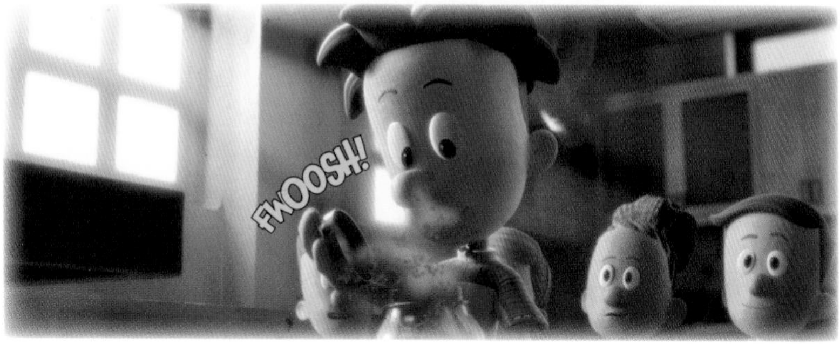
FWOOSH!

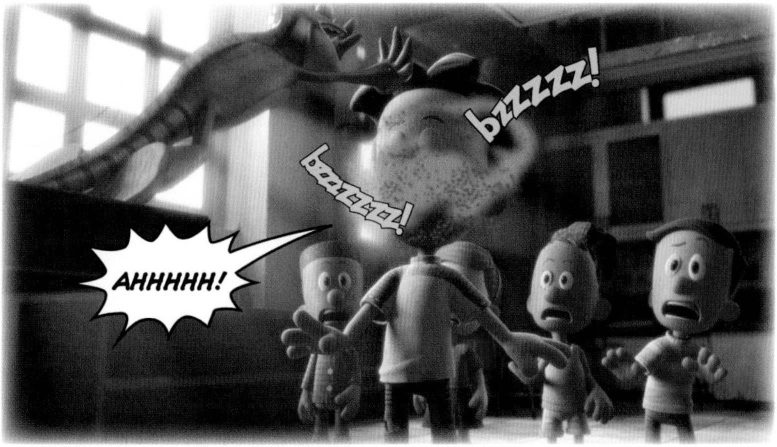
bzzzzz!
bzzzzzzz!
AHHHHH!

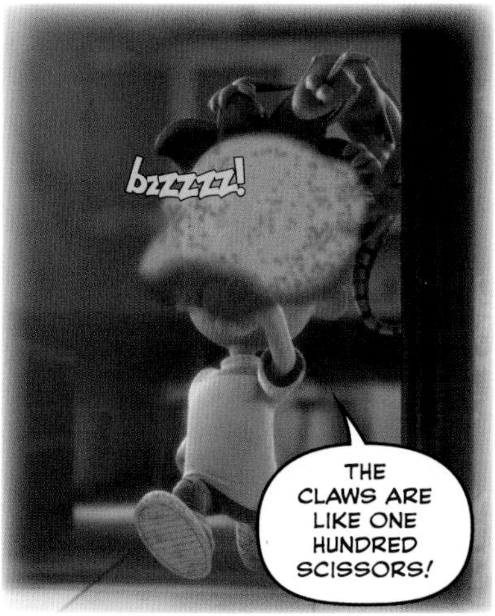
bzzzzz!
THE CLAWS ARE LIKE ONE HUNDRED SCISSORS!

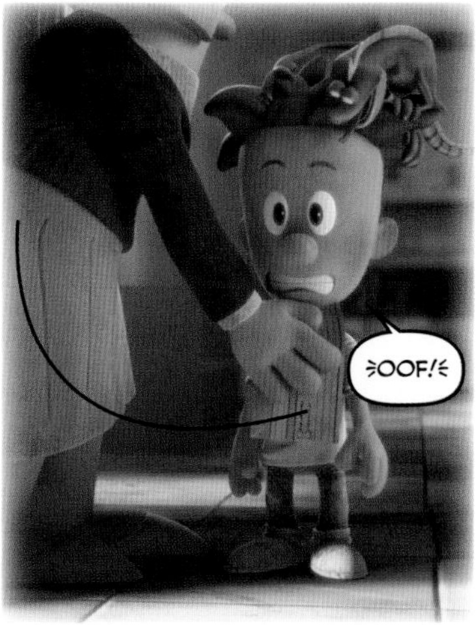
OOF!

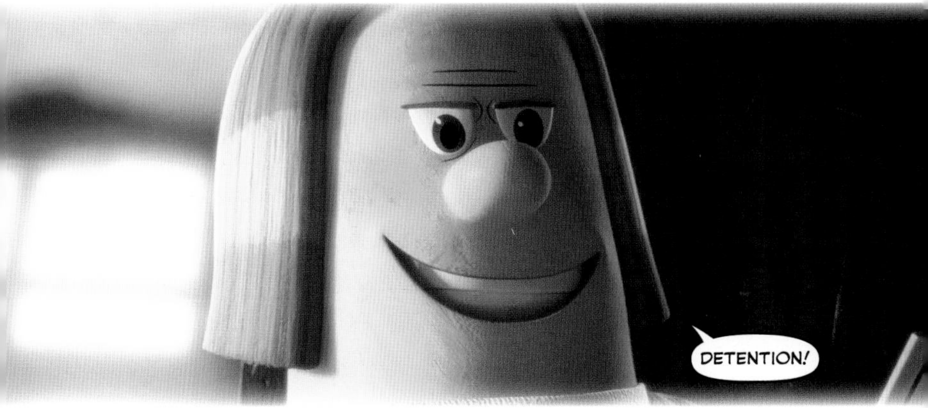
DETENTION!

DETENTION 3

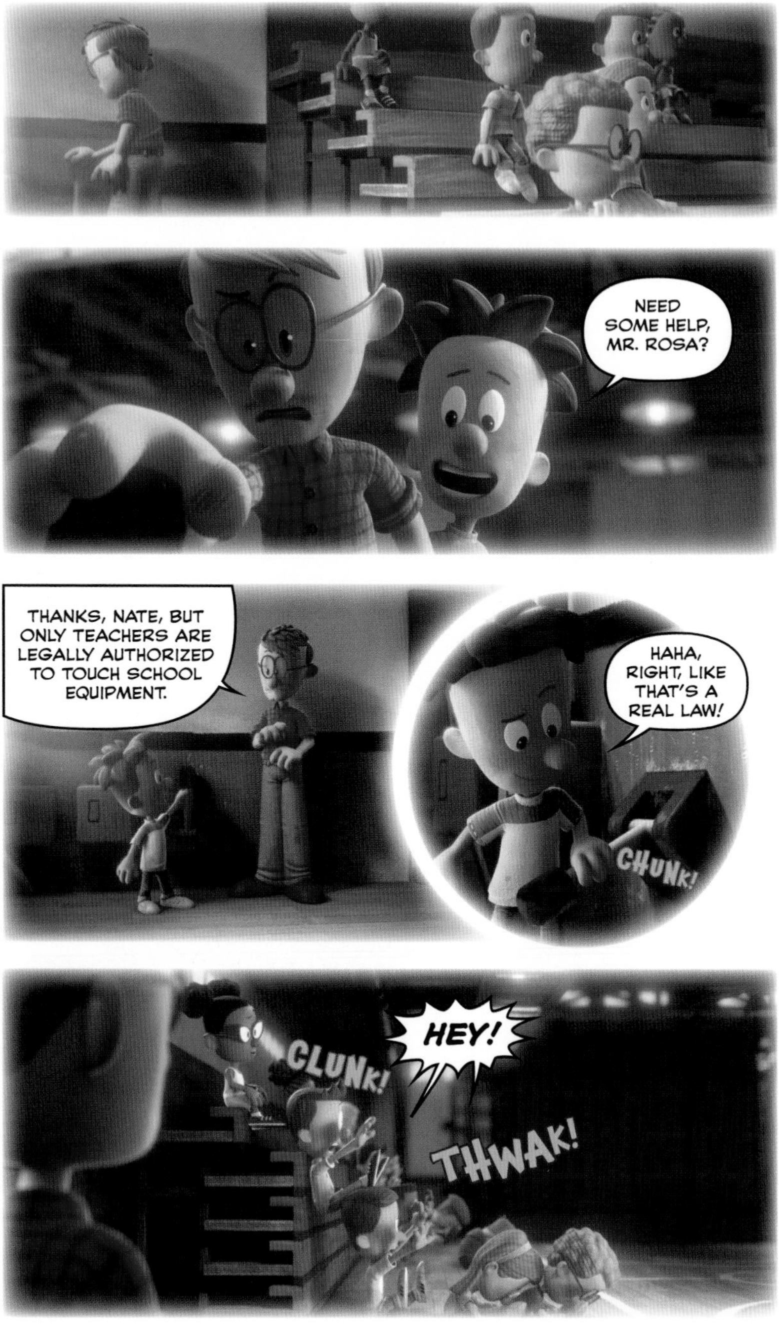

NEED SOME HELP, MR. ROSA?
THANKS, NATE, BUT ONLY TEACHERS ARE LEGALLY AUTHORIZED TO TOUCH SCHOOL EQUIPMENT.
HAHA, RIGHT, LIKE THAT'S A REAL LAW!
CHUNK!
HEY!
CLUNK!
THWAK!

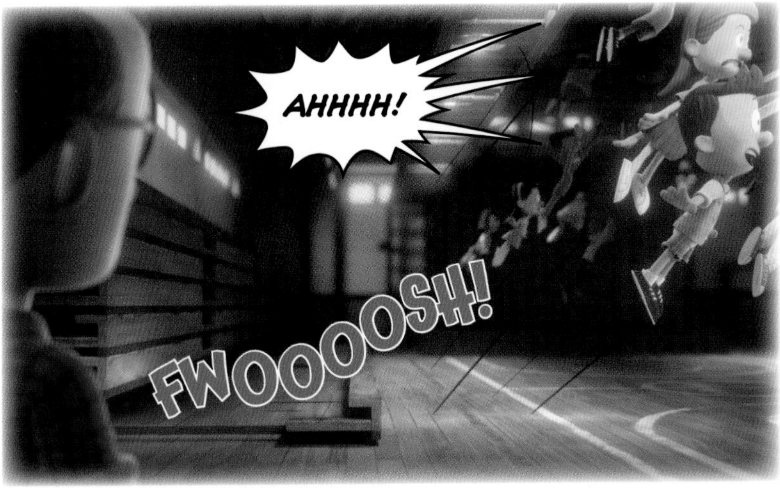
AHHHH!
FWOOOOSH!

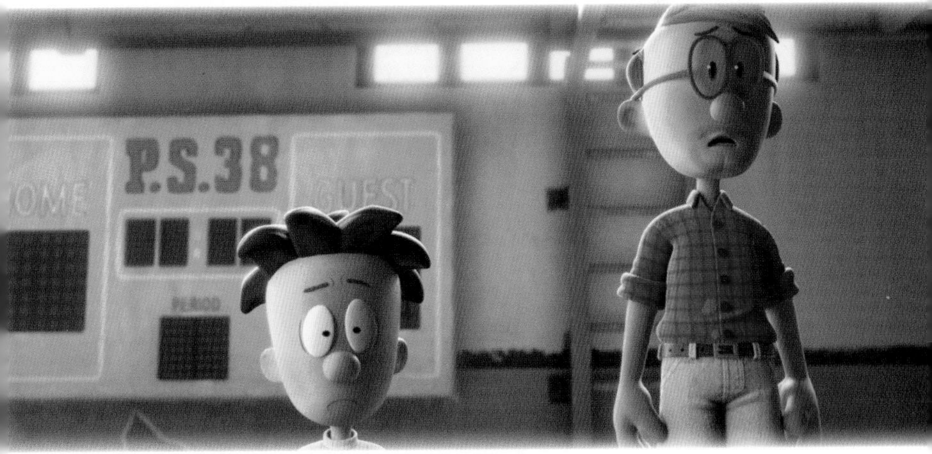
P.S.38
HOME
GUEST

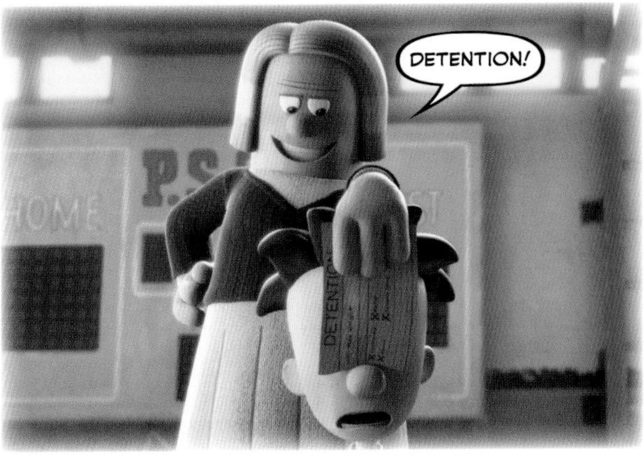
DETENTION!

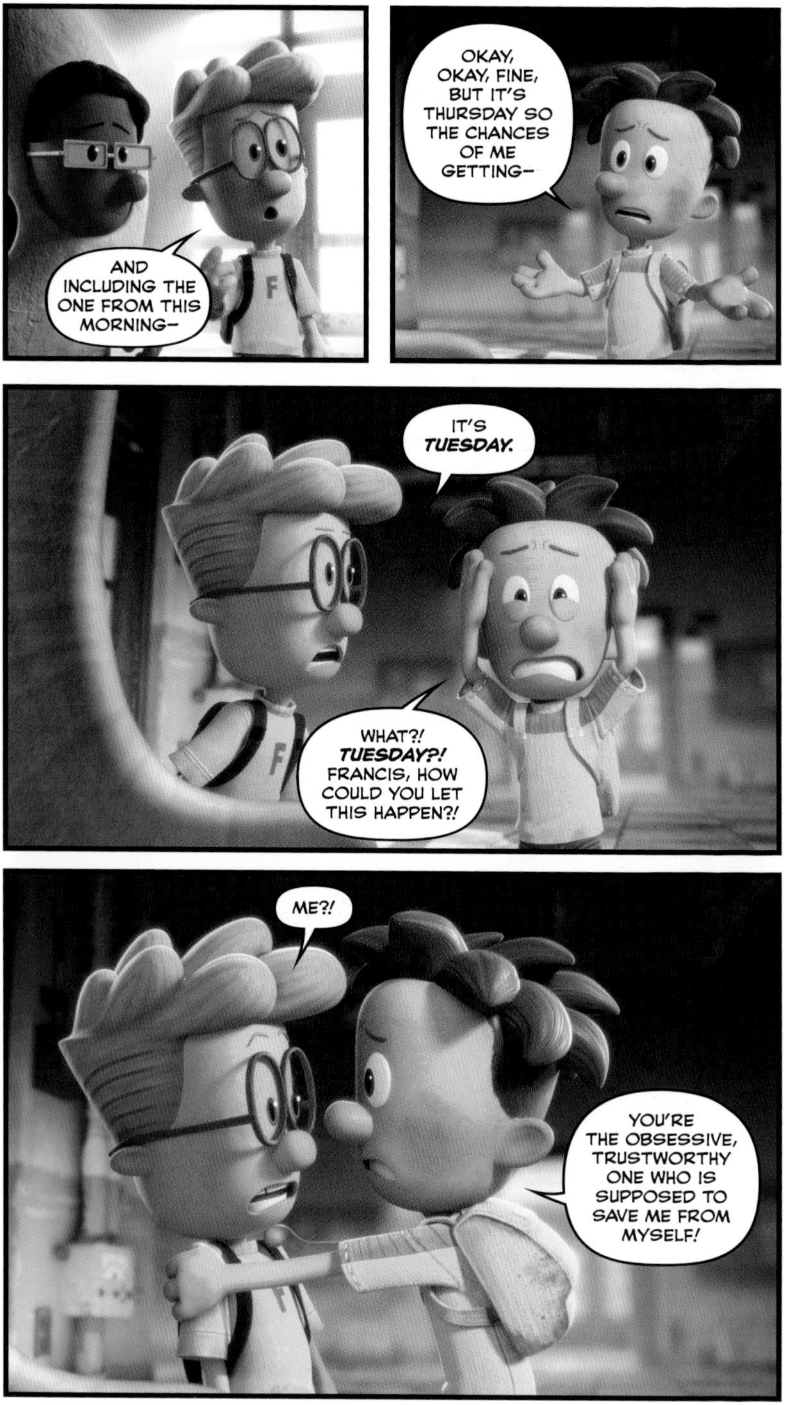
AND INCLUDING THE ONE FROM THIS MORNING—
OKAY, OKAY, FINE, BUT IT'S THURSDAY SO THE CHANCES OF ME GETTING—
IT'S *TUESDAY.*
WHAT?! *TUESDAY?!* FRANCIS, HOW COULD YOU LET THIS HAPPEN?!
ME?!
YOU'RE THE OBSESSIVE, TRUSTWORTHY ONE WHO IS SUPPOSED TO SAVE ME FROM MYSELF!

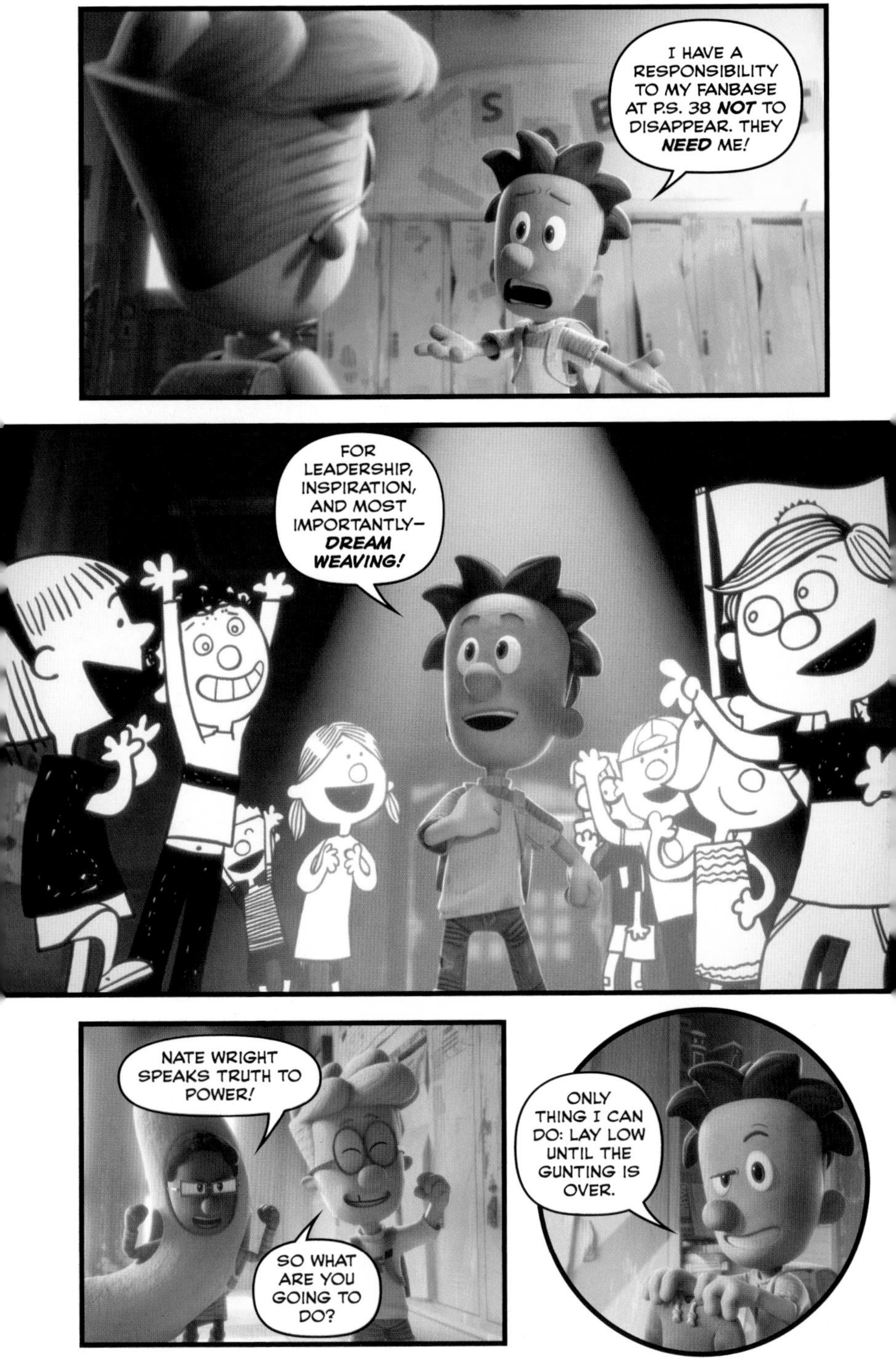
I HAVE A RESPONSIBILITY TO MY FANBASE AT P.S. 38 **NOT** TO DISAPPEAR. THEY **NEED** ME!
FOR LEADERSHIP, INSPIRATION, AND MOST IMPORTANTLY— **DREAM WEAVING!**
NATE WRIGHT SPEAKS TRUTH TO POWER!
SO WHAT ARE YOU GOING TO DO?
ONLY THING I CAN DO: LAY LOW UNTIL THE GUNTING IS OVER.

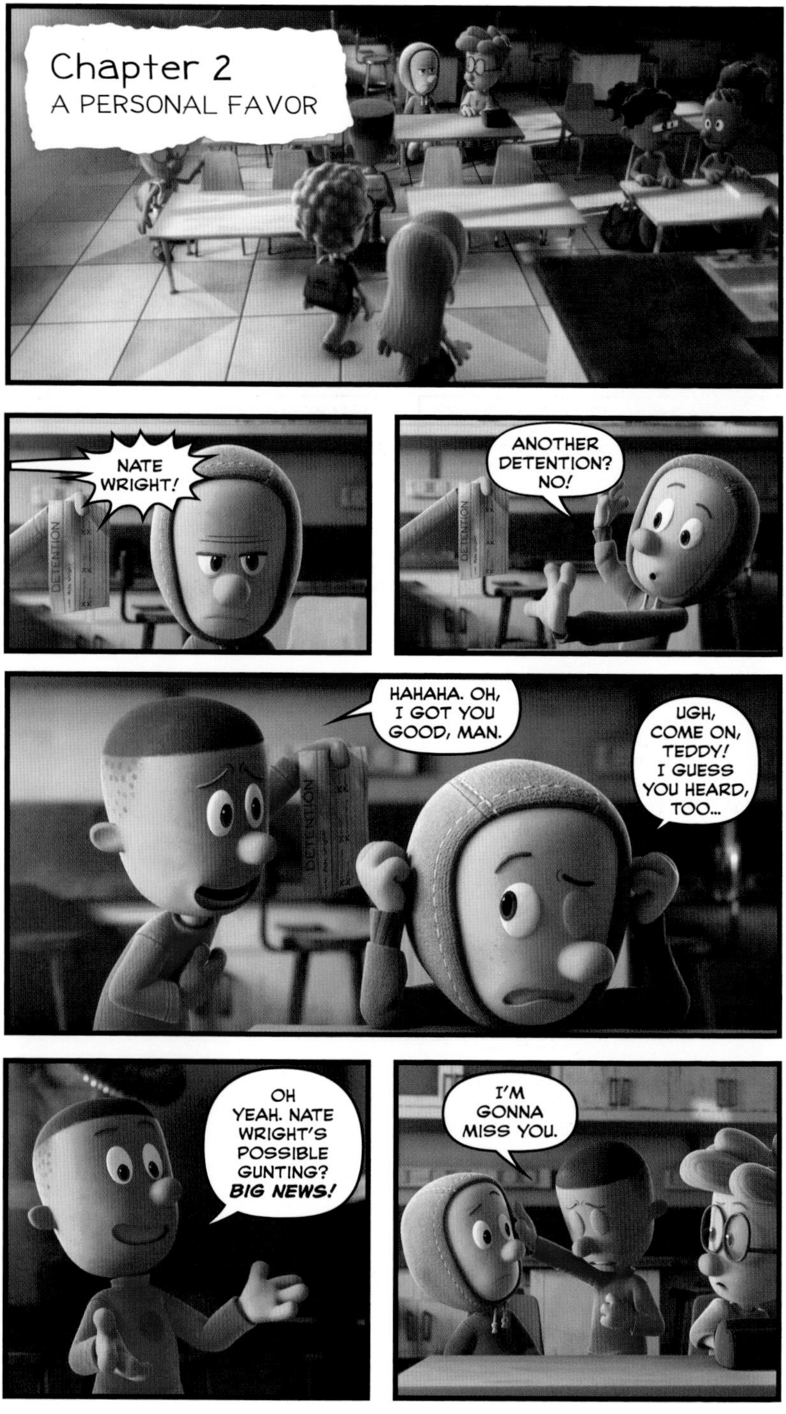
Chapter 2
A PERSONAL FAVOR
NATE WRIGHT!
DETENTION
ANOTHER DETENTION? NO!
DETENTION
HAHAHA. OH, I GOT YOU GOOD, MAN.
DETENTION
UGH, COME ON, TEDDY! I GUESS YOU HEARD, TOO...
OH YEAH. NATE WRIGHT'S POSSIBLE GUNTING? BIG NEWS!
I'M GONNA MISS YOU.

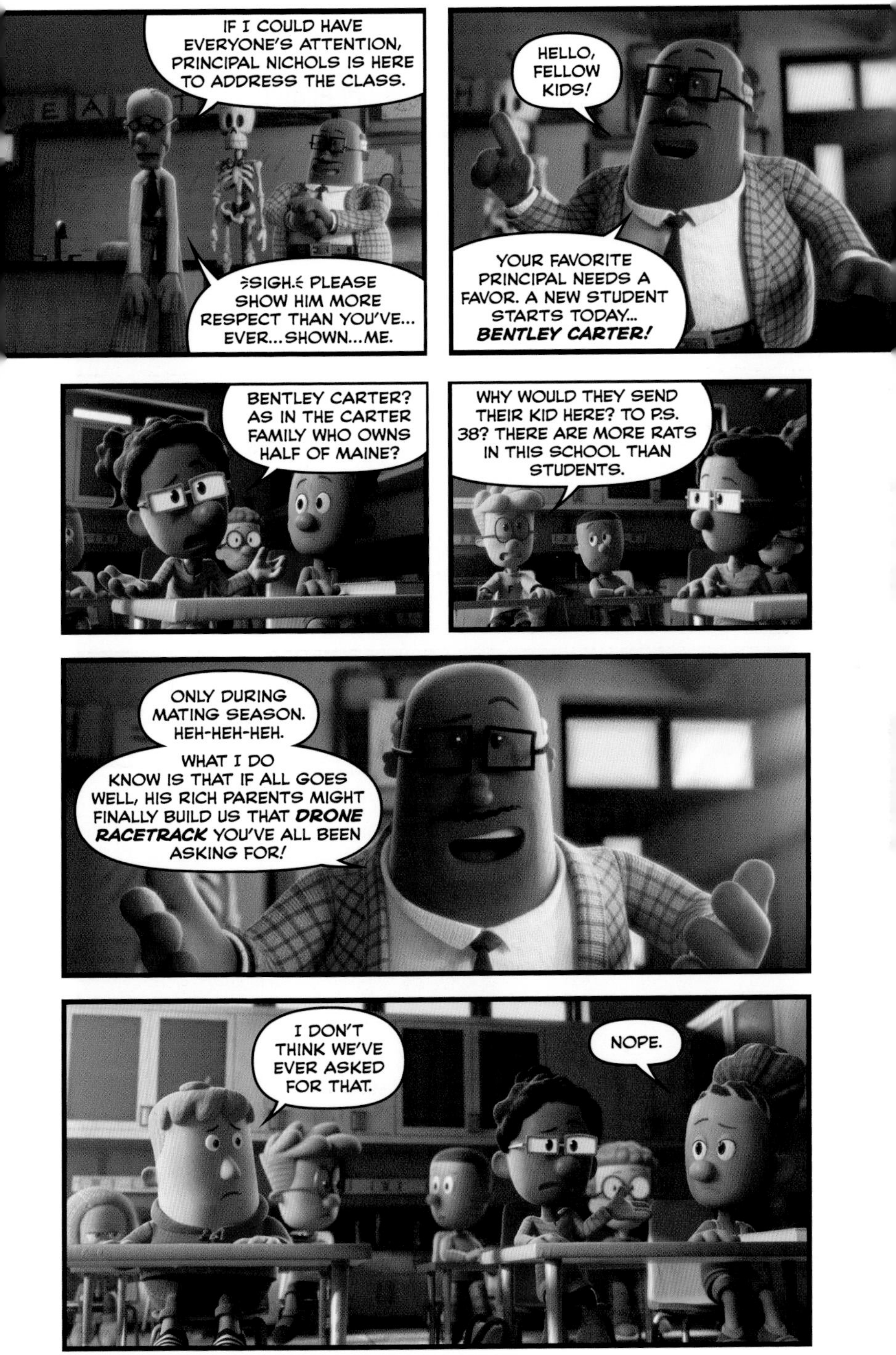
IF I COULD HAVE EVERYONE'S ATTENTION, PRINCIPAL NICHOLS IS HERE TO ADDRESS THE CLASS.
SIGH. PLEASE SHOW HIM MORE RESPECT THAN YOU'VE... EVER...SHOWN...ME.
HELLO, FELLOW KIDS!
YOUR FAVORITE PRINCIPAL NEEDS A FAVOR. A NEW STUDENT STARTS TODAY... ***BENTLEY CARTER!***
BENTLEY CARTER? AS IN THE CARTER FAMILY WHO OWNS HALF OF MAINE?
WHY WOULD THEY SEND THEIR KID HERE? TO P.S. 38? THERE ARE MORE RATS IN THIS SCHOOL THAN STUDENTS.
ONLY DURING MATING SEASON. HEH-HEH-HEH.
WHAT I DO KNOW IS THAT IF ALL GOES WELL, HIS RICH PARENTS MIGHT FINALLY BUILD US THAT ***DRONE RACETRACK*** YOU'VE ALL BEEN ASKING FOR!
I DON'T THINK WE'VE EVER ASKED FOR THAT.
NOPE.

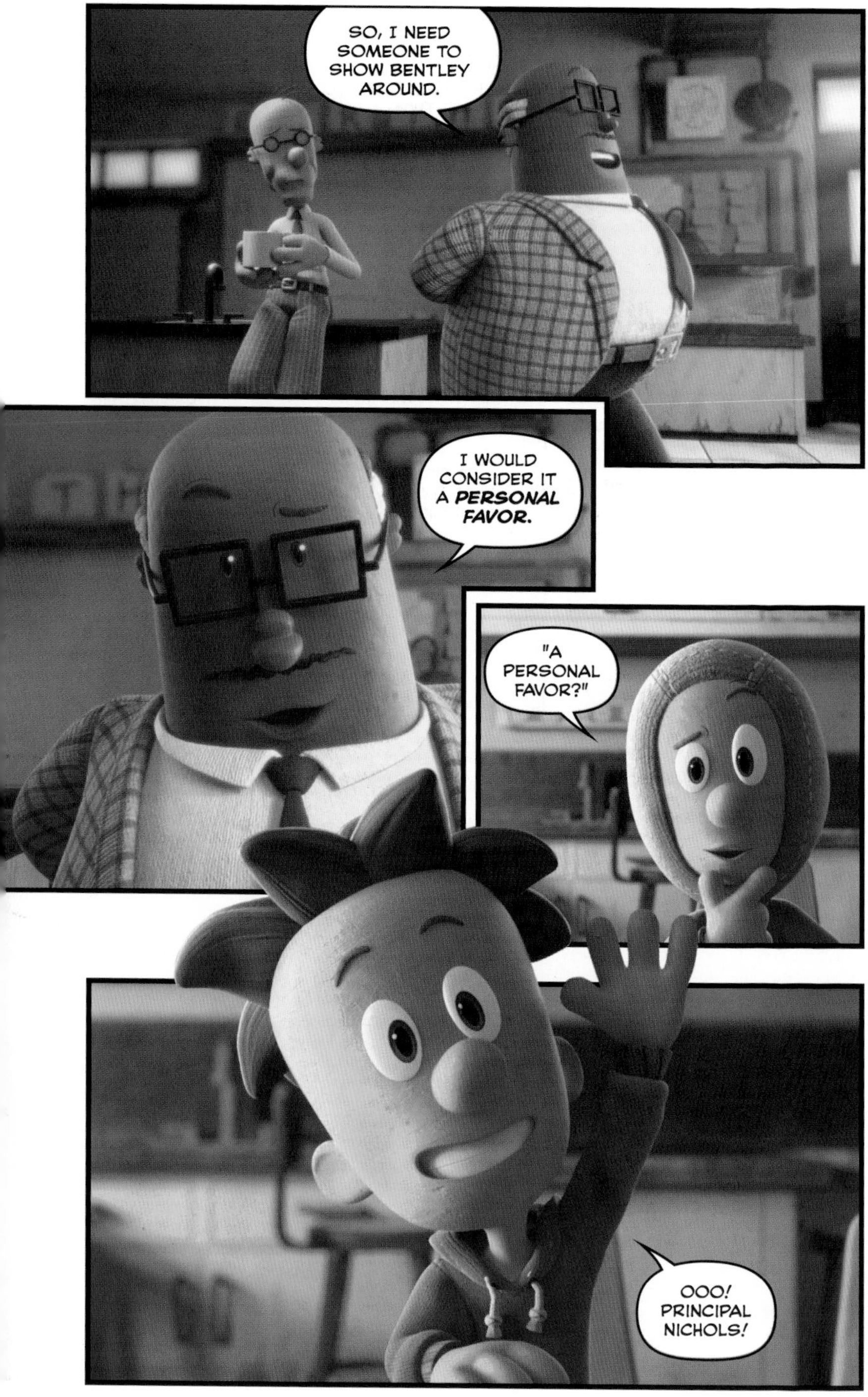
SO, I NEED SOMEONE TO SHOW BENTLEY AROUND.
I WOULD CONSIDER IT A *PERSONAL FAVOR.*
"A PERSONAL FAVOR?"
OOO! PRINCIPAL NICHOLS!

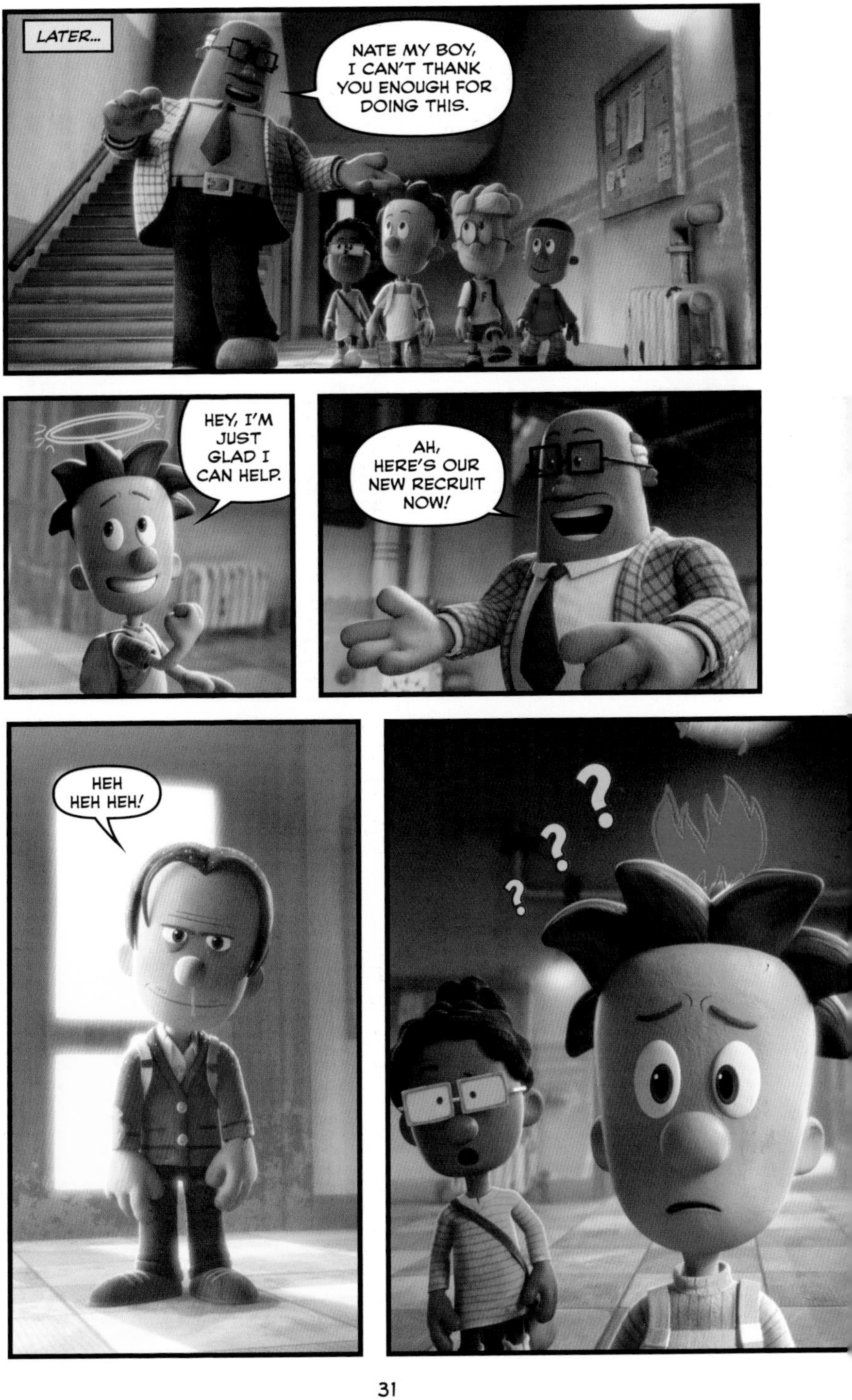
LATER...
NATE MY BOY, I CAN'T THANK YOU ENOUGH FOR DOING THIS.
HEY, I'M JUST GLAD I CAN HELP.
AH, HERE'S OUR NEW RECRUIT NOW!
HEH HEH HEH!
? ? ?

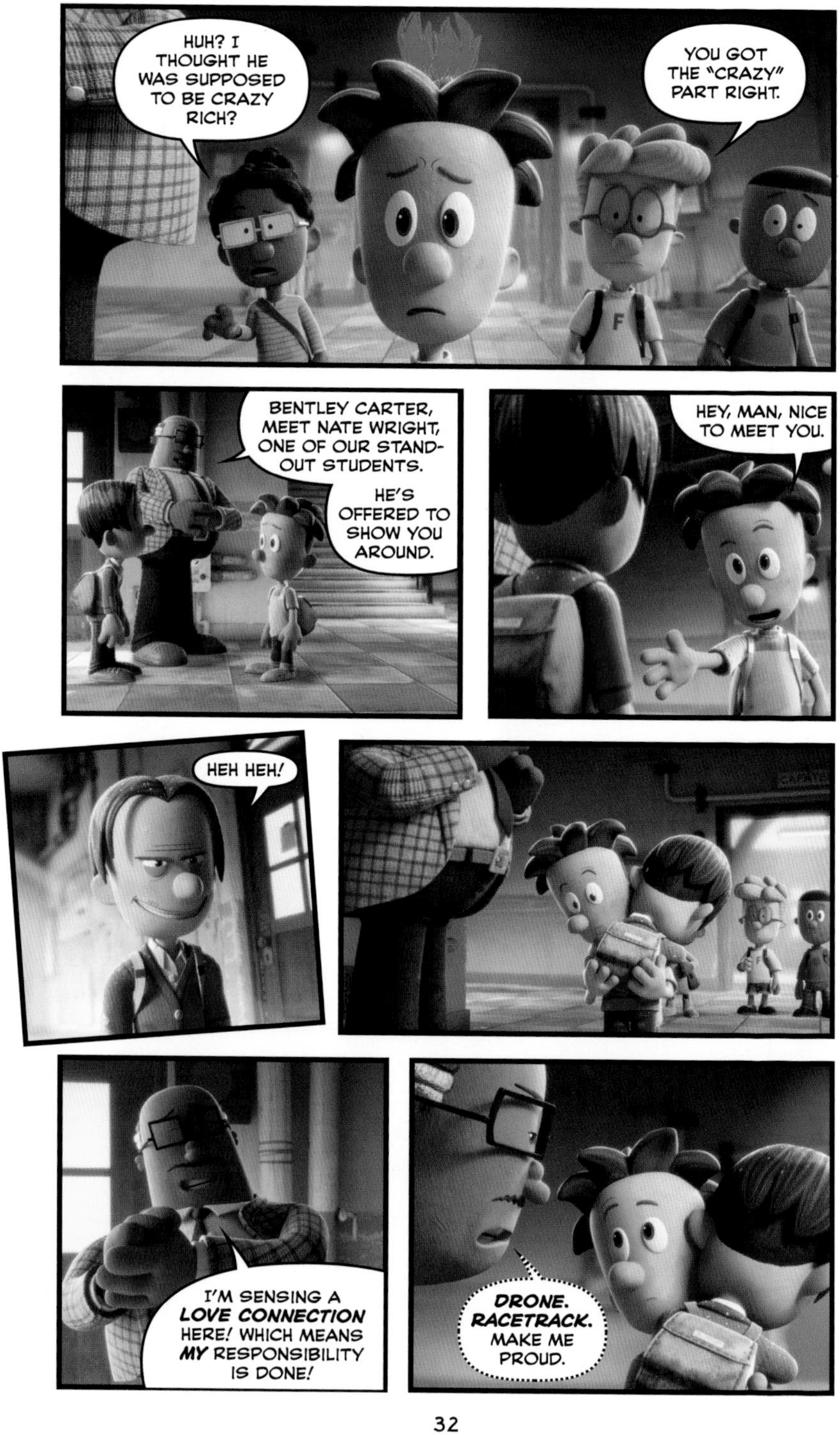
HUH? I THOUGHT HE WAS SUPPOSED TO BE CRAZY RICH?
YOU GOT THE "CRAZY" PART RIGHT.
BENTLEY CARTER, MEET NATE WRIGHT, ONE OF OUR STAND-OUT STUDENTS.
HE'S OFFERED TO SHOW YOU AROUND.
HEY, MAN, NICE TO MEET YOU.
HEH HEH!
I'M SENSING A LOVE CONNECTION HERE! WHICH MEANS MY RESPONSIBILITY IS DONE!
DRONE. RACETRACK. MAKE ME PROUD.

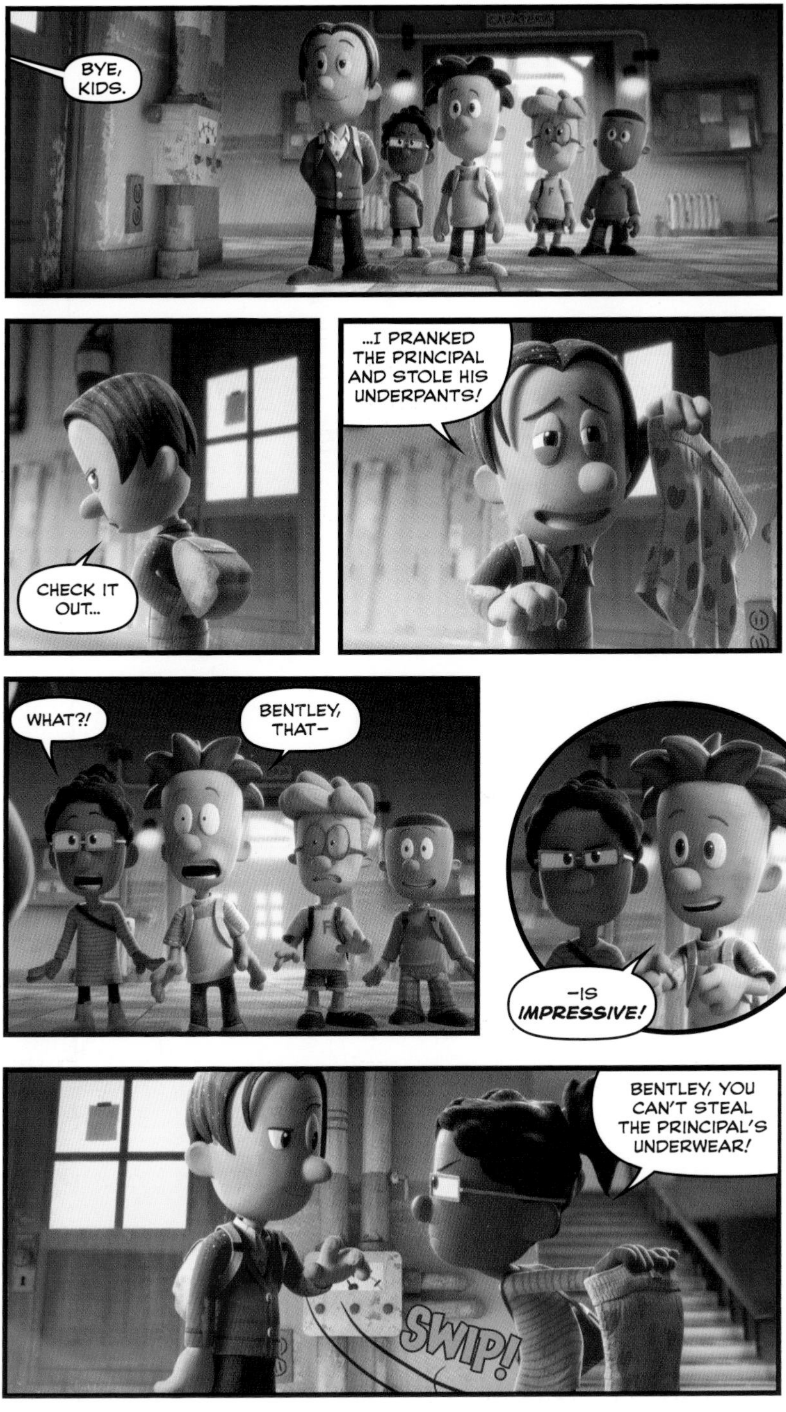
BYE, KIDS.
CHECK IT OUT...
...I PRANKED THE PRINCIPAL AND STOLE HIS UNDERPANTS!
WHAT?!
BENTLEY, THAT—
—IS *IMPRESSIVE!*
BENTLEY, YOU CAN'T STEAL THE PRINCIPAL'S UNDERWEAR!
SWIP!

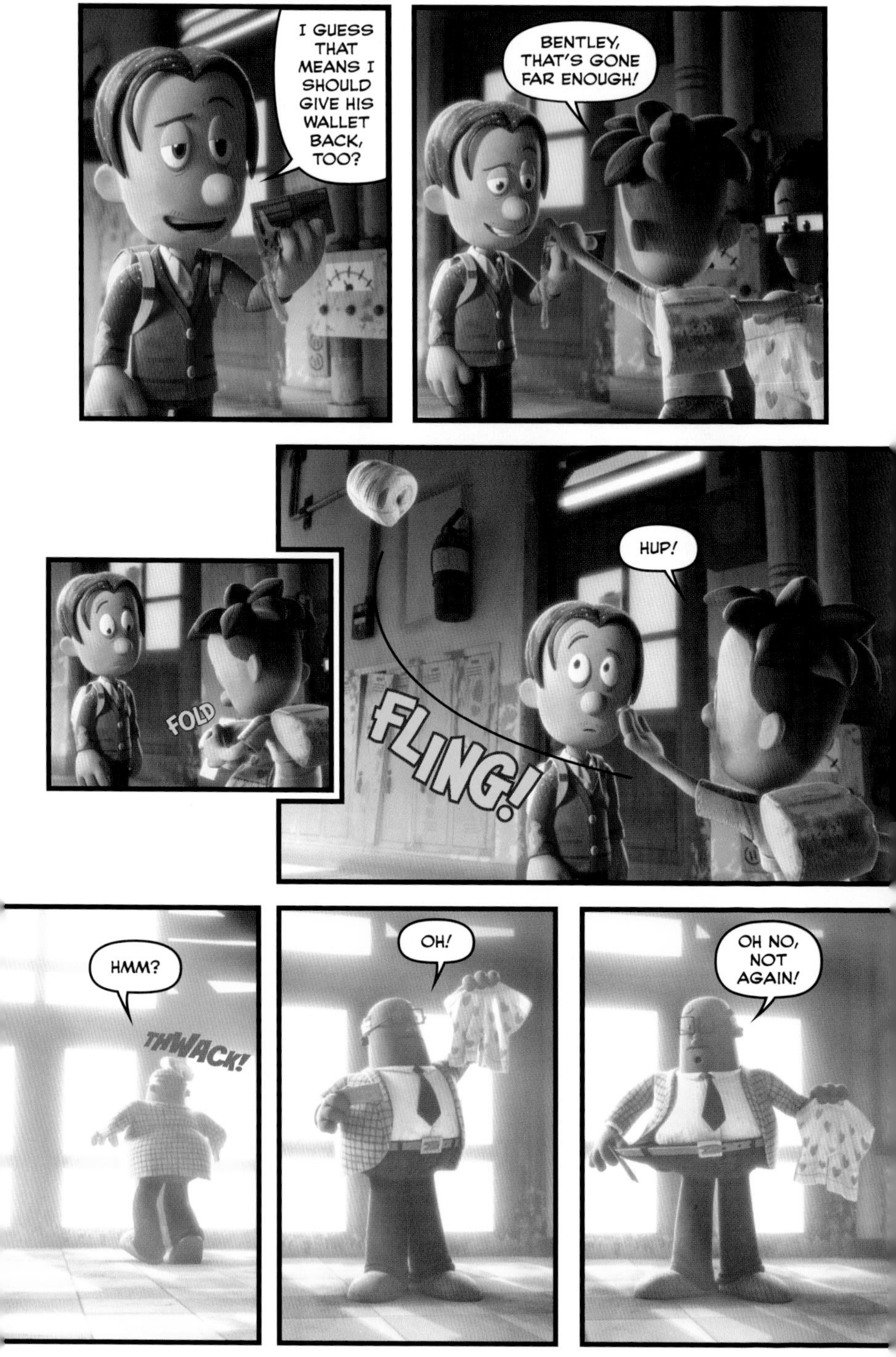
I GUESS THAT MEANS I SHOULD GIVE HIS WALLET BACK, TOO?
BENTLEY, THAT'S GONE FAR ENOUGH!
FOLD
HUP!
FLING!
HMM?
THWACK!
OH!
OH NO, NOT AGAIN!

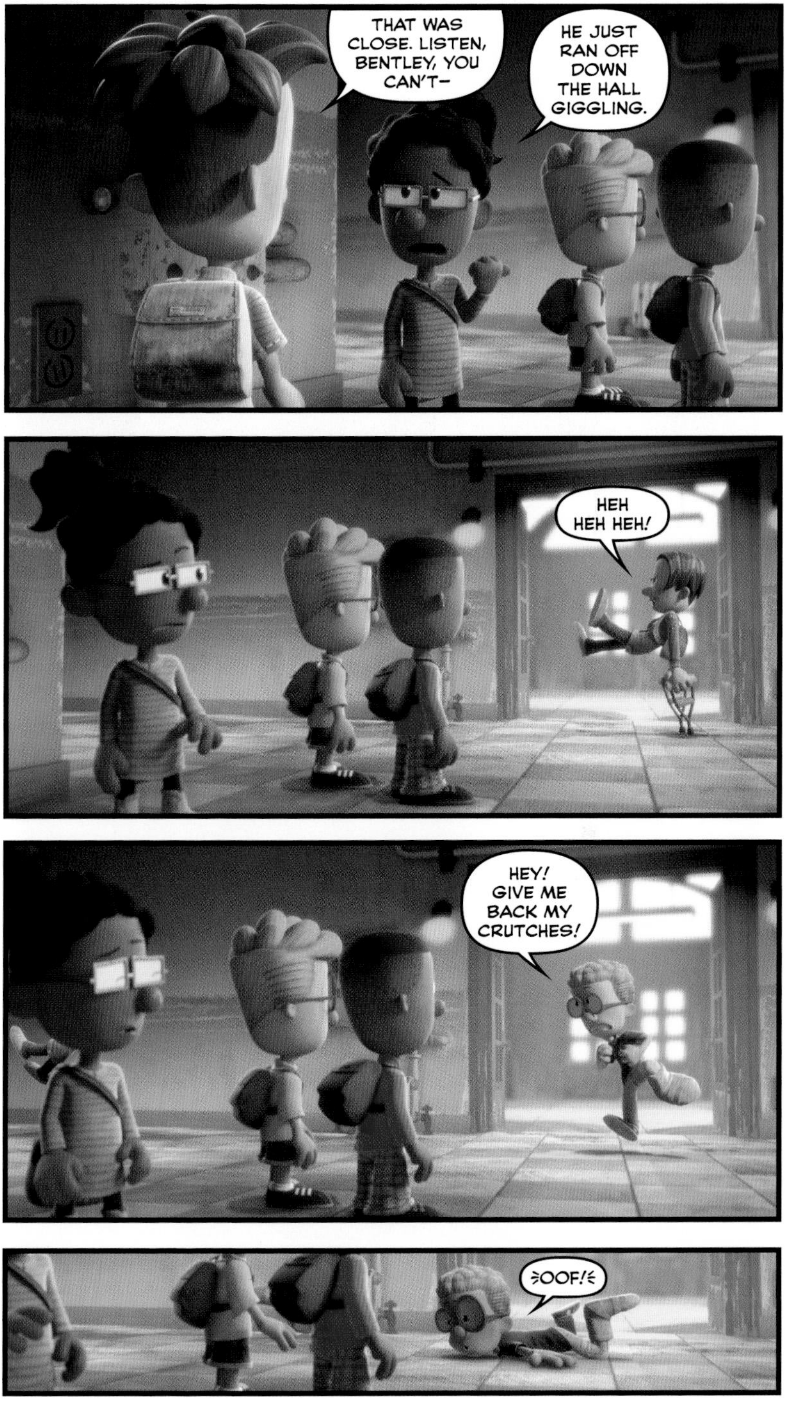
THAT WAS CLOSE. LISTEN, BENTLEY, YOU CAN'T–
HE JUST RAN OFF DOWN THE HALL GIGGLING.
HEH HEH HEH!
HEY! GIVE ME BACK MY CRUTCHES!
OOF!

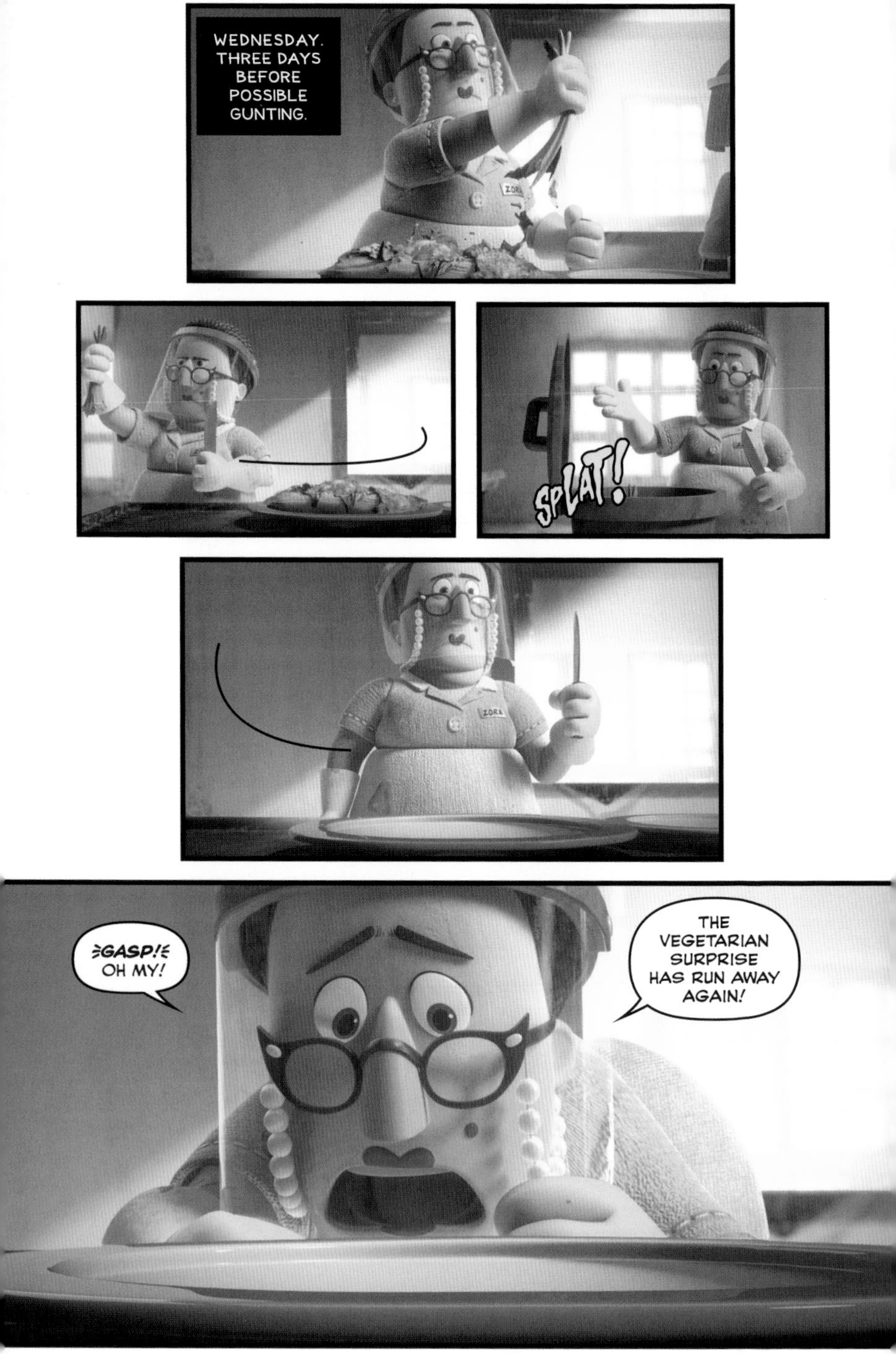
WEDNESDAY. THREE DAYS BEFORE POSSIBLE GUNTING.
ZORA
SPLAT!
ZORA
⋛GASP!⋚ OH MY!
THE VEGETARIAN SURPRISE HAS RUN AWAY AGAIN!

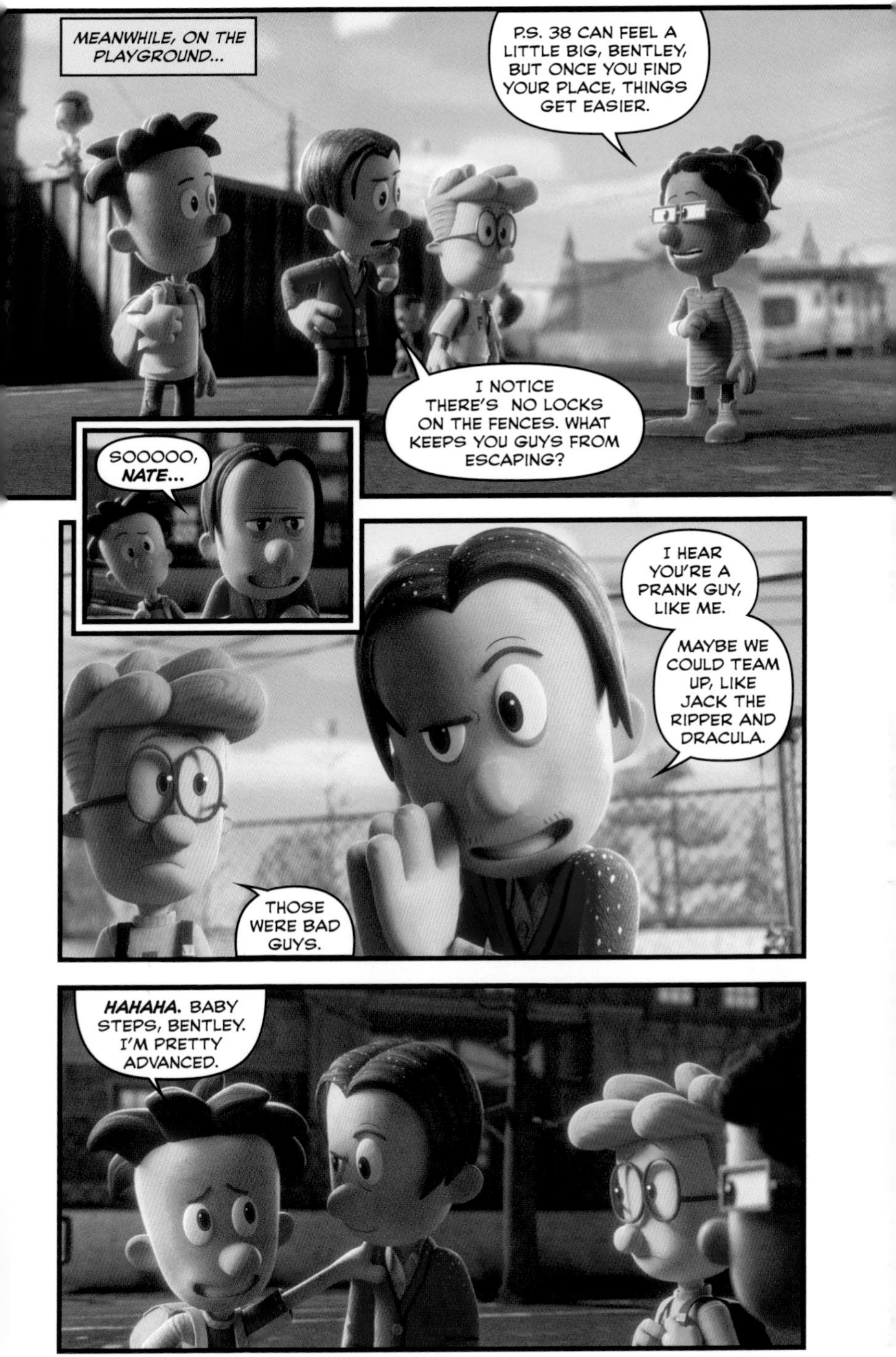

MEANWHILE, ON THE PLAYGROUND...
P.S. 38 CAN FEEL A LITTLE BIG, BENTLEY, BUT ONCE YOU FIND YOUR PLACE, THINGS GET EASIER.
I NOTICE THERE'S NO LOCKS ON THE FENCES. WHAT KEEPS YOU GUYS FROM ESCAPING?
SOOOOO, ***NATE...***
I HEAR YOU'RE A PRANK GUY, LIKE ME.
MAYBE WE COULD TEAM UP, LIKE JACK THE RIPPER AND DRACULA.
THOSE WERE BAD GUYS.
HAHAHA. BABY STEPS, BENTLEY. I'M PRETTY ADVANCED.

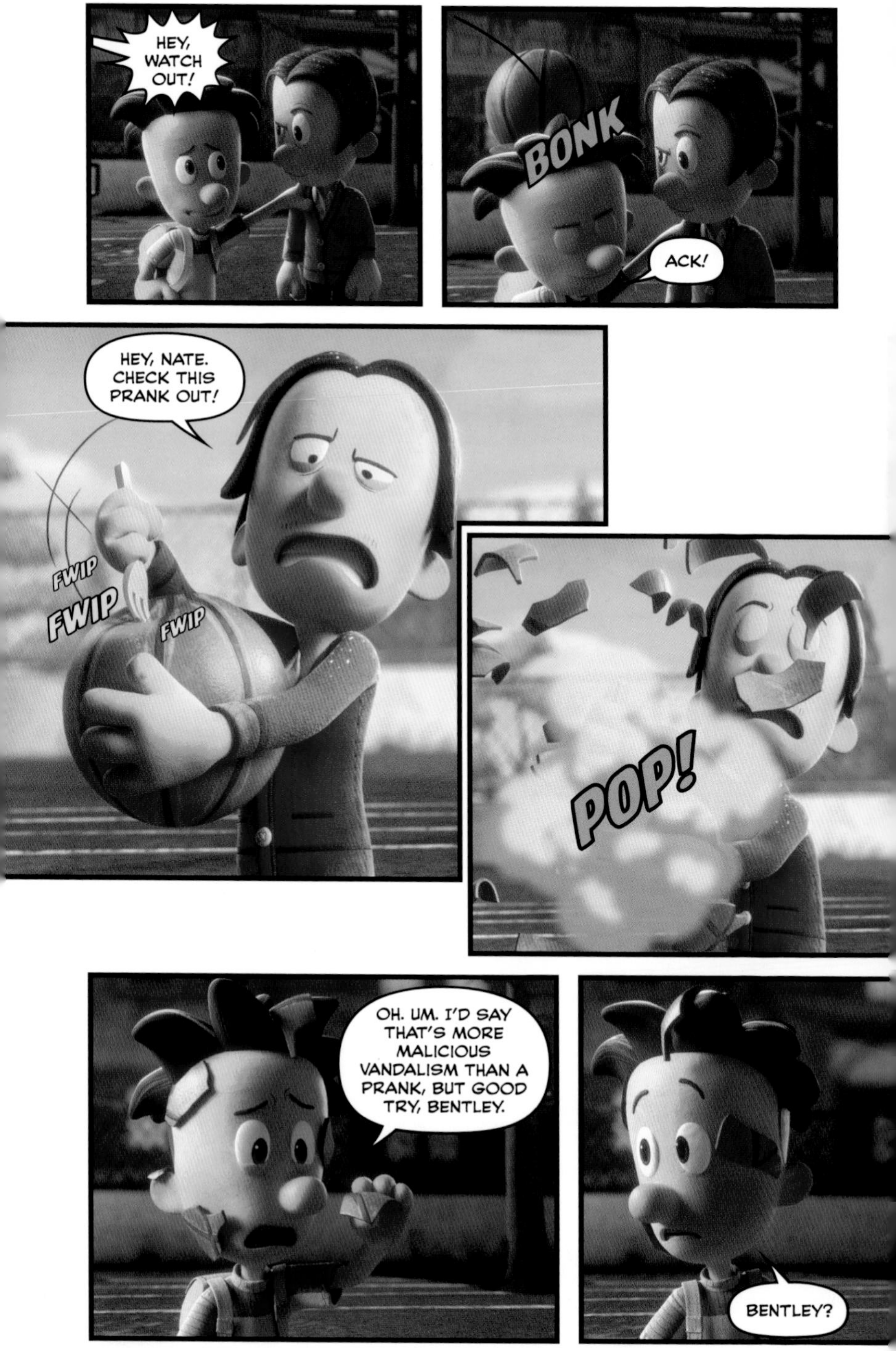
HEY, WATCH OUT!
BONK
ACK!
HEY, NATE. CHECK THIS PRANK OUT!
FWIP
FWIP
FWIP
POP!
OH. UM. I'D SAY THAT'S MORE MALICIOUS VANDALISM THAN A PRANK, BUT GOOD TRY, BENTLEY.
BENTLEY?

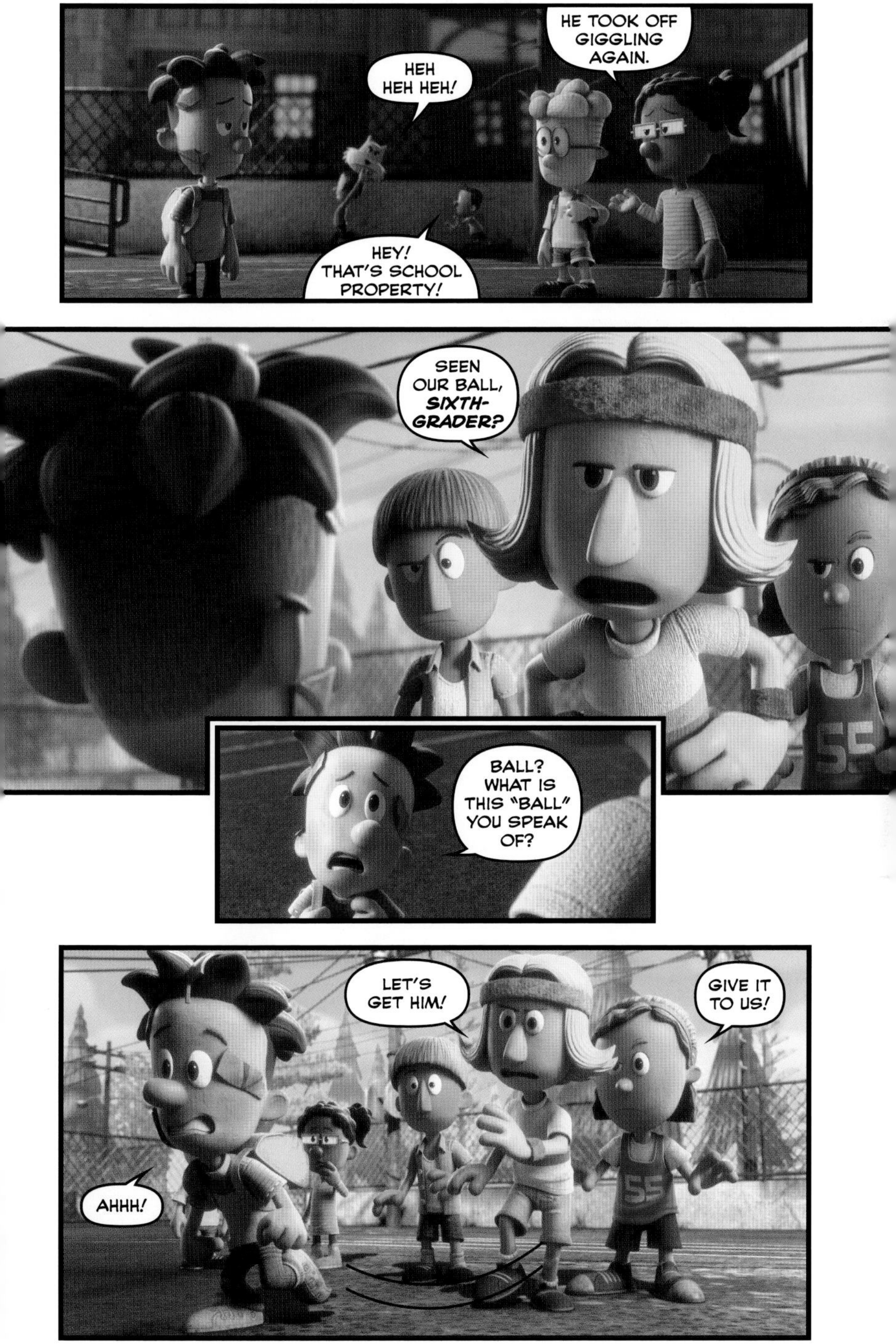
HEH HEH HEH!
HE TOOK OFF GIGGLING AGAIN.
HEY! THAT'S SCHOOL PROPERTY!
SEEN OUR BALL, *SIXTH-GRADER?*
BALL? WHAT IS THIS "BALL" YOU SPEAK OF?
LET'S GET HIM!
GIVE IT TO US!
AHHH!

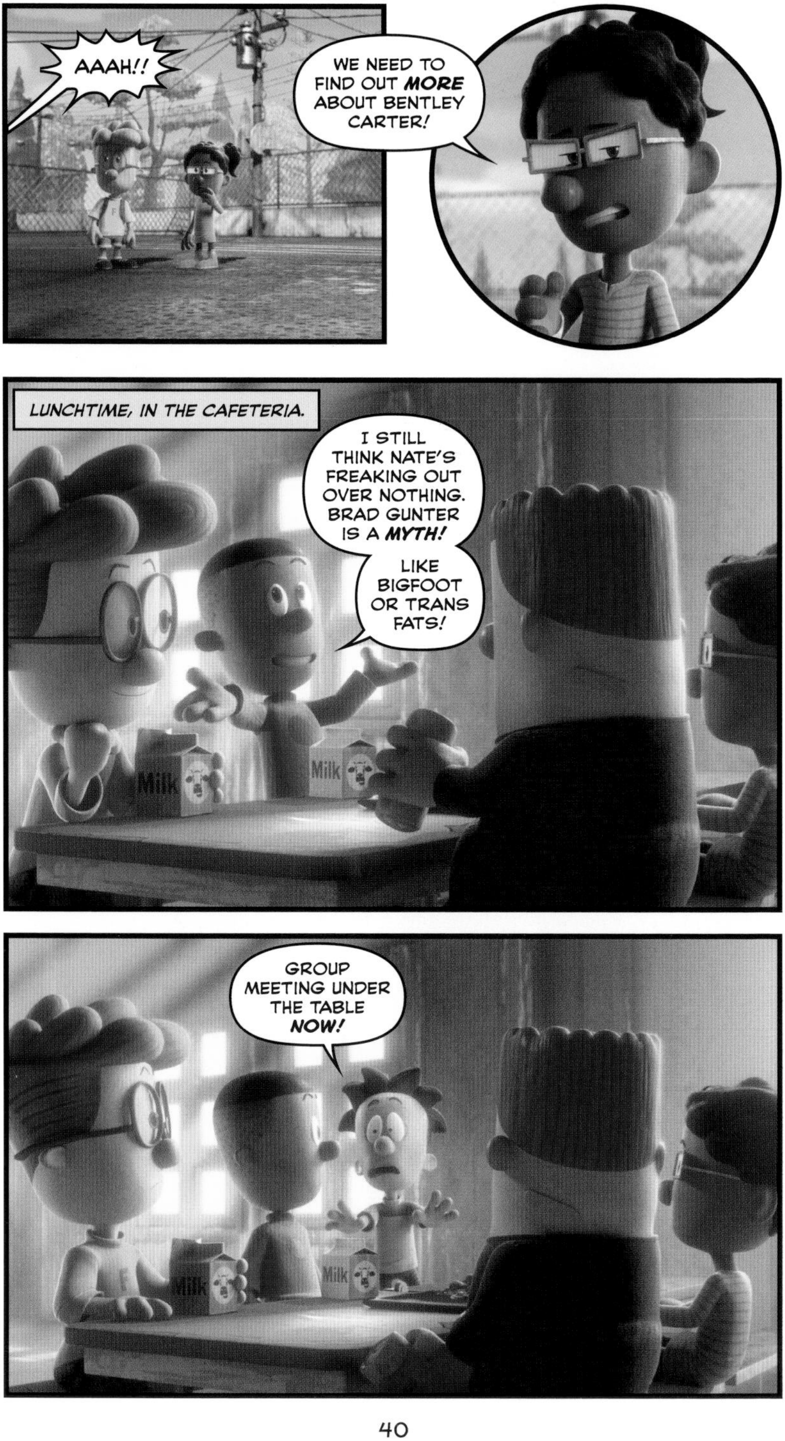
AAAH!!
WE NEED TO FIND OUT MORE ABOUT BENTLEY CARTER!
LUNCHTIME, IN THE CAFETERIA.
I STILL THINK NATE'S FREAKING OUT OVER NOTHING. BRAD GUNTER IS A MYTH!
LIKE BIGFOOT OR TRANS FATS!
GROUP MEETING UNDER THE TABLE NOW!

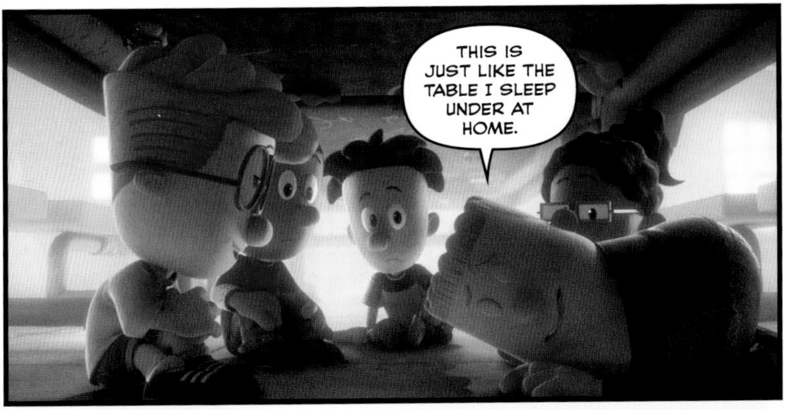
THIS IS JUST LIKE THE TABLE I SLEEP UNDER AT HOME.

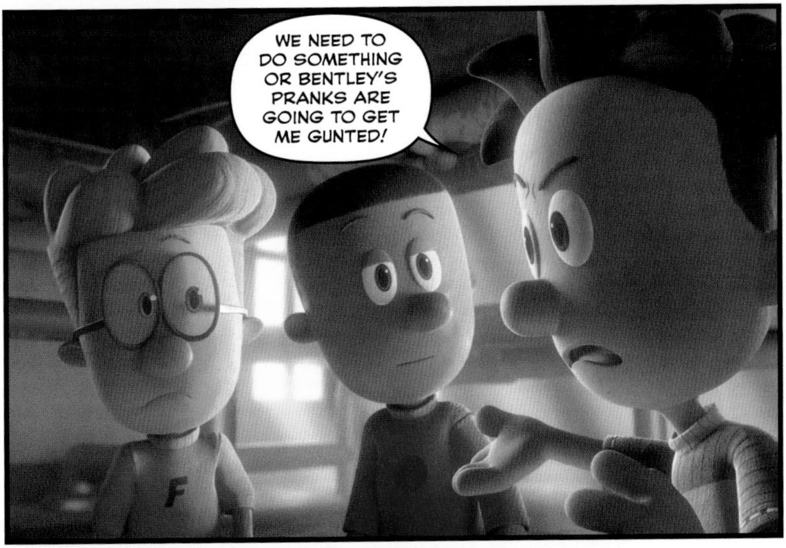
WE NEED TO DO SOMETHING OR BENTLEY'S PRANKS ARE GOING TO GET ME GUNTED!

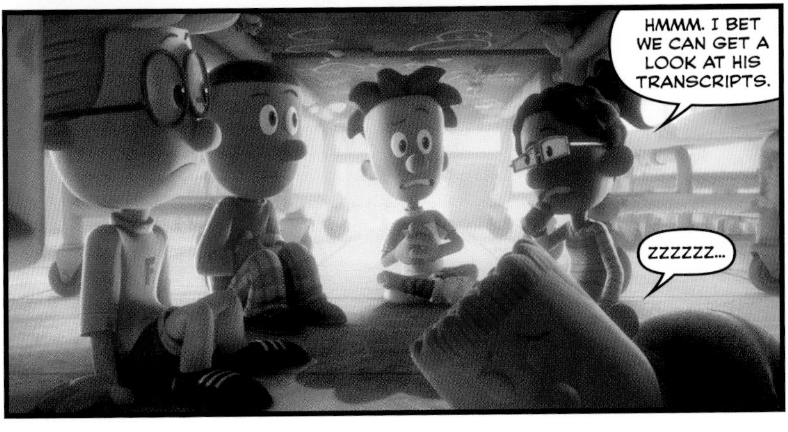
HMMM. I BET WE CAN GET A LOOK AT HIS TRANSCRIPTS.
ZZZZZZ...

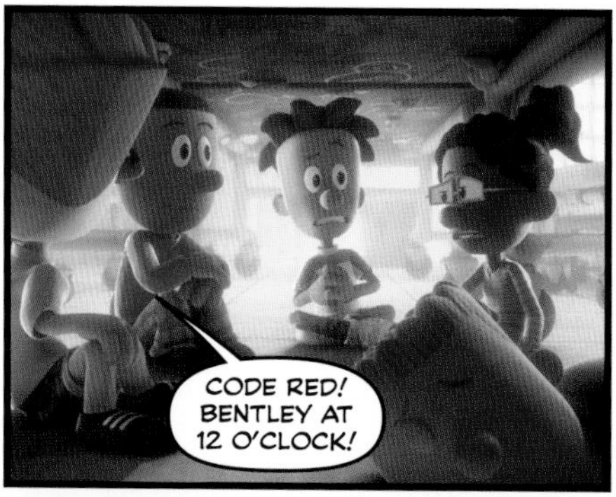
CODE RED! BENTLEY AT 12 O'CLOCK!

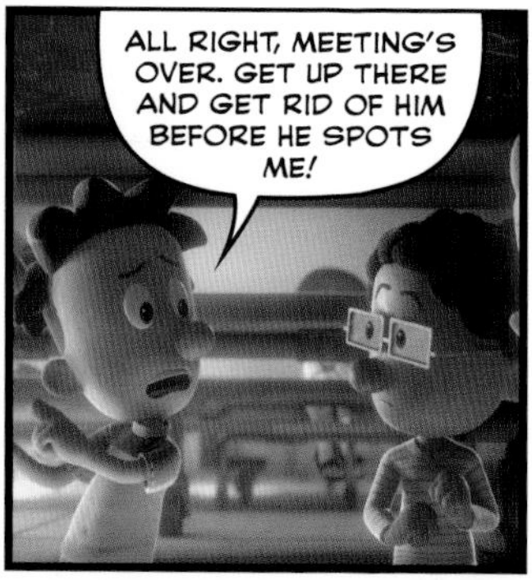
ALL RIGHT, MEETING'S OVER. GET UP THERE AND GET RID OF HIM BEFORE HE SPOTS ME!

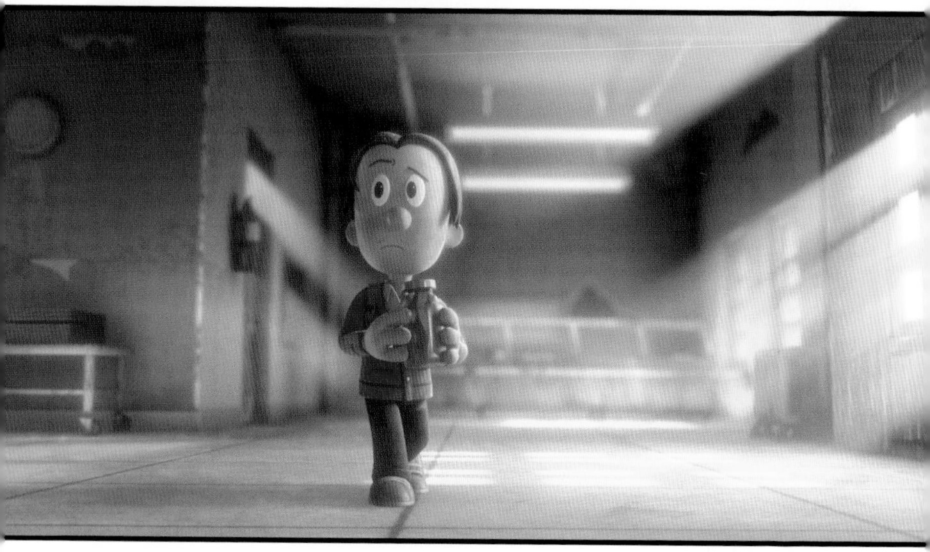

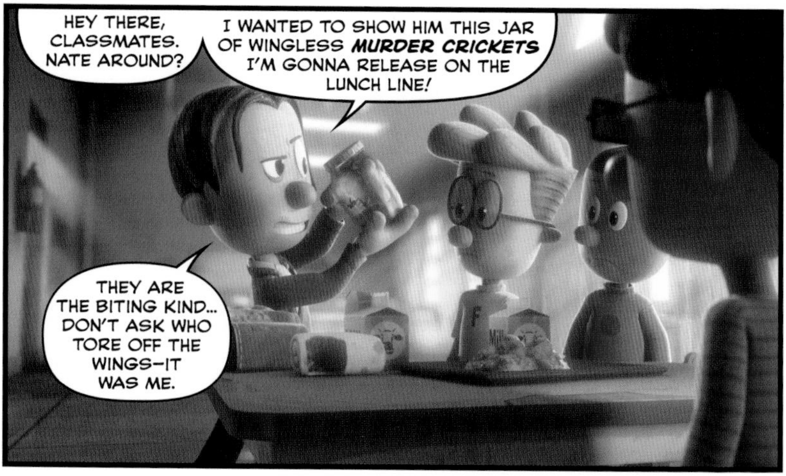
HEY THERE, CLASSMATES. NATE AROUND?
I WANTED TO SHOW HIM THIS JAR OF WINGLESS MURDER CRICKETS I'M GONNA RELEASE ON THE LUNCH LINE!
THEY ARE THE BITING KIND... DON'T ASK WHO TORE OFF THE WINGS—IT WAS ME.

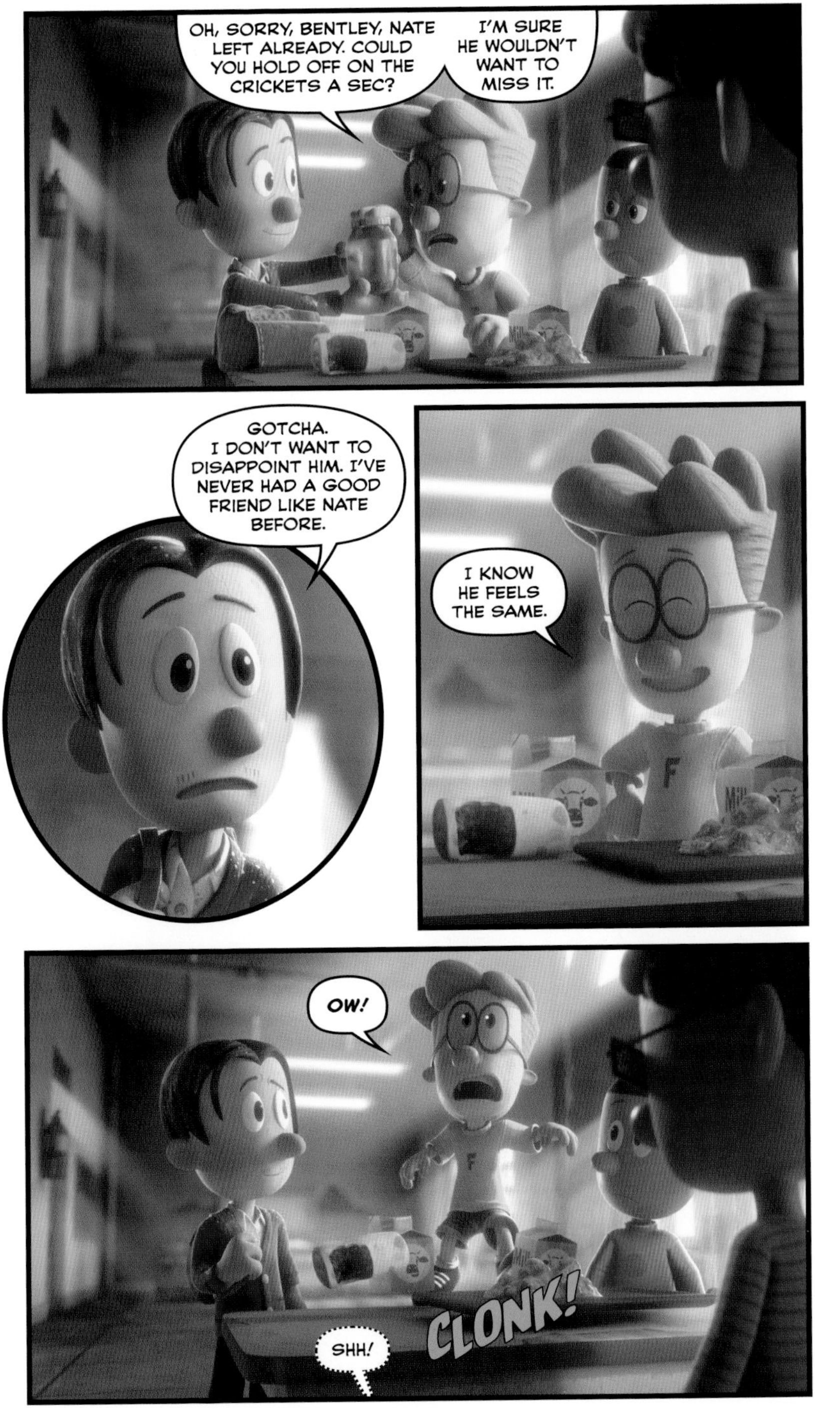
OH, SORRY, BENTLEY, NATE LEFT ALREADY. COULD YOU HOLD OFF ON THE CRICKETS A SEC?
I'M SURE HE WOULDN'T WANT TO MISS IT.
GOTCHA. I DON'T WANT TO DISAPPOINT HIM. I'VE NEVER HAD A GOOD FRIEND LIKE NATE BEFORE.
I KNOW HE FEELS THE SAME.
OW!
CLONK!
SHH!

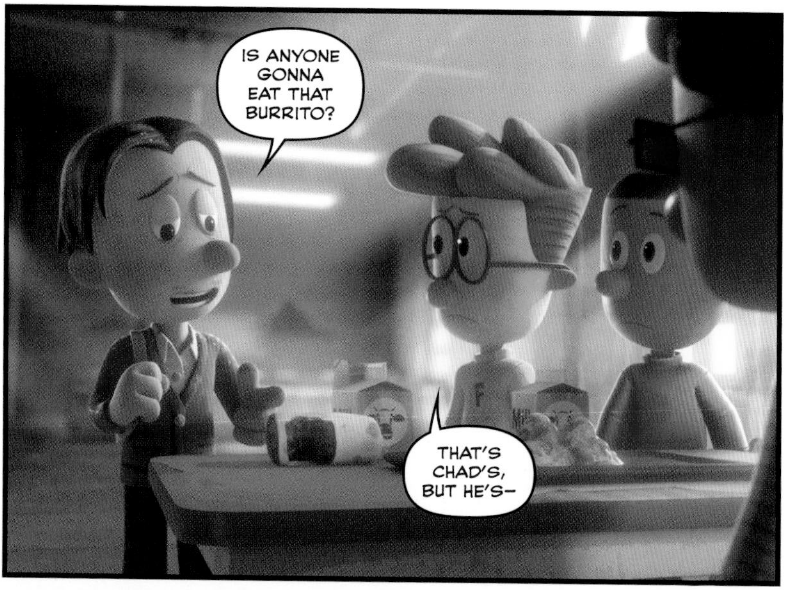
IS ANYONE GONNA EAT THAT BURRITO?
THAT'S CHAD'S, BUT HE'S—
Milk

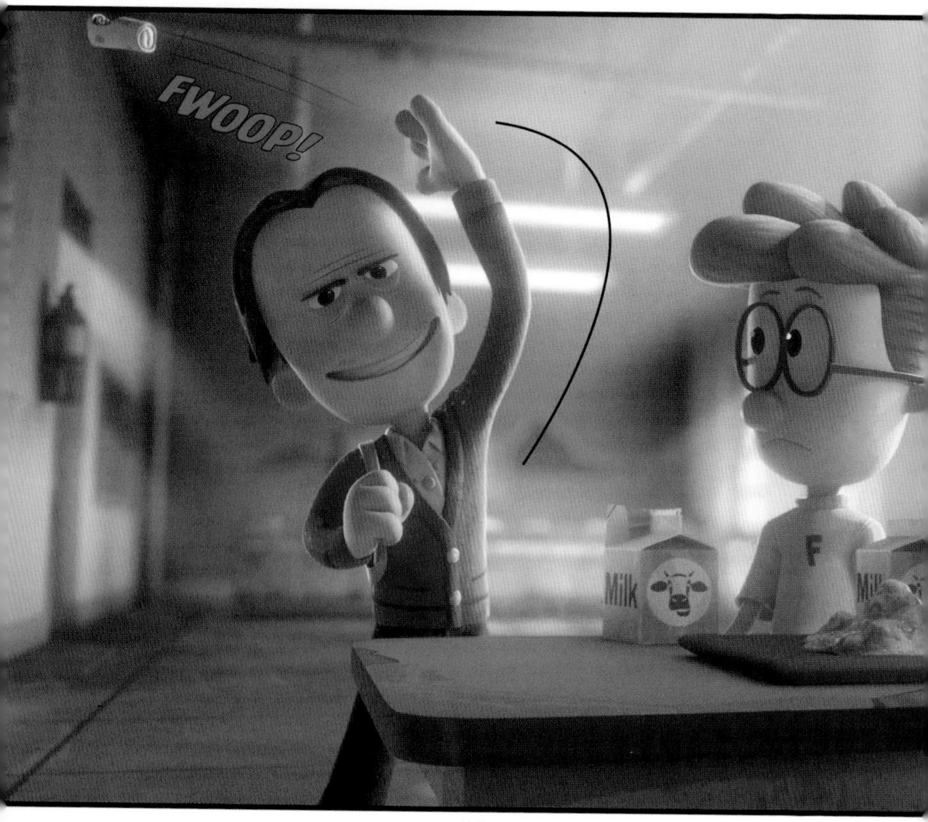
FWOOP!
Milk

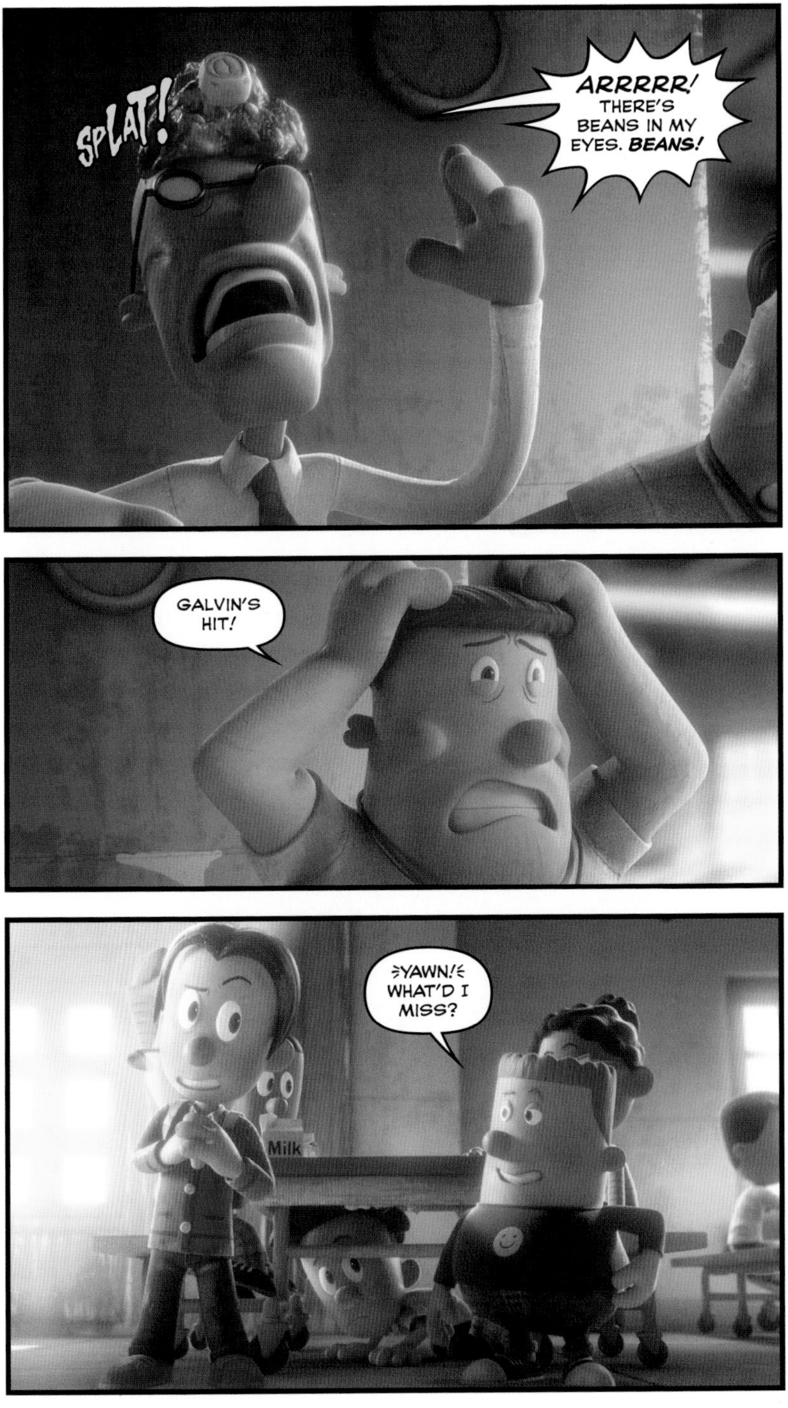
SPLAT!
ARRRRR! THERE'S BEANS IN MY EYES. BEANS!
GALVIN'S HIT!
≈YAWN!≈ WHAT'D I MISS?
Milk

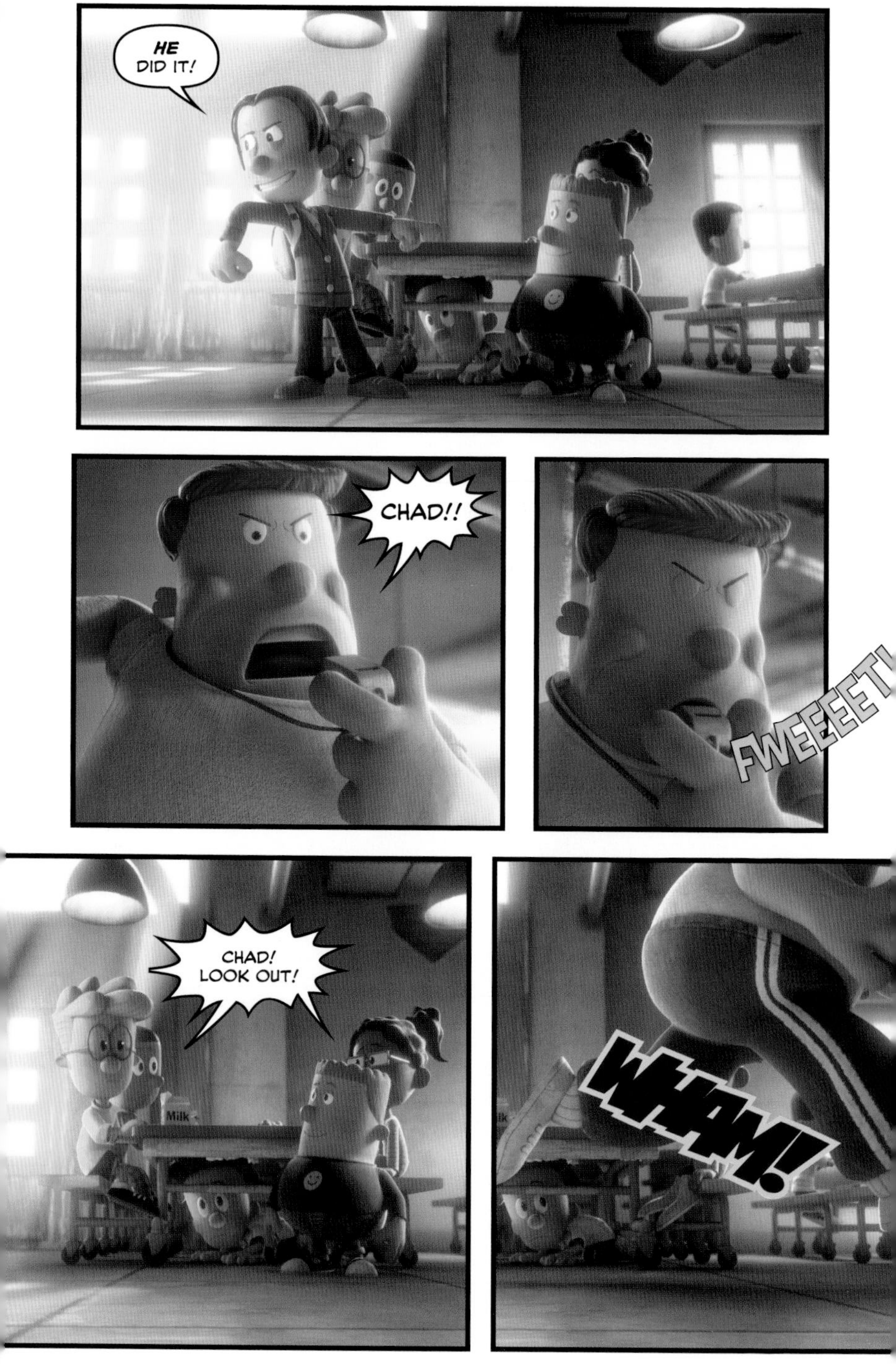
HE DID IT!
CHAD!!
FWEEEET!
CHAD! LOOK OUT!
WHAM!

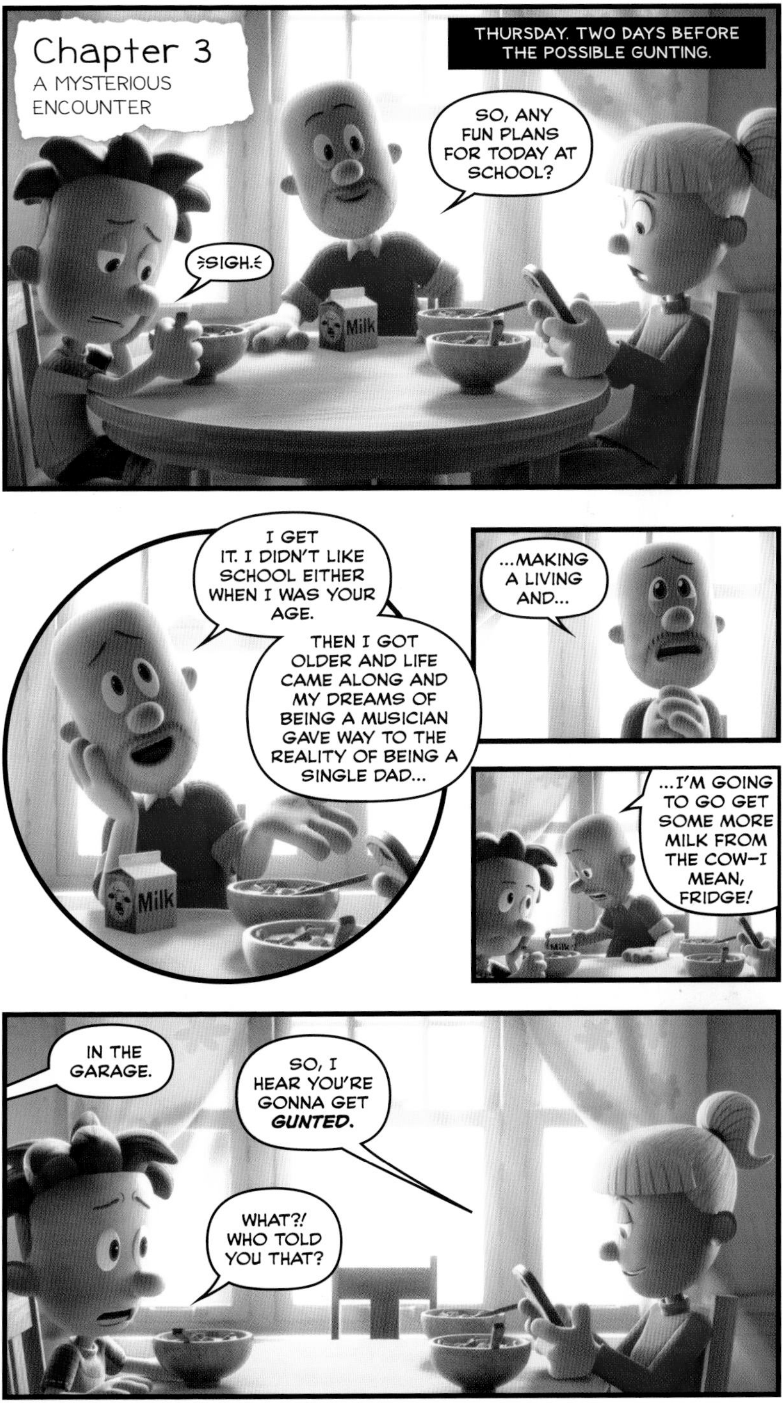

Chapter 3
A MYSTERIOUS ENCOUNTER
THURSDAY. TWO DAYS BEFORE THE POSSIBLE GUNTING.
SO, ANY FUN PLANS FOR TODAY AT SCHOOL?
SIGH.
Milk
I GET IT. I DIDN'T LIKE SCHOOL EITHER WHEN I WAS YOUR AGE.
THEN I GOT OLDER AND LIFE CAME ALONG AND MY DREAMS OF BEING A MUSICIAN GAVE WAY TO THE REALITY OF BEING A SINGLE DAD...
Milk
...MAKING A LIVING AND...
...I'M GOING TO GO GET SOME MORE MILK FROM THE COW—I MEAN, FRIDGE!
IN THE GARAGE.
SO, I HEAR YOU'RE GONNA GET ***GUNTED.***
WHAT?! WHO TOLD YOU THAT?

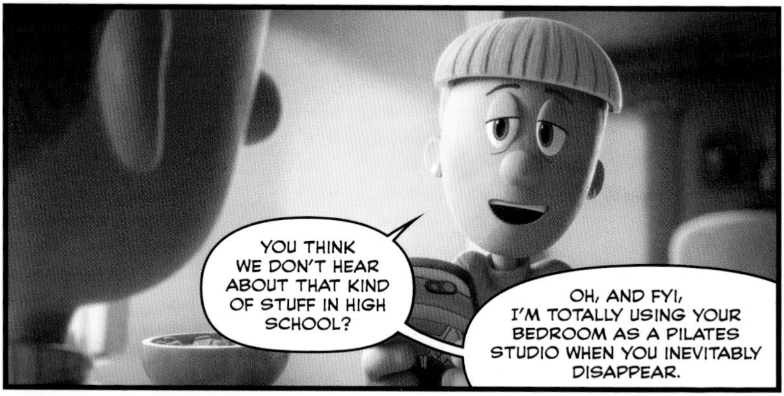
YOU THINK WE DON'T HEAR ABOUT THAT KIND OF STUFF IN HIGH SCHOOL?
OH, AND FYI, I'M TOTALLY USING YOUR BEDROOM AS A PILATES STUDIO WHEN YOU INEVITABLY DISAPPEAR.

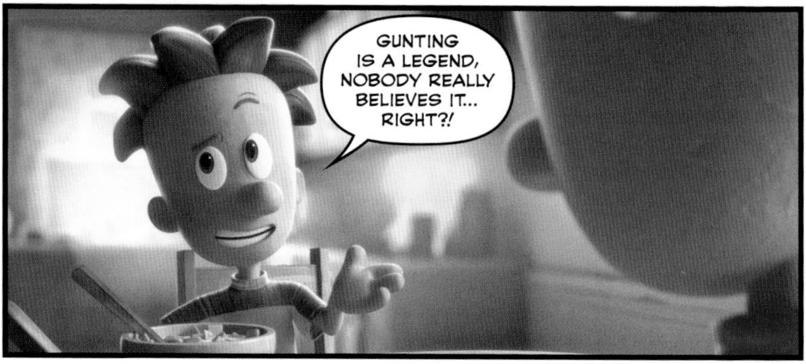
GUNTING IS A LEGEND, NOBODY REALLY BELIEVES IT... RIGHT?!

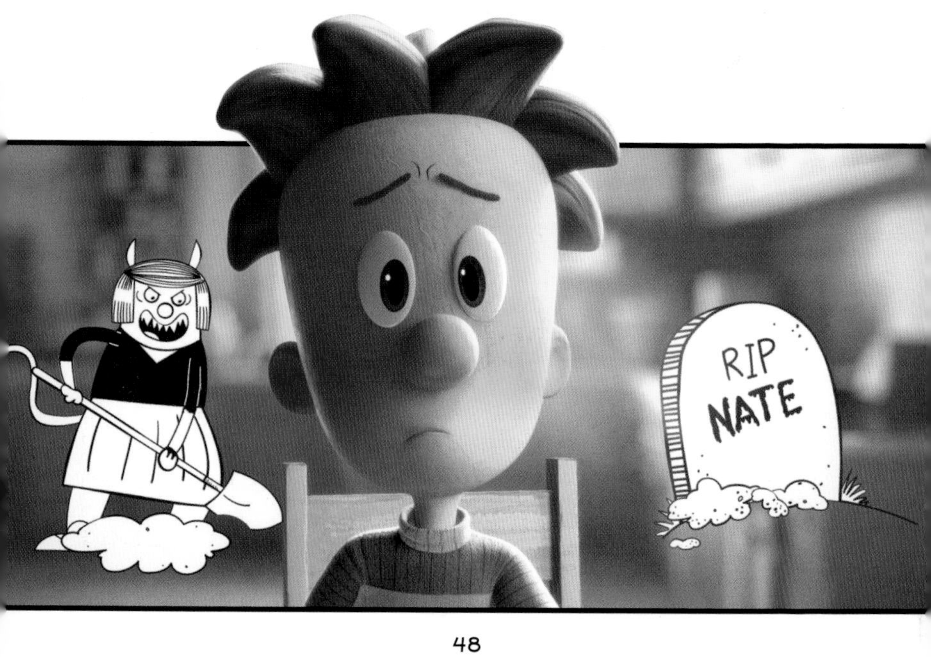
RIP NATE

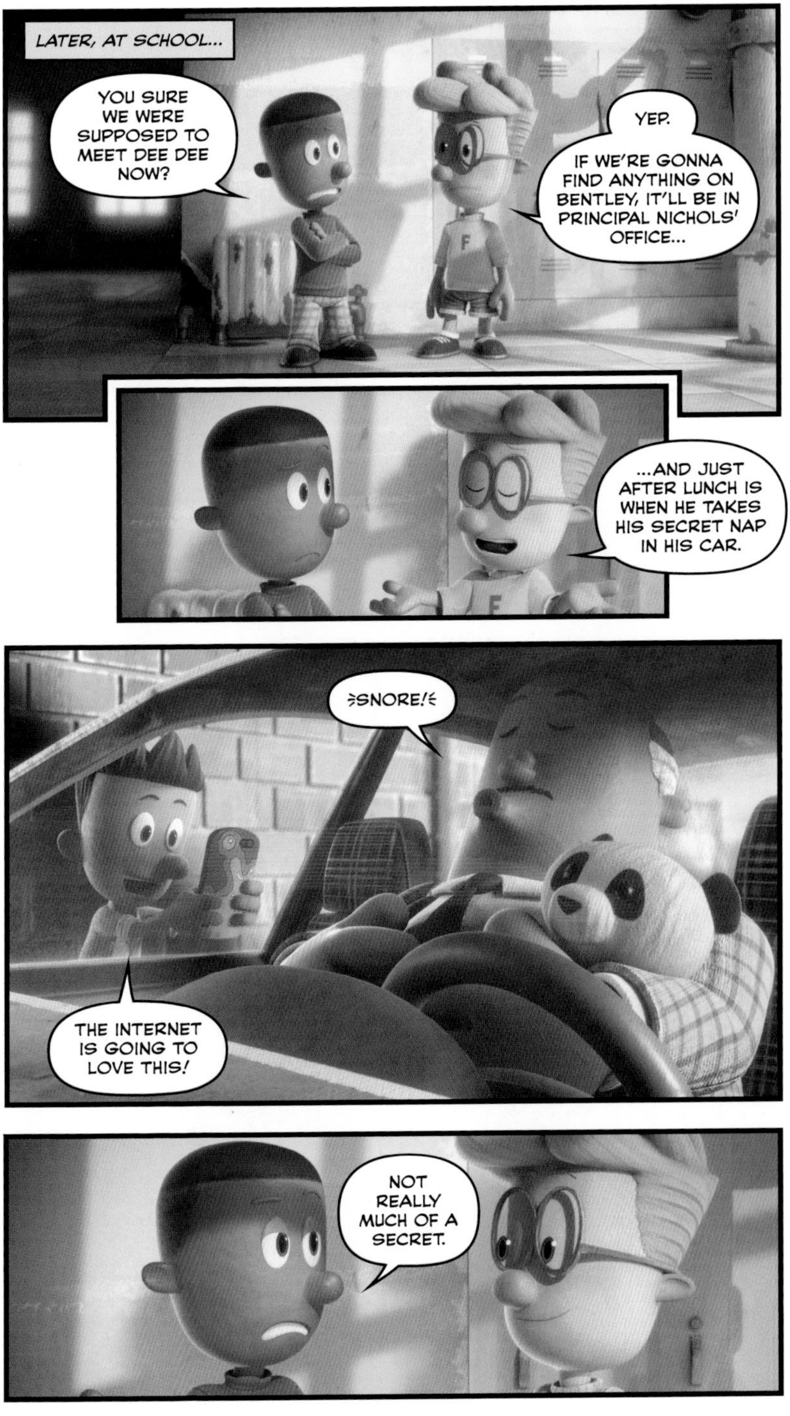
LATER, AT SCHOOL...
YOU SURE WE WERE SUPPOSED TO MEET DEE DEE NOW?
YEP.
IF WE'RE GONNA FIND ANYTHING ON BENTLEY, IT'LL BE IN PRINCIPAL NICHOLS' OFFICE...
...AND JUST AFTER LUNCH IS WHEN HE TAKES HIS SECRET NAP IN HIS CAR.
SNORE!
THE INTERNET IS GOING TO LOVE THIS!
NOT REALLY MUCH OF A SECRET.

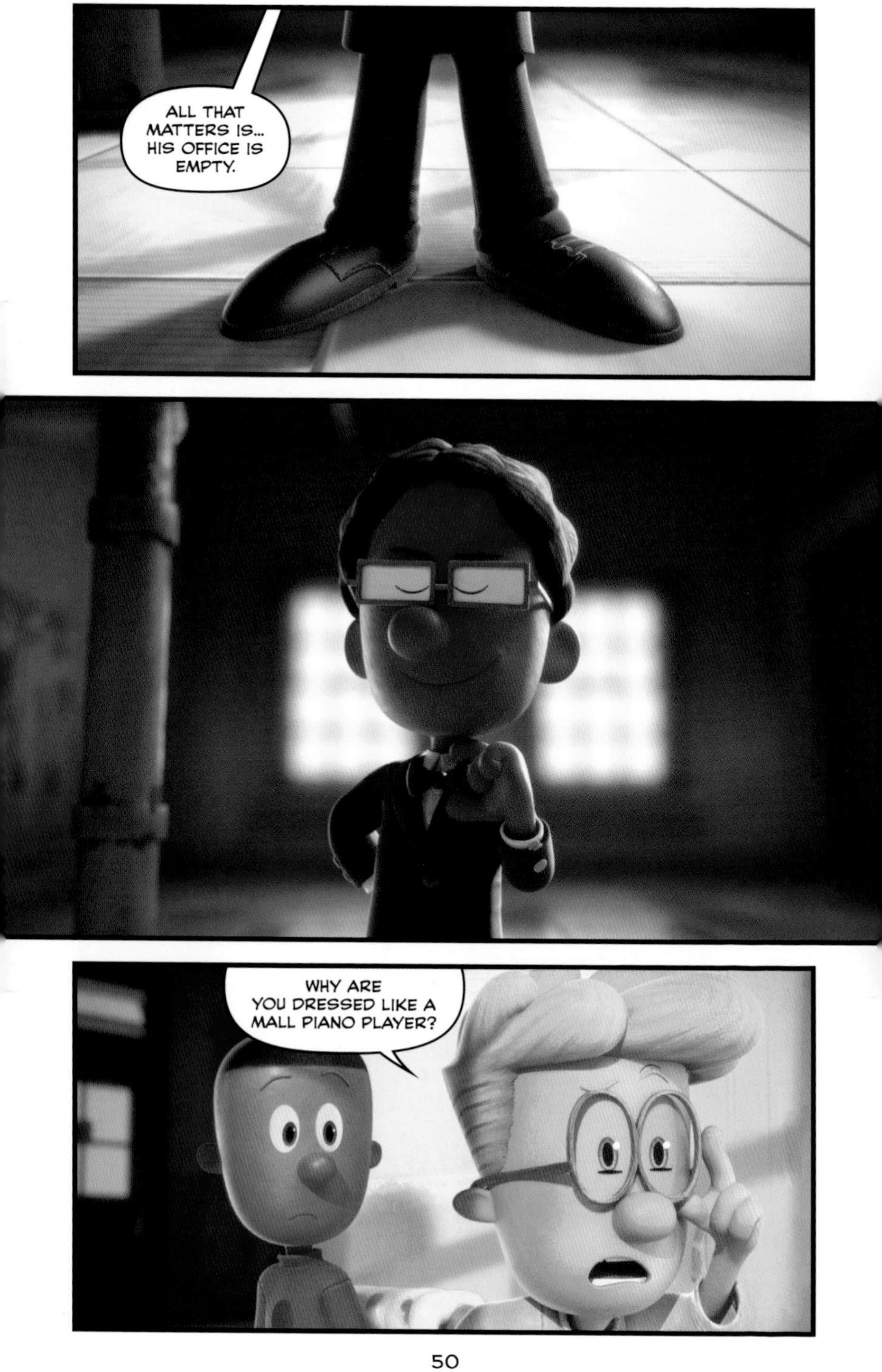
ALL THAT MATTERS IS... HIS OFFICE IS EMPTY.
WHY ARE YOU DRESSED LIKE A MALL PIANO PLAYER?

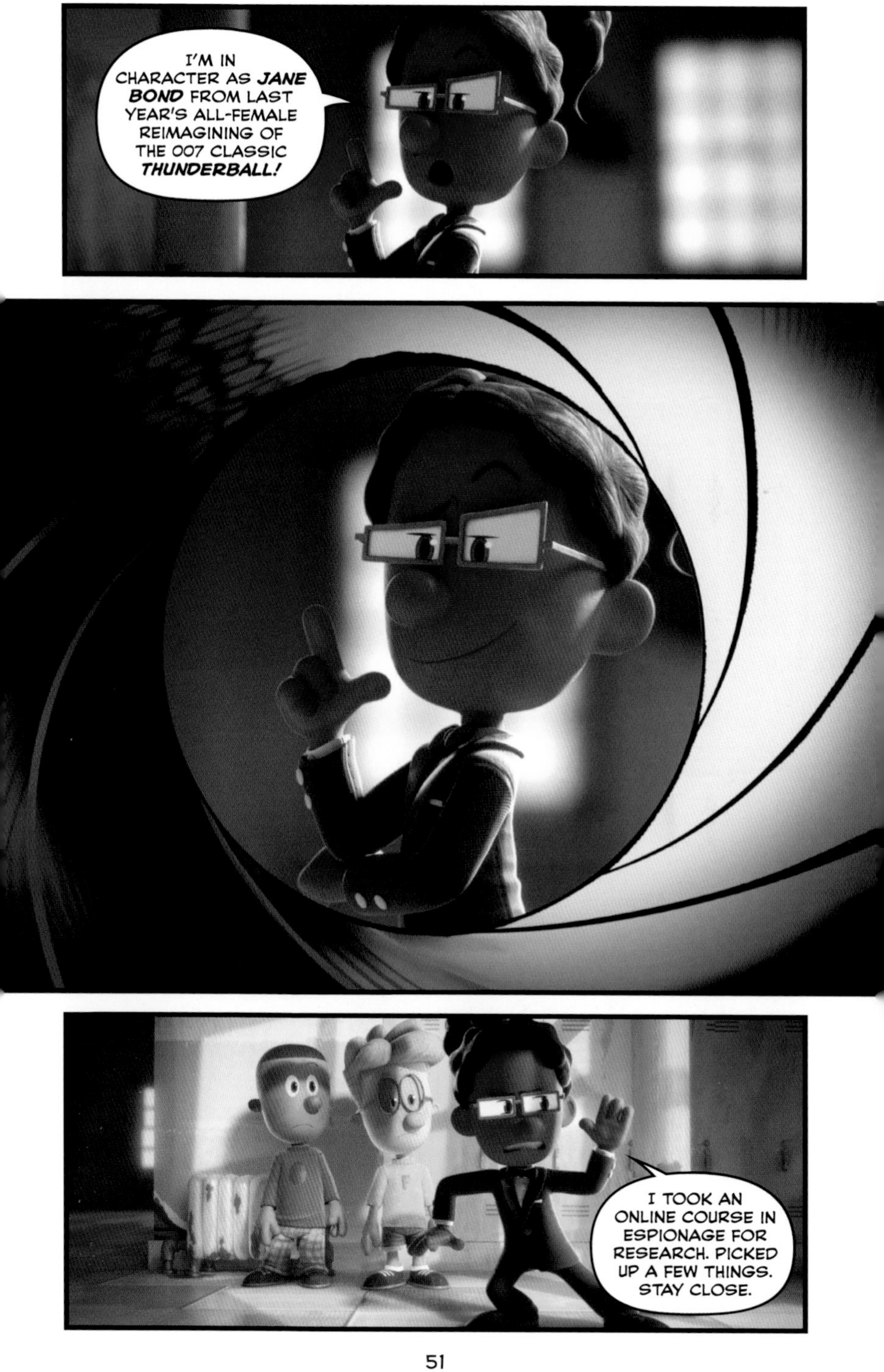
I'M IN CHARACTER AS JANE BOND FROM LAST YEAR'S ALL-FEMALE REIMAGINING OF THE 007 CLASSIC THUNDERBALL!
I TOOK AN ONLINE COURSE IN ESPIONAGE FOR RESEARCH. PICKED UP A FEW THINGS. STAY CLOSE.

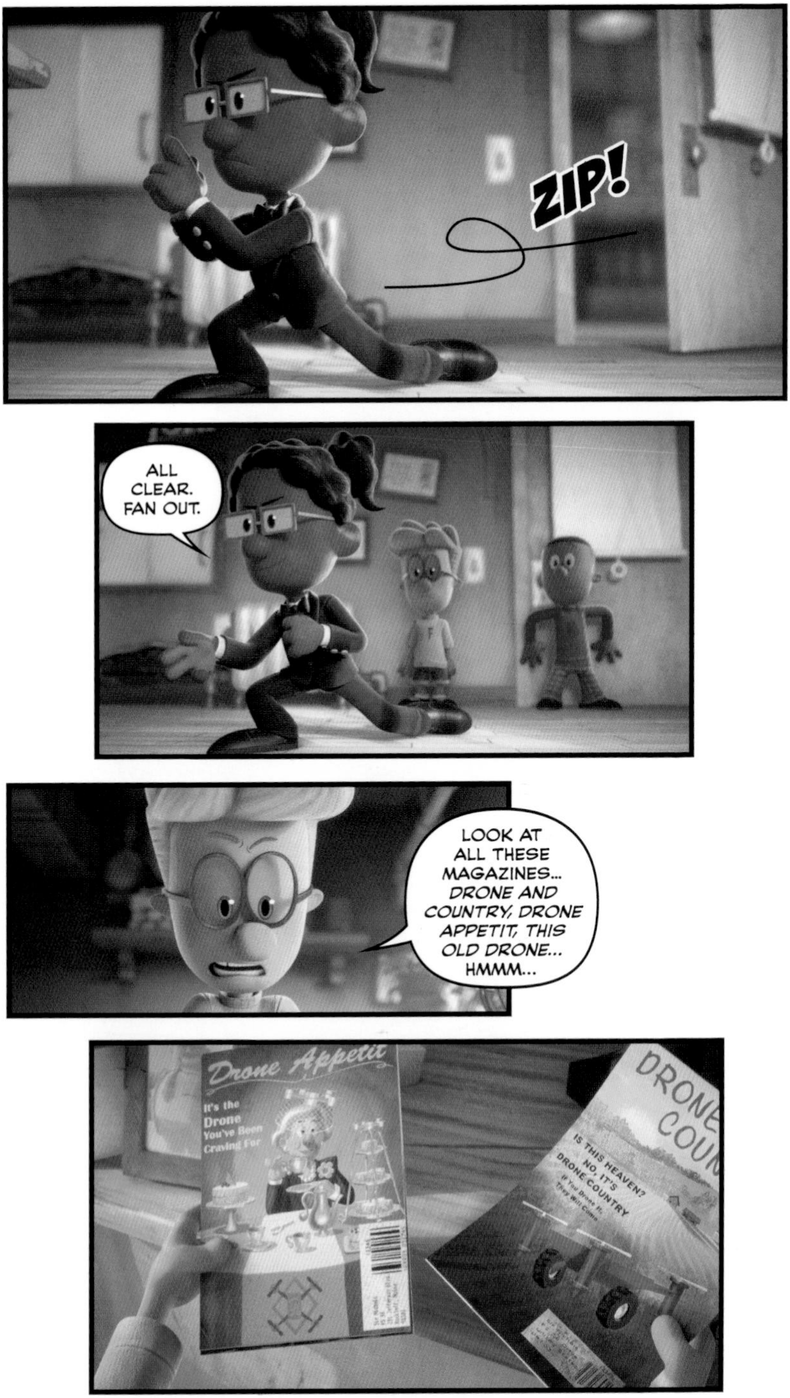
ZIP!
ALL CLEAR. FAN OUT.
LOOK AT ALL THESE MAGAZINES... *DRONE AND COUNTRY, DRONE APPETIT, THIS OLD DRONE*... HMMM...
Drone Appetit
It's the Drone You've Been Craving For
DRONE COUN
IS THIS HEAVEN? NO, IT'S DRONE COUNTRY
If You Drone It, They Will Come

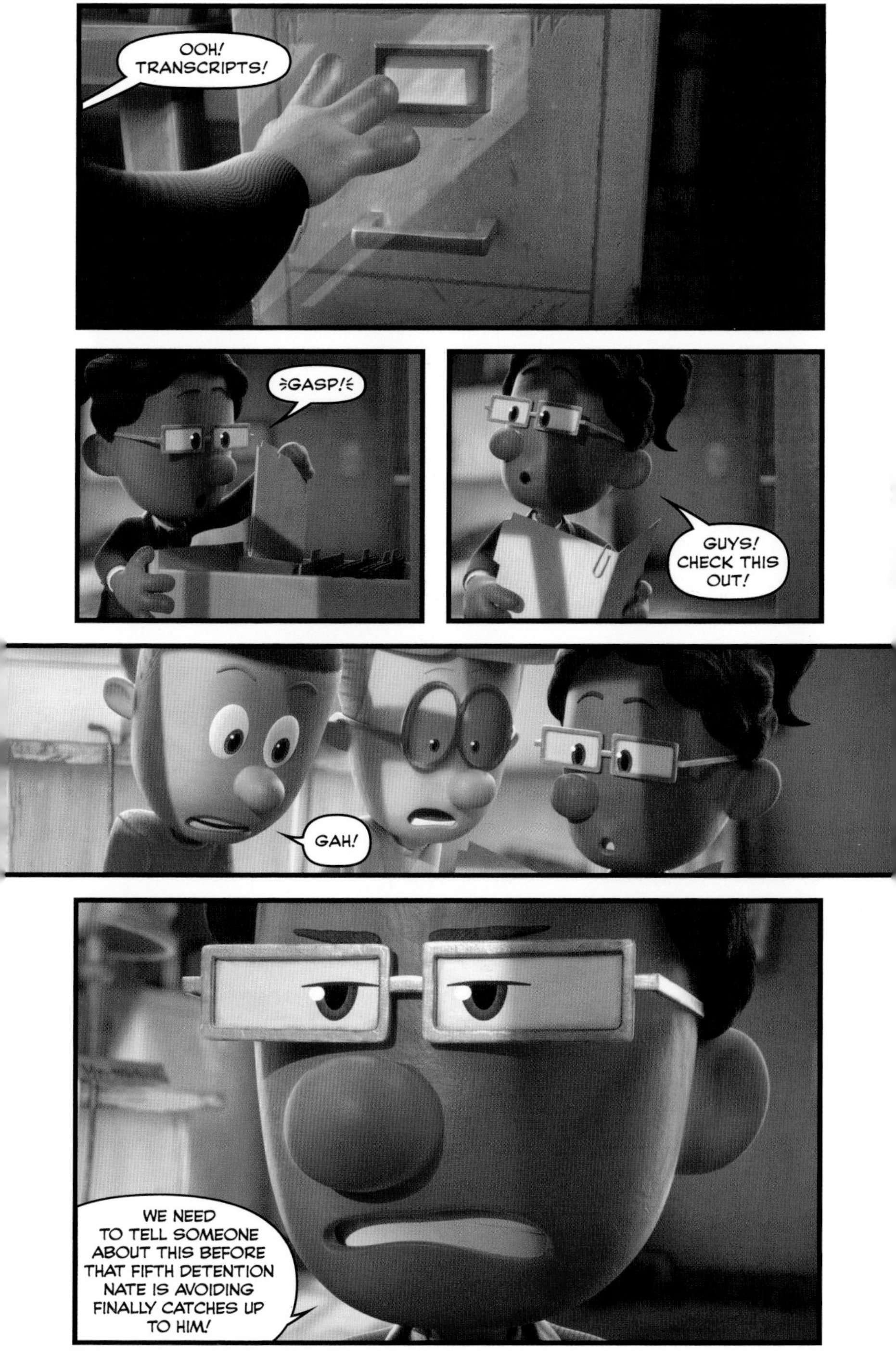
OOH! TRANSCRIPTS!
GASP!
GUYS! CHECK THIS OUT!
GAH!
WE NEED TO TELL SOMEONE ABOUT THIS BEFORE THAT FIFTH DETENTION NATE IS AVOIDING FINALLY CATCHES UP TO HIM!

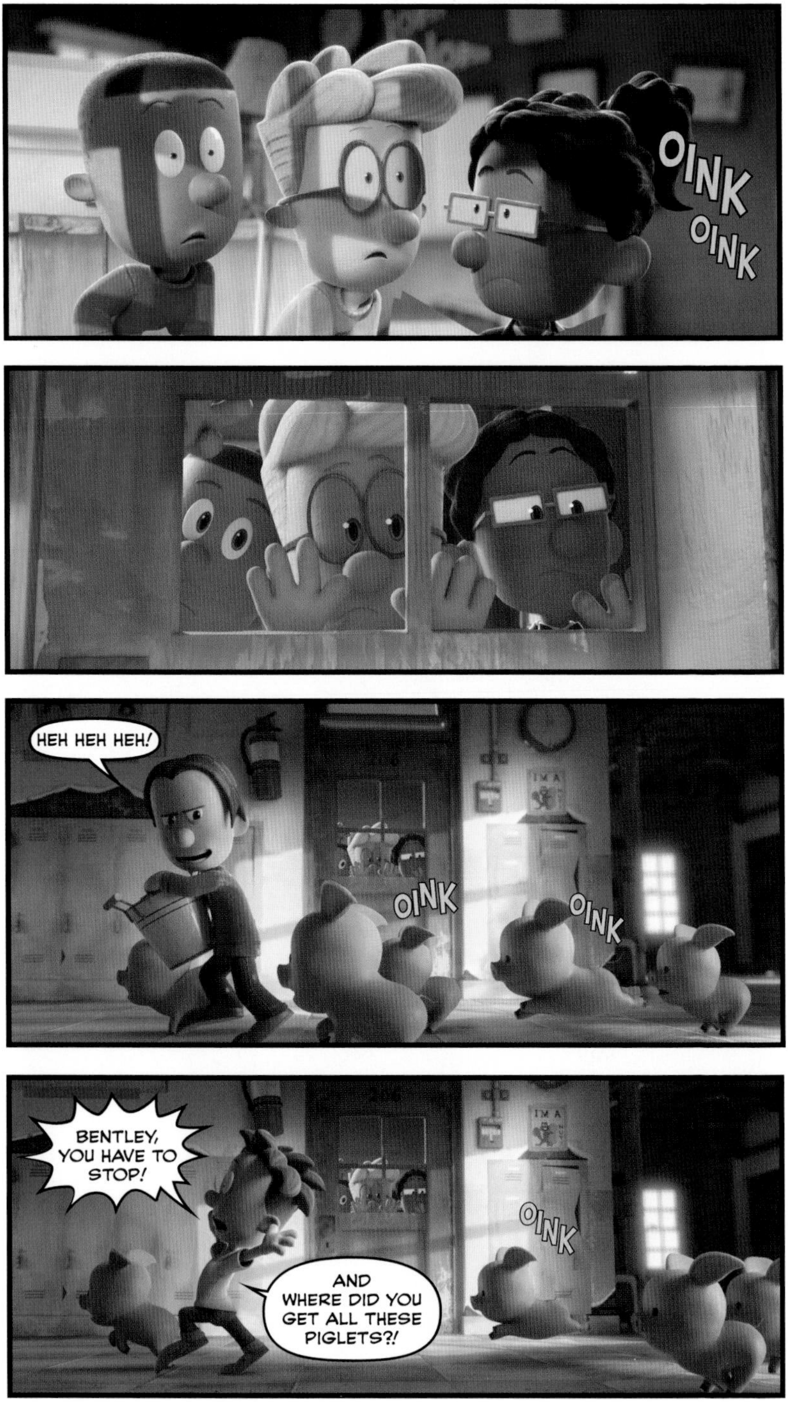
OINK
OINK
HEH HEH HEH!
OINK
OINK
BENTLEY, YOU HAVE TO STOP!
OINK
AND WHERE DID YOU GET ALL THESE PIGLETS?!

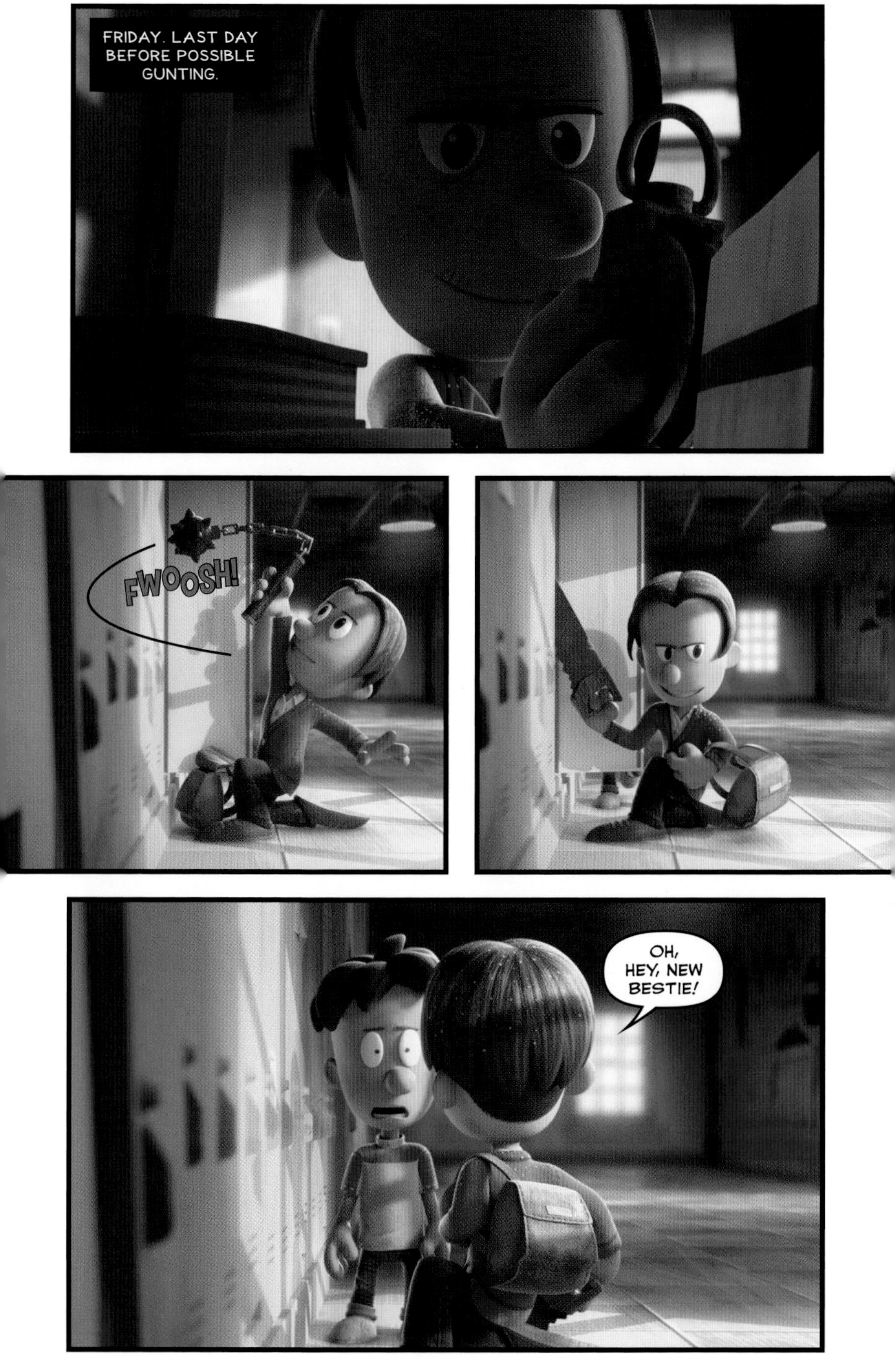
FRIDAY. LAST DAY BEFORE POSSIBLE GUNTING.
FWOOSH!
OH, HEY, NEW BESTIE!

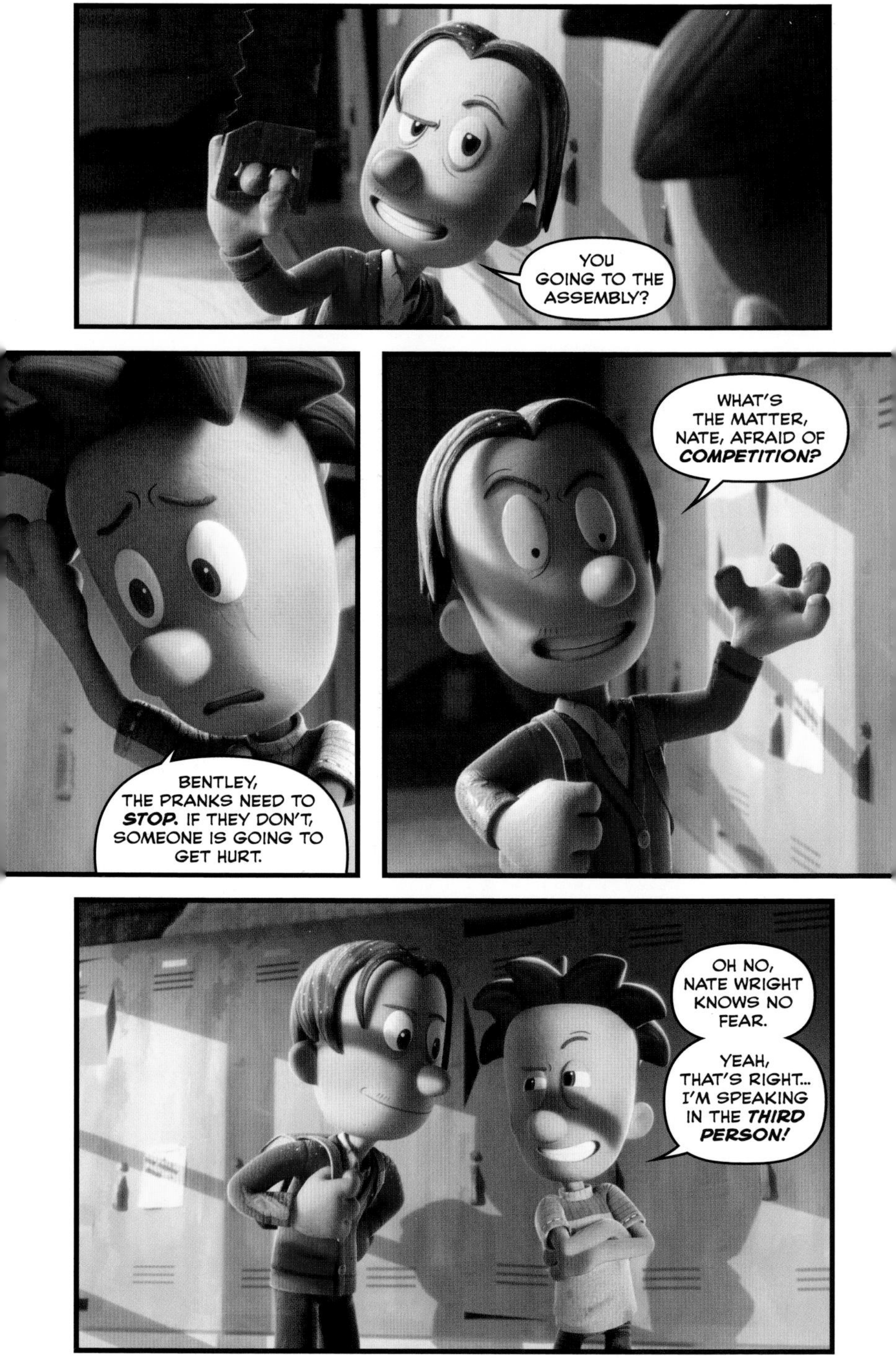
YOU GOING TO THE ASSEMBLY?
BENTLEY, THE PRANKS NEED TO **STOP.** IF THEY DON'T, SOMEONE IS GOING TO GET HURT.
WHAT'S THE MATTER, NATE, AFRAID OF ***COMPETITION?***
OH NO, NATE WRIGHT KNOWS NO FEAR.
YEAH, THAT'S RIGHT... I'M SPEAKING IN THE ***THIRD PERSON!***

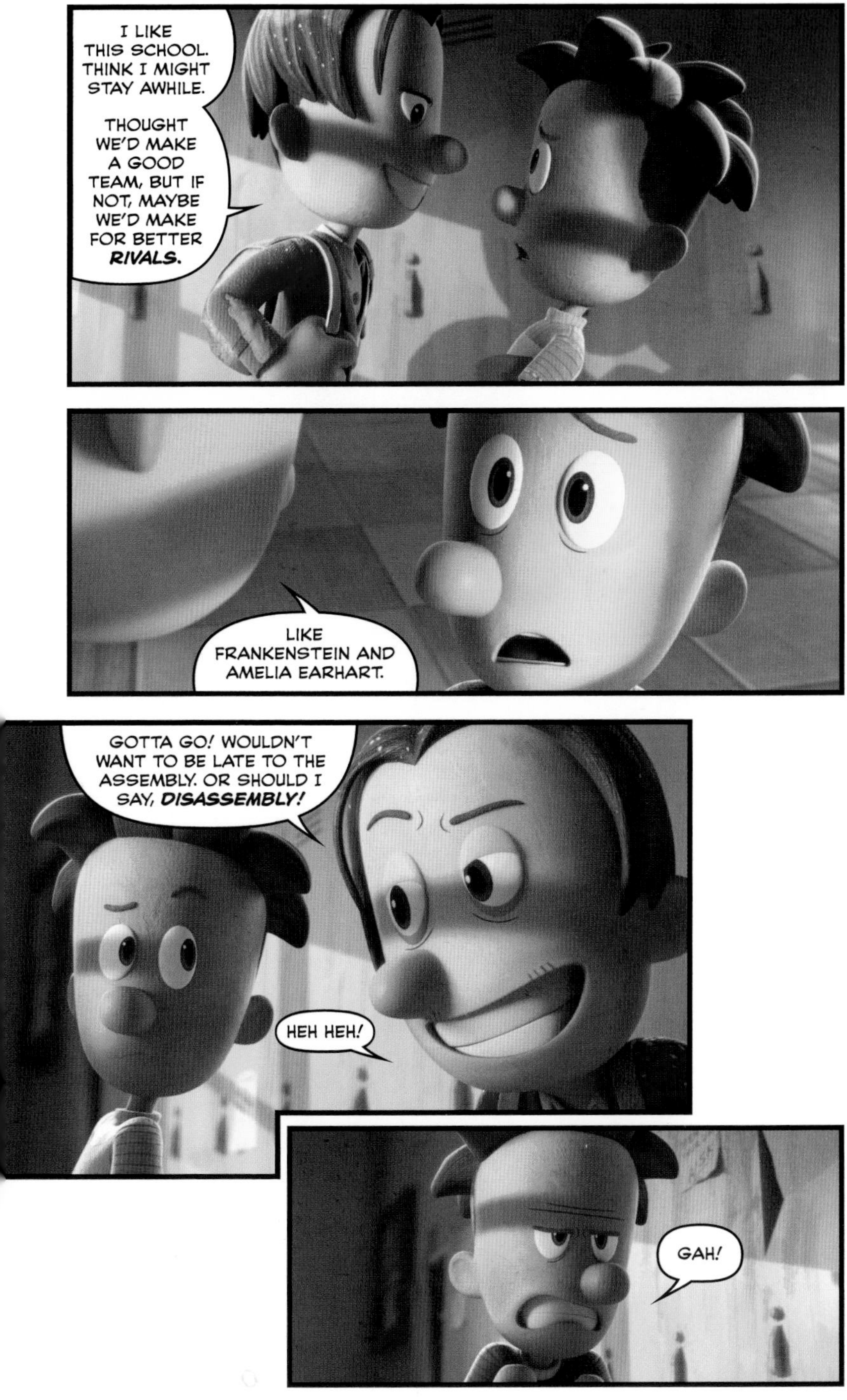
I LIKE THIS SCHOOL. THINK I MIGHT STAY AWHILE.
THOUGHT WE'D MAKE A GOOD TEAM, BUT IF NOT, MAYBE WE'D MAKE FOR BETTER ***RIVALS.***
LIKE FRANKENSTEIN AND AMELIA EARHART.
GOTTA GO! WOULDN'T WANT TO BE LATE TO THE ASSEMBLY. OR SHOULD I SAY, ***DISASSEMBLY!***
HEH HEH!
GAH!

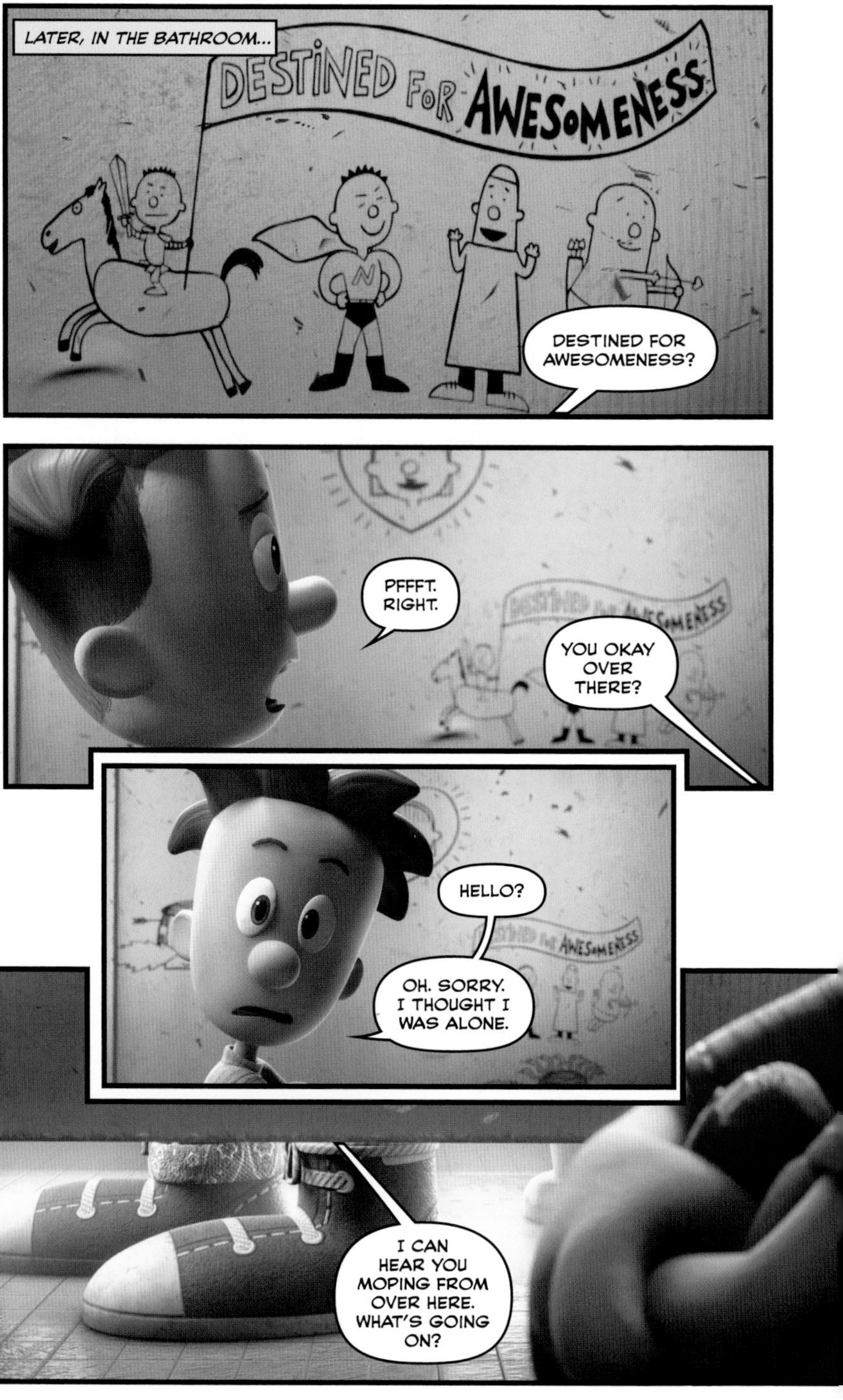
LATER, IN THE BATHROOM...
DESTINED FOR AWESOMENESS
DESTINED FOR AWESOMENESS?
PFFFT. RIGHT.
YOU OKAY OVER THERE?
HELLO?
OH. SORRY. I THOUGHT I WAS ALONE.
I CAN HEAR YOU MOPING FROM OVER HERE. WHAT'S GOING ON?

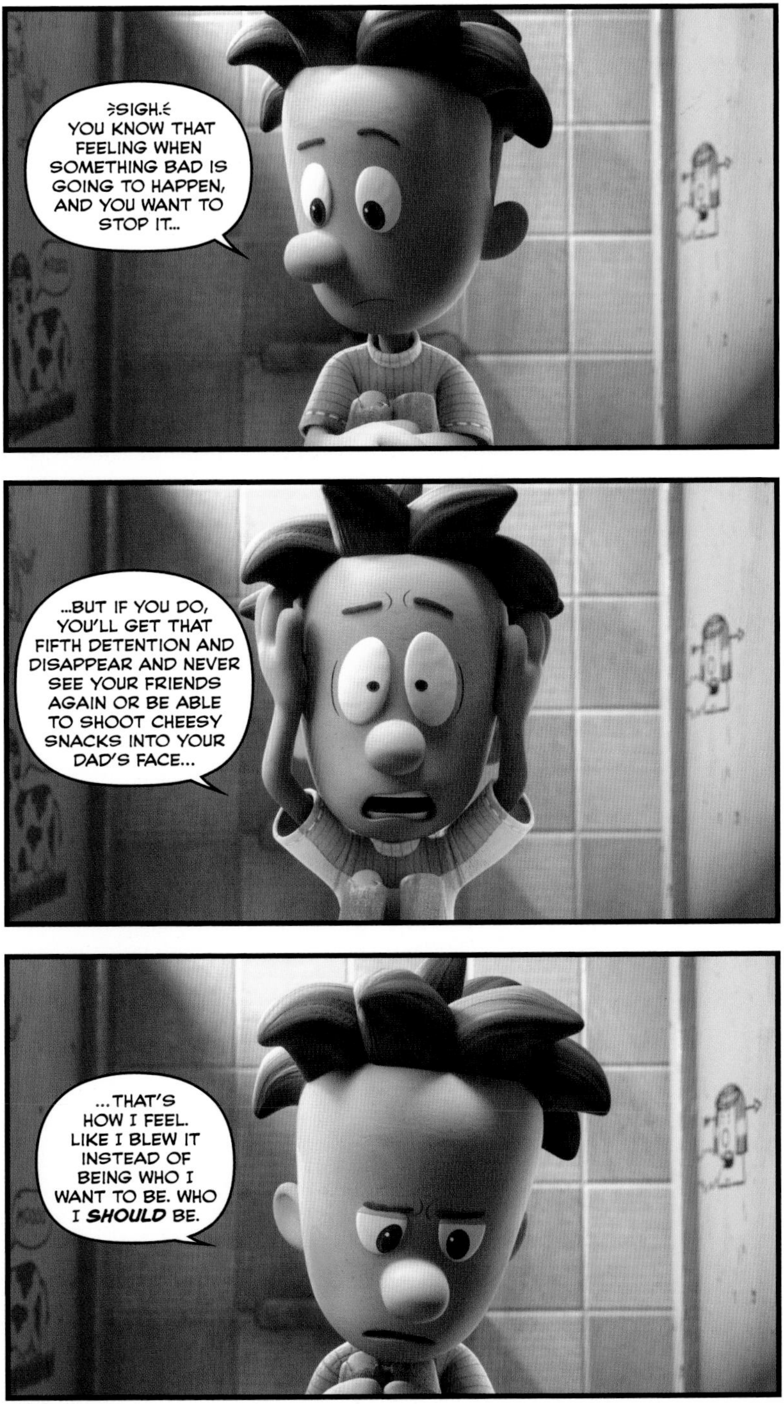

⋟SIGH.⋞ YOU KNOW THAT FEELING WHEN SOMETHING BAD IS GOING TO HAPPEN, AND YOU WANT TO STOP IT...
...BUT IF YOU DO, YOU'LL GET THAT FIFTH DETENTION AND DISAPPEAR AND NEVER SEE YOUR FRIENDS AGAIN OR BE ABLE TO SHOOT CHEESY SNACKS INTO YOUR DAD'S FACE...
...THAT'S HOW I FEEL. LIKE I BLEW IT INSTEAD OF BEING WHO I WANT TO BE. WHO I ***SHOULD*** BE.

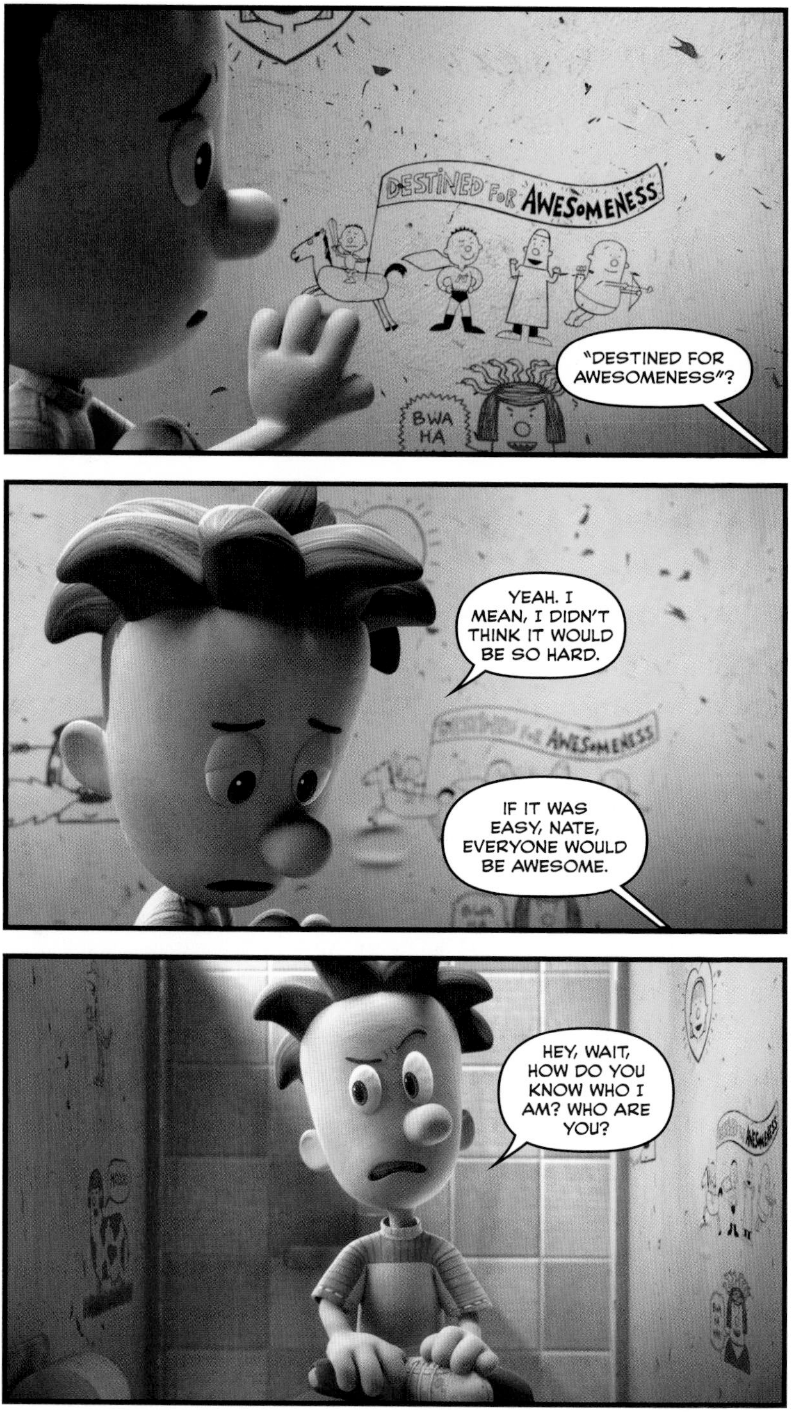
DESTINED FOR AWESOMENESS
BWA HA
"DESTINED FOR AWESOMENESS"?
YEAH. I MEAN, I DIDN'T THINK IT WOULD BE SO HARD.
IF IT WAS EASY, NATE, EVERYONE WOULD BE AWESOME.
HEY, WAIT, HOW DO YOU KNOW WHO I AM? WHO ARE YOU?

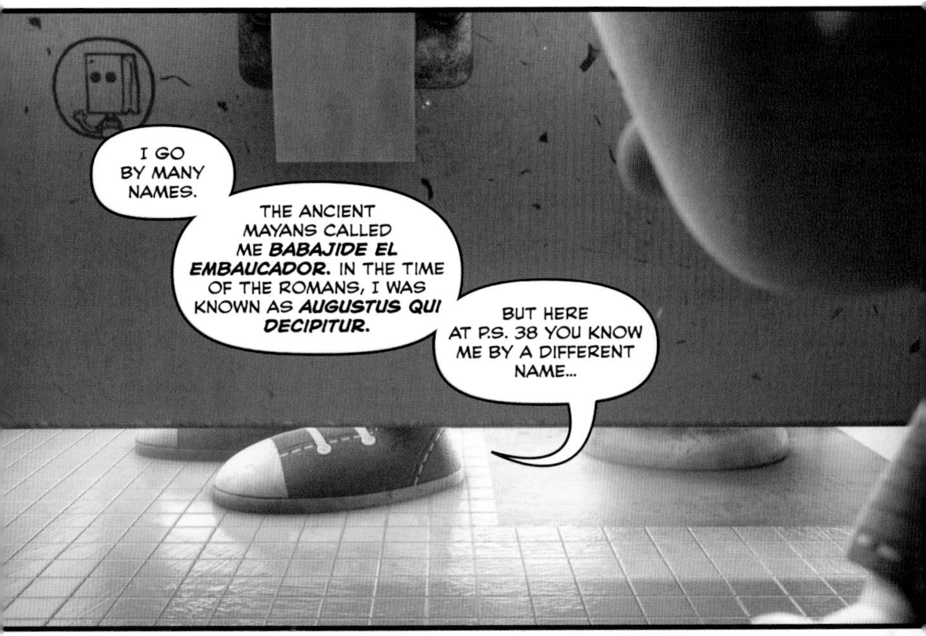
I GO BY MANY NAMES.
THE ANCIENT MAYANS CALLED ME BABAJIDE EL EMBAUCADOR. IN THE TIME OF THE ROMANS, I WAS KNOWN AS AUGUSTUS QUI DECIPITUR.
BUT HERE AT P.S. 38 YOU KNOW ME BY A DIFFERENT NAME...

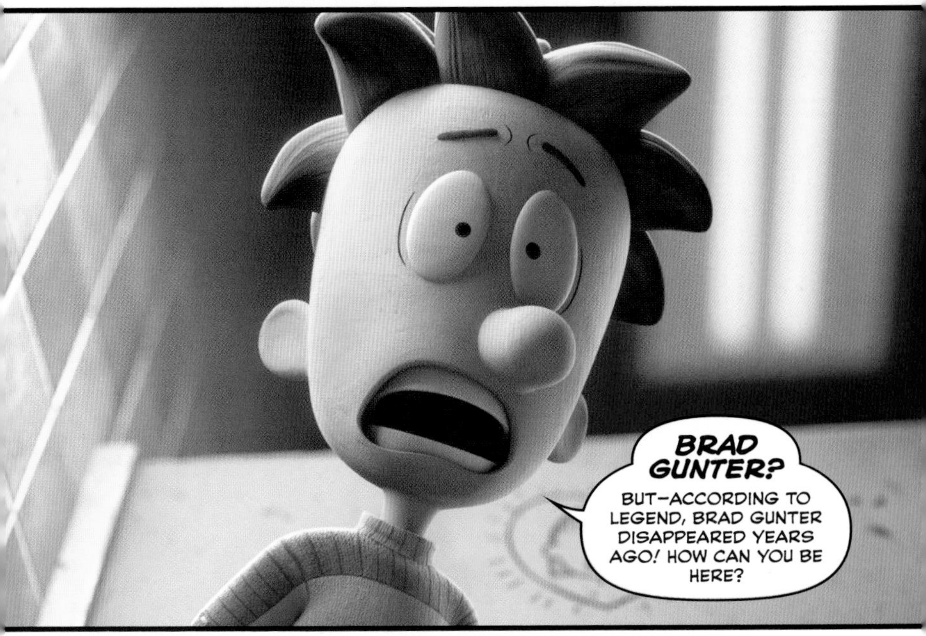
BRAD GUNTER? BUT—ACCORDING TO LEGEND, BRAD GUNTER DISAPPEARED YEARS AGO! HOW CAN YOU BE HERE?

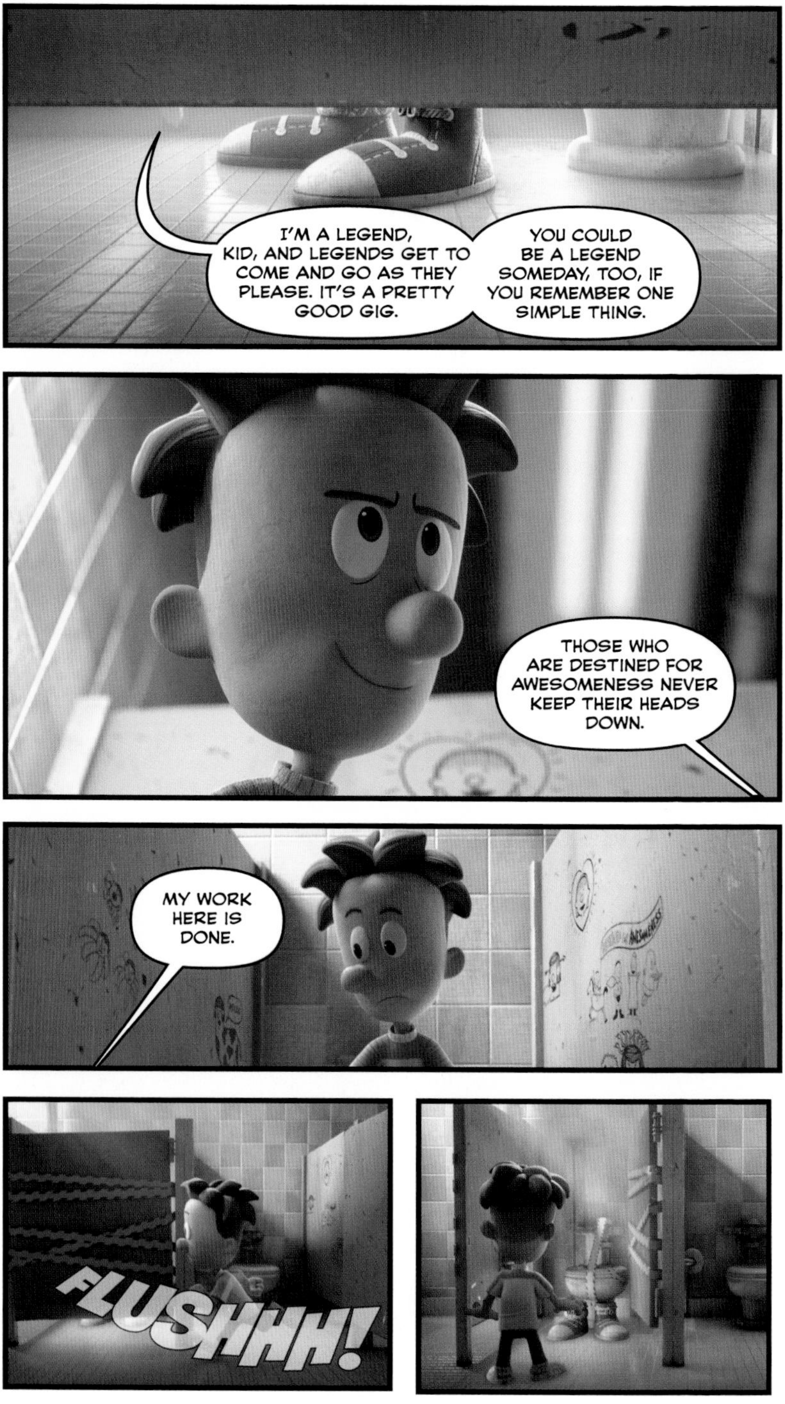
I'M A LEGEND, KID, AND LEGENDS GET TO COME AND GO AS THEY PLEASE. IT'S A PRETTY GOOD GIG.
YOU COULD BE A LEGEND SOMEDAY, TOO, IF YOU REMEMBER ONE SIMPLE THING.
THOSE WHO ARE DESTINED FOR AWESOMENESS NEVER KEEP THEIR HEADS DOWN.
MY WORK HERE IS DONE.
FLUSHHH!

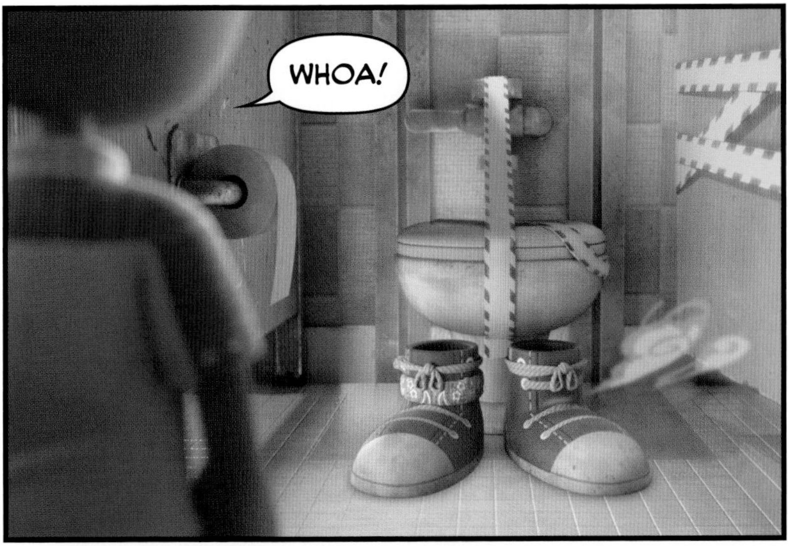
WHOA!

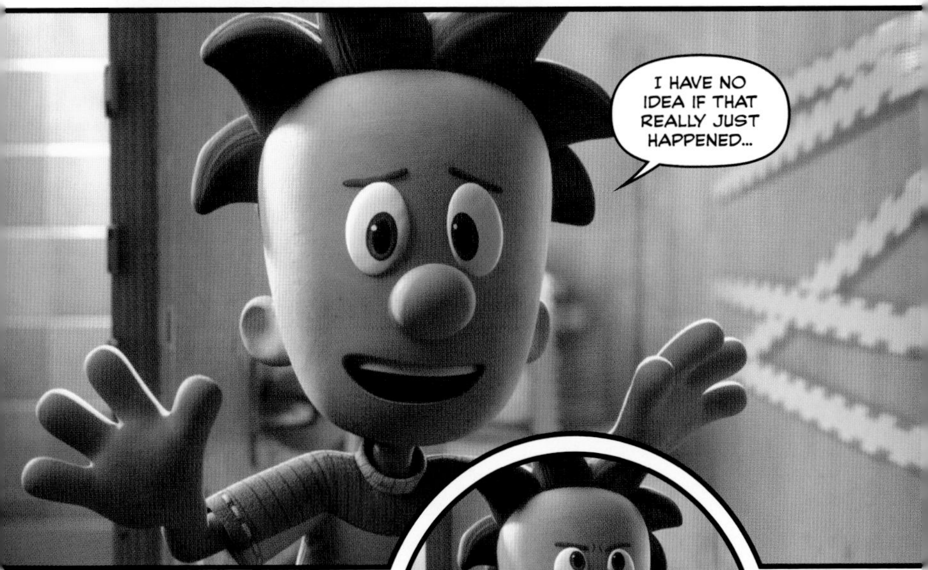
I HAVE NO IDEA IF THAT REALLY JUST HAPPENED...

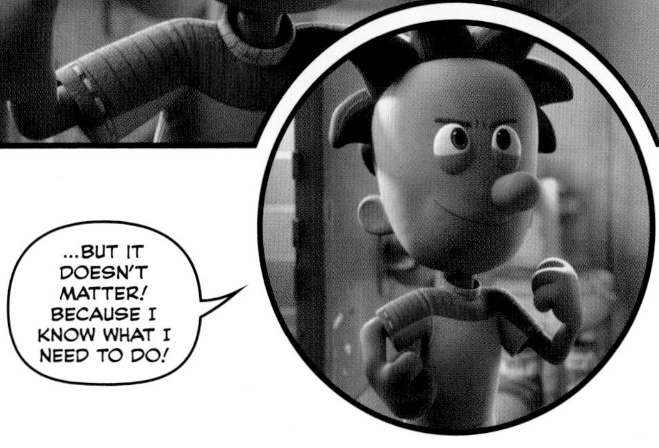
...BUT IT DOESN'T MATTER! BECAUSE I KNOW WHAT I NEED TO DO!

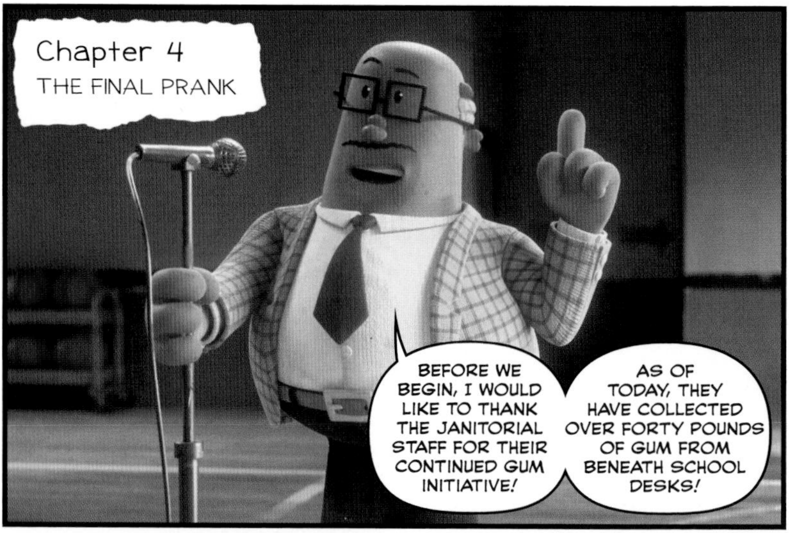
Chapter 4
THE FINAL PRANK
BEFORE WE BEGIN, I WOULD LIKE TO THANK THE JANITORIAL STAFF FOR THEIR CONTINUED GUM INITIATIVE!
AS OF TODAY, THEY HAVE COLLECTED OVER FORTY POUNDS OF GUM FROM BENEATH SCHOOL DESKS!

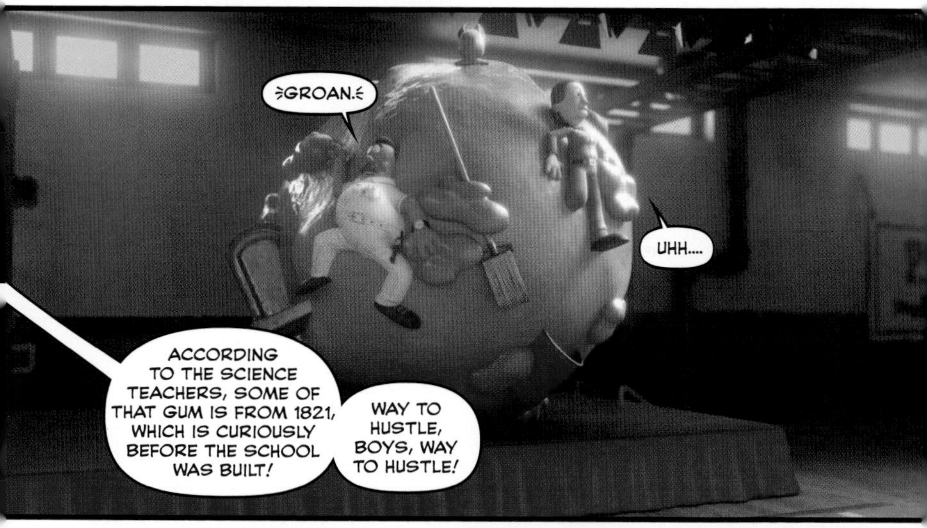
GROAN.
UHH....
ACCORDING TO THE SCIENCE TEACHERS, SOME OF THAT GUM IS FROM 1821, WHICH IS CURIOUSLY BEFORE THE SCHOOL WAS BUILT!
WAY TO HUSTLE, BOYS, WAY TO HUSTLE!

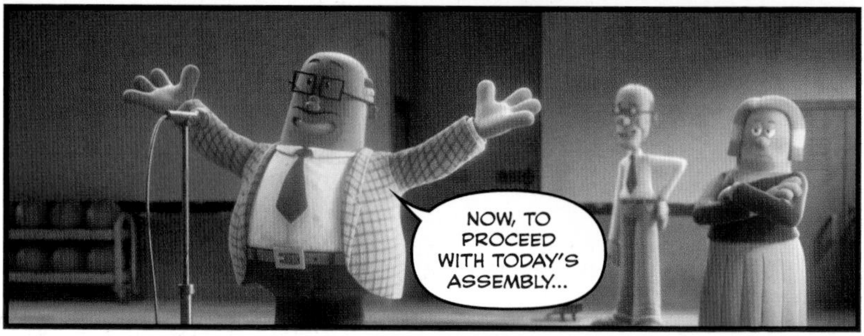
NOW, TO PROCEED WITH TODAY'S ASSEMBLY...

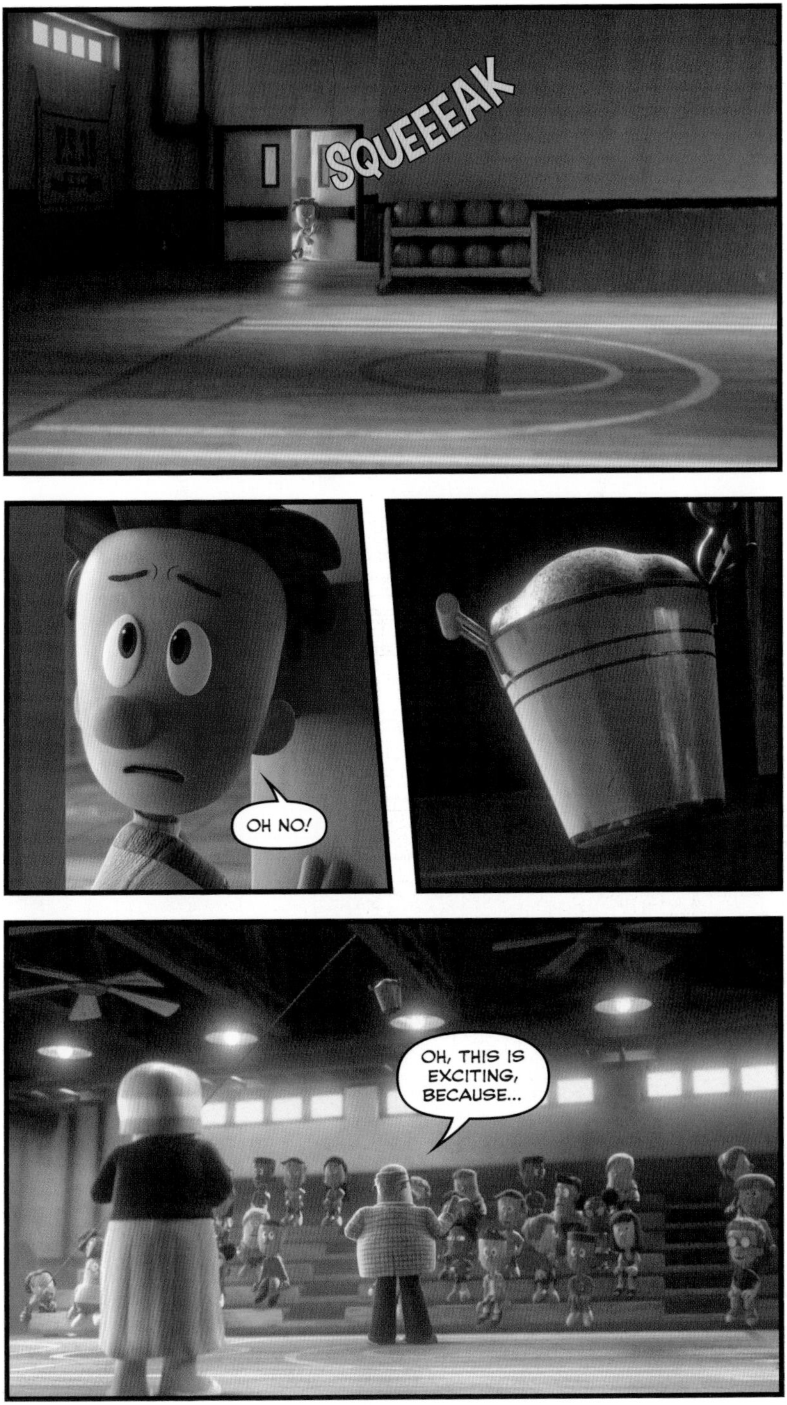
SQUEEEAK
OH NO!
OH, THIS IS EXCITING, BECAUSE...

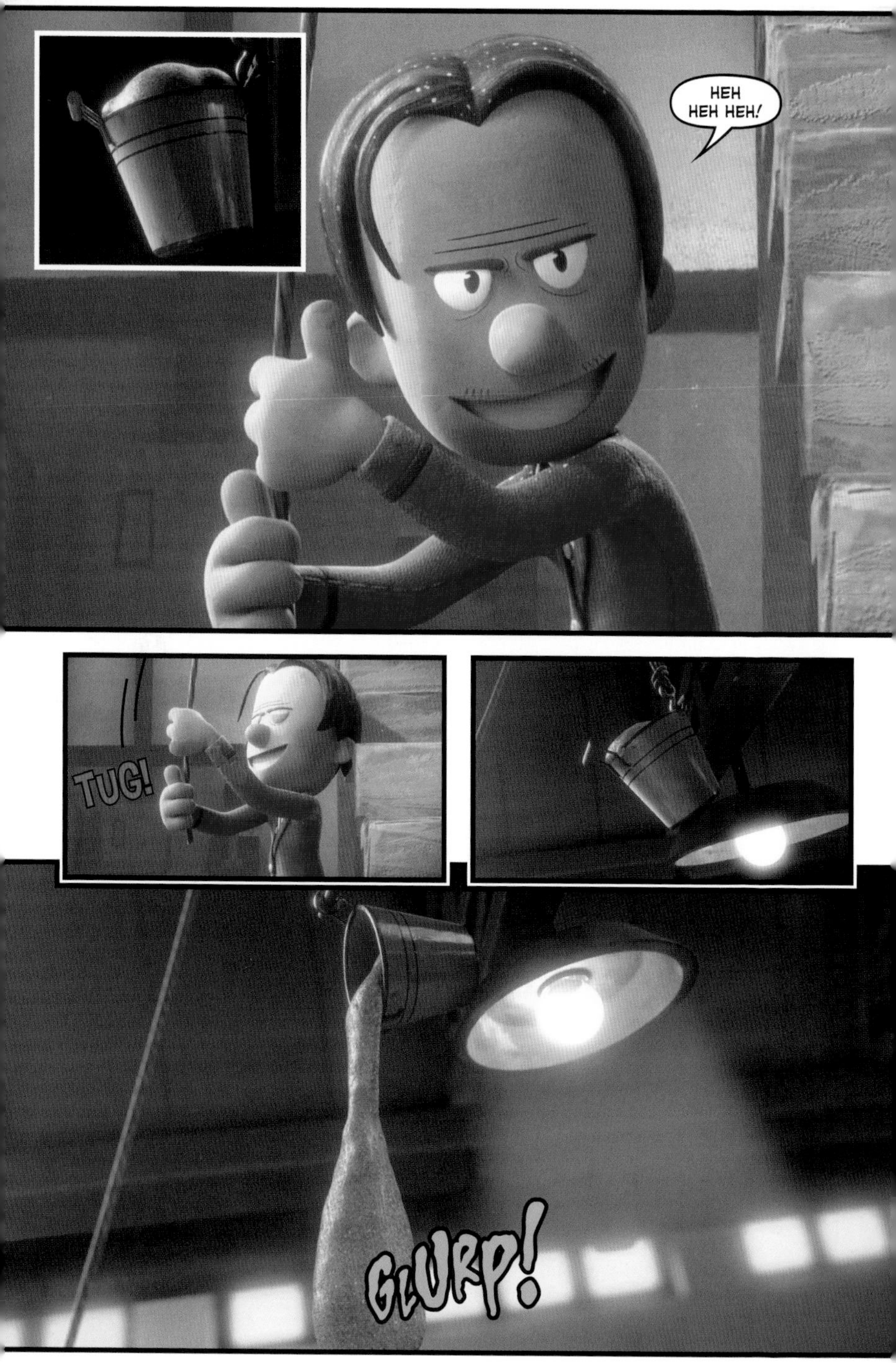
HEH
HEH HEH!
TUG!
GLURP!

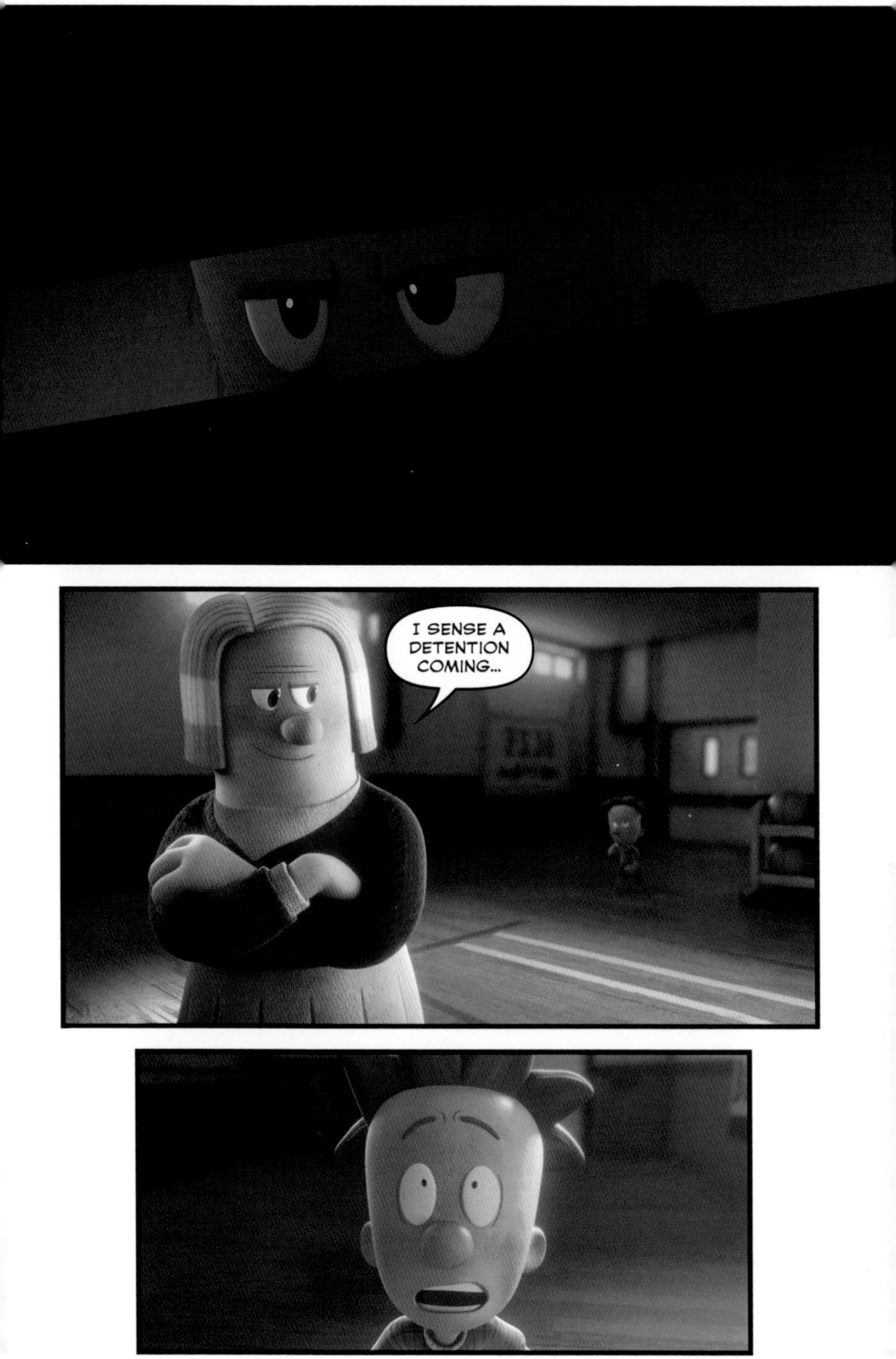
I SENSE A DETENTION COMING...

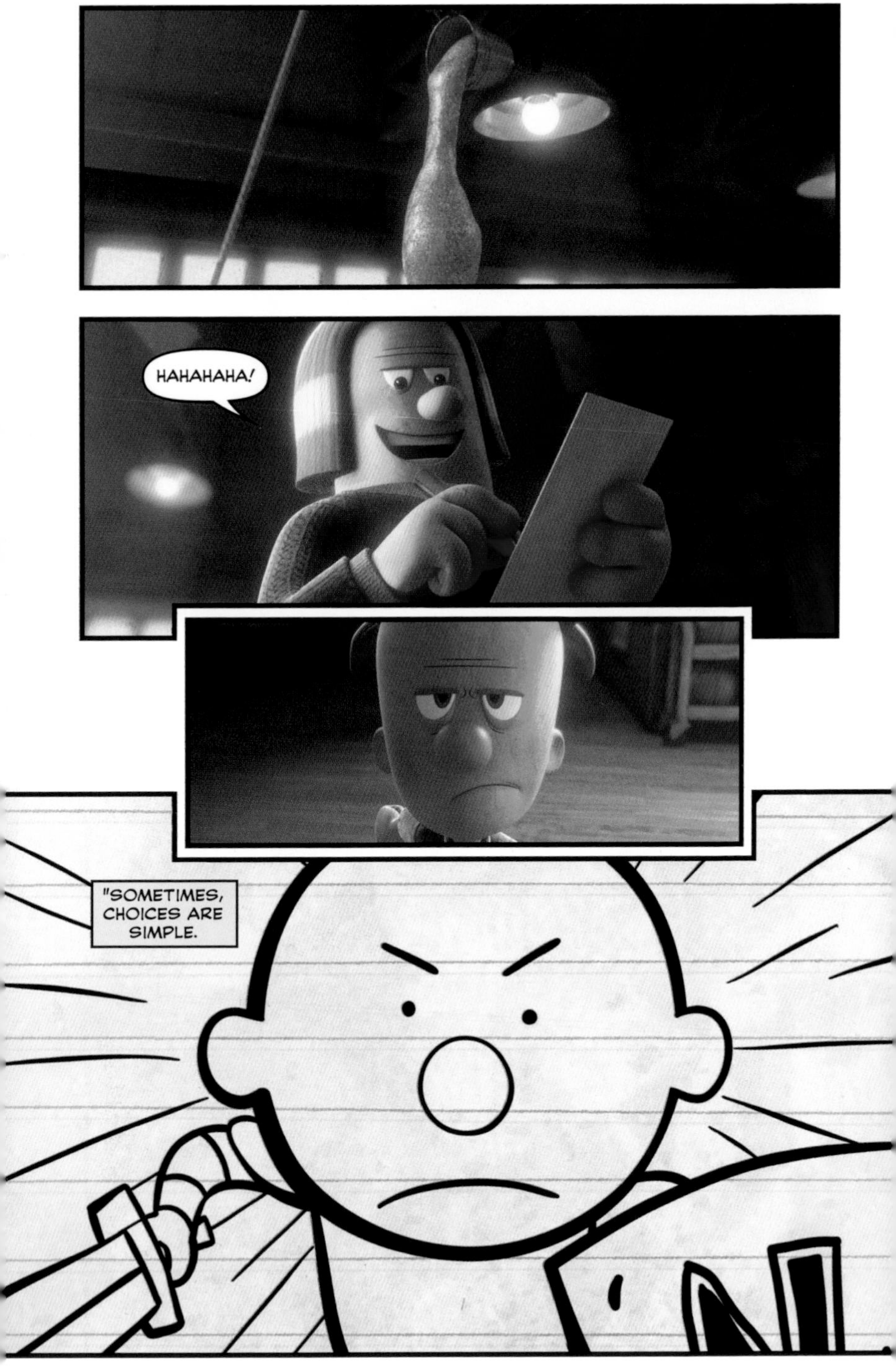
HAHAHAHA!
"SOMETIMES, CHOICES ARE SIMPLE.

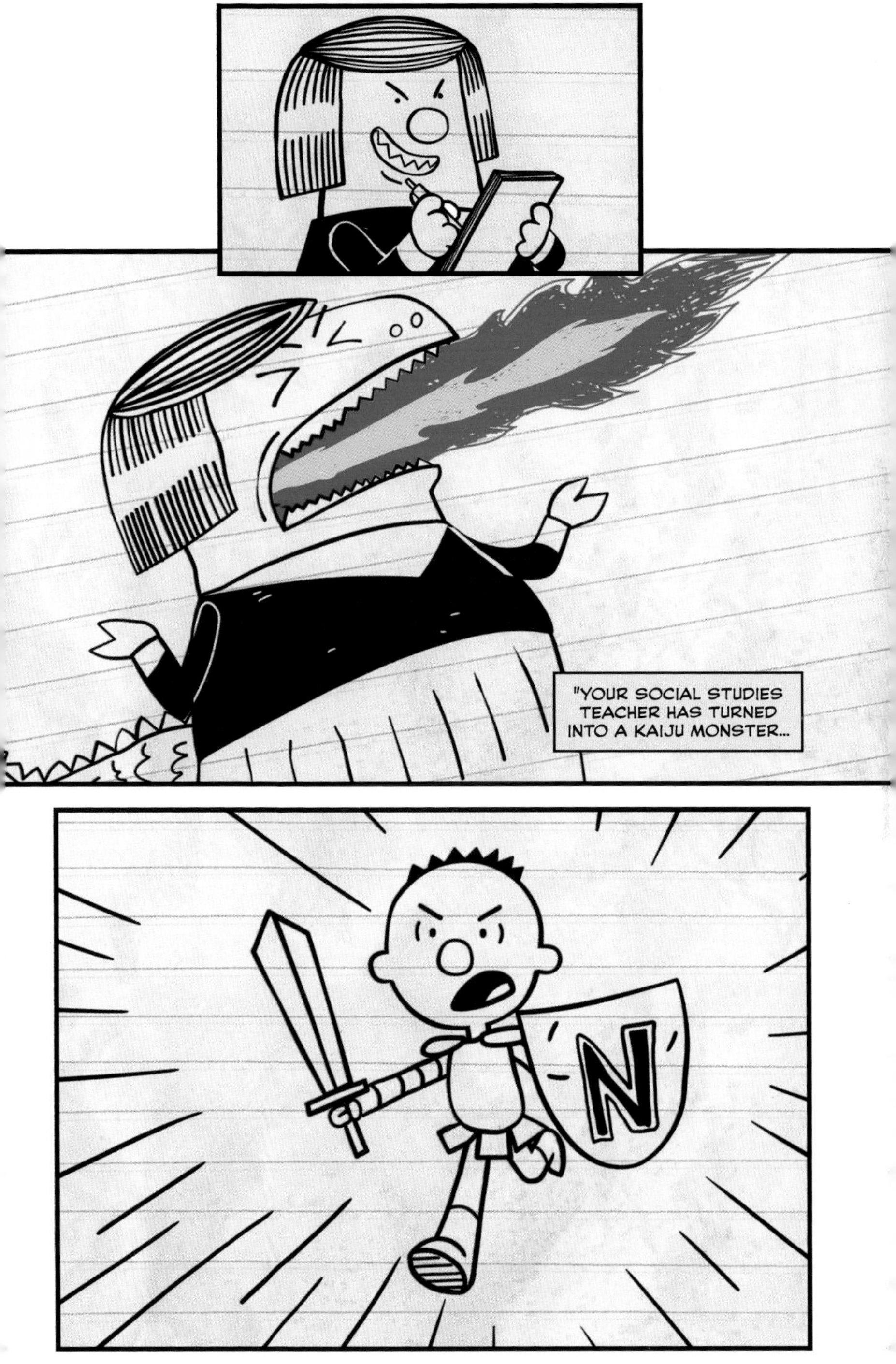
"YOUR SOCIAL STUDIES
TEACHER HAS TURNED
INTO A KAIJU MONSTER...
N

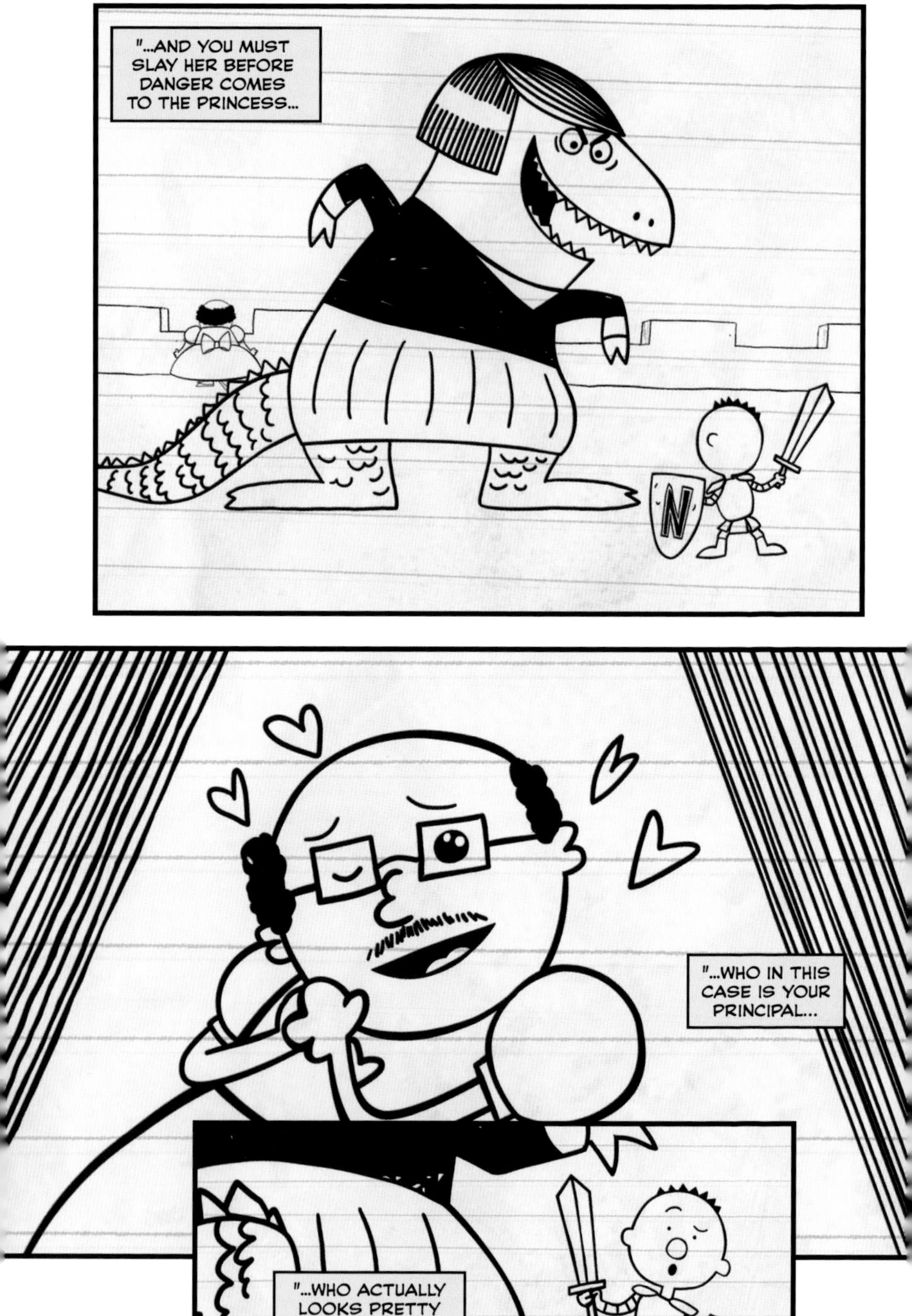
"...AND YOU MUST SLAY HER BEFORE DANGER COMES TO THE PRINCESS...
N
"...WHO IN THIS CASE IS YOUR PRINCIPAL...
"...WHO ACTUALLY LOOKS PRETTY GOOD IN A DRESS.

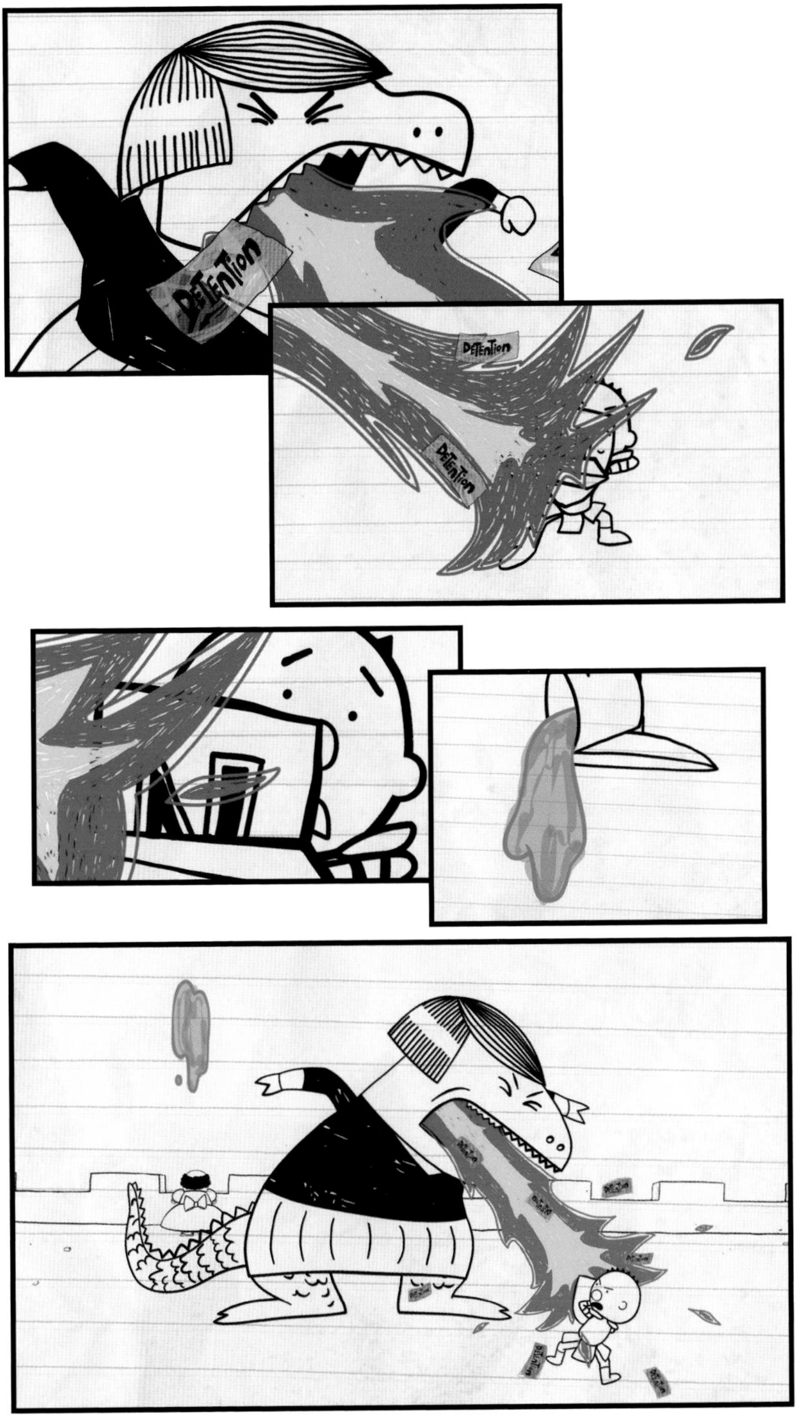
DETENTION
DETENTION
DETENTION

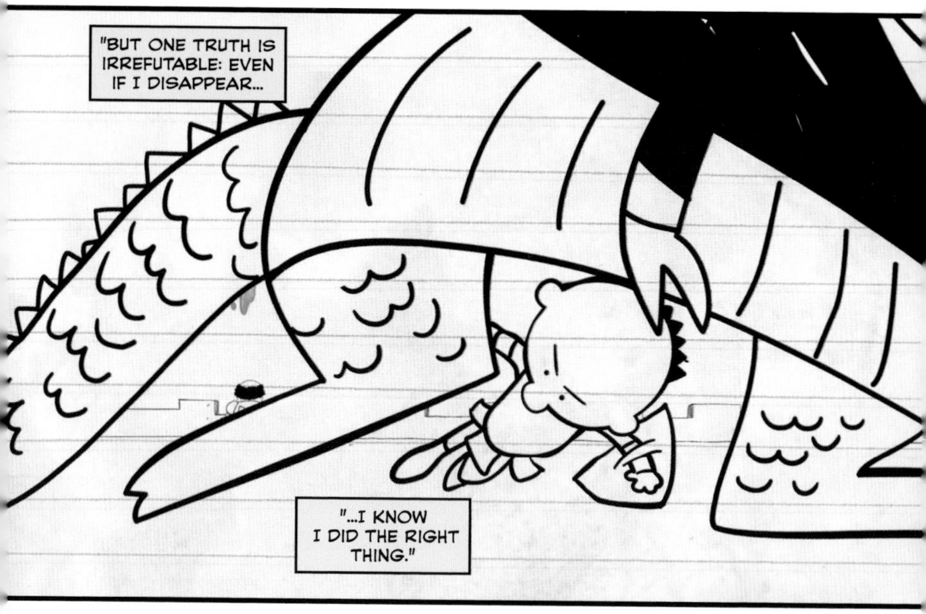
"BUT ONE TRUTH IS IRREFUTABLE: EVEN IF I DISAPPEAR...
"...I KNOW I DID THE RIGHT THING."

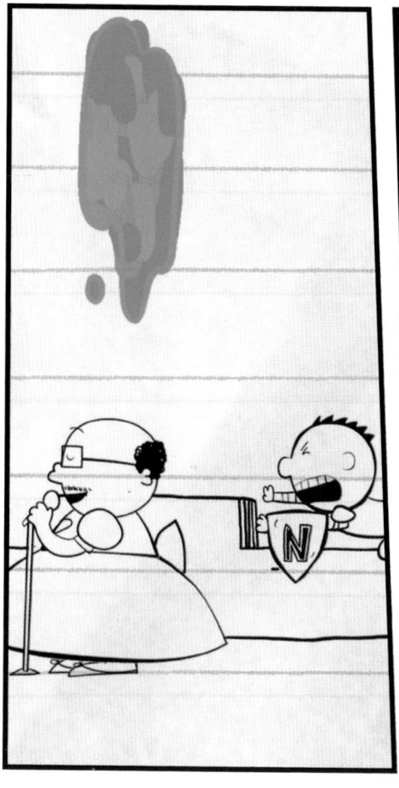
N

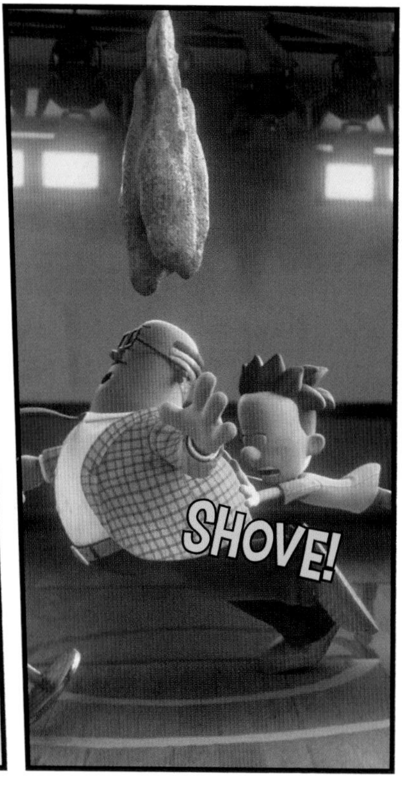
SHOVE!

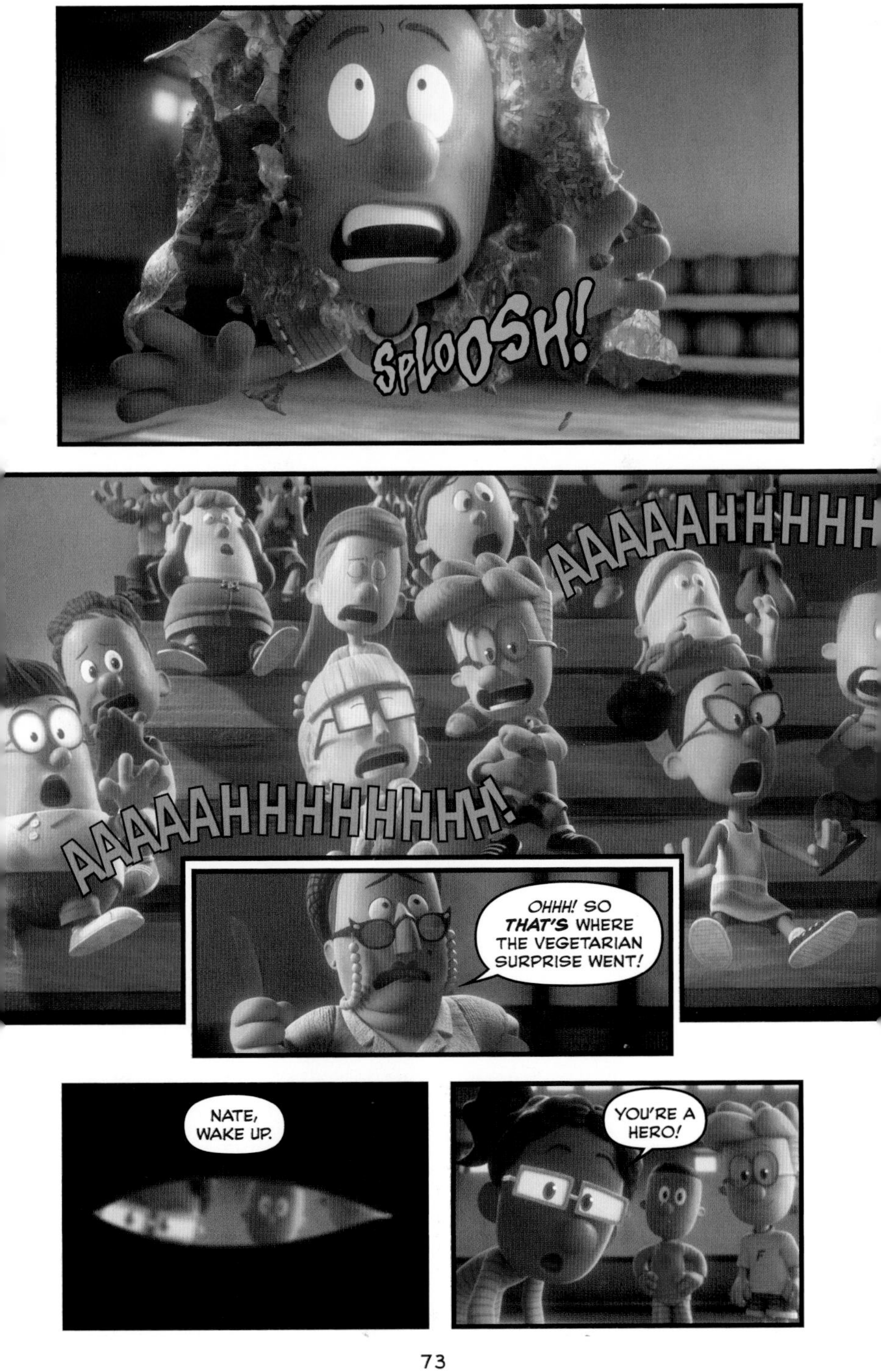
SPLOOSH!
AAAAAHHHHH
AAAAAHHHHHHHHH!
OHHH! SO THAT'S WHERE THE VEGETARIAN SURPRISE WENT!
NATE, WAKE UP.
YOU'RE A HERO!

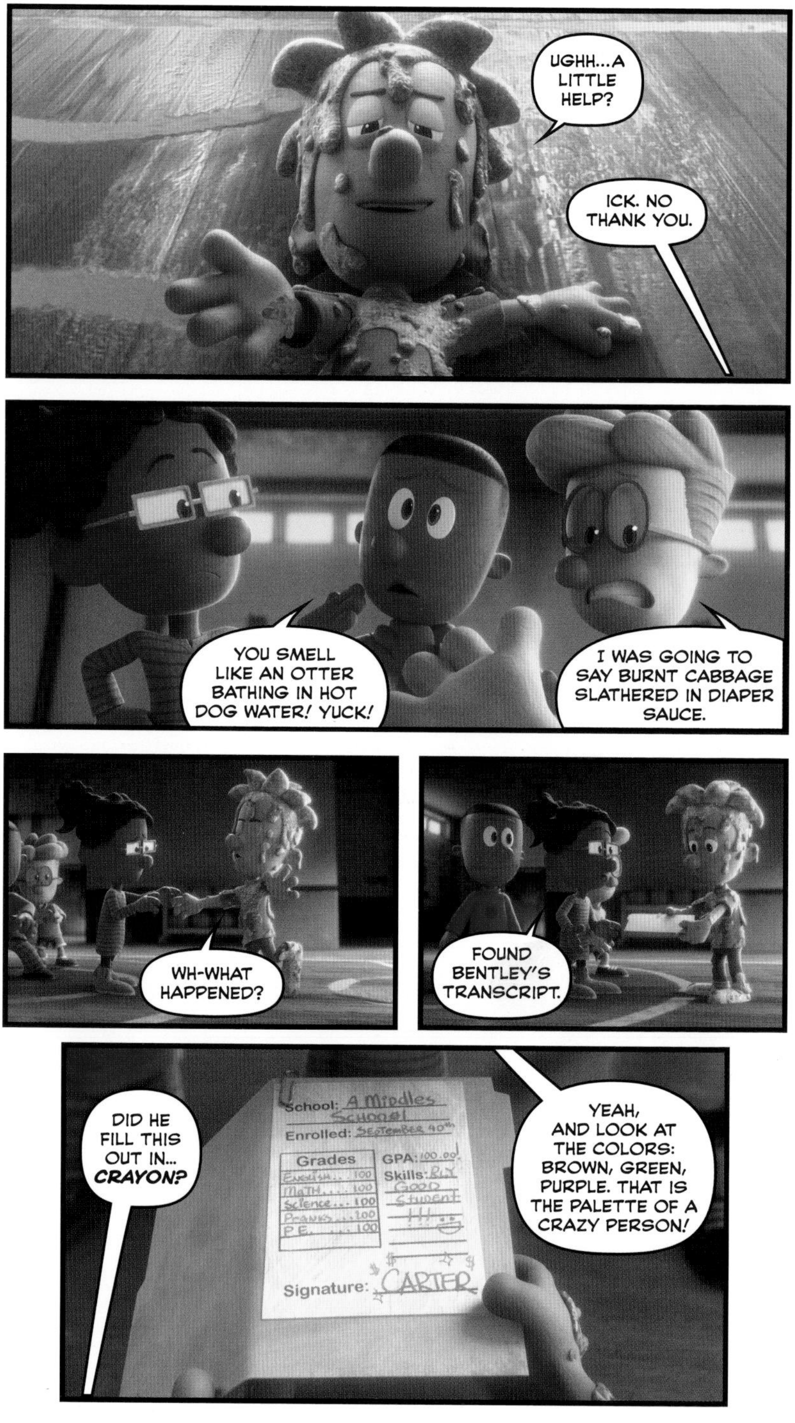
UGHH...A LITTLE HELP?
ICK. NO THANK YOU.
YOU SMELL LIKE AN OTTER BATHING IN HOT DOG WATER! YUCK!
I WAS GOING TO SAY BURNT CABBAGE SLATHERED IN DIAPER SAUCE.
WH-WHAT HAPPENED?
FOUND BENTLEY'S TRANSCRIPT.
DID HE FILL THIS OUT IN... ***CRAYON?***
School:
Enrolled:
Grades
GPA:
Skills:
Signature: CARTER
YEAH, AND LOOK AT THE COLORS: BROWN, GREEN, PURPLE. THAT IS THE PALETTE OF A CRAZY PERSON!

CHECK OUT THE PHOTO ABOVE HIS NAME.
Name: Bentley Carter
D.O.B.: 2/3/45
M/F: m
NICHOLS MUST HAVE BEEN SO EXCITED ABOUT GETTING A RICH KID IN THIS SCHOOL HE NEVER LOOKED AT HIS TRANSCRIPTS!
YOU CAN'T PROVE THAT.
SO IF BENTLEY'S NOT BENTLEY— WHO *IS* BENTLEY?
HIS REAL NAME IS ***MERL LAZENBEE*** AND HE'S AN ESCAPEE FROM THE INSTITUTION FOR ***CRIMINALLY INSANE TWEENS!***
HE'S DONE THIS SAME THING BEFORE AT OTHER SCHOOLS.

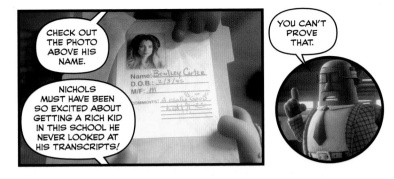

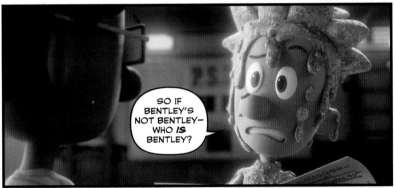

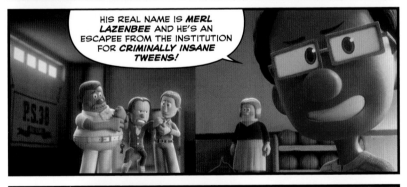

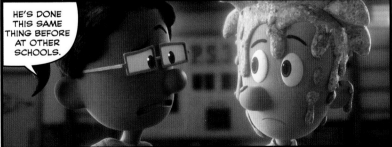

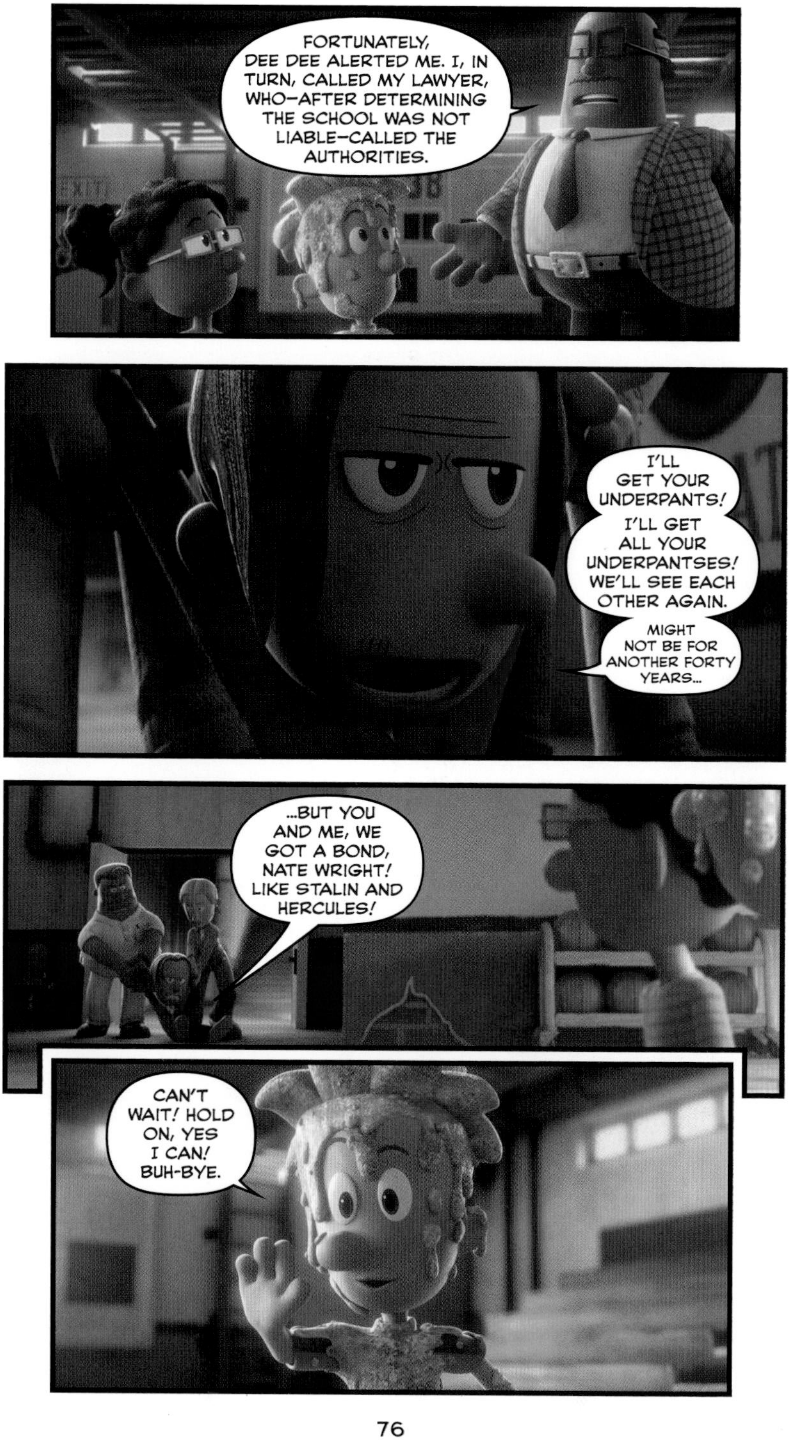
FORTUNATELY, DEE DEE ALERTED ME. I, IN TURN, CALLED MY LAWYER, WHO—AFTER DETERMINING THE SCHOOL WAS NOT LIABLE—CALLED THE AUTHORITIES.
I'LL GET YOUR UNDERPANTS!
I'LL GET ALL YOUR UNDERPANTSES! WE'LL SEE EACH OTHER AGAIN.
MIGHT NOT BE FOR ANOTHER FORTY YEARS...
...BUT YOU AND ME, WE GOT A BOND, NATE WRIGHT! LIKE STALIN AND HERCULES!
CAN'T WAIT! HOLD ON, YES I CAN! BUH-BYE.

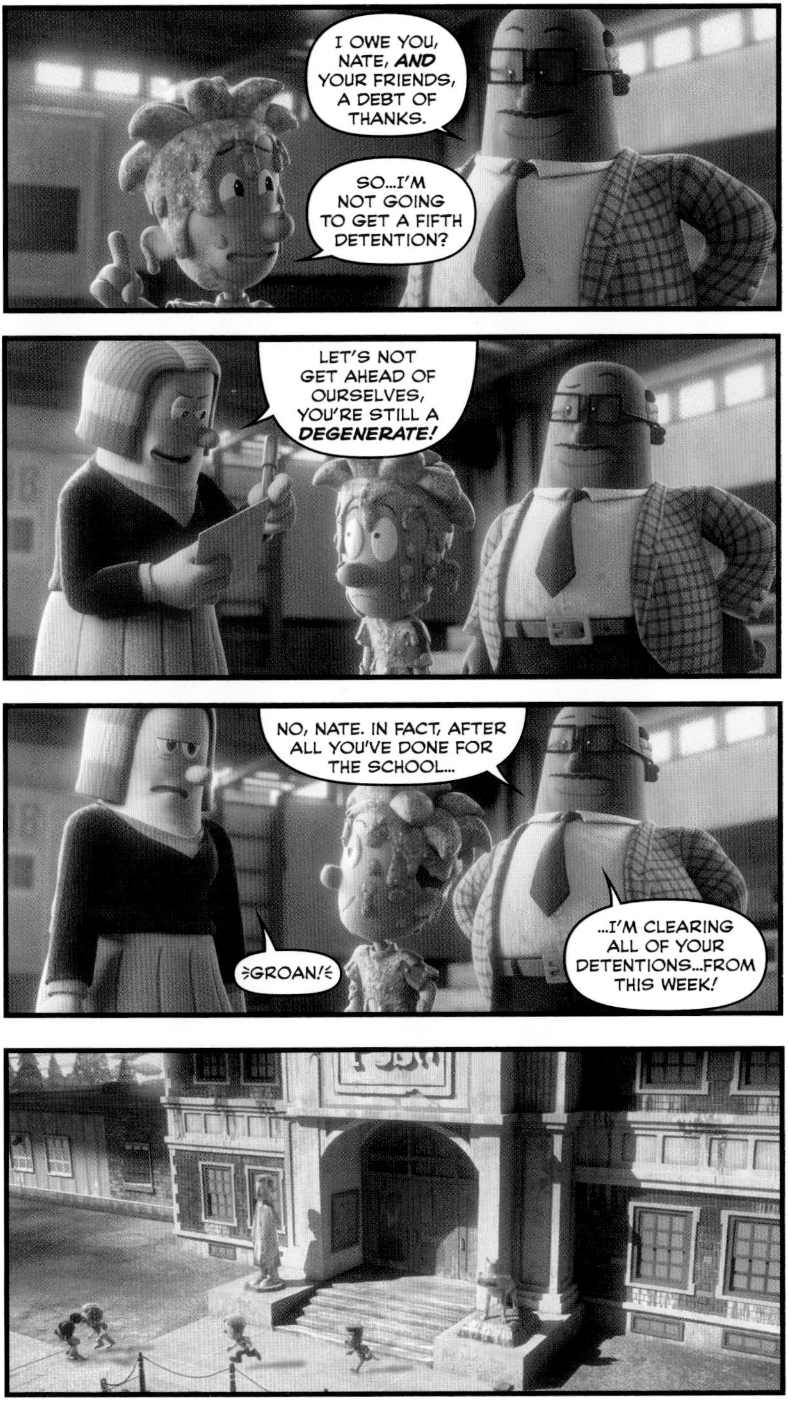
I OWE YOU, NATE, **AND** YOUR FRIENDS, A DEBT OF THANKS.
SO...I'M NOT GOING TO GET A FIFTH DETENTION?
LET'S NOT GET AHEAD OF OURSELVES, YOU'RE STILL A ***DEGENERATE!***
NO, NATE. IN FACT, AFTER ALL YOU'VE DONE FOR THE SCHOOL...
GROAN!
...I'M CLEARING ALL OF YOUR DETENTIONS...FROM THIS WEEK!

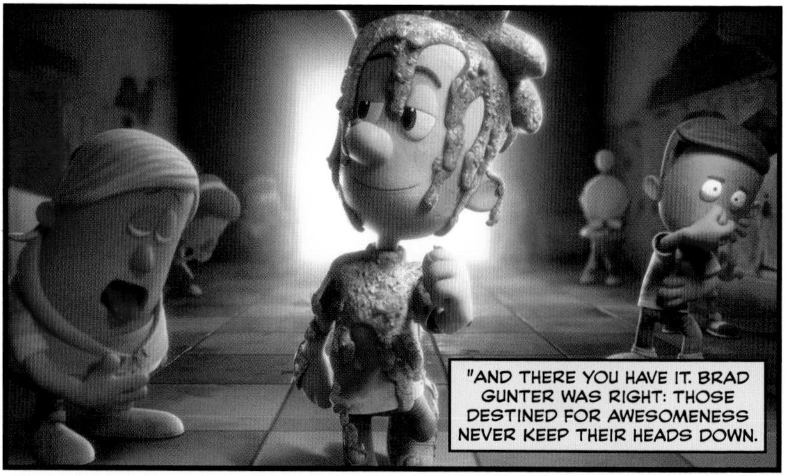
"AND THERE YOU HAVE IT. BRAD GUNTER WAS RIGHT: THOSE DESTINED FOR AWESOMENESS NEVER KEEP THEIR HEADS DOWN.

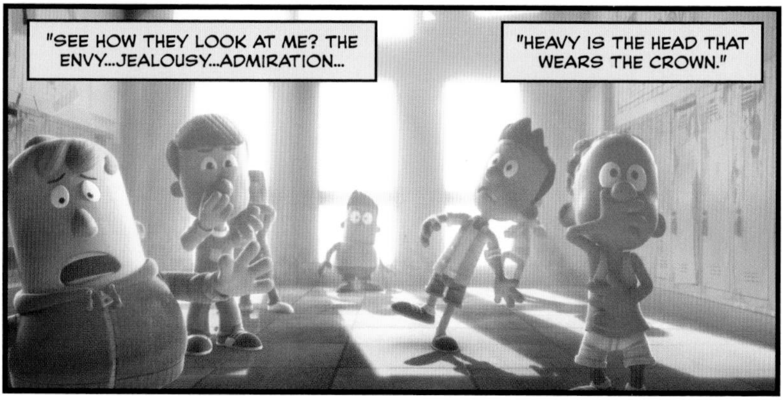
"SEE HOW THEY LOOK AT ME? THE ENVY...JEALOUSY...ADMIRATION...
"HEAVY IS THE HEAD THAT WEARS THE CROWN."

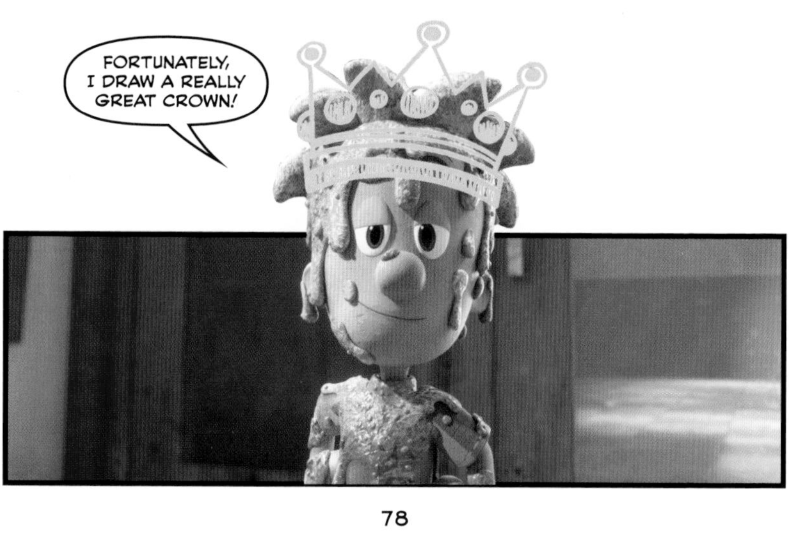
FORTUNATELY, I DRAW A REALLY GREAT CROWN!

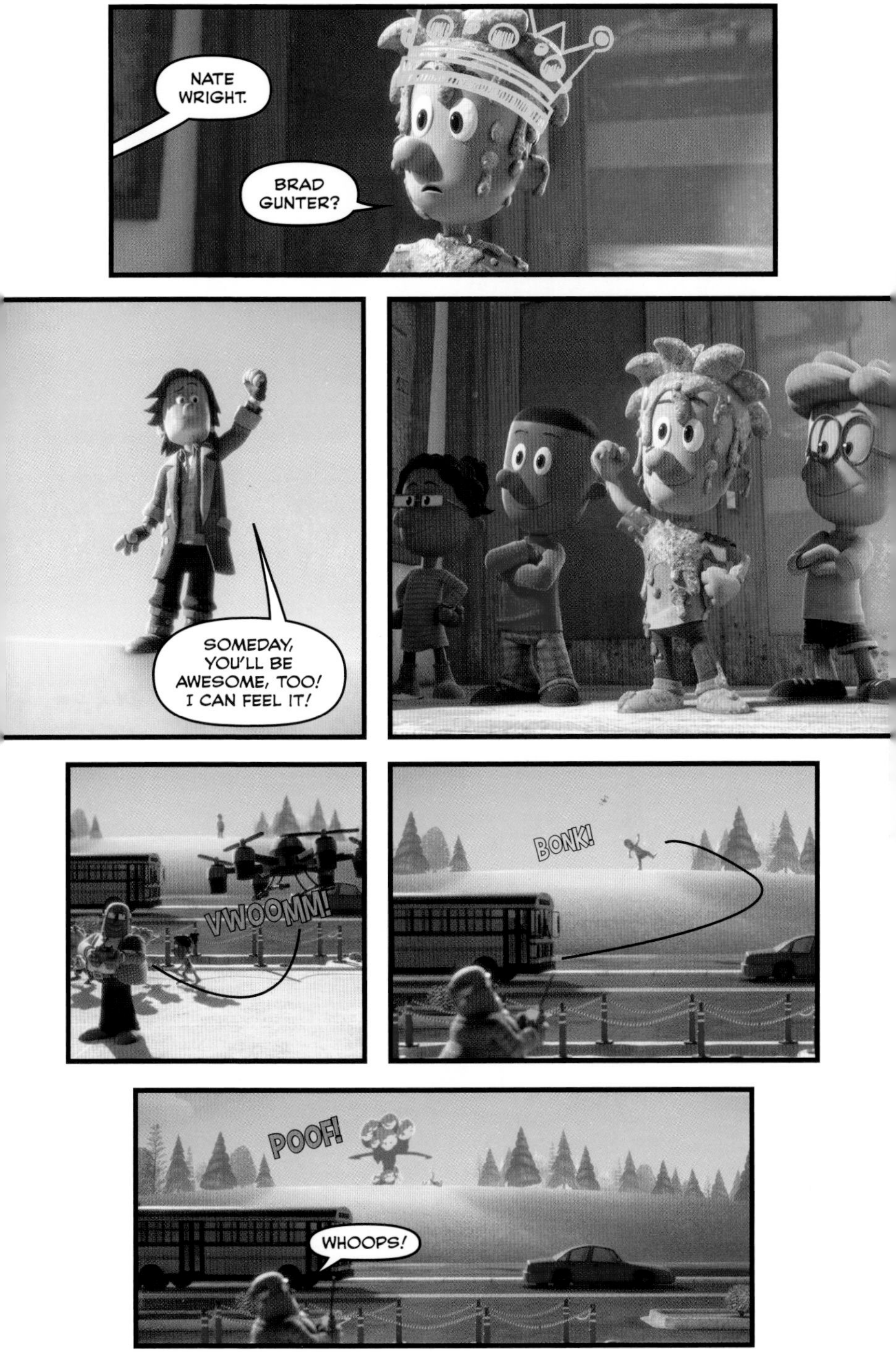
NATE WRIGHT.
BRAD GUNTER?
SOMEDAY, YOU'LL BE AWESOME, TOO! I CAN FEEL IT!
VWOOMM!
BONK!
POOF!
WHOOPS!

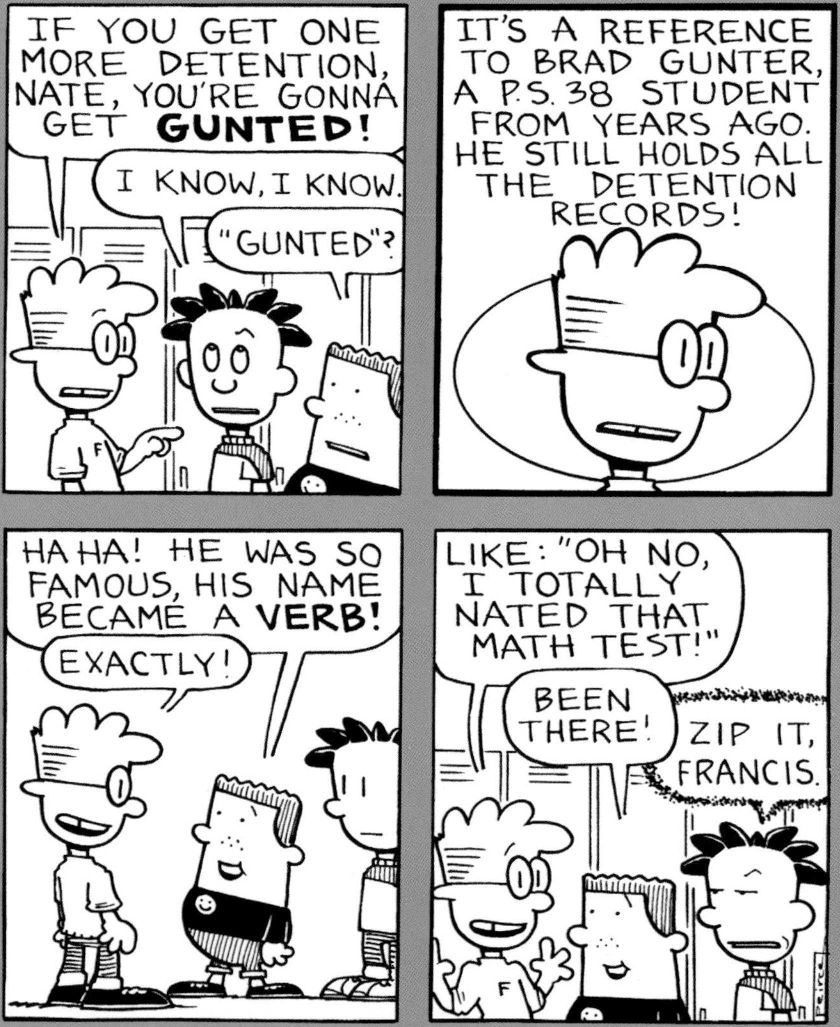

IF YOU GET ONE MORE DETENTION, NATE, YOU'RE GONNA GET **GUNTED**!
I KNOW, I KNOW.
"GUNTED"?
IT'S A REFERENCE TO BRAD GUNTER, A P.S. 38 STUDENT FROM YEARS AGO. HE STILL HOLDS ALL THE DETENTION RECORDS!
HA HA! HE WAS SO FAMOUS, HIS NAME BECAME A **VERB**!
EXACTLY!
LIKE: "OH NO, I TOTALLY NATED THAT MATH TEST!"
BEEN THERE!
ZIP IT, FRANCIS.
PEIRCE

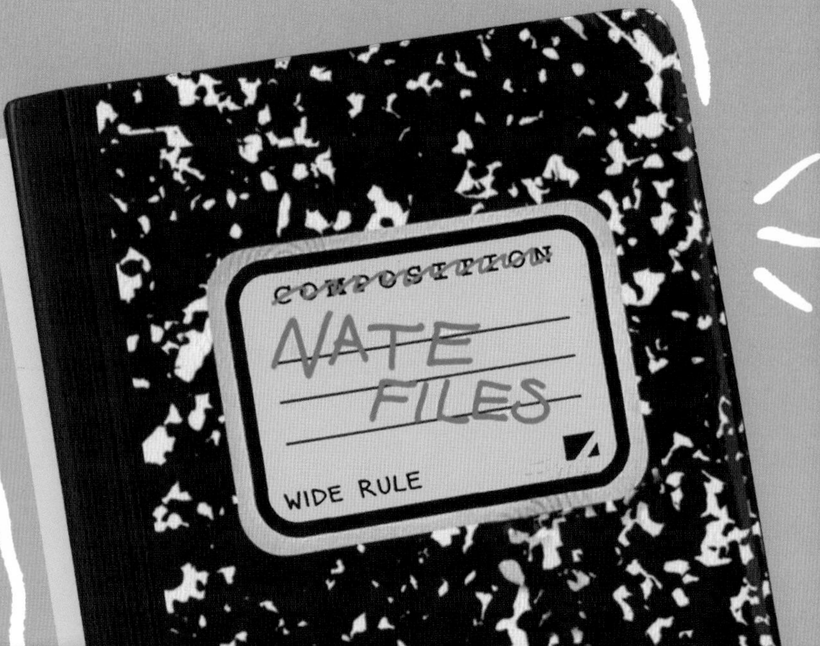
COMPOSITION
NATE
FILES
WIDE RULE

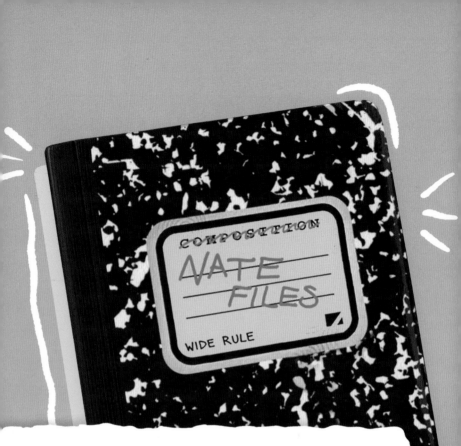

Go Nate!
It's Your Birthday

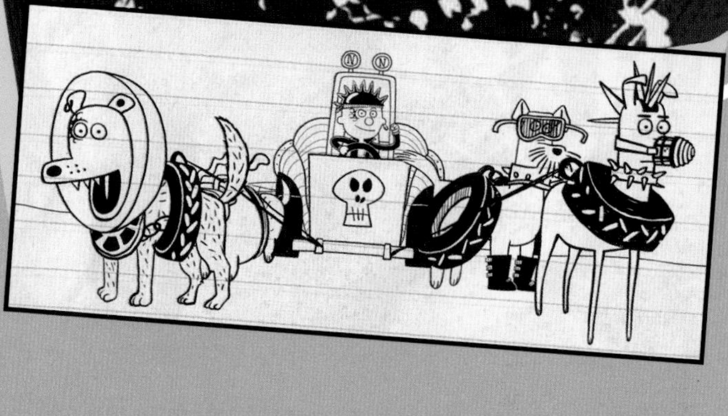

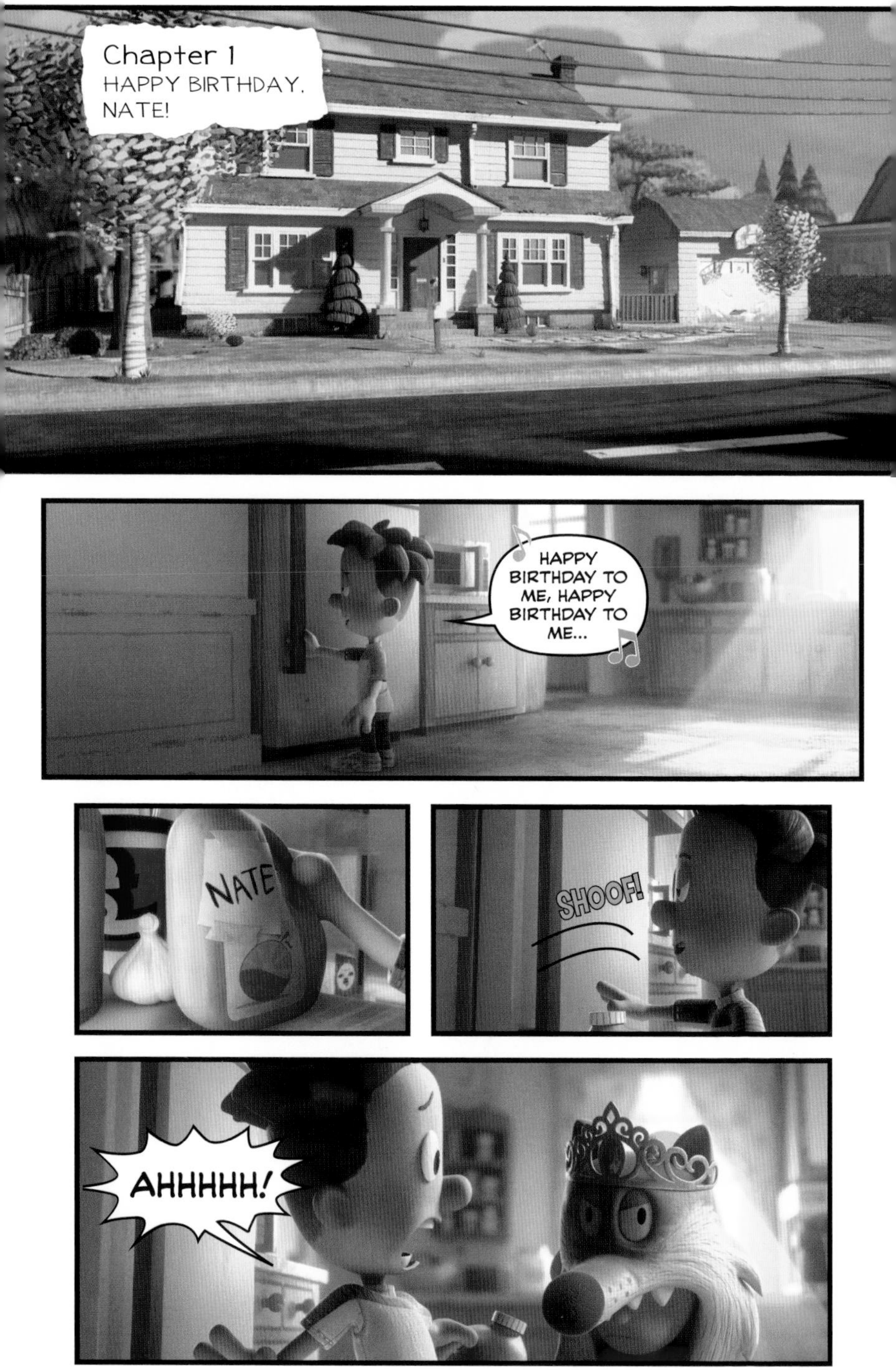
Chapter 1
HAPPY BIRTHDAY, NATE!
HAPPY BIRTHDAY TO ME, HAPPY BIRTHDAY TO ME...
NATE
SHOOF!
AHHHHH!

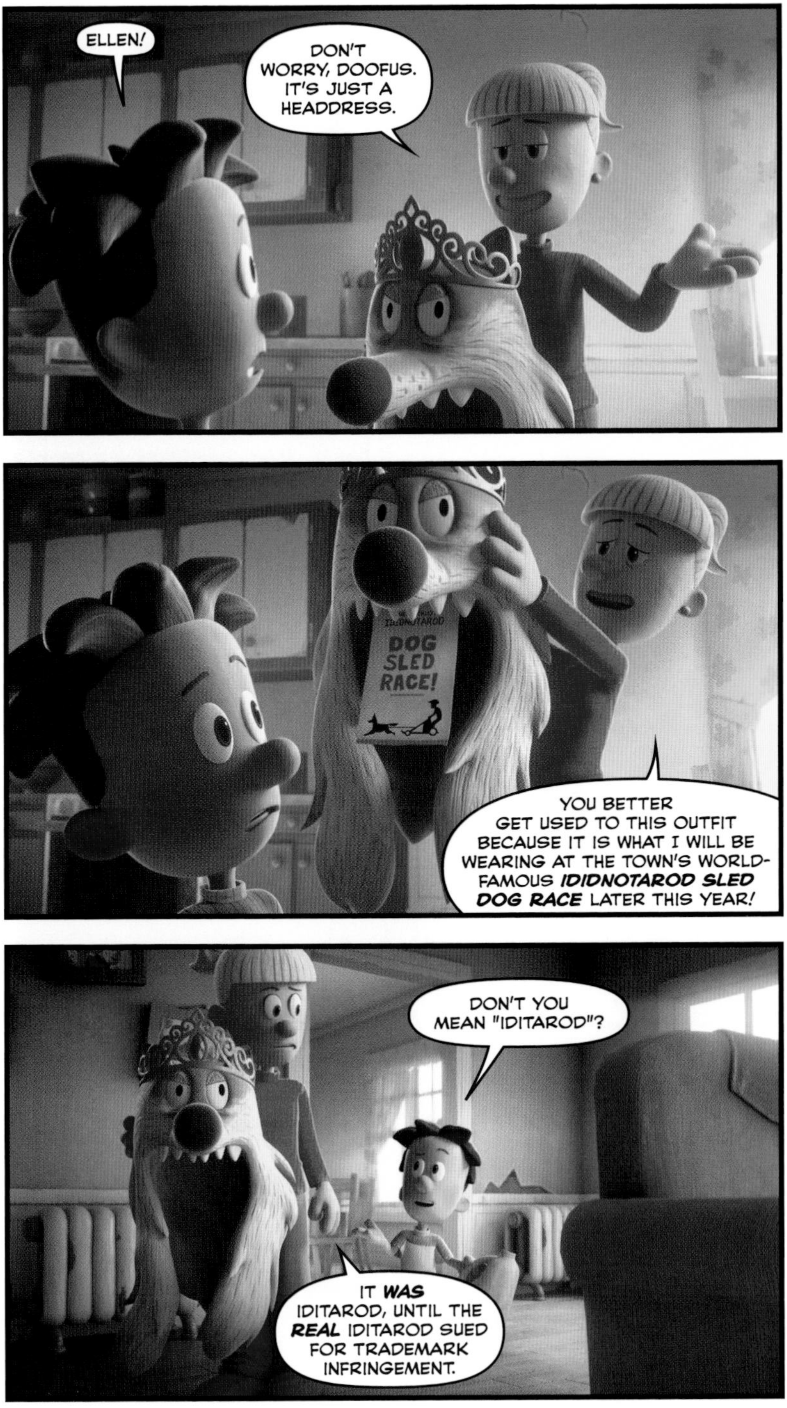
ELLEN!
DON'T WORRY, DOOFUS. IT'S JUST A HEADDRESS.
IDIDNOTAROD
DOG SLED RACE!
YOU BETTER GET USED TO THIS OUTFIT BECAUSE IT IS WHAT I WILL BE WEARING AT THE TOWN'S WORLD-FAMOUS ***IDIDNOTAROD SLED DOG RACE*** LATER THIS YEAR!
DON'T YOU MEAN "IDITAROD"?
IT ***WAS*** IDITAROD, UNTIL THE ***REAL*** IDITAROD SUED FOR TRADEMARK INFRINGEMENT.

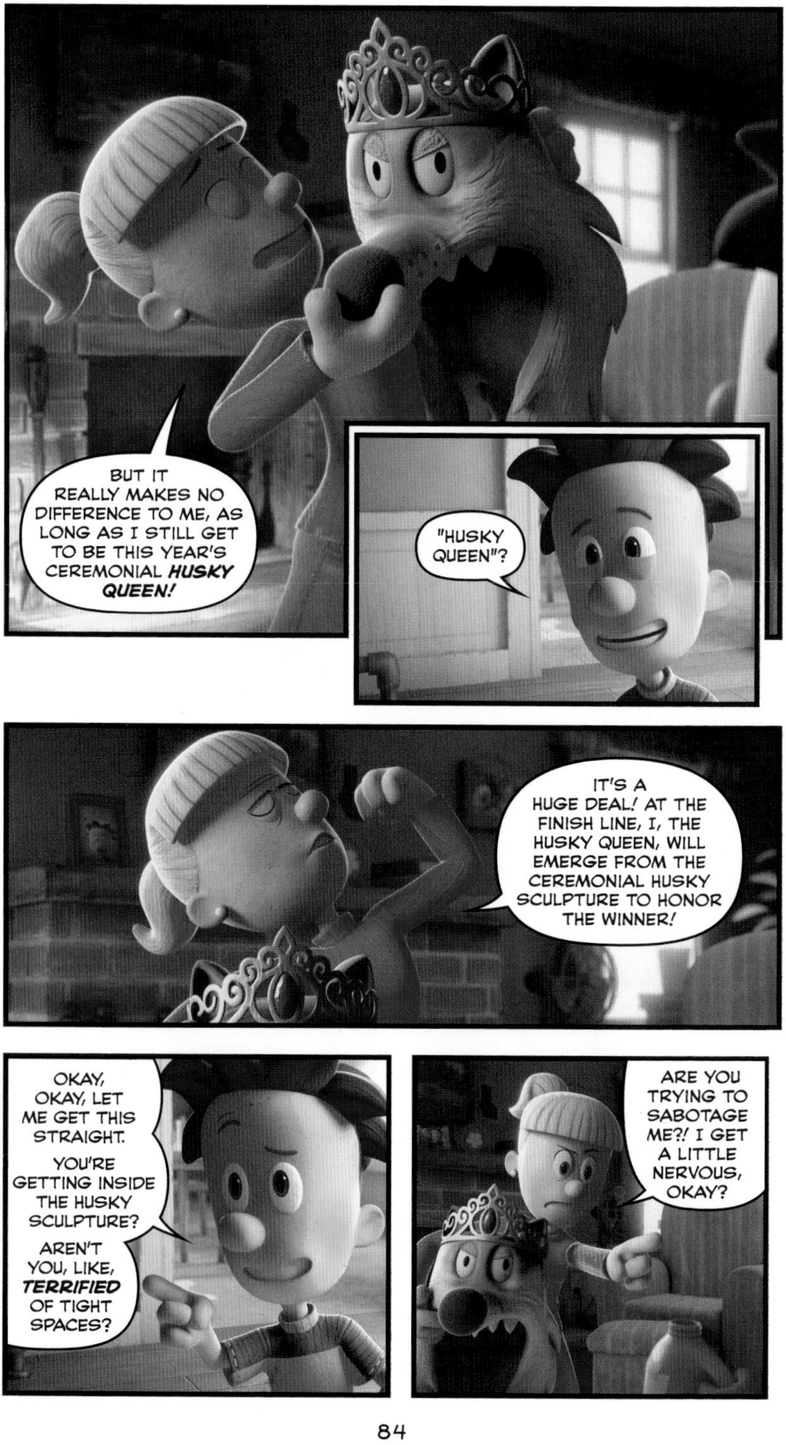
BUT IT REALLY MAKES NO DIFFERENCE TO ME, AS LONG AS I STILL GET TO BE THIS YEAR'S CEREMONIAL HUSKY QUEEN!
"HUSKY QUEEN"?
IT'S A HUGE DEAL! AT THE FINISH LINE, I, THE HUSKY QUEEN, WILL EMERGE FROM THE CEREMONIAL HUSKY SCULPTURE TO HONOR THE WINNER!
OKAY, OKAY, LET ME GET THIS STRAIGHT.
YOU'RE GETTING INSIDE THE HUSKY SCULPTURE?
AREN'T YOU, LIKE, TERRIFIED OF TIGHT SPACES?
ARE YOU TRYING TO SABOTAGE ME?! I GET A LITTLE NERVOUS, OKAY?

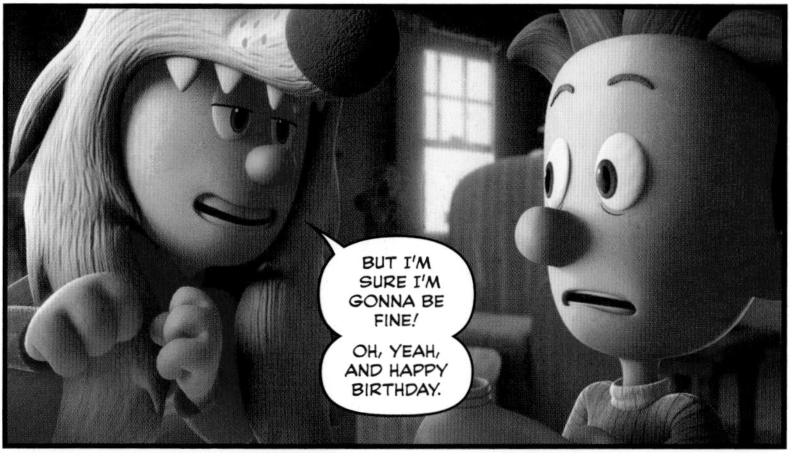
BUT I'M SURE I'M GONNA BE FINE!
OH, YEAH, AND HAPPY BIRTHDAY.

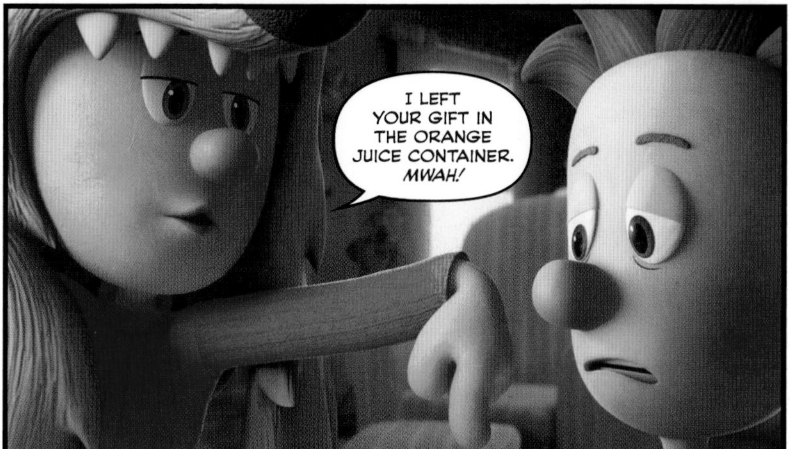
I LEFT YOUR GIFT IN THE ORANGE JUICE CONTAINER. *MWAH!*

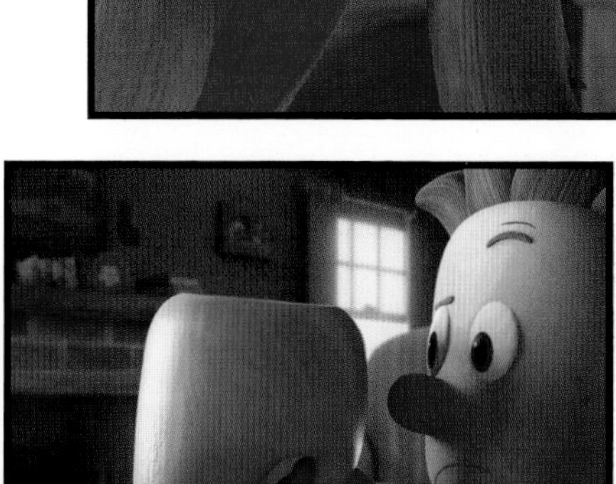

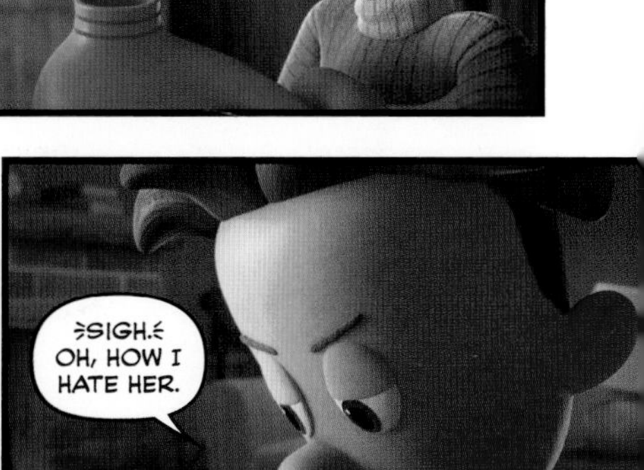
⪢SIGH.⪡ OH, HOW I HATE HER.

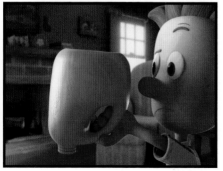

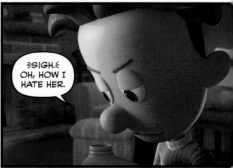

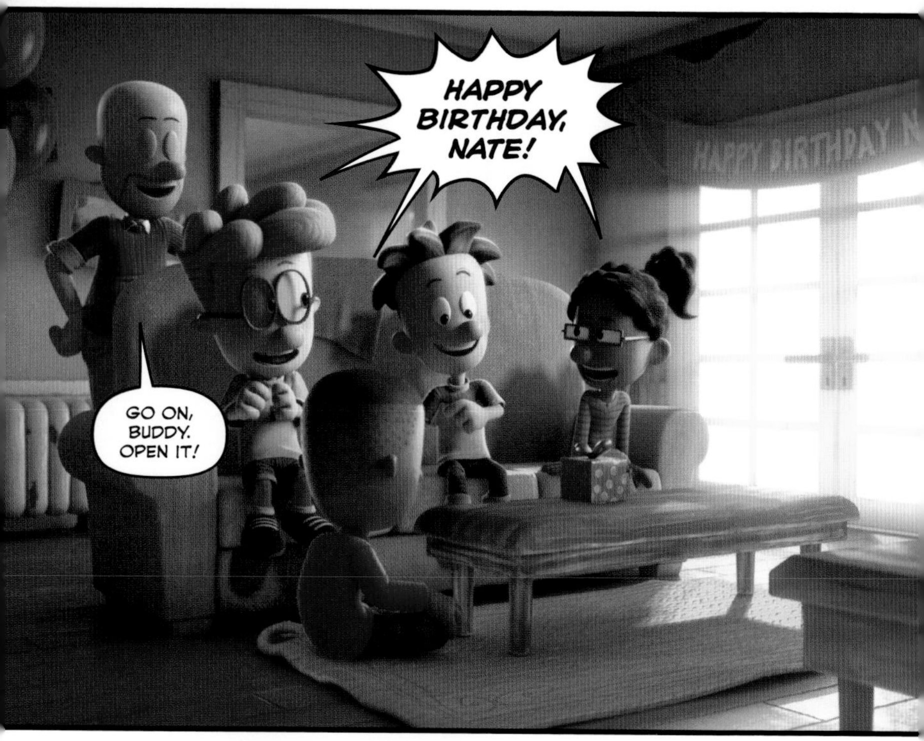
HAPPY BIRTHDAY, NATE!
HAPPY BIRTHDAY N
GO ON, BUDDY. OPEN IT!

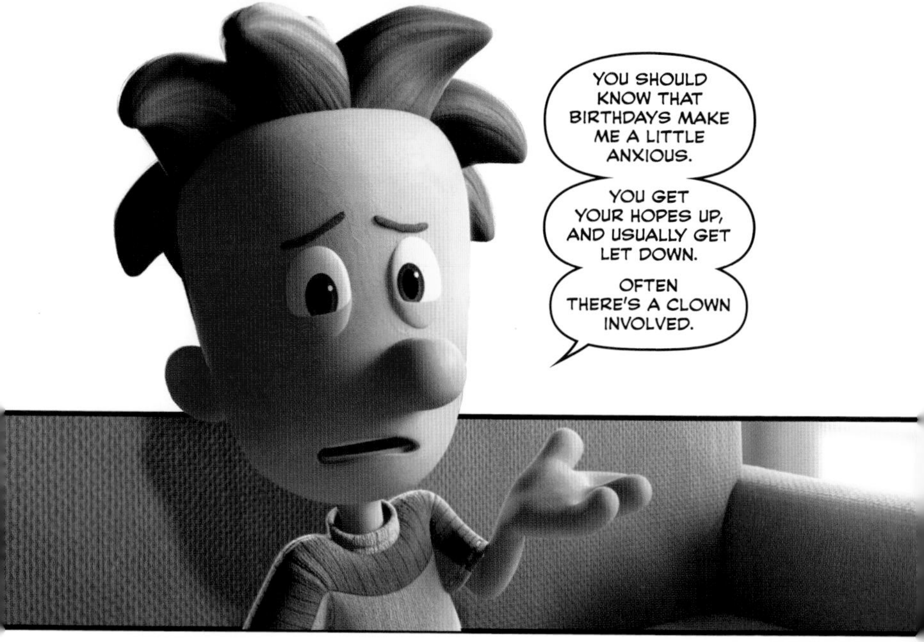
YOU SHOULD KNOW THAT BIRTHDAYS MAKE ME A LITTLE ANXIOUS.
YOU GET YOUR HOPES UP, AND USUALLY GET LET DOWN.
OFTEN THERE'S A CLOWN INVOLVED.

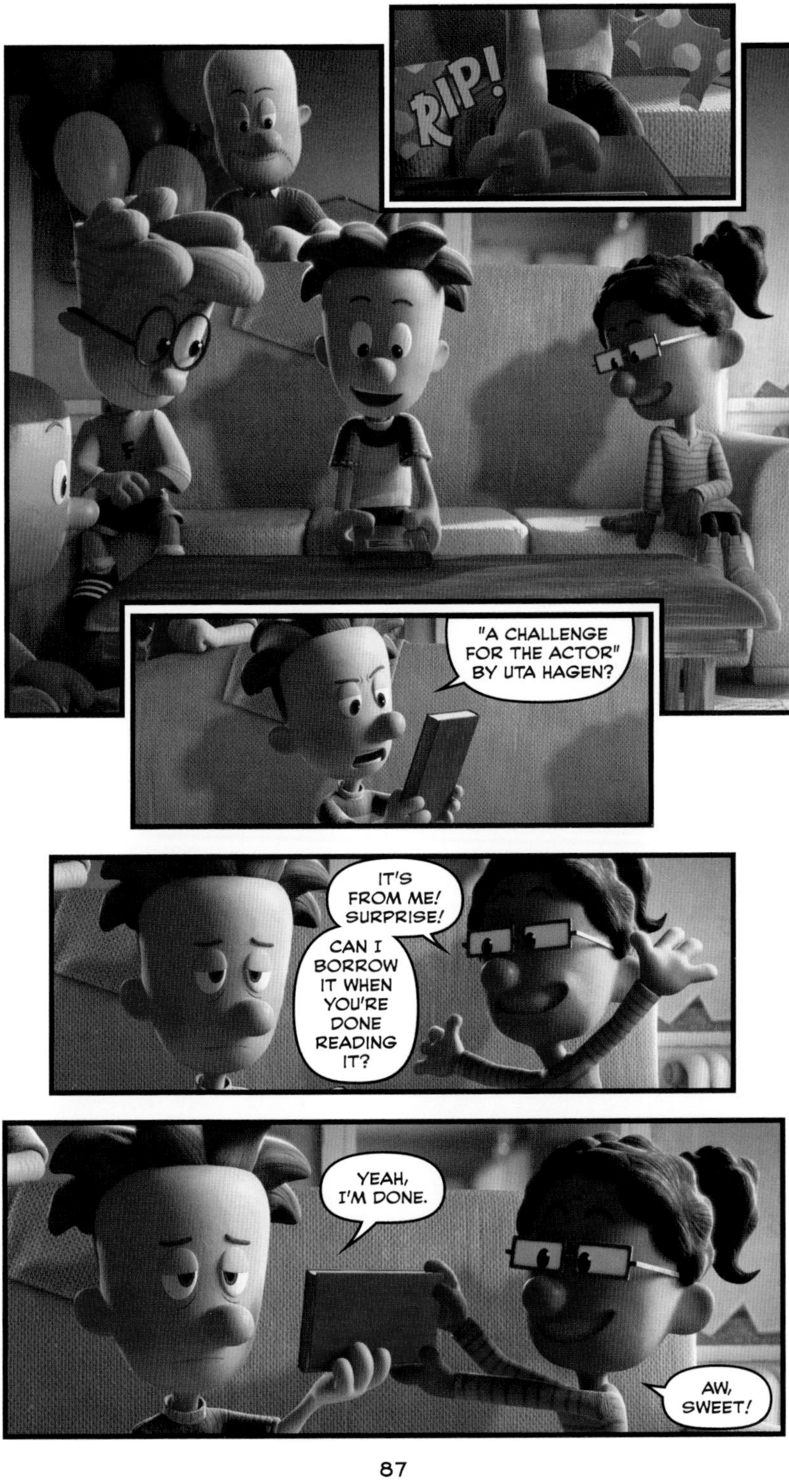
RIP!
"A CHALLENGE FOR THE ACTOR" BY UTA HAGEN?
IT'S FROM ME! SURPRISE!
CAN I BORROW IT WHEN YOU'RE DONE READING IT?
YEAH, I'M DONE.
AW, SWEET!

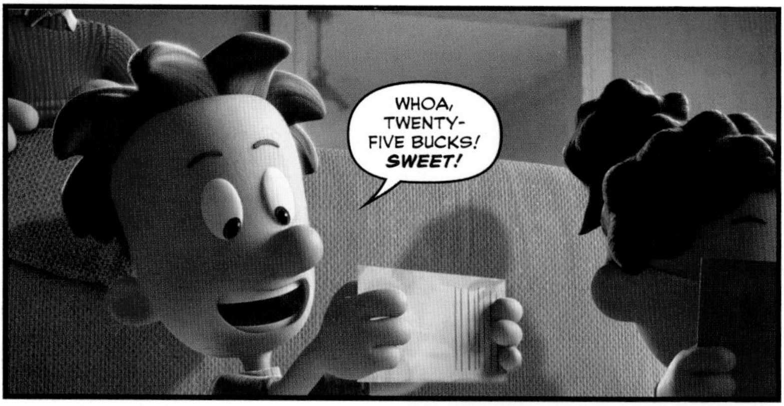
WHOA, TWENTY-FIVE BUCKS! **SWEET!**

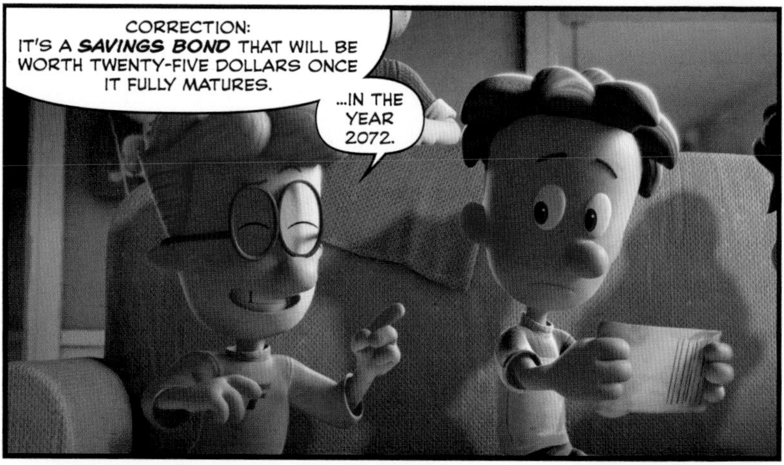
CORRECTION: IT'S A **SAVINGS BOND** THAT WILL BE WORTH TWENTY-FIVE DOLLARS ONCE IT FULLY MATURES.
...IN THE YEAR 2072.

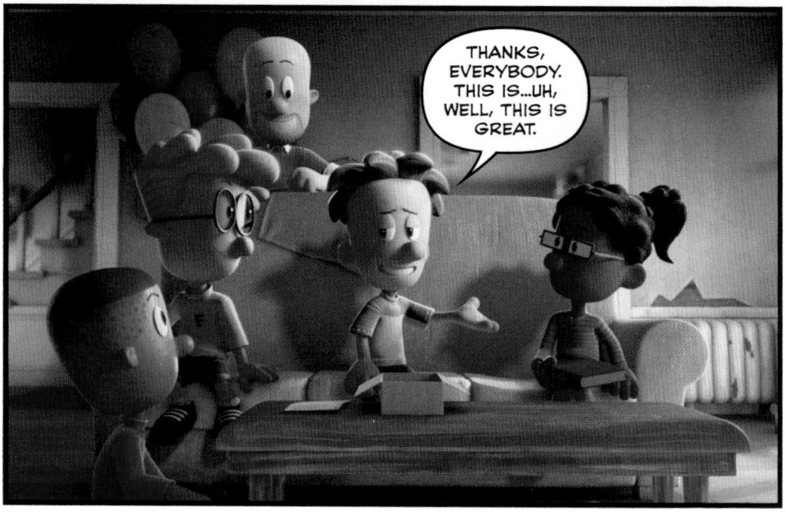
THANKS, EVERYBODY. THIS IS...UH, WELL, THIS IS GREAT.

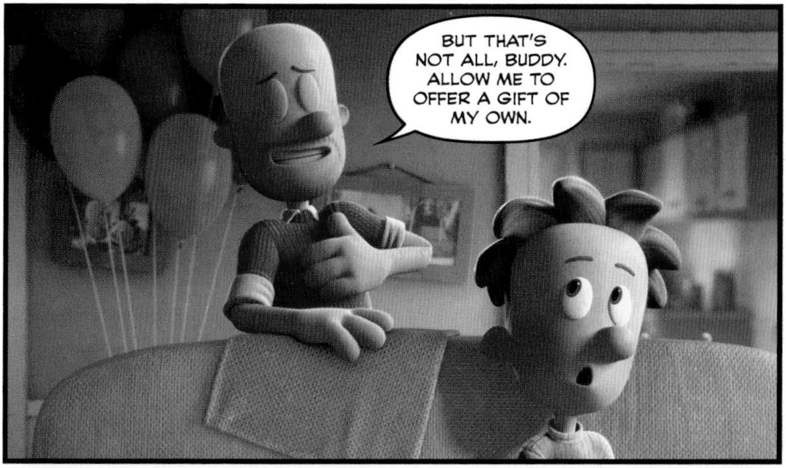
BUT THAT'S NOT ALL, BUDDY. ALLOW ME TO OFFER A GIFT OF MY OWN.

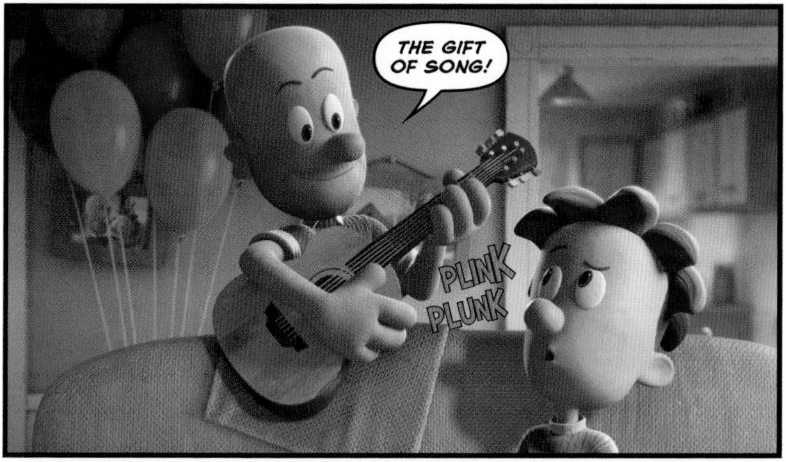
THE GIFT OF SONG!
PLINK
PLUNK

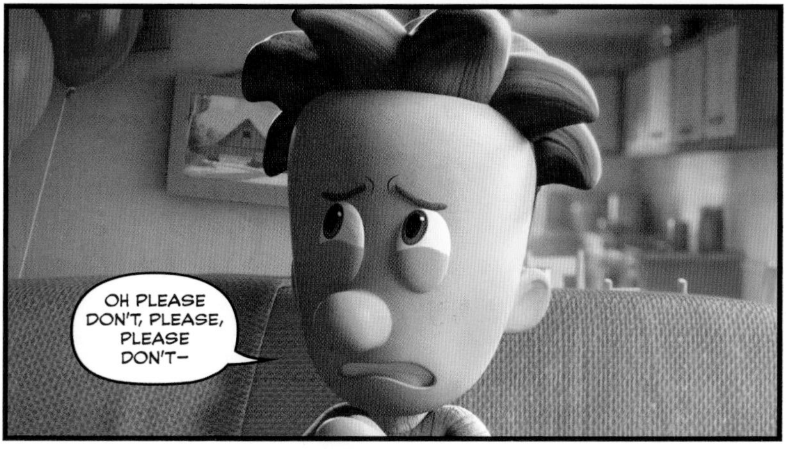
OH PLEASE DON'T, PLEASE, PLEASE DON'T–

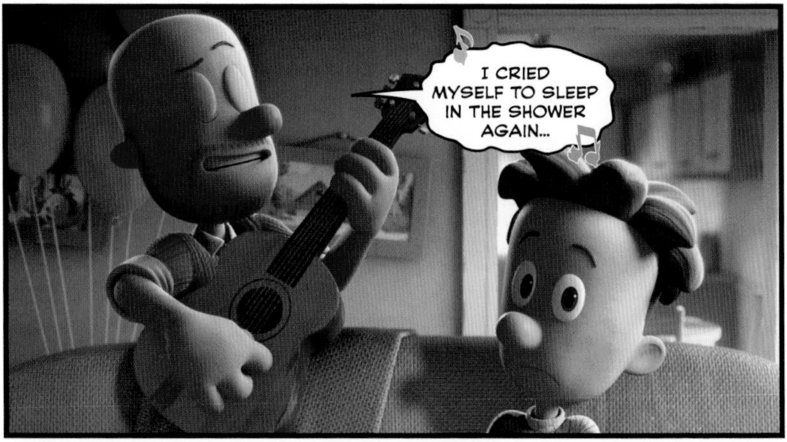
I CRIED MYSELF TO SLEEP IN THE SHOWER AGAIN...

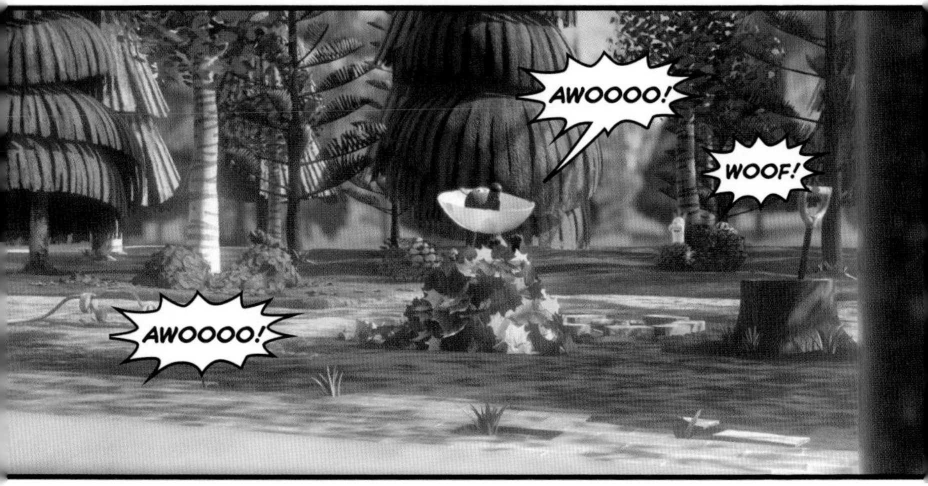
AWOOOO!
WOOF!
AWOOOO!

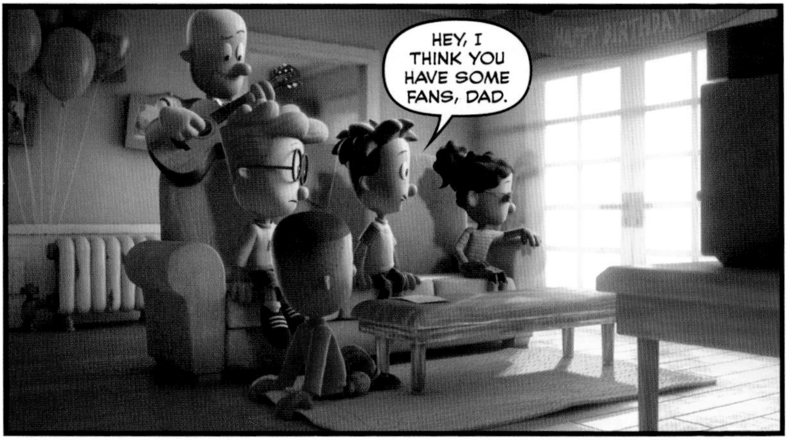
HEY, I THINK YOU HAVE SOME FANS, DAD.

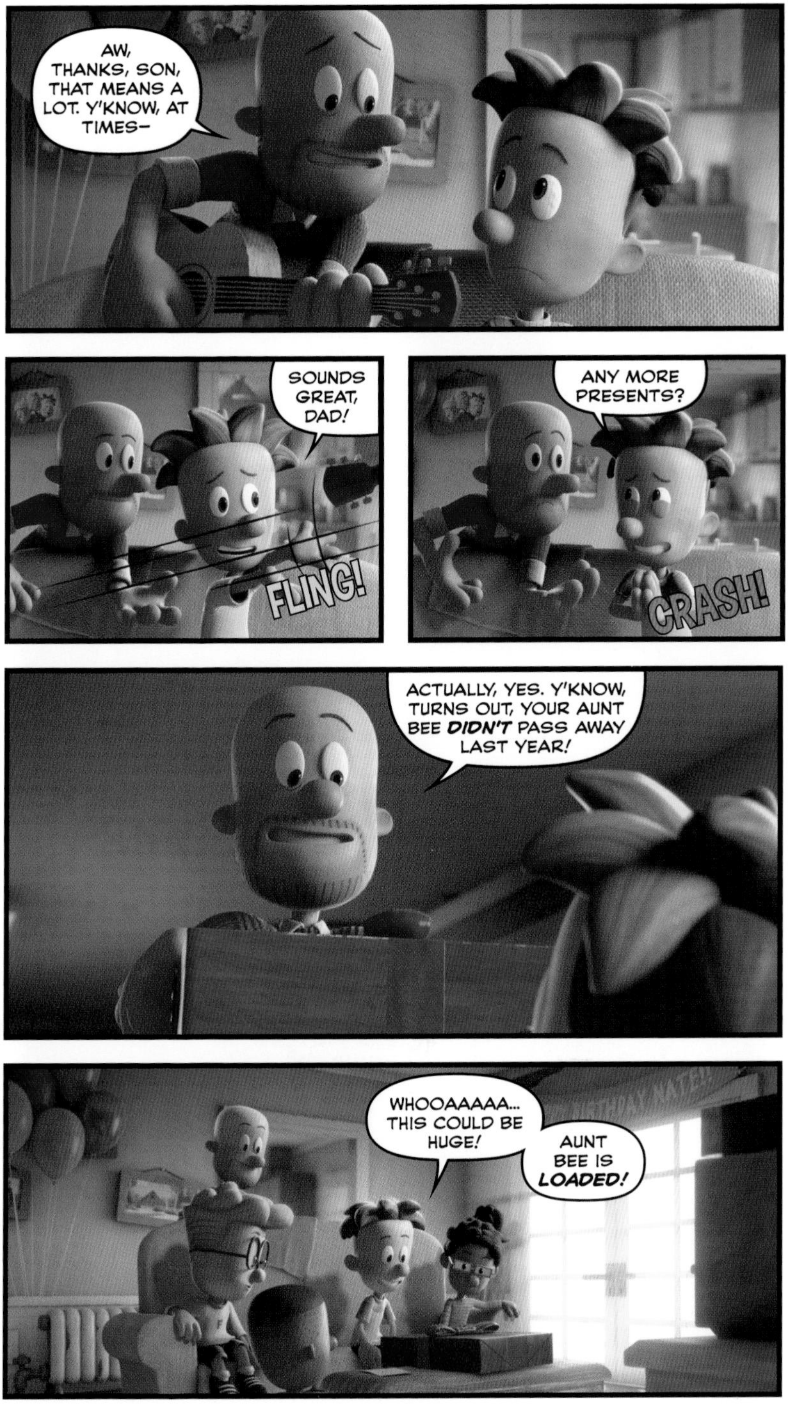
AW, THANKS, SON, THAT MEANS A LOT. Y'KNOW, AT TIMES—
SOUNDS GREAT, DAD!
FLING!
ANY MORE PRESENTS?
CRASH!
ACTUALLY, YES. Y'KNOW, TURNS OUT, YOUR AUNT BEE ***DIDN'T*** PASS AWAY LAST YEAR!
WHOOAAAAA... THIS COULD BE HUGE!
AUNT BEE IS ***LOADED!***

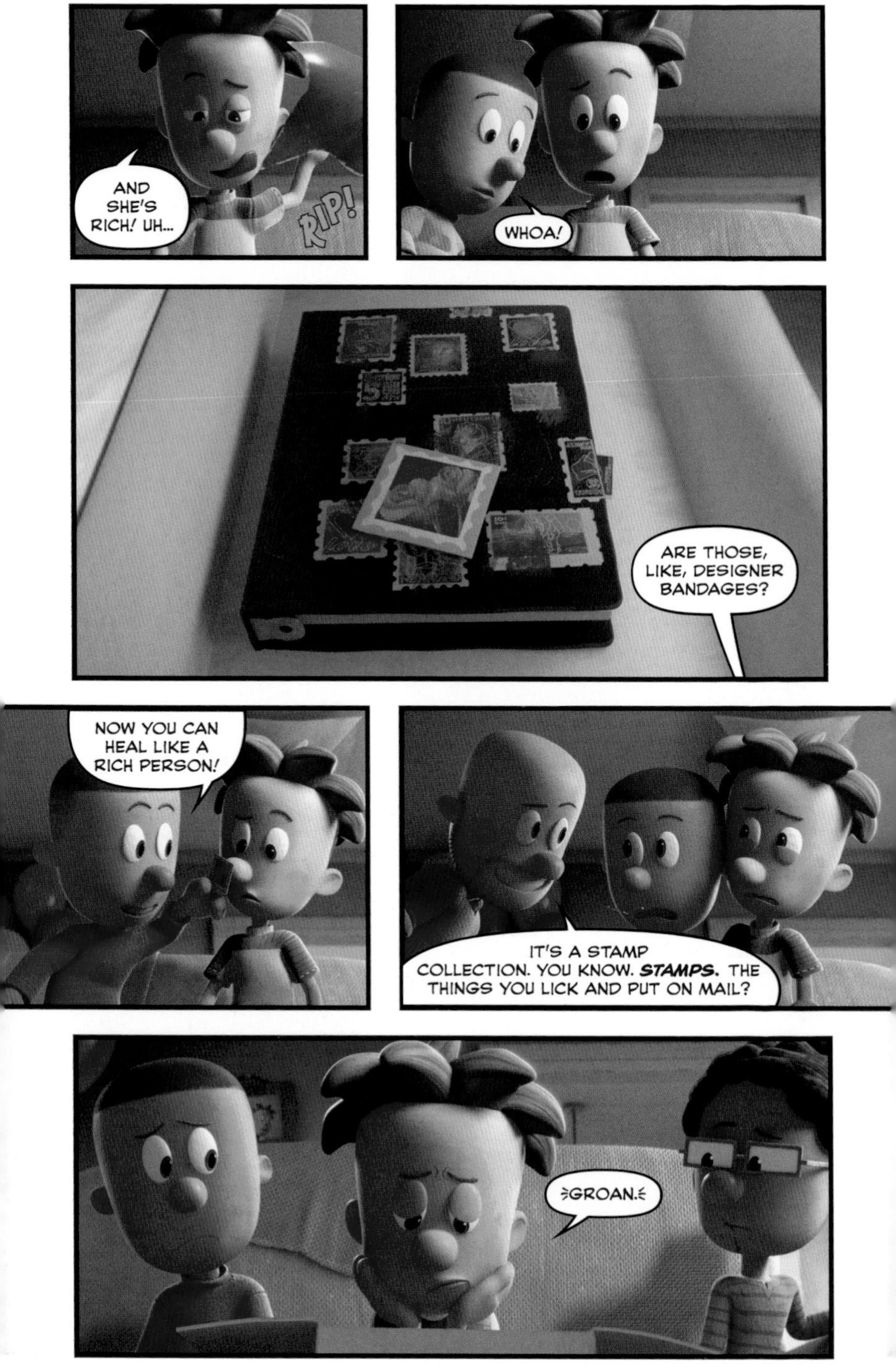
AND SHE'S RICH! UH...
RIP!
WHOA!
ARE THOSE, LIKE, DESIGNER BANDAGES?
NOW YOU CAN HEAL LIKE A RICH PERSON!
IT'S A STAMP COLLECTION. YOU KNOW. ***STAMPS.*** THE THINGS YOU LICK AND PUT ON MAIL?
GROAN.

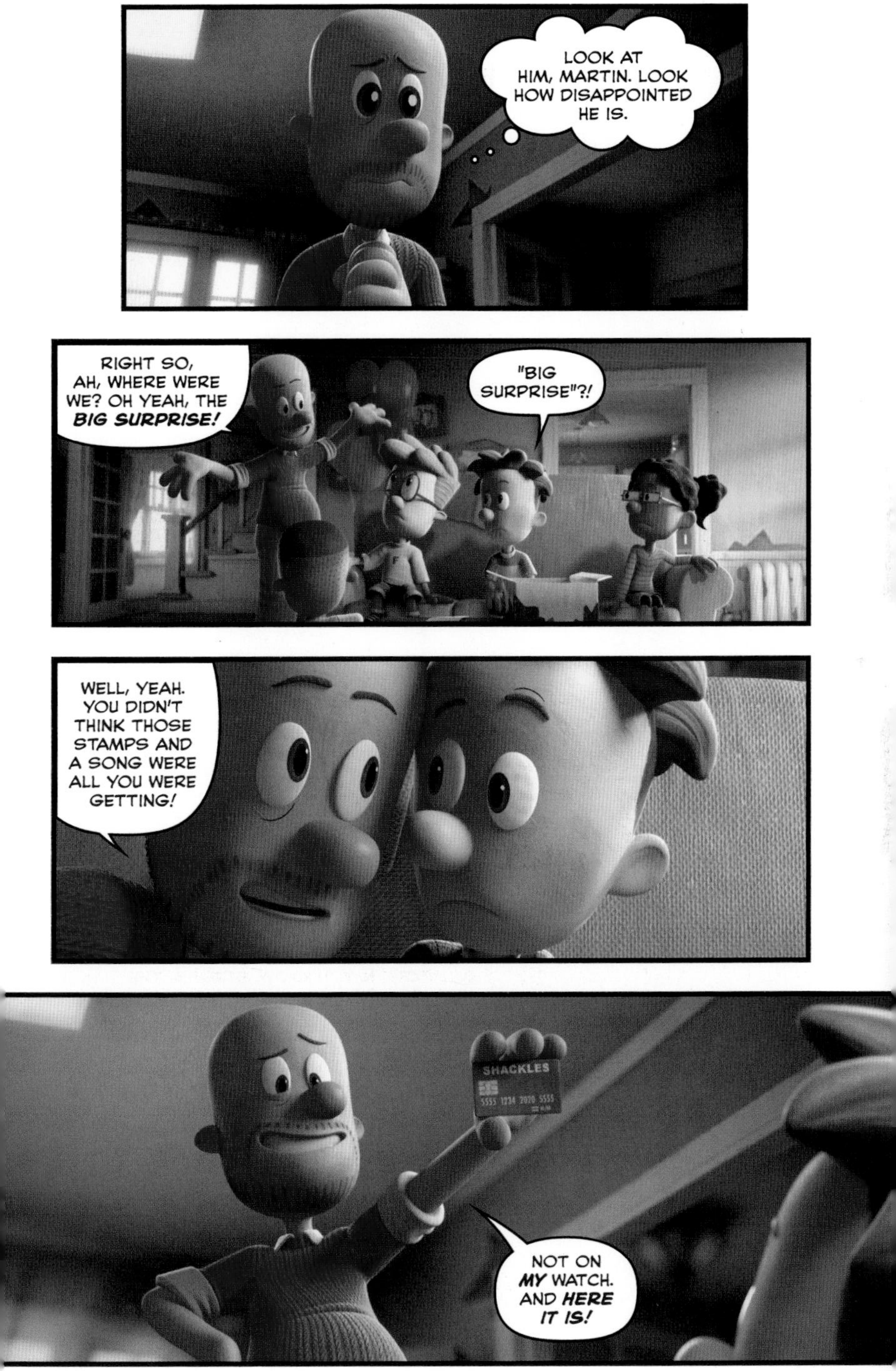
LOOK AT HIM, MARTIN. LOOK HOW DISAPPOINTED HE IS.
RIGHT SO, AH, WHERE WERE WE? OH YEAH, THE ***BIG SURPRISE!***
"BIG SURPRISE"?!
WELL, YEAH. YOU DIDN'T THINK THOSE STAMPS AND A SONG WERE ALL YOU WERE GETTING!
SHACKLES
NOT ON ***MY*** WATCH. AND ***HERE IT IS!***

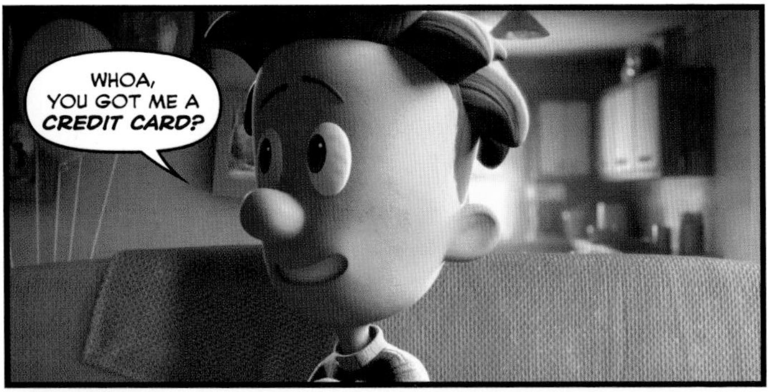
WHOA, YOU GOT ME A *CREDIT CARD?*

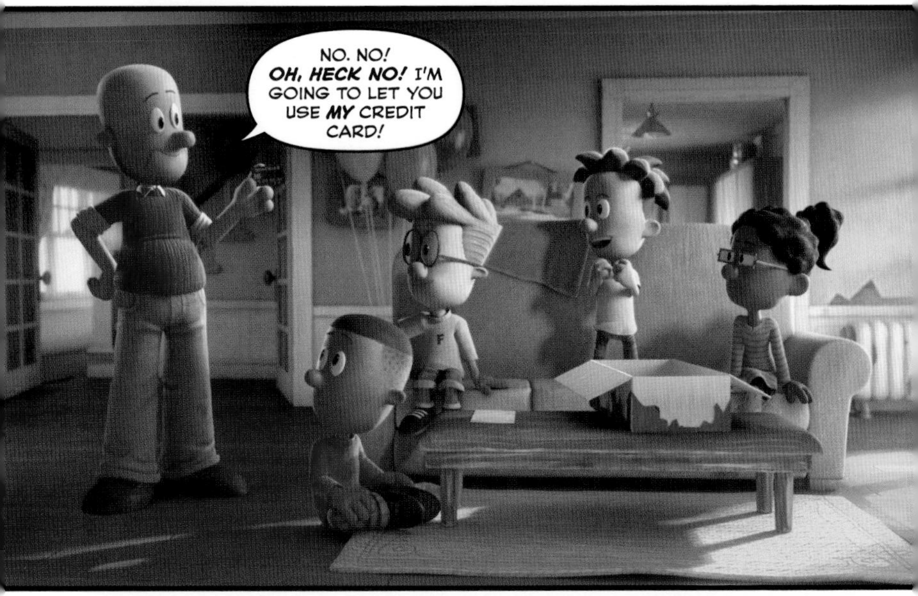
NO. NO! ***OH, HECK NO!*** I'M GOING TO LET YOU USE ***MY*** CREDIT CARD!

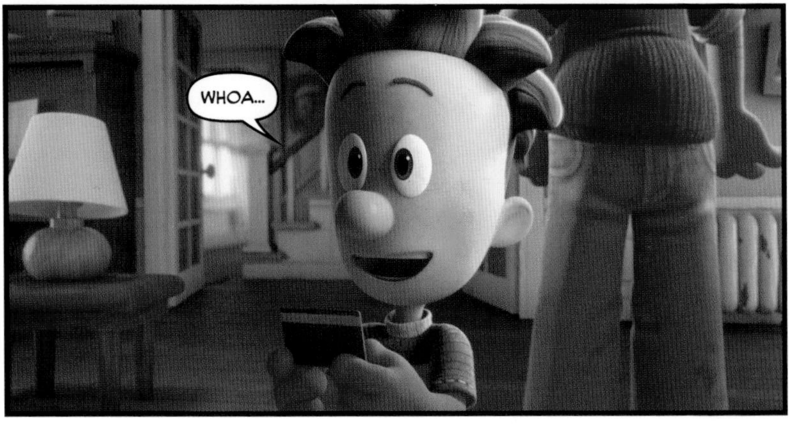
WHOA...

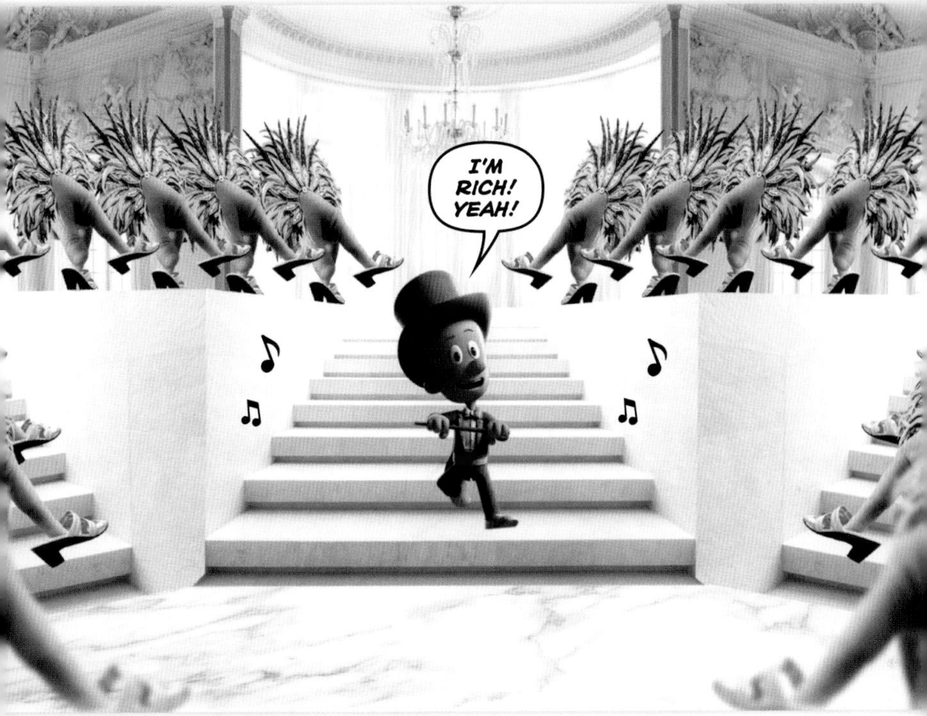
I'M RICH! YEAH!

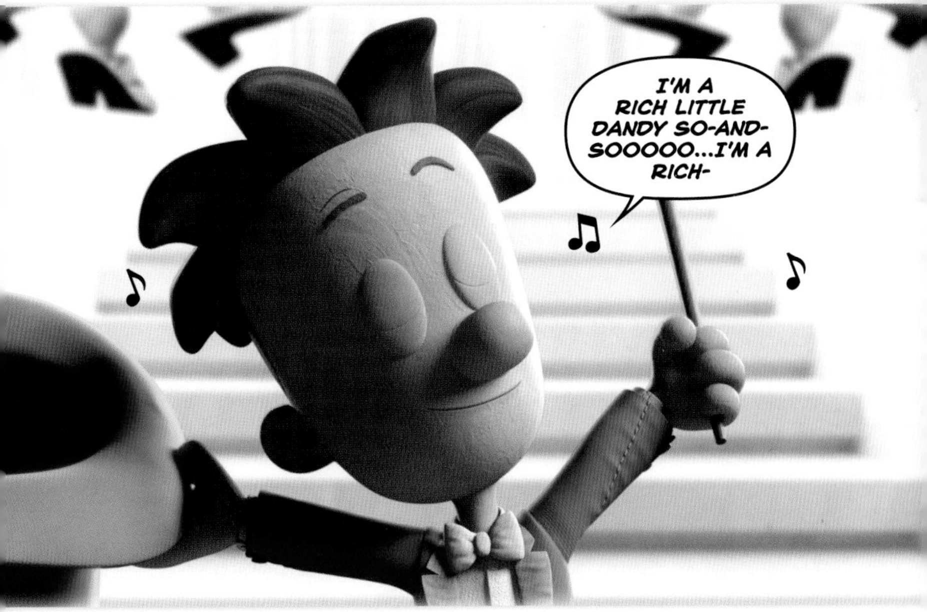
I'M A RICH LITTLE DANDY SO-AND-SOOOOO...I'M A RICH-

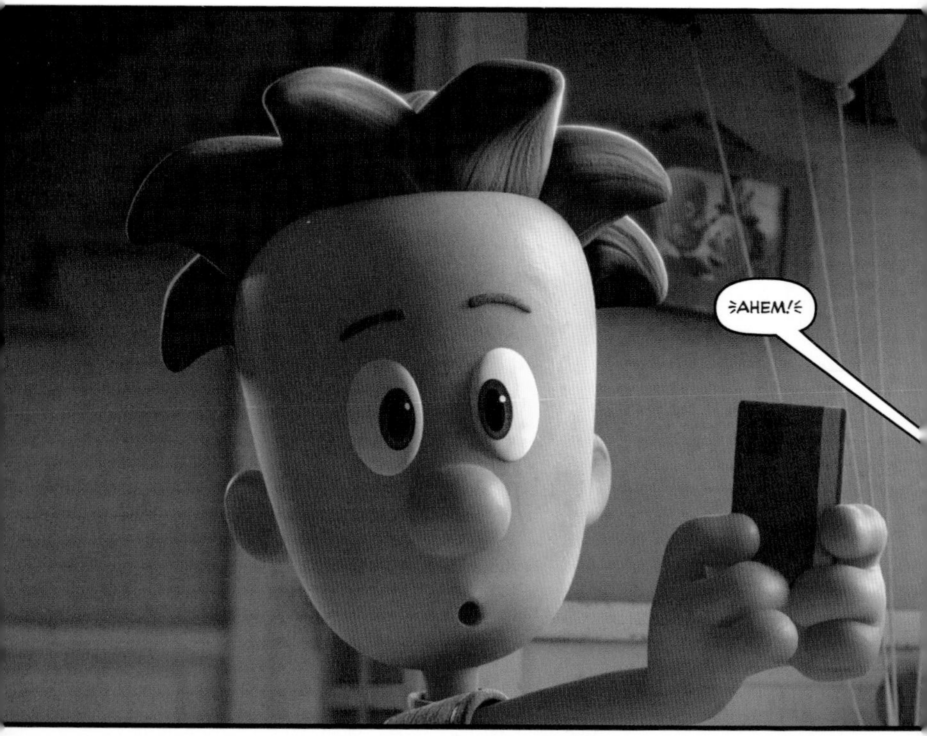
AHEM!

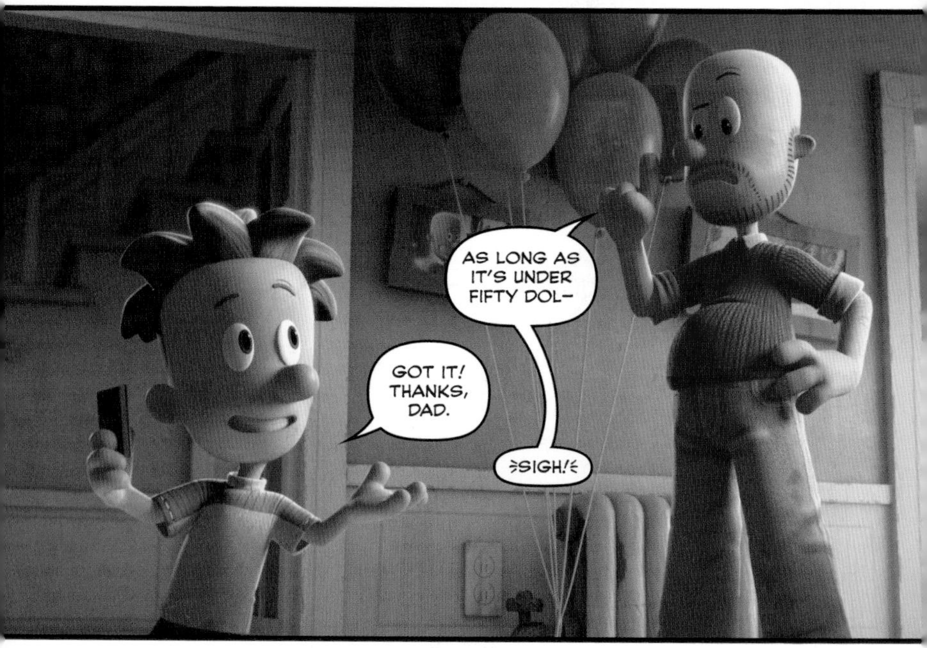
AS LONG AS IT'S UNDER FIFTY DOL-
GOT IT! THANKS, DAD.
SIGH!

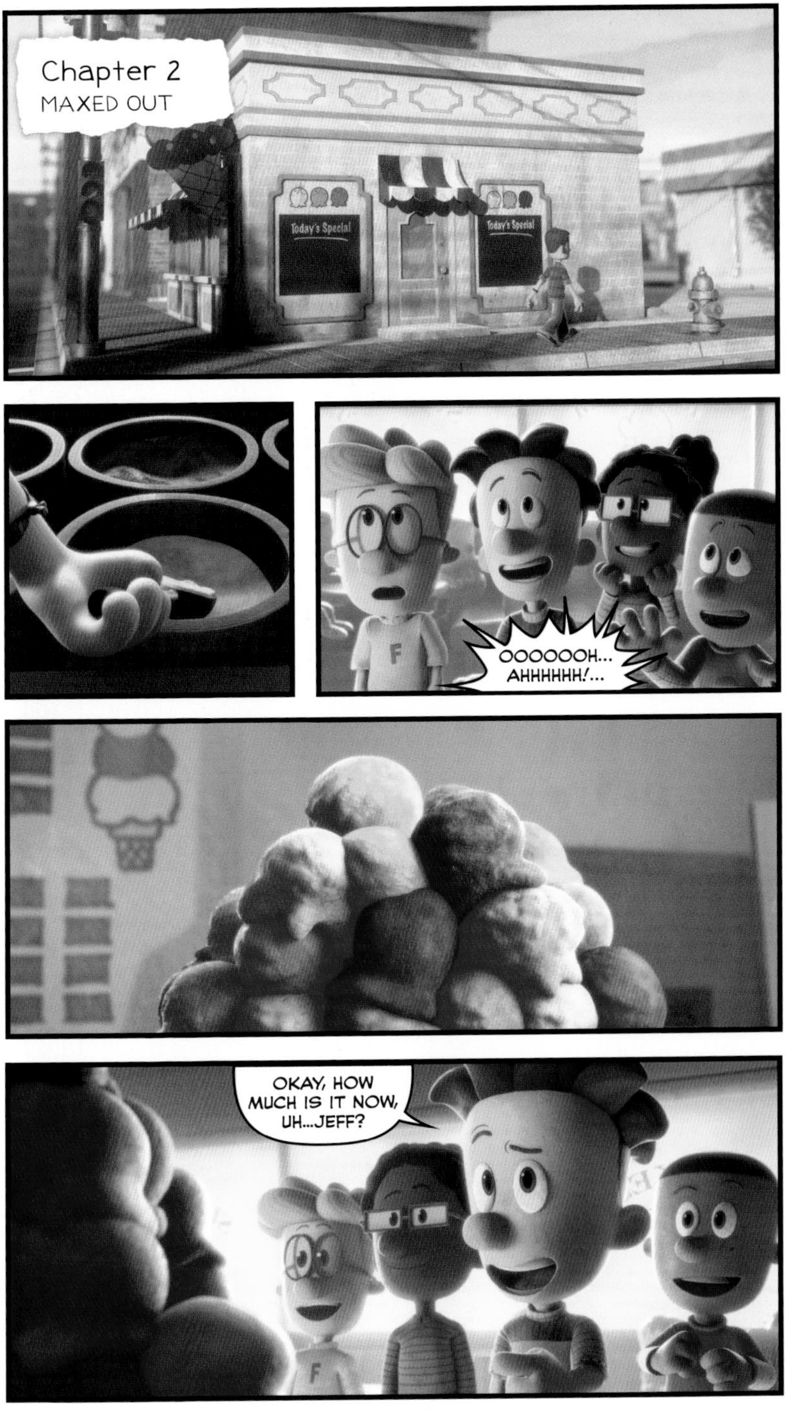
Chapter 2
MAXED OUT
Today's Special
Today's Special
OOOOOOH... AHHHHHH!...
OKAY, HOW MUCH IS IT NOW, UH...JEFF?

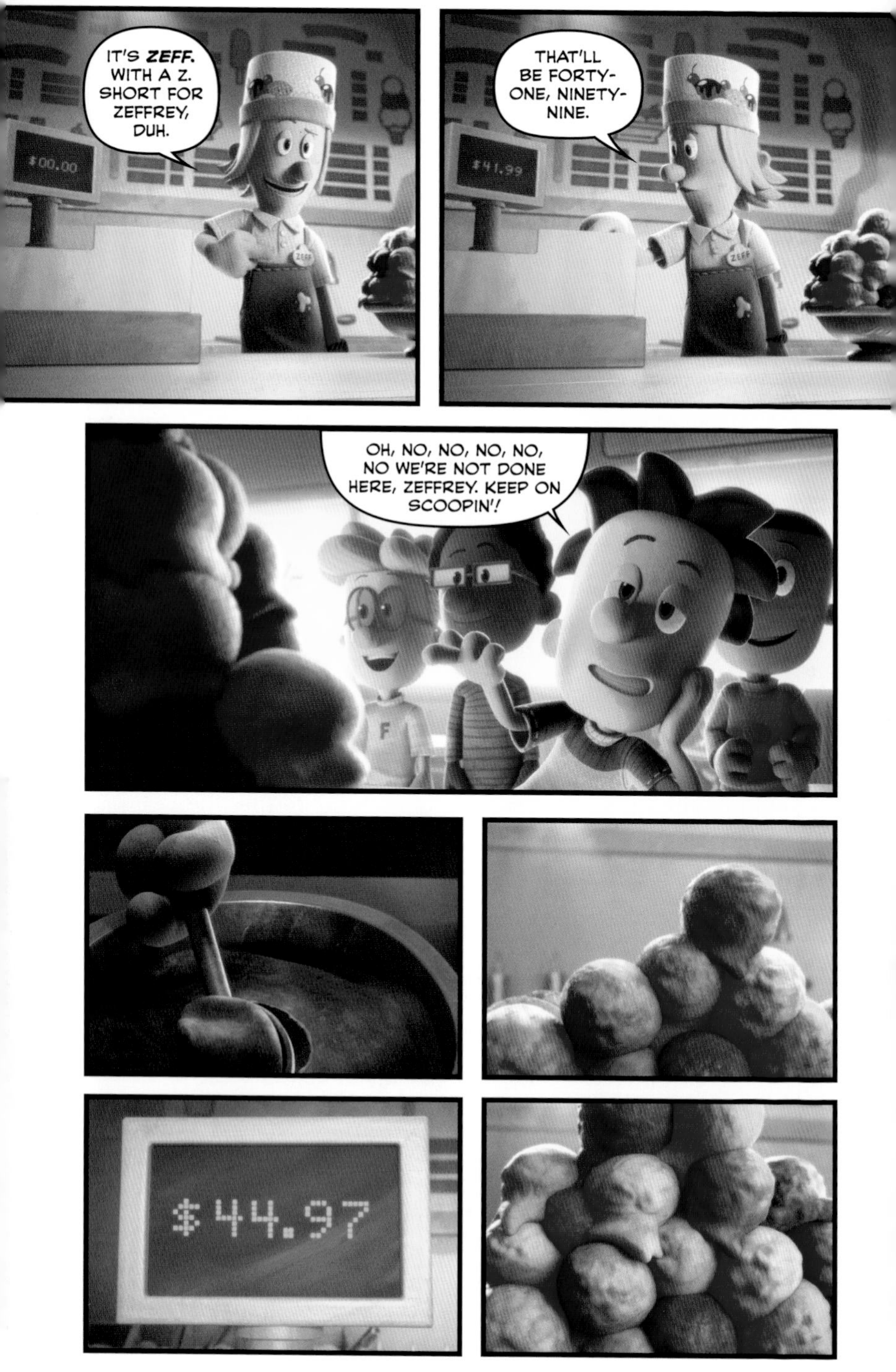
IT'S **ZEFF.** WITH A Z. SHORT FOR ZEFFREY, DUH.
$00.00
THAT'LL BE FORTY-ONE, NINETY-NINE.
$41.99
OH, NO, NO, NO, NO, NO WE'RE NOT DONE HERE, ZEFFREY. KEEP ON SCOOPIN'!
$44.97

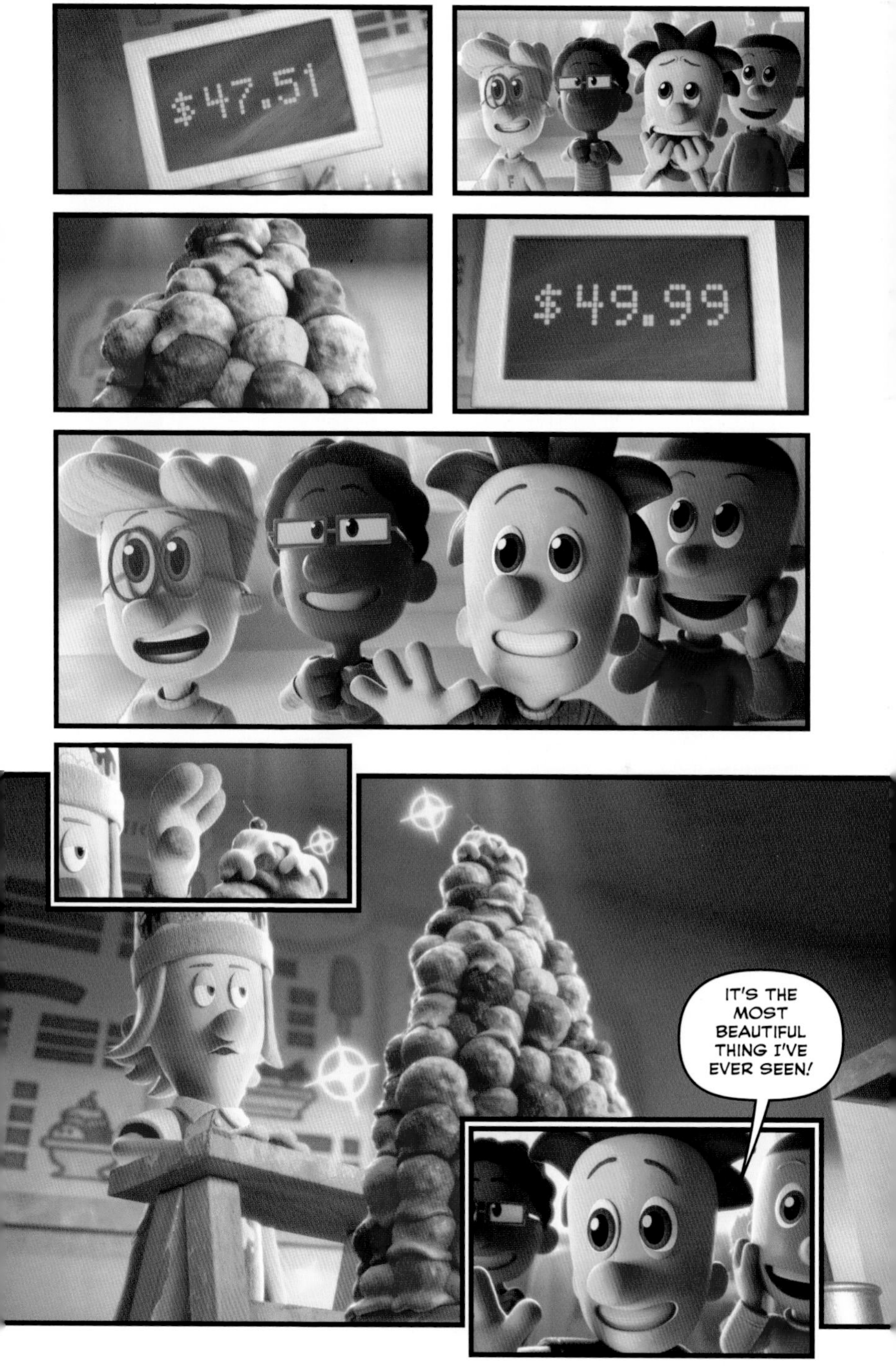
$47.51
$49.99
IT'S THE MOST BEAUTIFUL THING I'VE EVER SEEN!

100

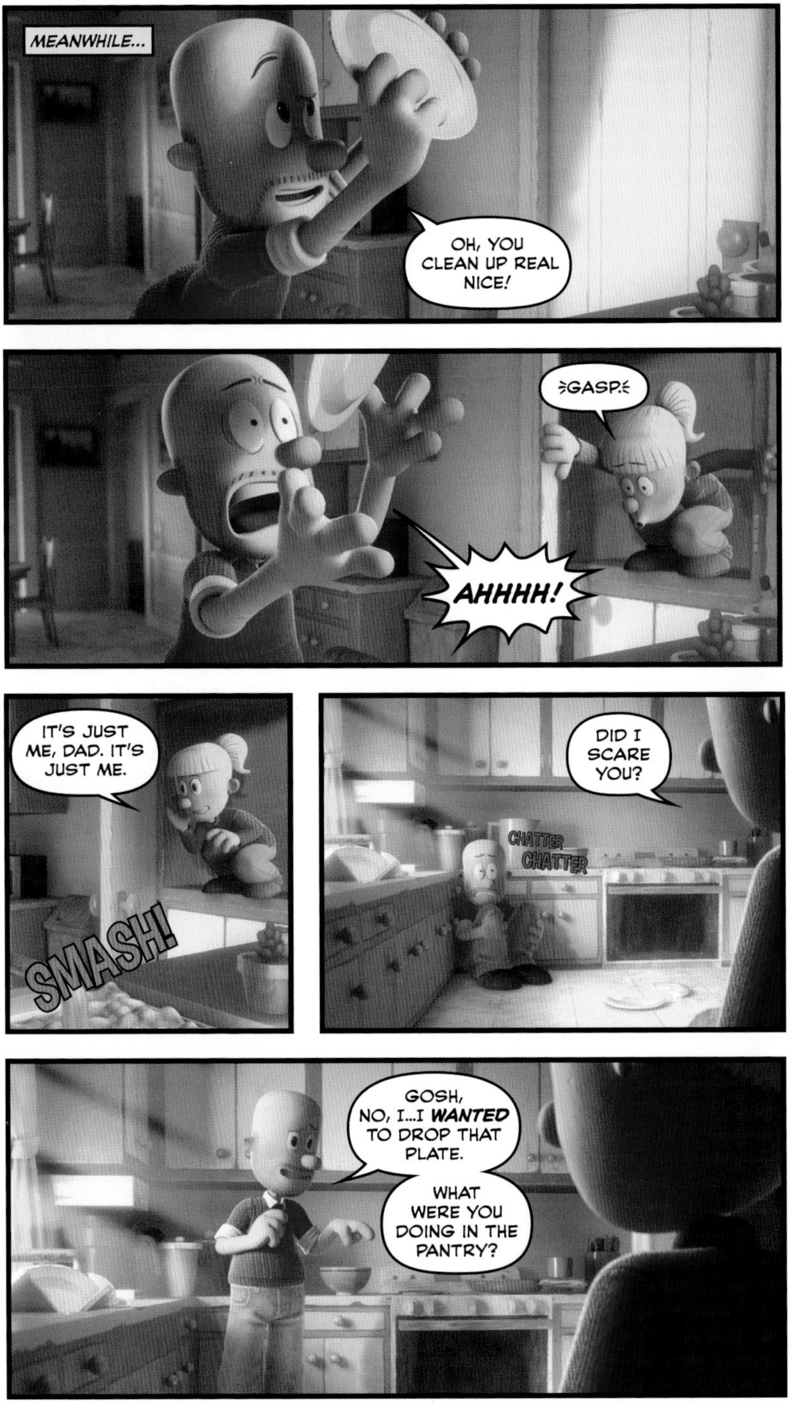
MEANWHILE...
OH, YOU CLEAN UP REAL NICE!
GASP.
AHHHH!
IT'S JUST ME, DAD. IT'S JUST ME.
SMASH!
DID I SCARE YOU?
CHATTER CHATTER
GOSH, NO, I...I *WANTED* TO DROP THAT PLATE.
WHAT WERE YOU DOING IN THE PANTRY?

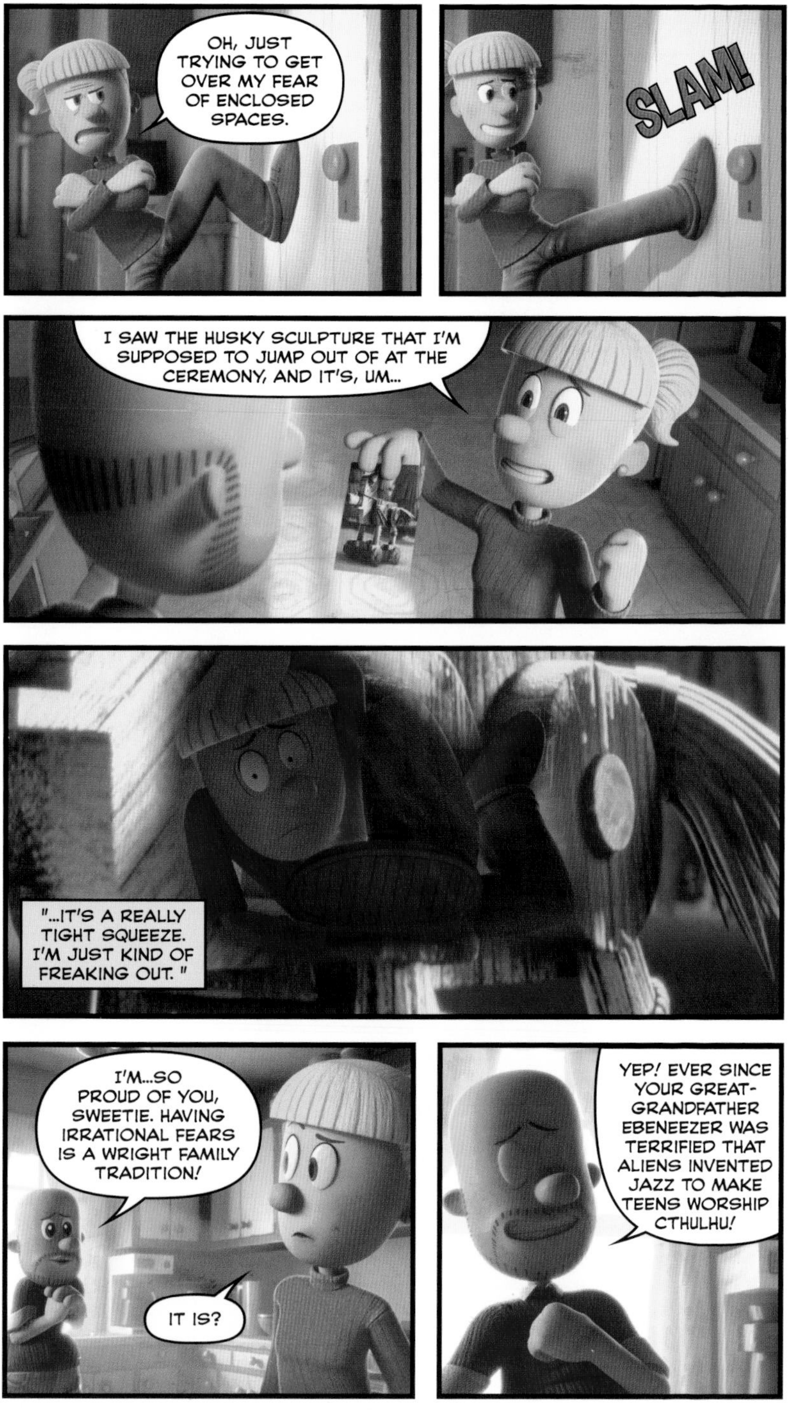
OH, JUST TRYING TO GET OVER MY FEAR OF ENCLOSED SPACES.
SLAM!
I SAW THE HUSKY SCULPTURE THAT I'M SUPPOSED TO JUMP OUT OF AT THE CEREMONY, AND IT'S, UM...
"...IT'S A REALLY TIGHT SQUEEZE. I'M JUST KIND OF FREAKING OUT."
I'M...SO PROUD OF YOU, SWEETIE. HAVING IRRATIONAL FEARS IS A WRIGHT FAMILY TRADITION!
IT IS?
YEP! EVER SINCE YOUR GREAT-GRANDFATHER EBENEEZER WAS TERRIFIED THAT ALIENS INVENTED JAZZ TO MAKE TEENS WORSHIP CTHULHU!

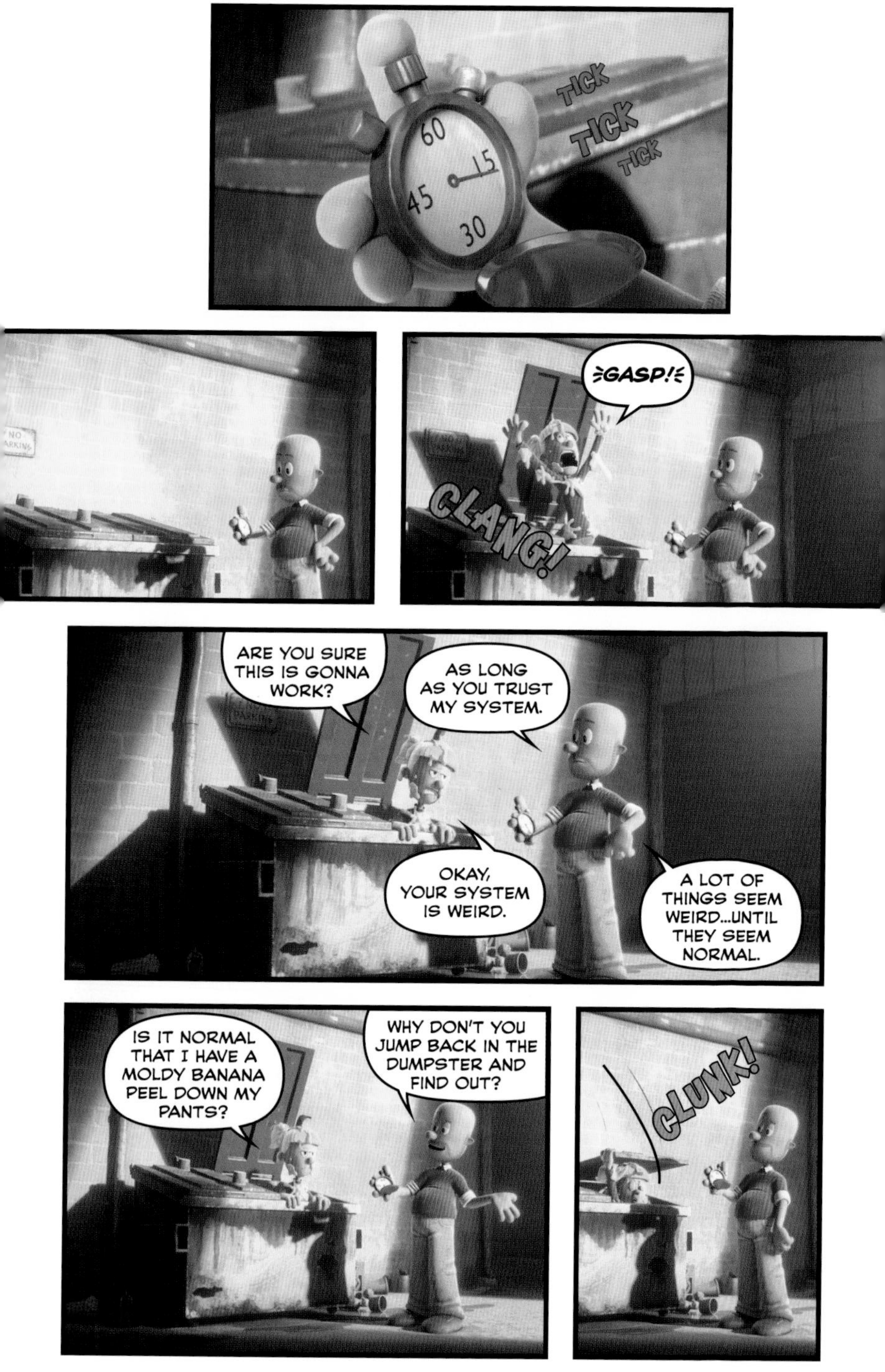
TICK
TICK
TICK
GASP!
CLANG!
ARE YOU SURE THIS IS GONNA WORK?
AS LONG AS YOU TRUST MY SYSTEM.
OKAY, YOUR SYSTEM IS WEIRD.
A LOT OF THINGS SEEM WEIRD...UNTIL THEY SEEM NORMAL.
IS IT NORMAL THAT I HAVE A MOLDY BANANA PEEL DOWN MY PANTS?
WHY DON'T YOU JUMP BACK IN THE DUMPSTER AND FIND OUT?
CLUNK!

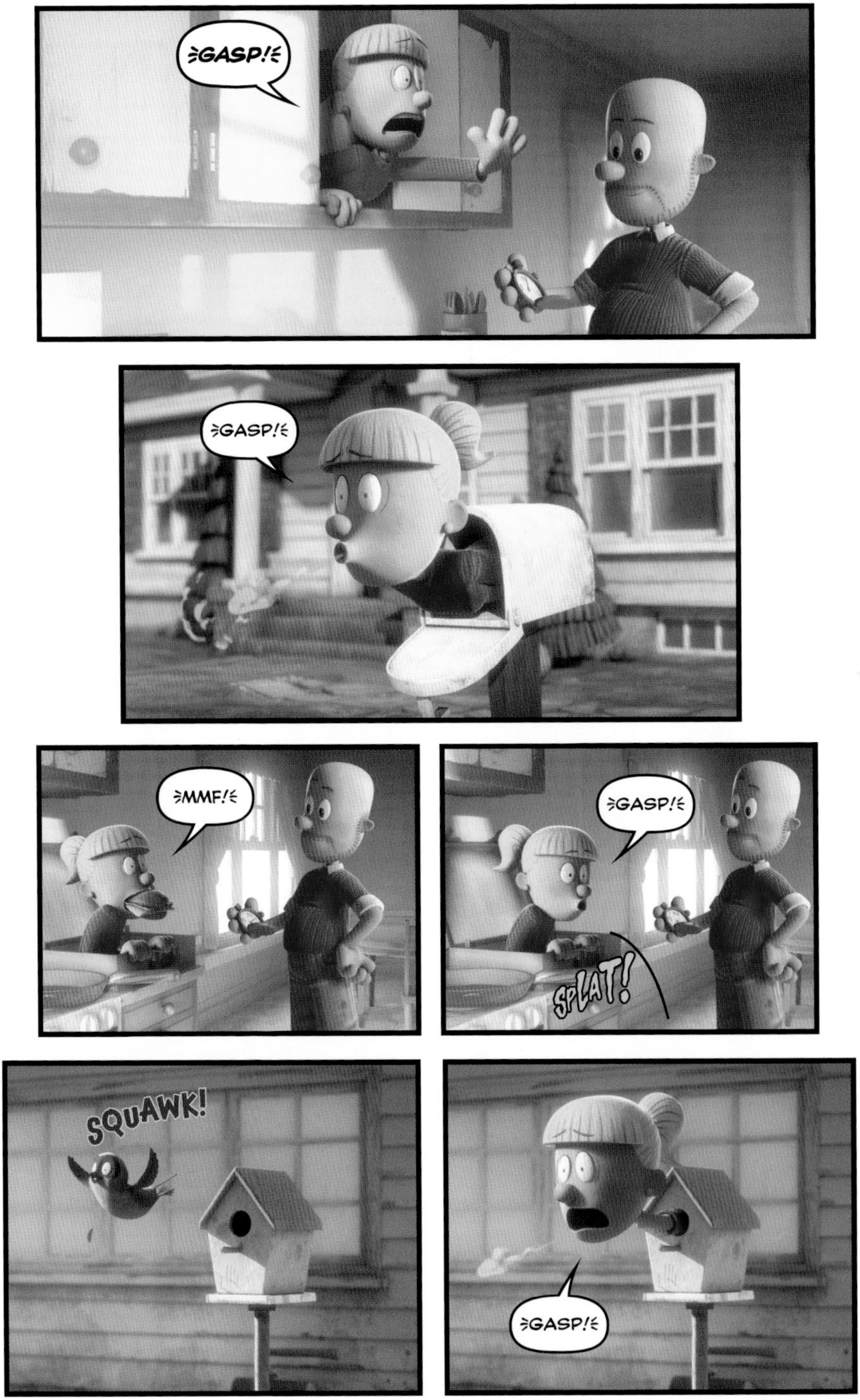
GASP!
GASP!
MMF!
GASP!
SPLAT!
SQUAWK!
GASP!

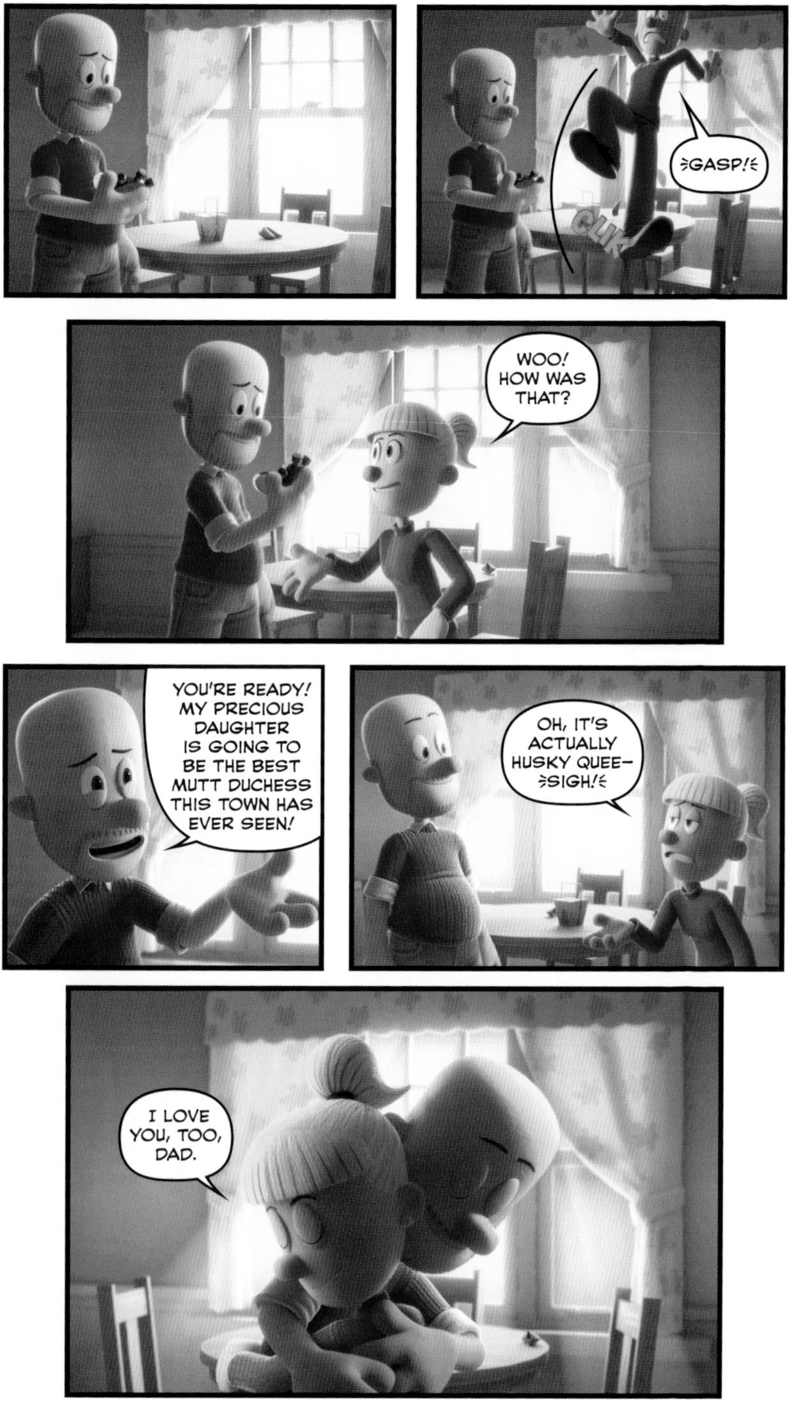

>GASP!<
CLIK
WOO! HOW WAS THAT?
YOU'RE READY! MY PRECIOUS DAUGHTER IS GOING TO BE THE BEST MUTT DUCHESS THIS TOWN HAS EVER SEEN!
OH, IT'S ACTUALLY HUSKY QUEE— >SIGH!<
I LOVE YOU, TOO, DAD.

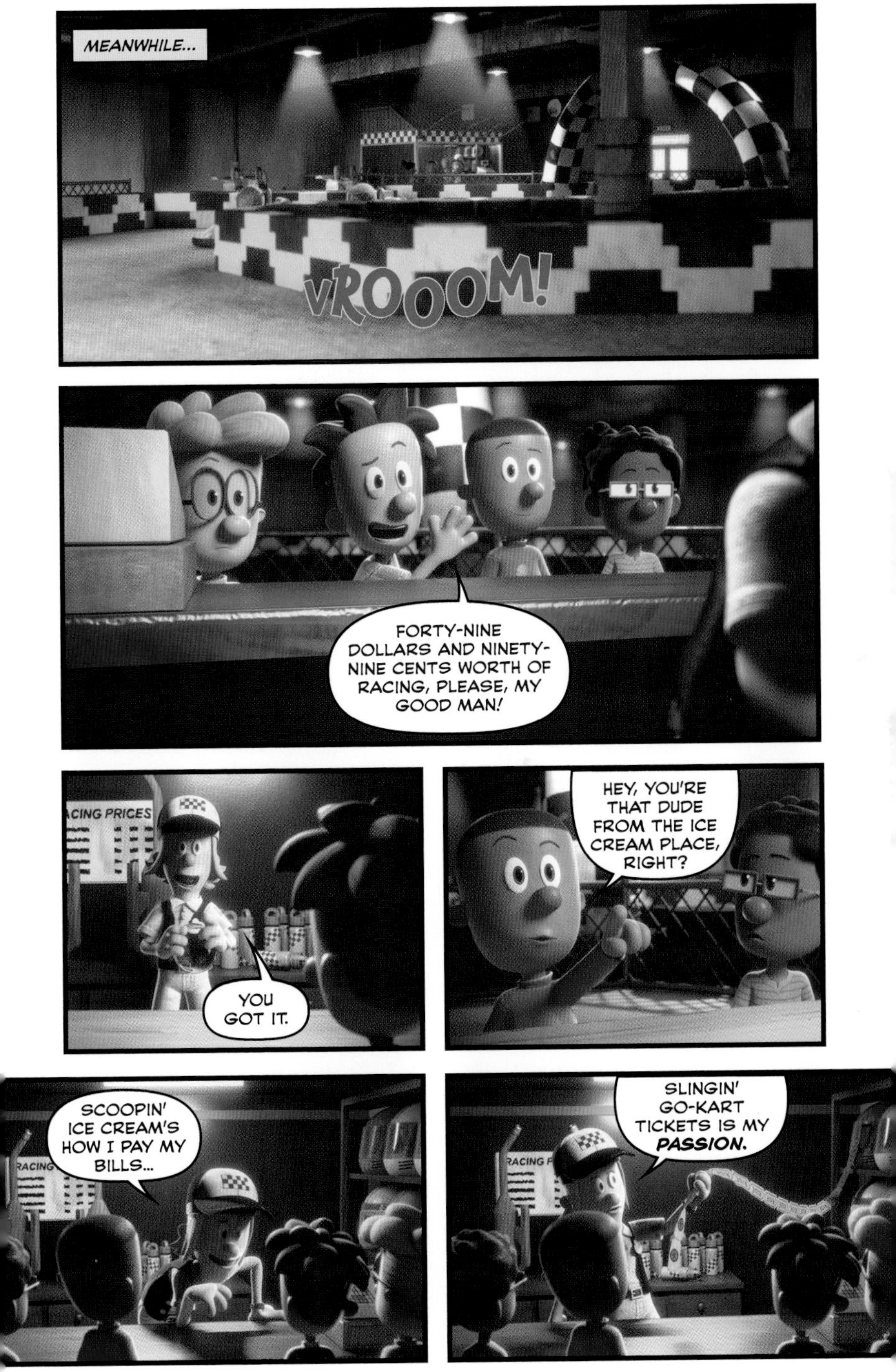
MEANWHILE...
VROOOM!
FORTY-NINE DOLLARS AND NINETY-NINE CENTS WORTH OF RACING, PLEASE, MY GOOD MAN!
RACING PRICES
YOU GOT IT.
HEY, YOU'RE THAT DUDE FROM THE ICE CREAM PLACE, RIGHT?
SCOOPIN' ICE CREAM'S HOW I PAY MY BILLS...
SLINGIN' GO-KART TICKETS IS MY ***PASSION.***

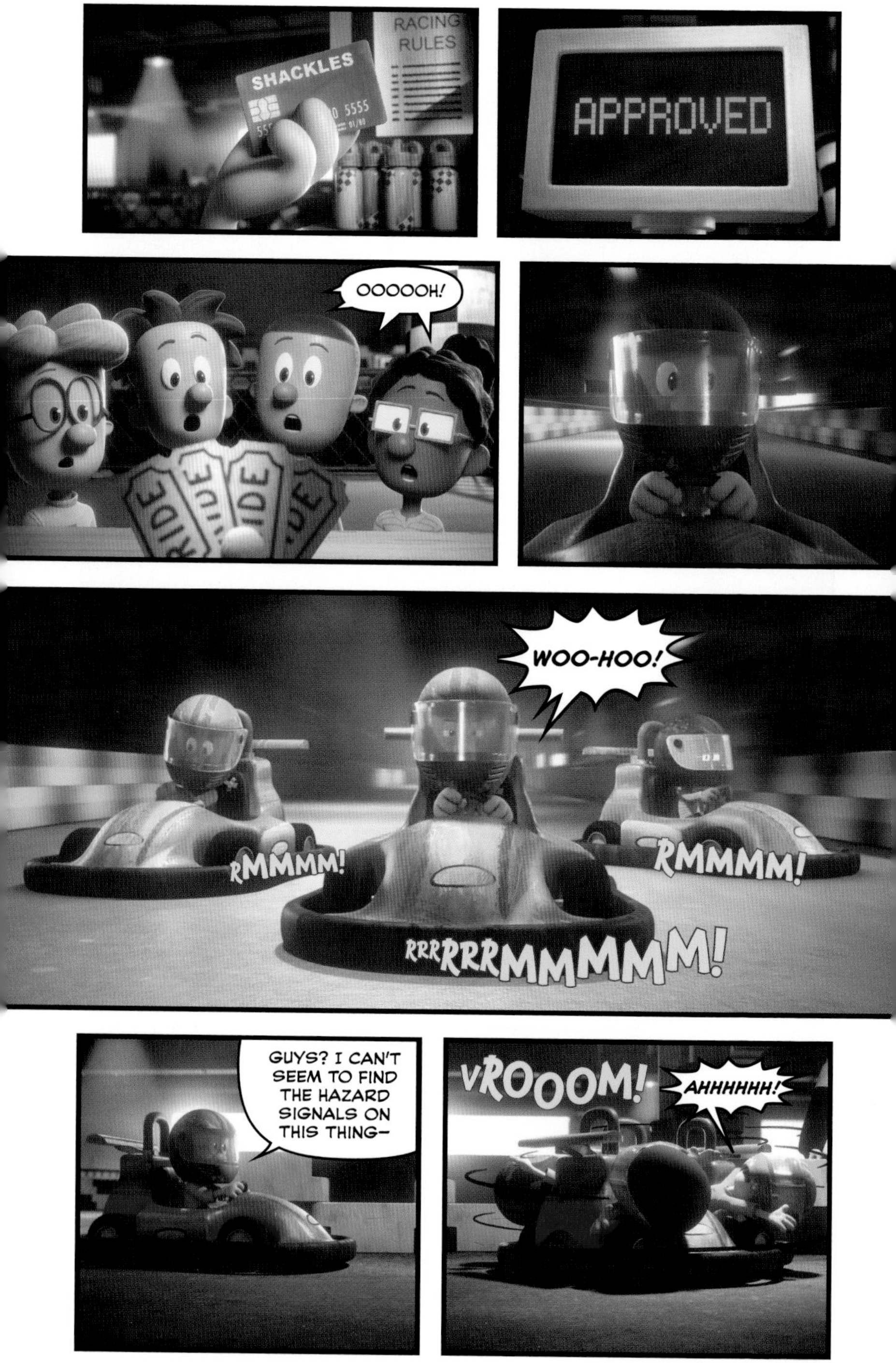
SHACKLES
RACING RULES
APPROVED
OOOOOH!
WOO-HOO!
RMMMM!
RMMMM!
RRRRRRMMMMMM!
GUYS? I CAN'T SEEM TO FIND THE HAZARD SIGNALS ON THIS THING—
VROOOM!
AHHHHHH!

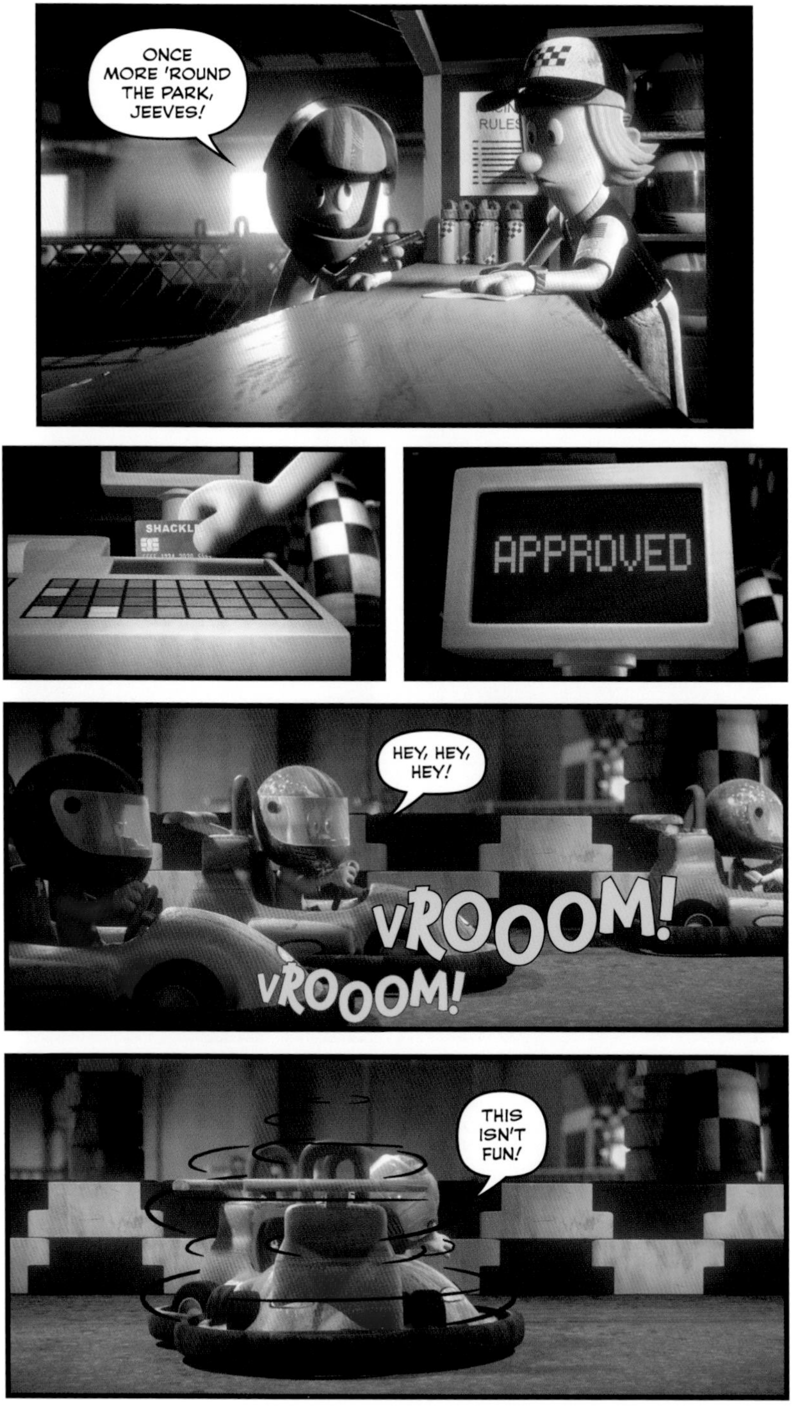
ONCE MORE 'ROUND THE PARK, JEEVES!
RULES
SHACKL
APPROVED
HEY, HEY, HEY!
VROOOM!
VROOOM!
THIS ISN'T FUN!

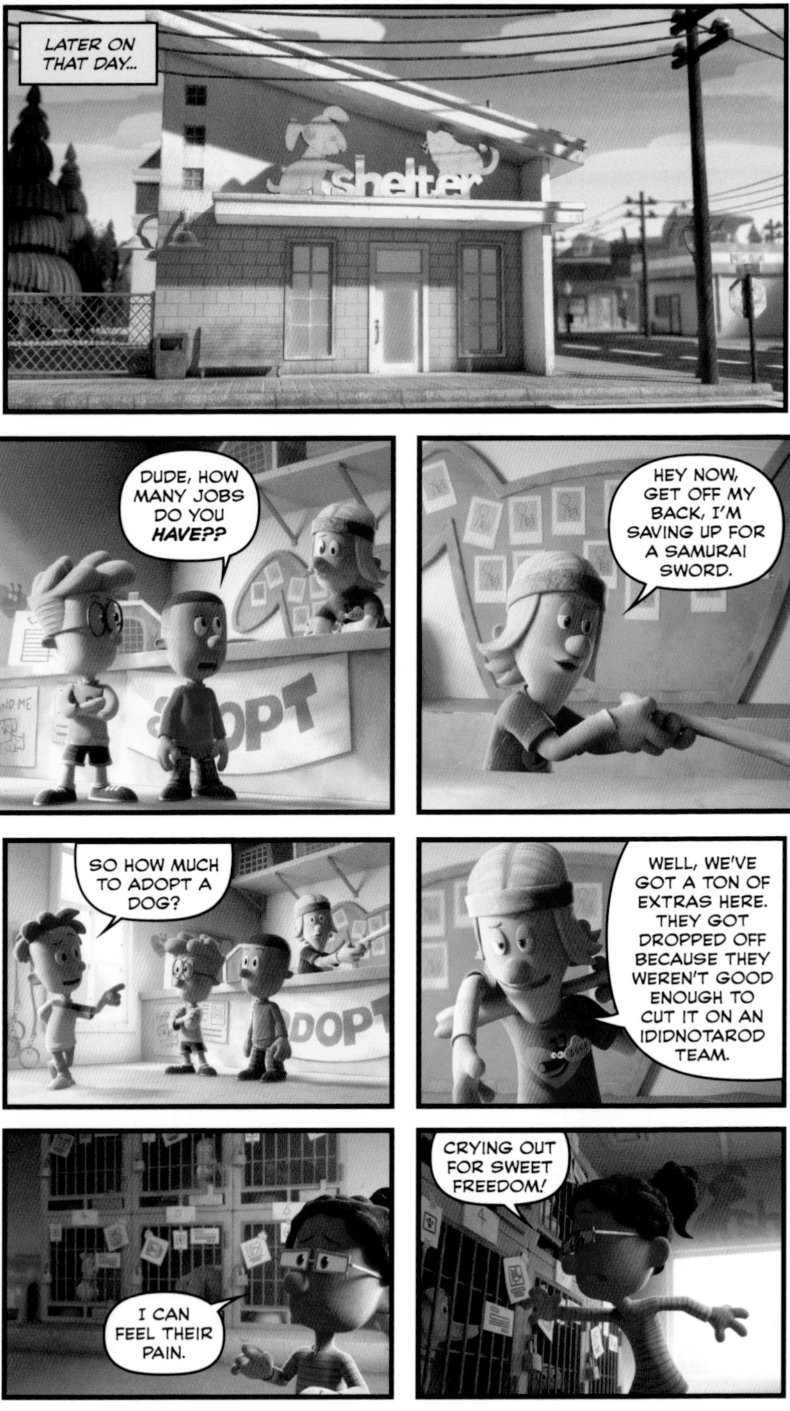
LATER ON THAT DAY...
shelter
DUDE, HOW MANY JOBS DO YOU *HAVE??*
ADOPT
FIND ME
HEY NOW, GET OFF MY BACK, I'M SAVING UP FOR A SAMURAI SWORD.
SO HOW MUCH TO ADOPT A DOG?
WELL, WE'VE GOT A TON OF EXTRAS HERE. THEY GOT DROPPED OFF BECAUSE THEY WEREN'T GOOD ENOUGH TO CUT IT ON AN IDIDNOTAROD TEAM.
I CAN FEEL THEIR PAIN.
CRYING OUT FOR SWEET FREEDOM!

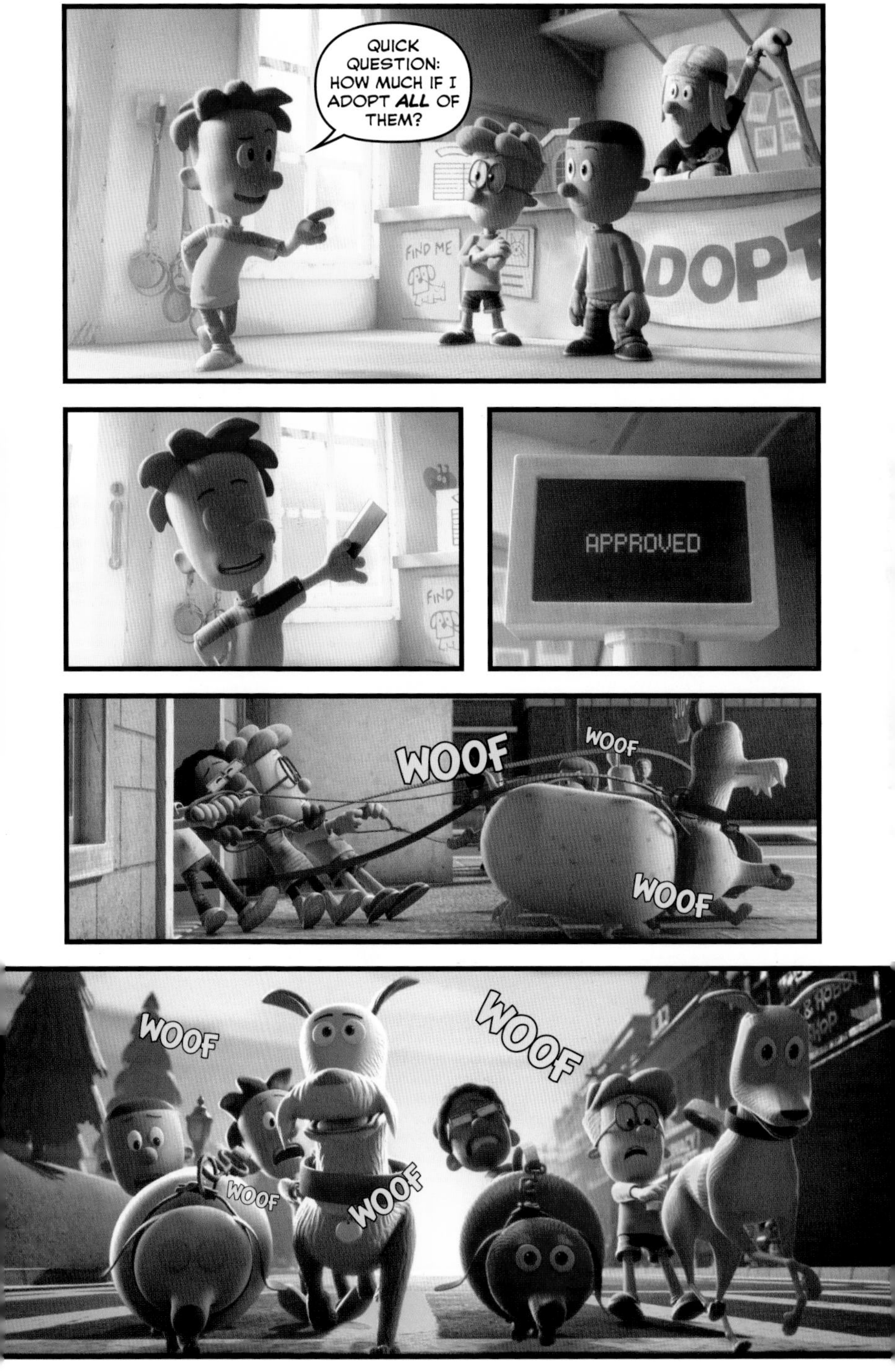
QUICK QUESTION: HOW MUCH IF I ADOPT **ALL** OF THEM?
FIND ME
FIND
APPROVED
WOOF
WOOF
WOOF
WOOF
WOOF
WOOF
WOOF

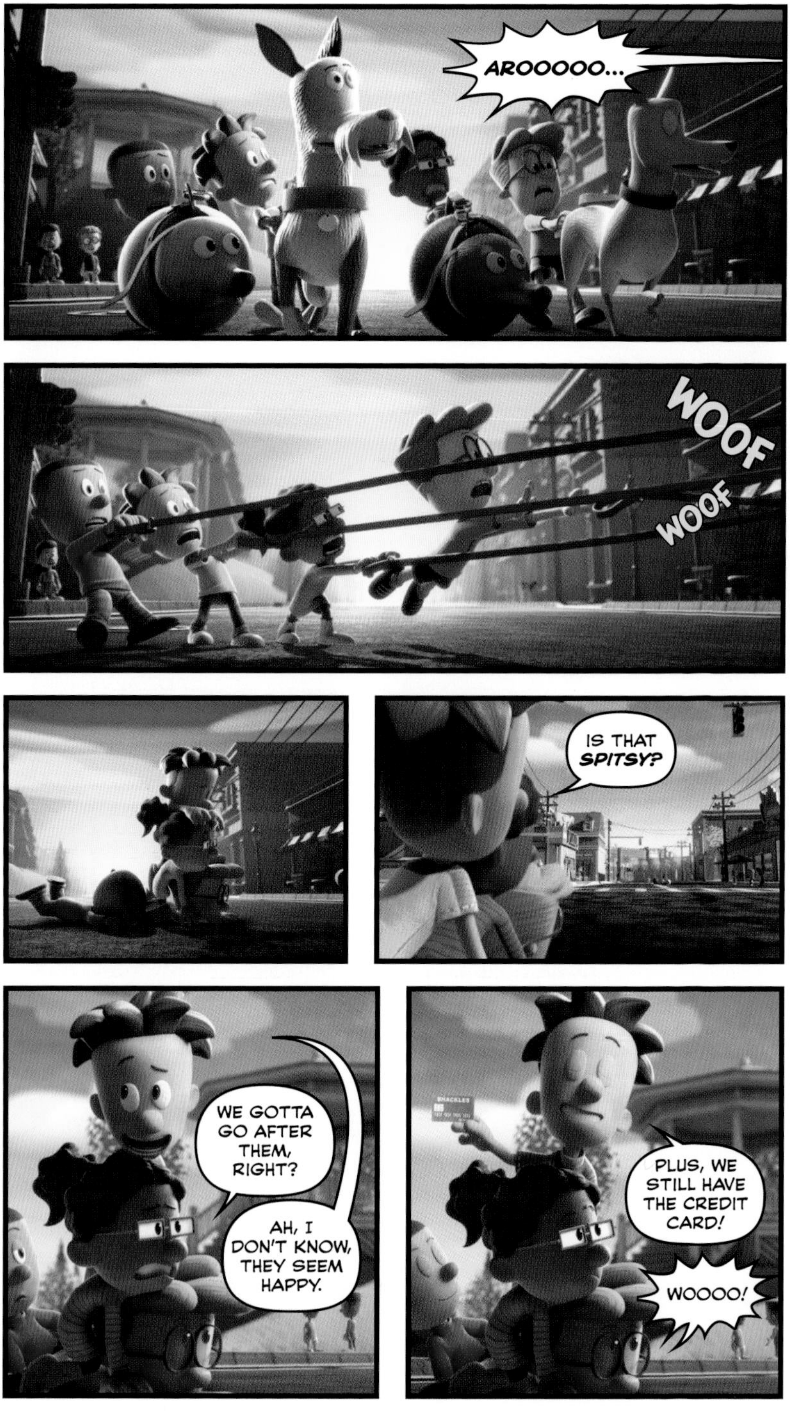
AROOOOO...
WOOF
WOOF
IS THAT SPITSY?
WE GOTTA GO AFTER THEM, RIGHT?
AH, I DON'T KNOW, THEY SEEM HAPPY.
PLUS, WE STILL HAVE THE CREDIT CARD!
WOOOO!

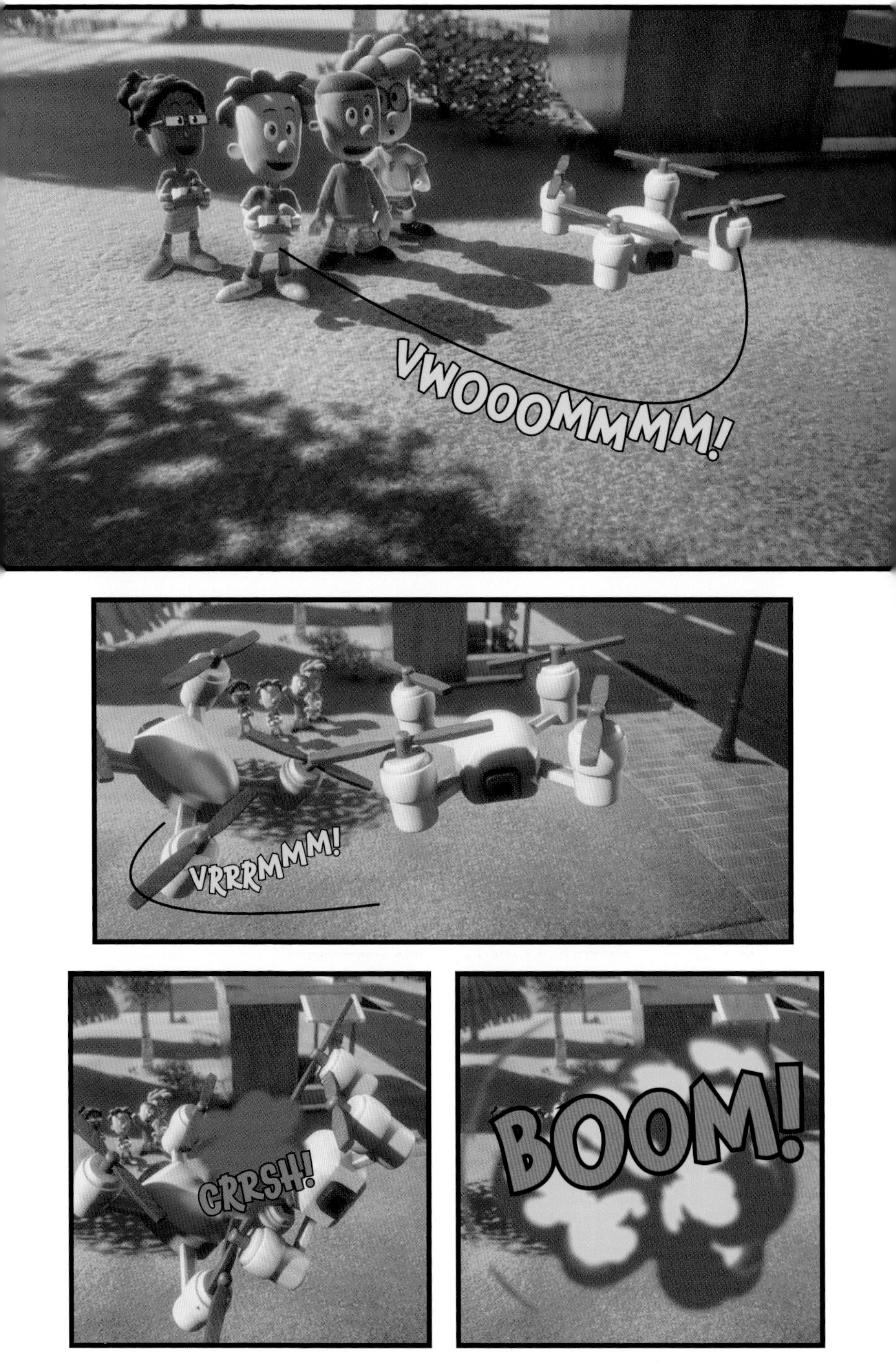
VWOOOMMMMM!
VRRRMMM!
CRRSH!
BOOM!

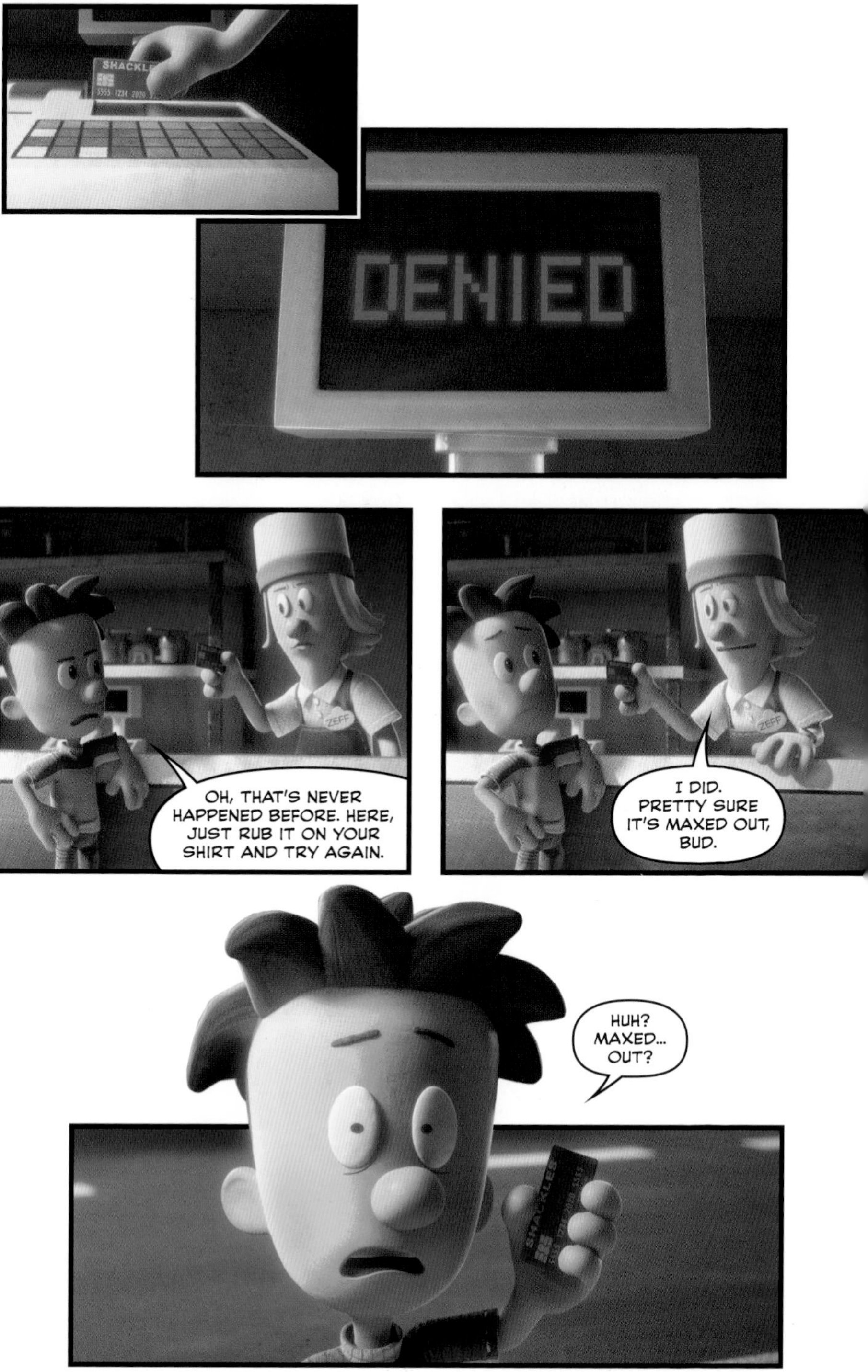
DENIED
OH, THAT'S NEVER HAPPENED BEFORE. HERE, JUST RUB IT ON YOUR SHIRT AND TRY AGAIN.
I DID. PRETTY SURE IT'S MAXED OUT, BUD.
HUH? MAXED... OUT?

Chapter 3
WHO LET THE DOGS OUT?

NO, NO, MY DAD'S GOING TO KILL ME!

¡DIOS MÍO! TO BE FINANCIALLY RUINED BY YOUR OWN SON...I JUST HOPE HIS WEAK HEART CAN HANDLE THIS.

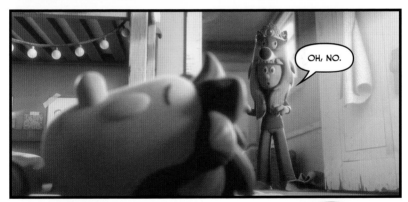

OH, NO.

NATE, IS EVERYTHING OKAY?

...SHE ASKED, HOPING THE ANSWER WAS NO.

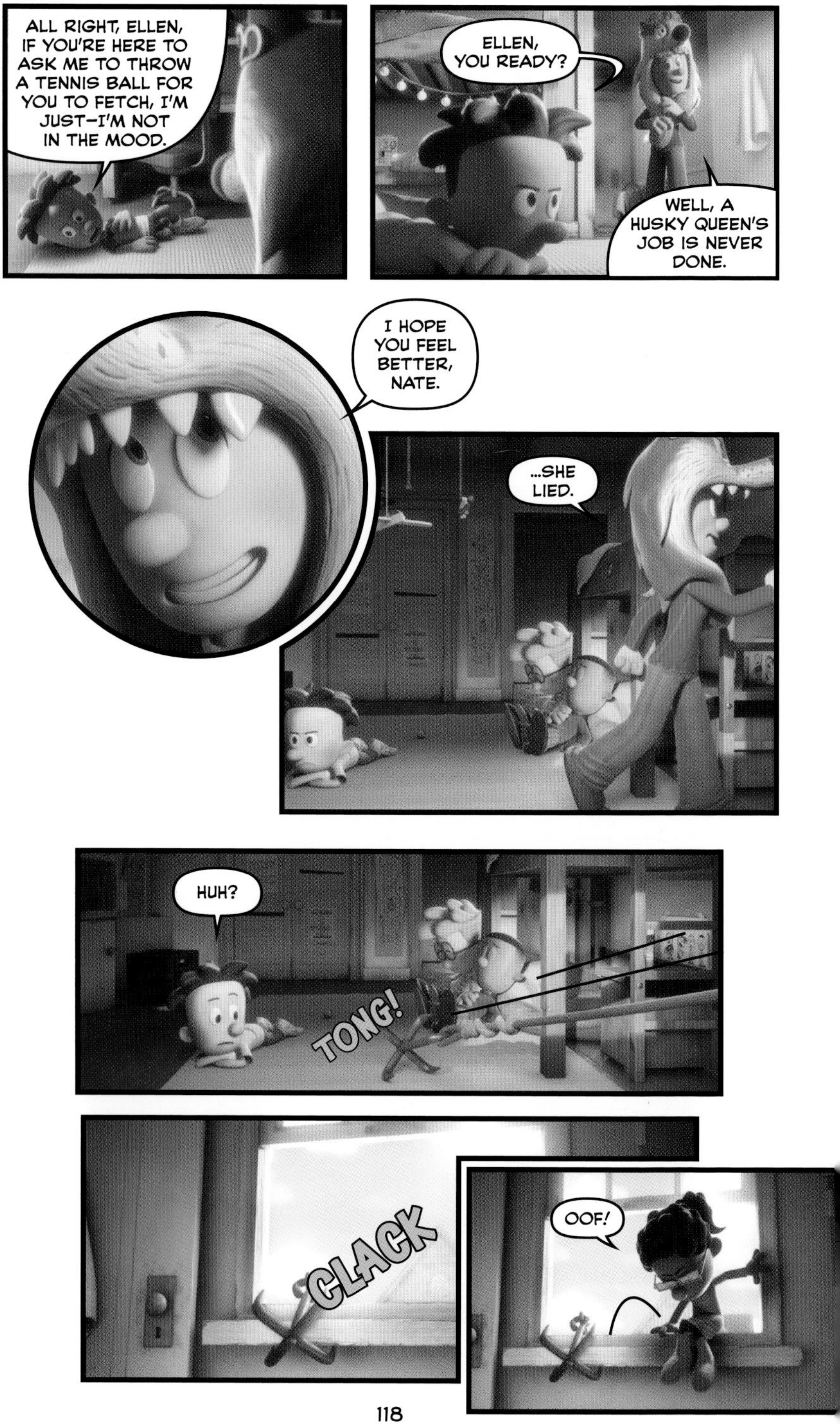
ALL RIGHT, ELLEN, IF YOU'RE HERE TO ASK ME TO THROW A TENNIS BALL FOR YOU TO FETCH, I'M JUST—I'M NOT IN THE MOOD.
ELLEN, YOU READY?
WELL, A HUSKY QUEEN'S JOB IS NEVER DONE.
I HOPE YOU FEEL BETTER, NATE.
...SHE LIED.
HUH?
TONG!
CLACK
OOF!

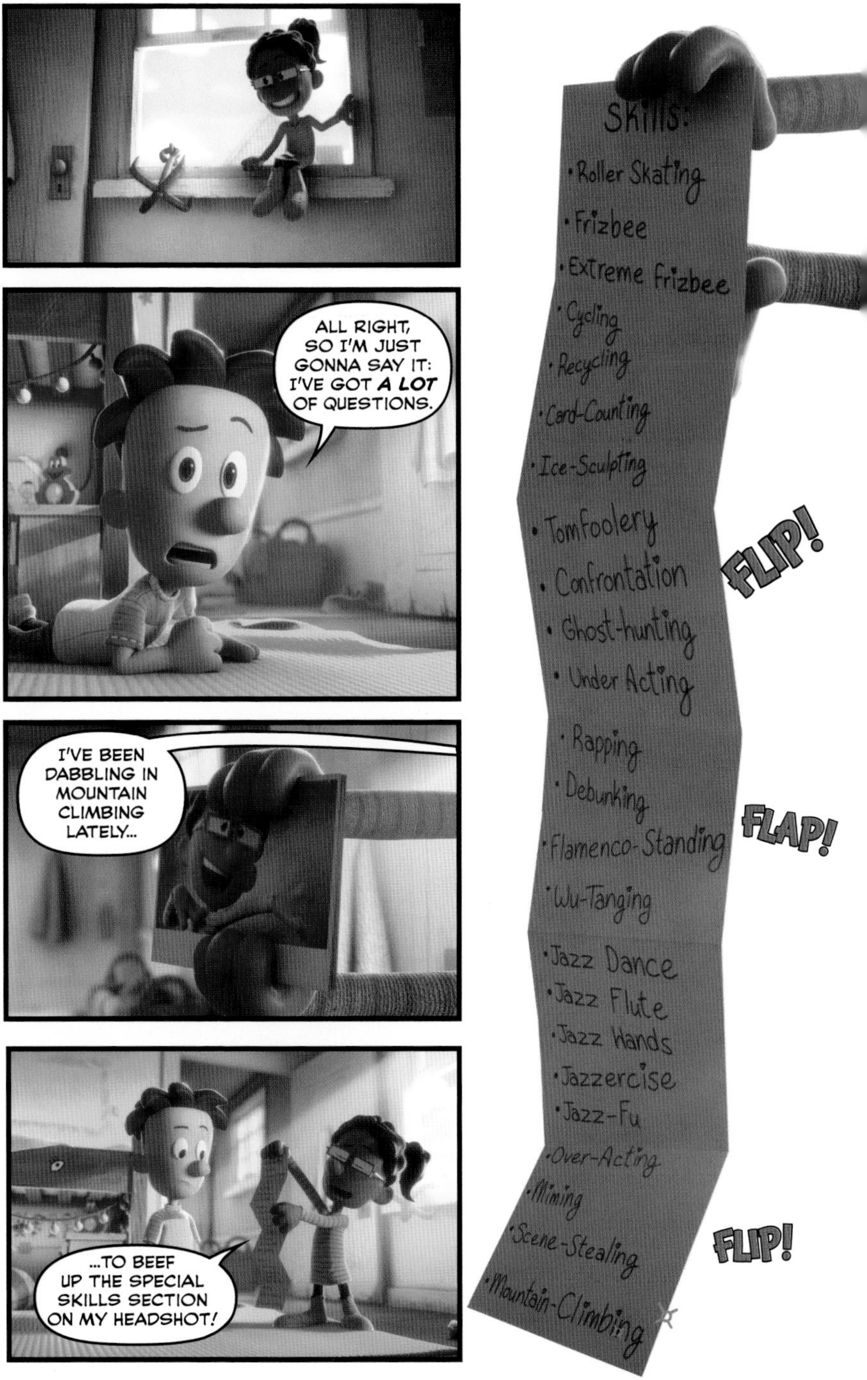
ALL RIGHT, SO I'M JUST GONNA SAY IT: I'VE GOT **A LOT** OF QUESTIONS.
I'VE BEEN DABBLING IN MOUNTAIN CLIMBING LATELY...
...TO BEEF UP THE SPECIAL SKILLS SECTION ON MY HEADSHOT!
Skills:
•Roller Skating
•Frizbee
•Extreme frizbee
•Cycling
•Recycling
•Card-Counting
•Ice-Sculpting
•Tomfoolery
•Confrontation
•Ghost-hunting
•Under Acting
•Rapping
•Debunking
•Flamenco-Standing
•Wu-Tanging
•Jazz Dance
•Jazz Flute
•Jazz Hands
•Jazzercise
•Jazz-Fu
•Over-Acting
•Miming
•Scene-Stealing
•Mountain-Climbing
FLIP!
FLAP!
FLIP!

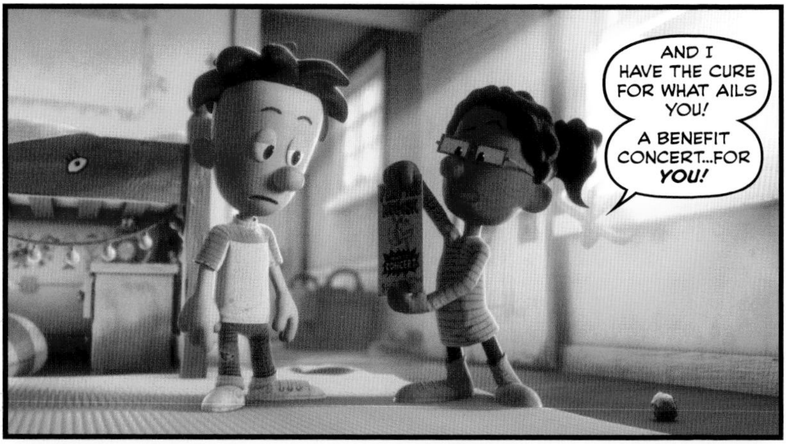
AND I HAVE THE CURE FOR WHAT AILS YOU!
A BENEFIT CONCERT...FOR *YOU!*

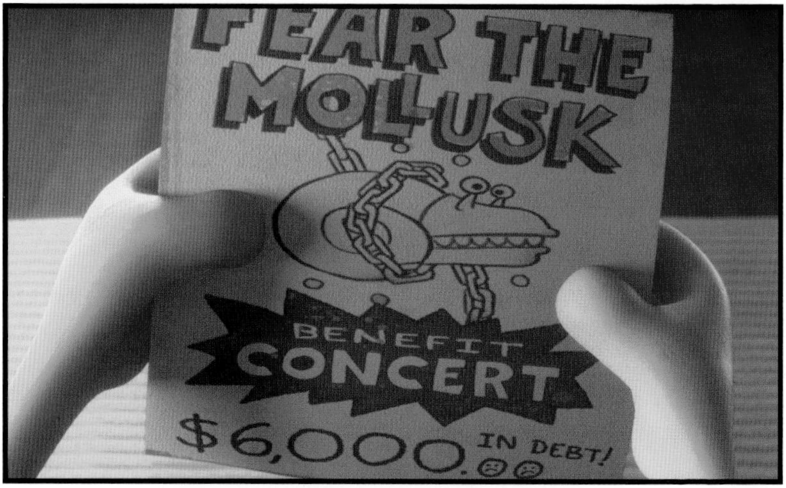
FEAR THE MOLLUSK
BENEFIT CONCERT
$6,000. IN DEBT!

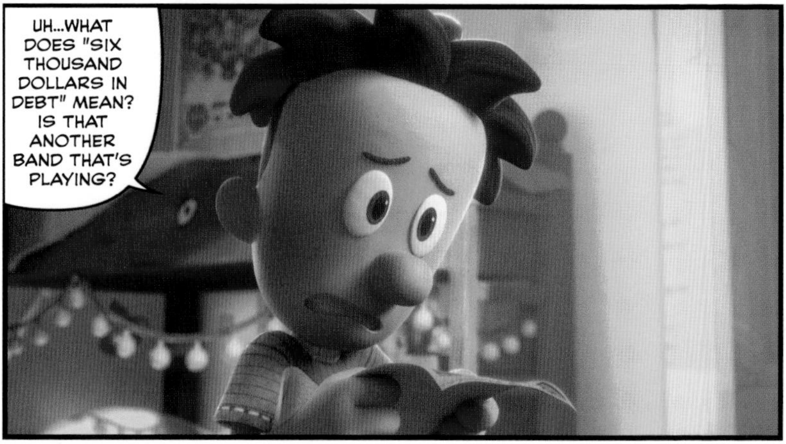
UH...WHAT DOES "SIX THOUSAND DOLLARS IN DEBT" MEAN? IS THAT ANOTHER BAND THAT'S PLAYING?

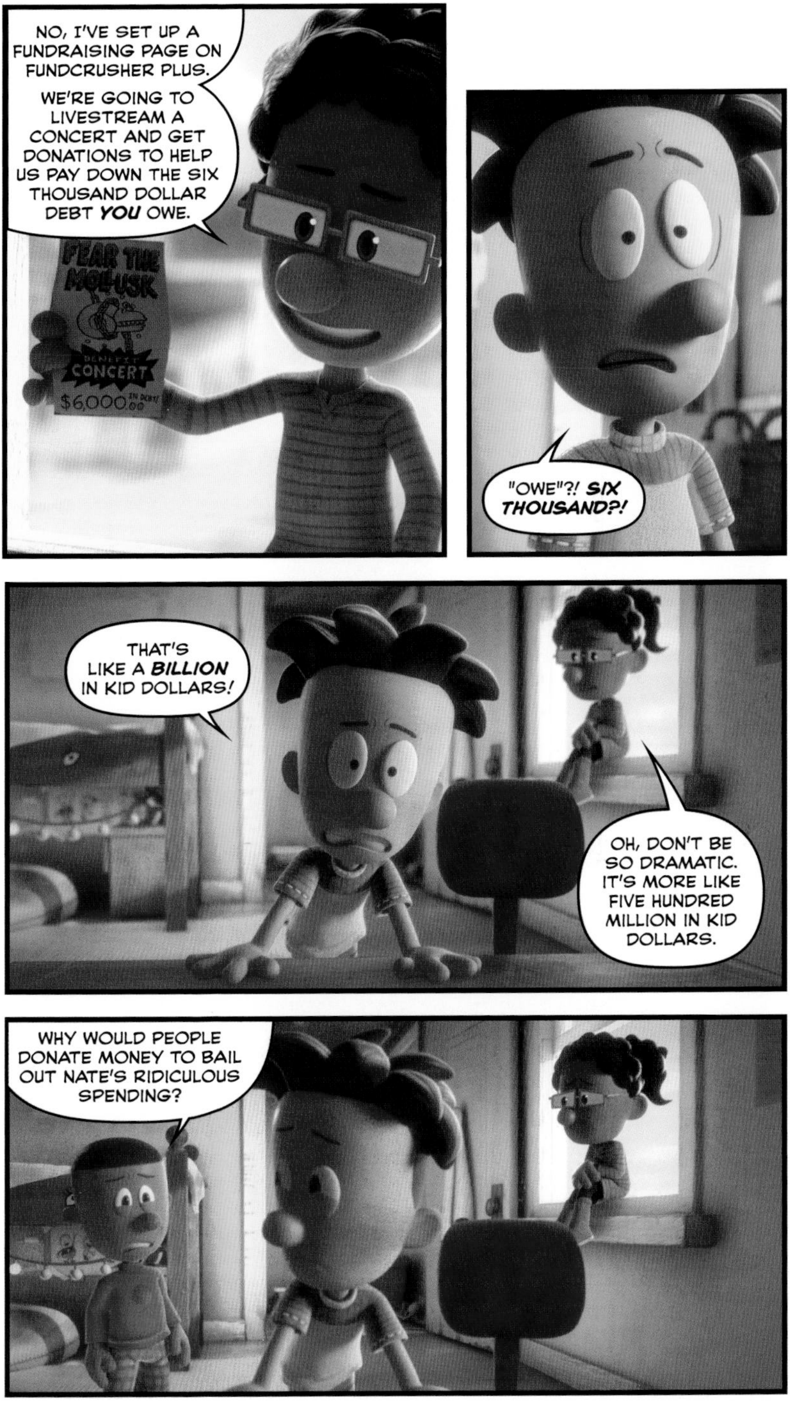
NO, I'VE SET UP A FUNDRAISING PAGE ON FUNDCRUSHER PLUS.
WE'RE GOING TO LIVESTREAM A CONCERT AND GET DONATIONS TO HELP US PAY DOWN THE SIX THOUSAND DOLLAR DEBT *YOU* OWE.
FEAR THE MOLLUSK
CONCERT
$6,000.00
"OWE"?! ***SIX THOUSAND?!***
THAT'S LIKE A ***BILLION*** IN KID DOLLARS!
OH, DON'T BE SO DRAMATIC. IT'S MORE LIKE FIVE HUNDRED MILLION IN KID DOLLARS.
WHY WOULD PEOPLE DONATE MONEY TO BAIL OUT NATE'S RIDICULOUS SPENDING?

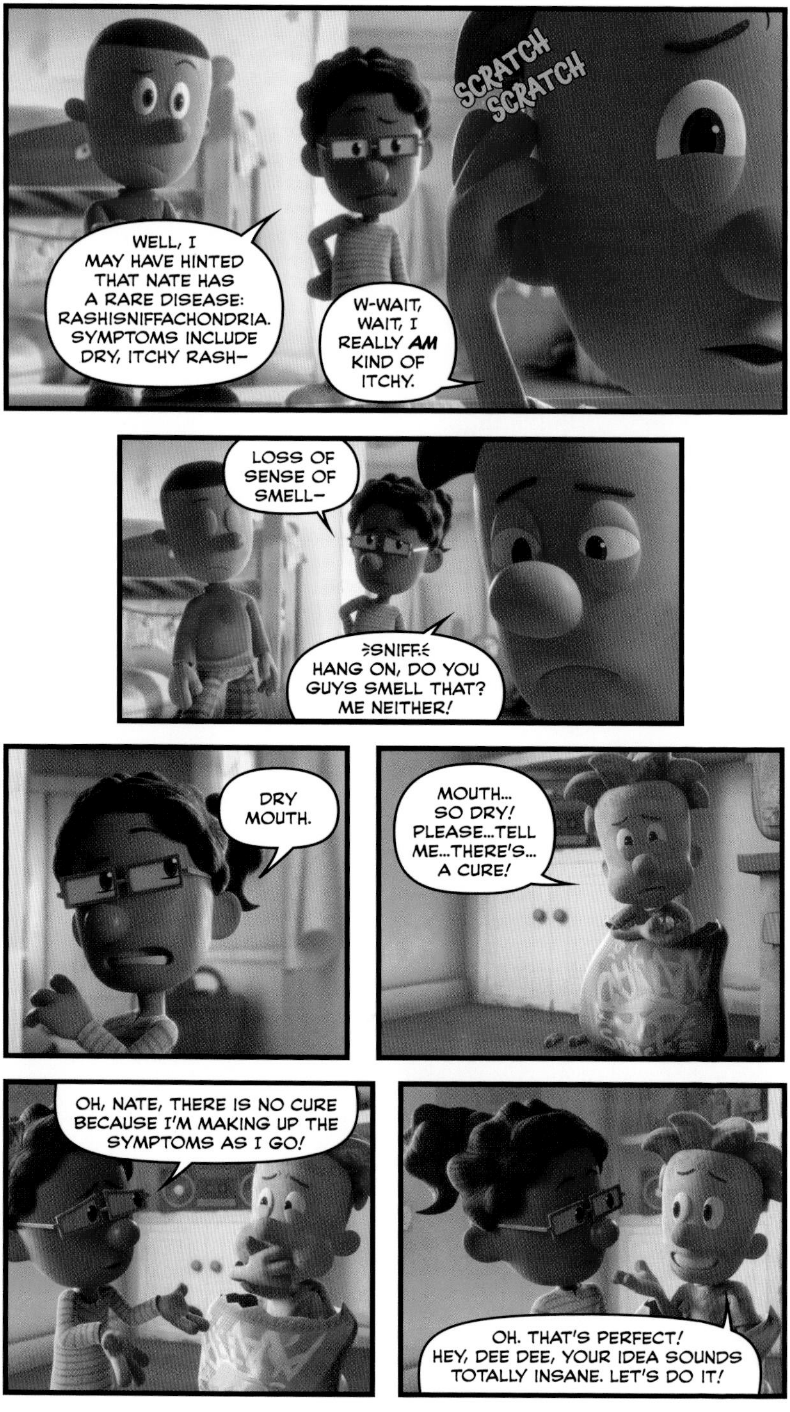
SCRATCH SCRATCH
WELL, I MAY HAVE HINTED THAT NATE HAS A RARE DISEASE: RASHISNIFFACHONDRIA. SYMPTOMS INCLUDE DRY, ITCHY RASH–
W-WAIT, WAIT, I REALLY *AM* KIND OF ITCHY.
LOSS OF SENSE OF SMELL–
SNIFF HANG ON, DO YOU GUYS SMELL THAT? ME NEITHER!
DRY MOUTH.
MOUTH... SO DRY! PLEASE...TELL ME...THERE'S... A CURE!
OH, NATE, THERE IS NO CURE BECAUSE I'M MAKING UP THE SYMPTOMS AS I GO!
OH. THAT'S PERFECT! HEY, DEE DEE, YOUR IDEA SOUNDS TOTALLY INSANE. LET'S DO IT!

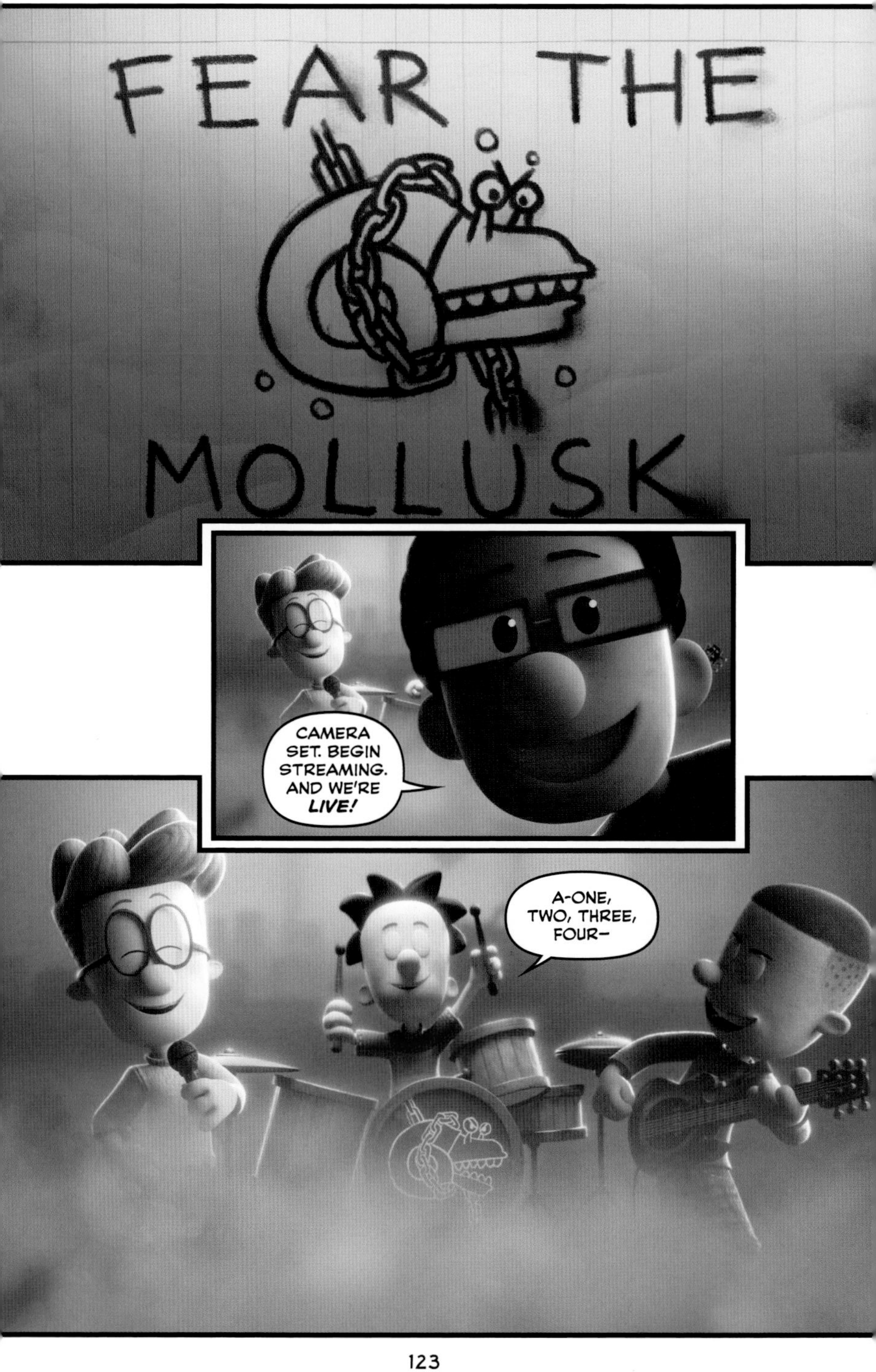
FEAR THE
MOLLUSK
CAMERA SET. BEGIN STREAMING. AND WE'RE *LIVE!*
A-ONE, TWO, THREE, FOUR—

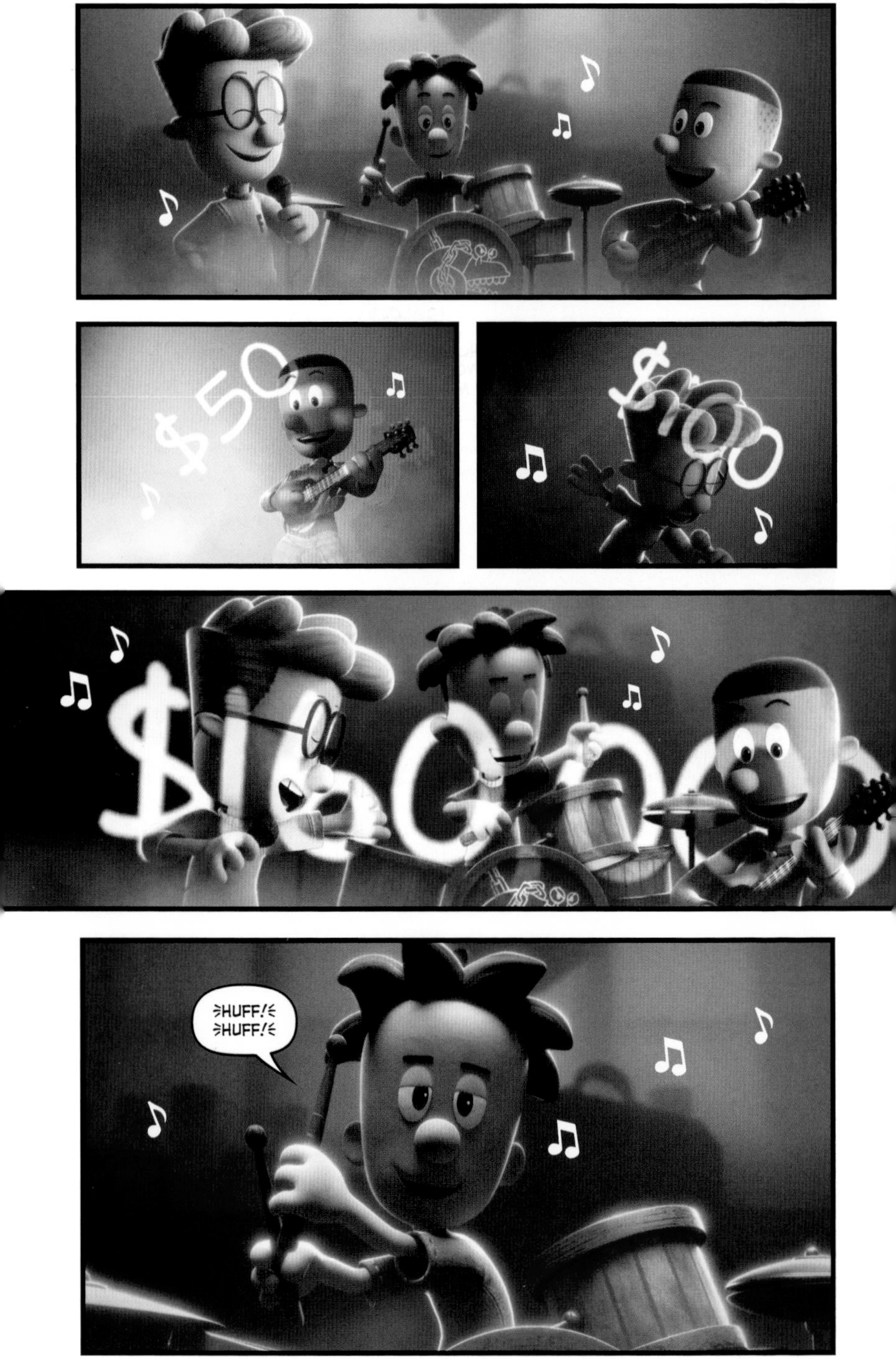
$50
$100
HUFF! HUFF!

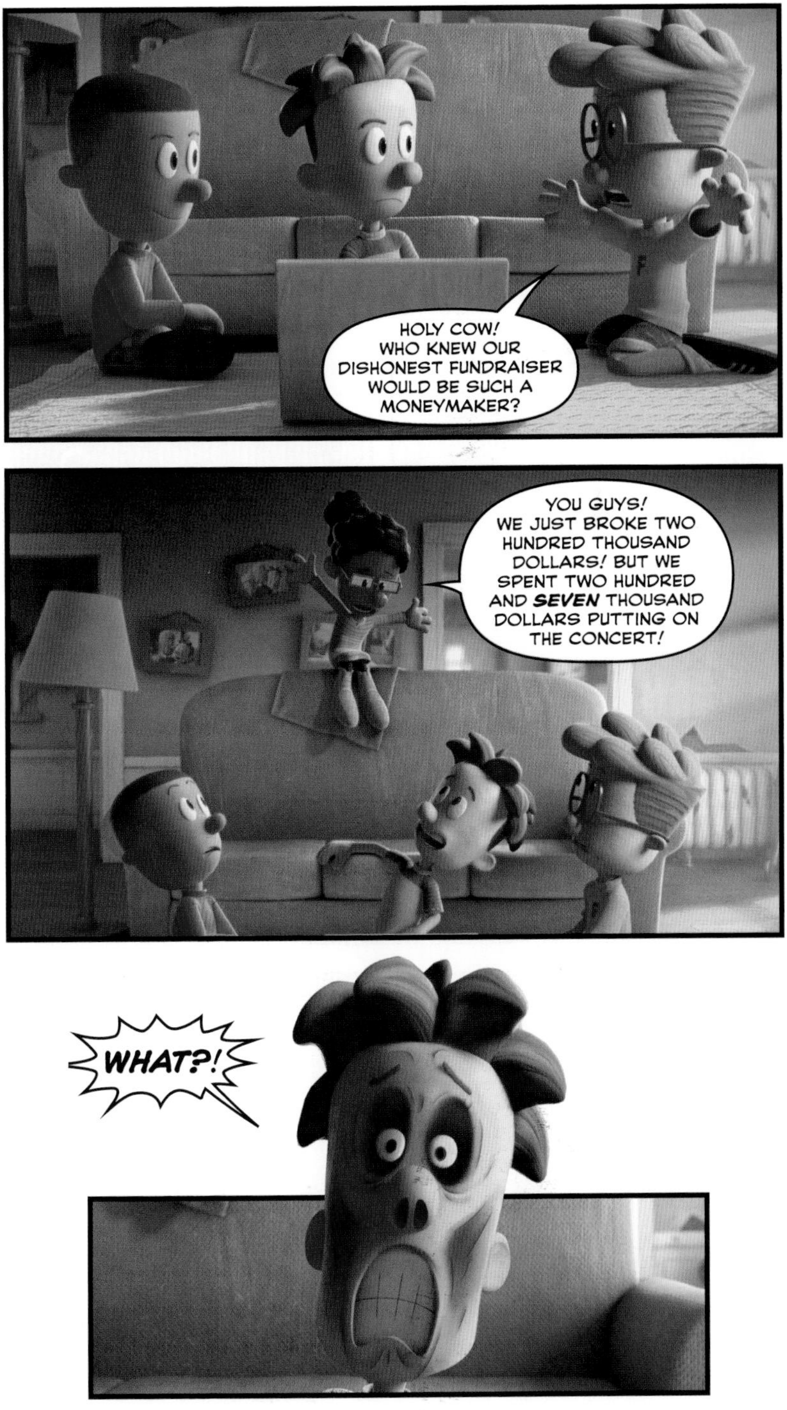
HOLY COW! WHO KNEW OUR DISHONEST FUNDRAISER WOULD BE SUCH A MONEYMAKER?
YOU GUYS! WE JUST BROKE TWO HUNDRED THOUSAND DOLLARS! BUT WE SPENT TWO HUNDRED AND SEVEN THOUSAND DOLLARS PUTTING ON THE CONCERT!
WHAT?!

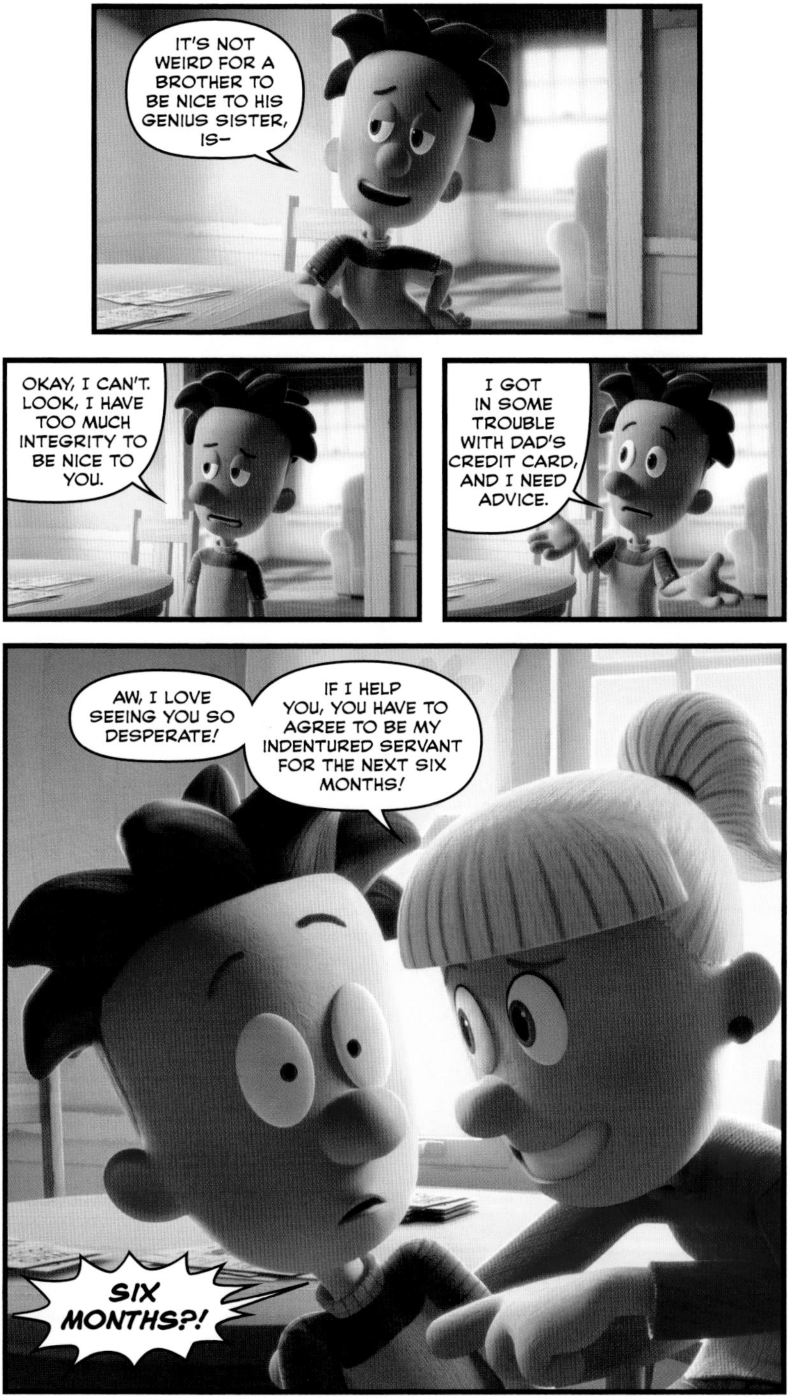
IT'S NOT WEIRD FOR A BROTHER TO BE NICE TO HIS GENIUS SISTER, IS–
OKAY, I CAN'T. LOOK, I HAVE TOO MUCH INTEGRITY TO BE NICE TO YOU.
I GOT IN SOME TROUBLE WITH DAD'S CREDIT CARD, AND I NEED ADVICE.
AW, I LOVE SEEING YOU SO DESPERATE!
IF I HELP YOU, YOU HAVE TO AGREE TO BE MY INDENTURED SERVANT FOR THE NEXT SIX MONTHS!
SIX MONTHS?!

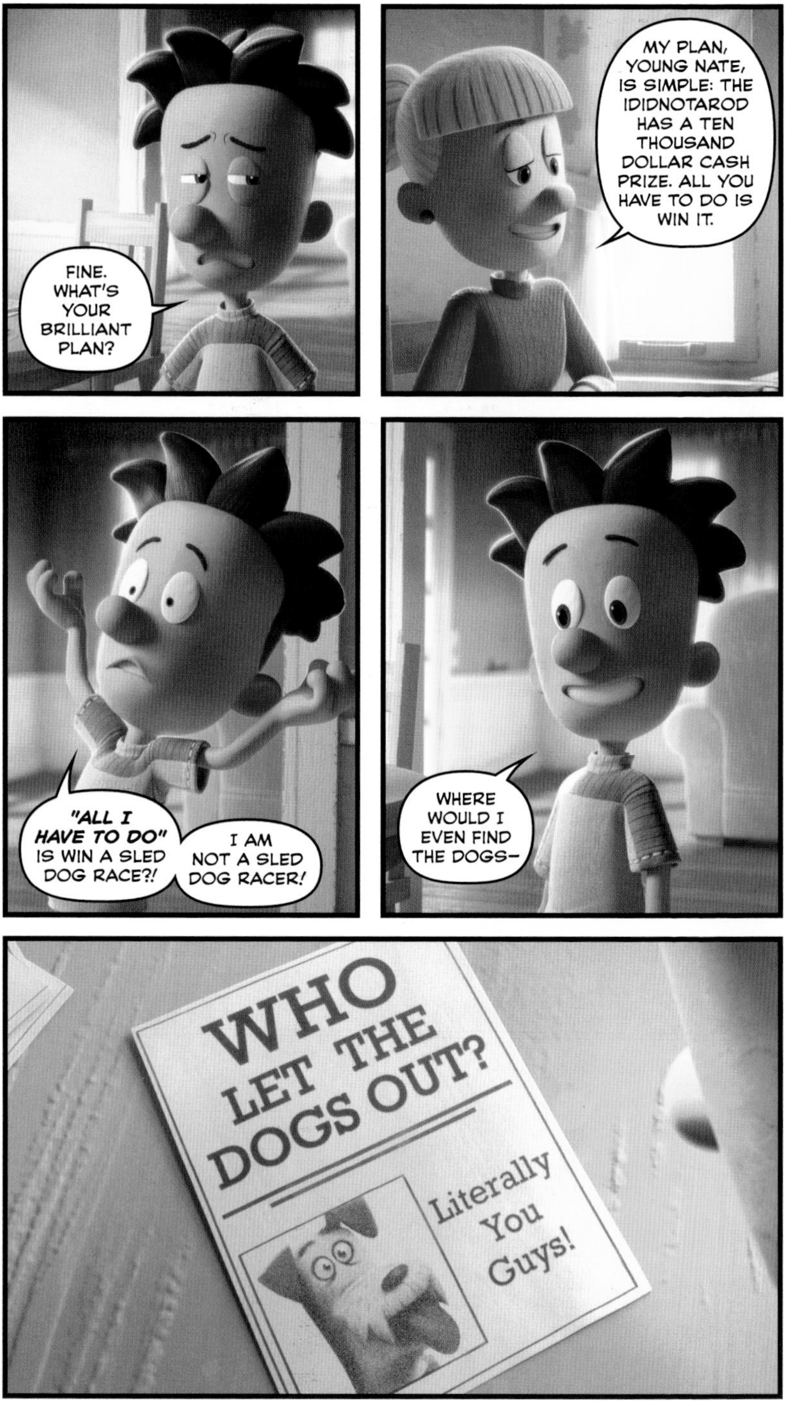
FINE. WHAT'S YOUR BRILLIANT PLAN?
MY PLAN, YOUNG NATE, IS SIMPLE: THE IDIDNOTAROD HAS A TEN THOUSAND DOLLAR CASH PRIZE. ALL YOU HAVE TO DO IS WIN IT.
"ALL I HAVE TO DO" IS WIN A SLED DOG RACE?!
I AM NOT A SLED DOG RACER!
WHERE WOULD I EVEN FIND THE DOGS–
WHO LET THE DOGS OUT?
Literally You Guys!

129

CHAD, WHAT THE HECK?!

WHAT? I'M JUST ENJOYING A CRUNCHY SNACK! WHAT ARE YOU GUYS DOING?

WE'RE TRYING TO RECRUIT A TEAM OF SLED DOGS TO WIN THE IDIDNOTAROD.

IT COULD BE GOING BETTER.

OH! YOU GUYS NEED AN ALPHA. WHEN MY PARENTS WERE CRATE-TRAINING ME, I LEARNED THAT DOGS ARE ALWAYS LOOKING FOR AN ALPHA. I'M STILL LOOKING FOR MINE.

HMMM... I THINK I KNOW JUST THE ALPHA!

...SO YOU SEE, SPITSY, WE NEED YOUR HELP.

WE NEED YOU TO BECOME THE STRONG LEADER YOU WERE MEANT TO BE.

130

Chapter 4
THE RACE IS ON!

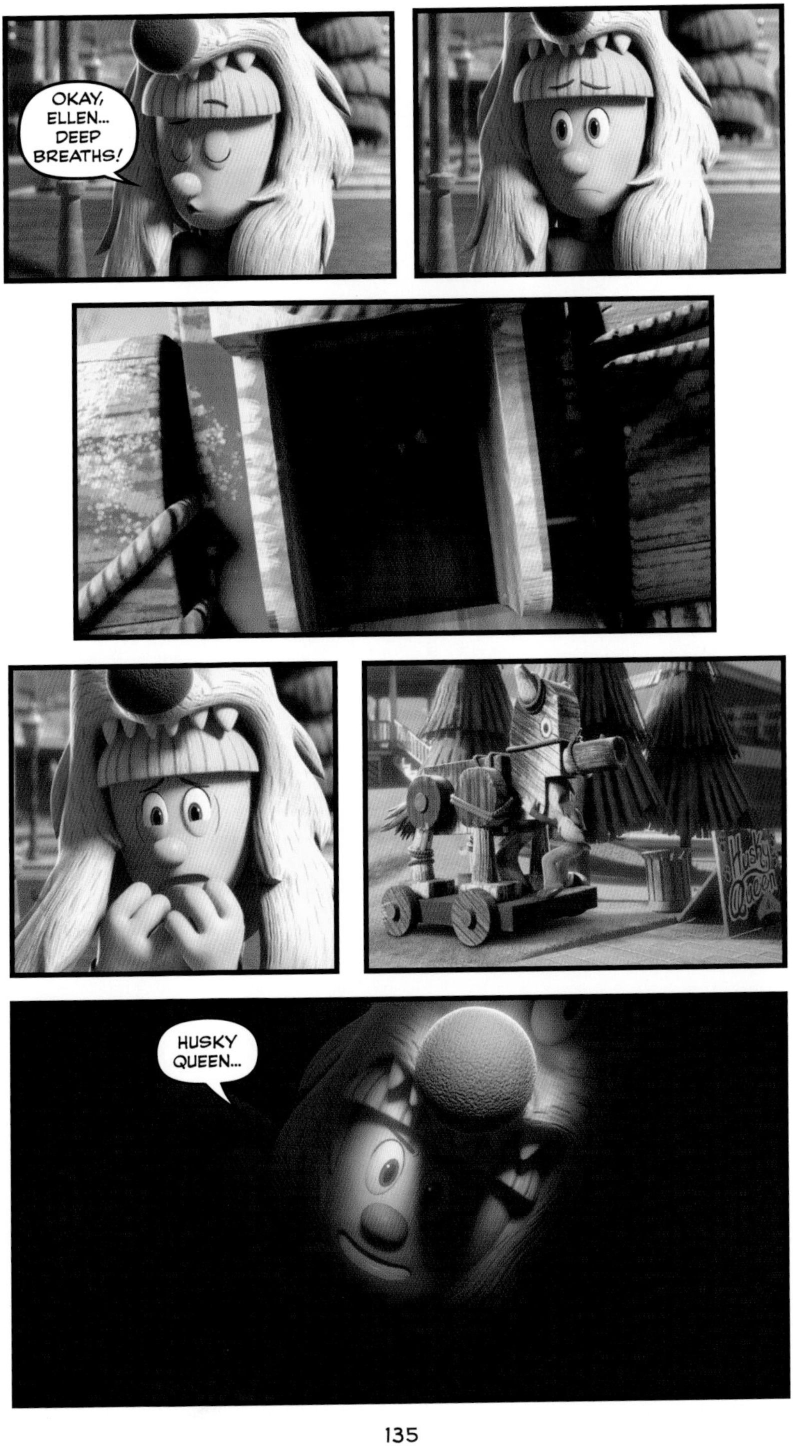
OKAY, ELLEN... DEEP BREATHS!
HUSKY QUEEN...

137

140

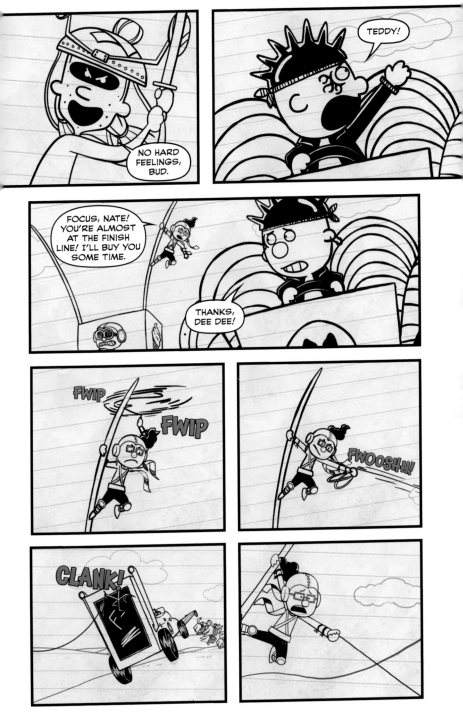

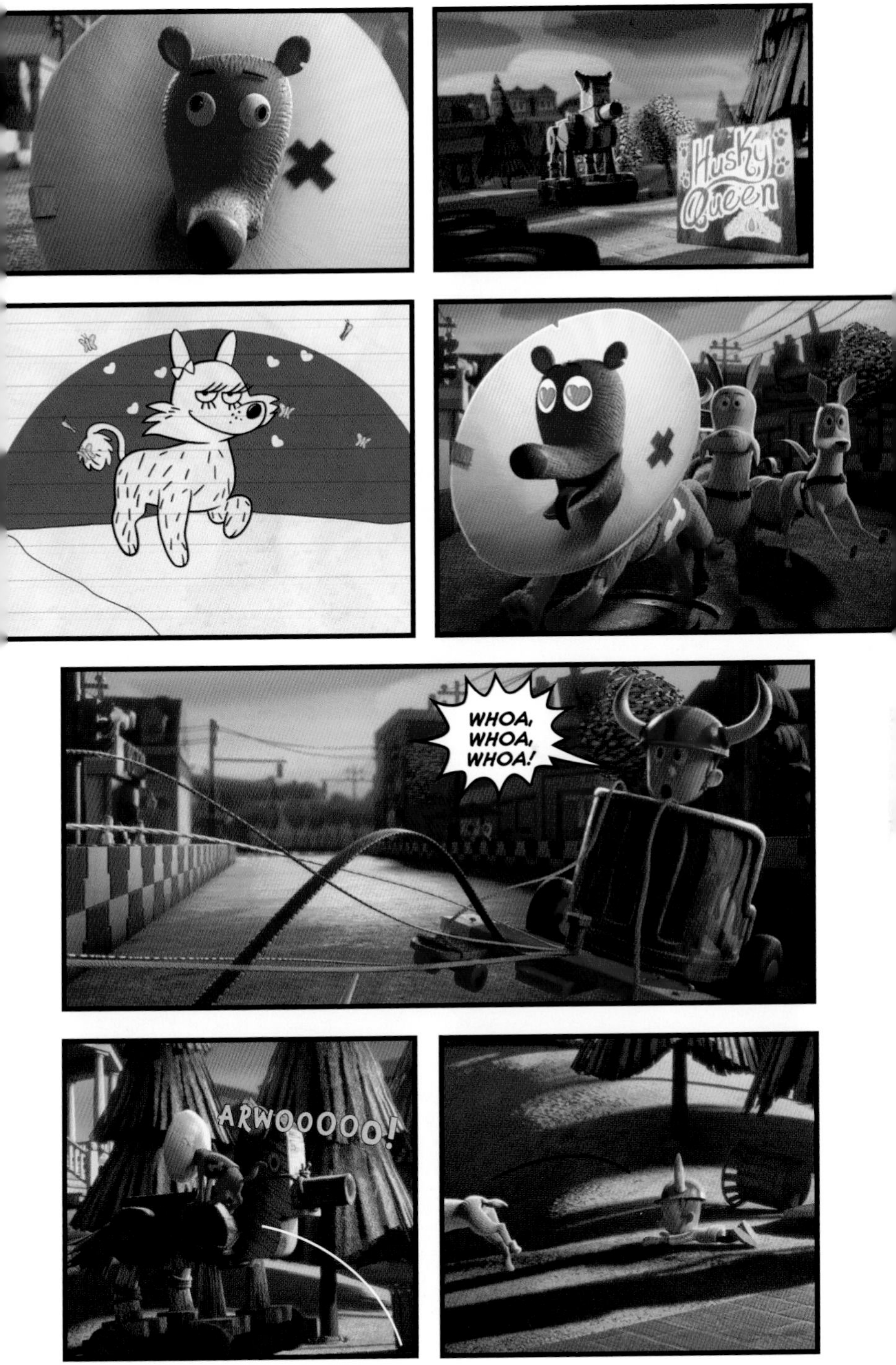
Husky Queen
WHOA, WHOA, WHOA!
ARWOOOOOO!

144

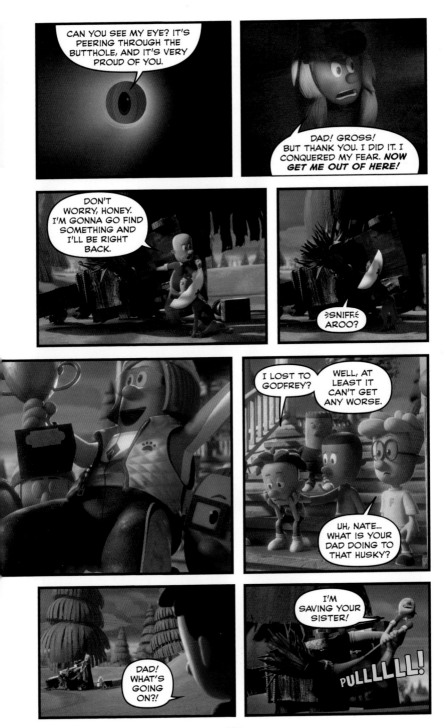

146

147

148

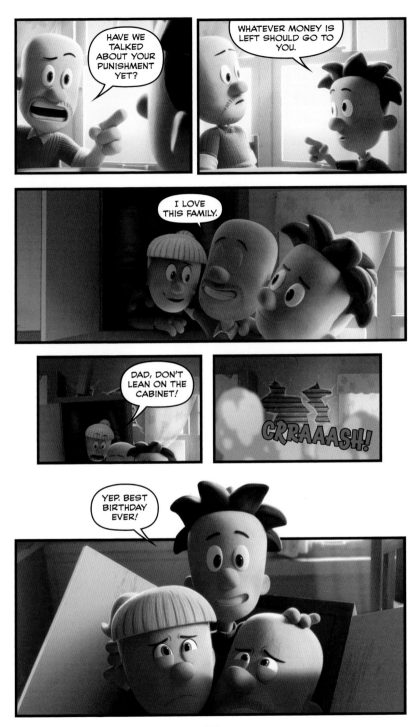

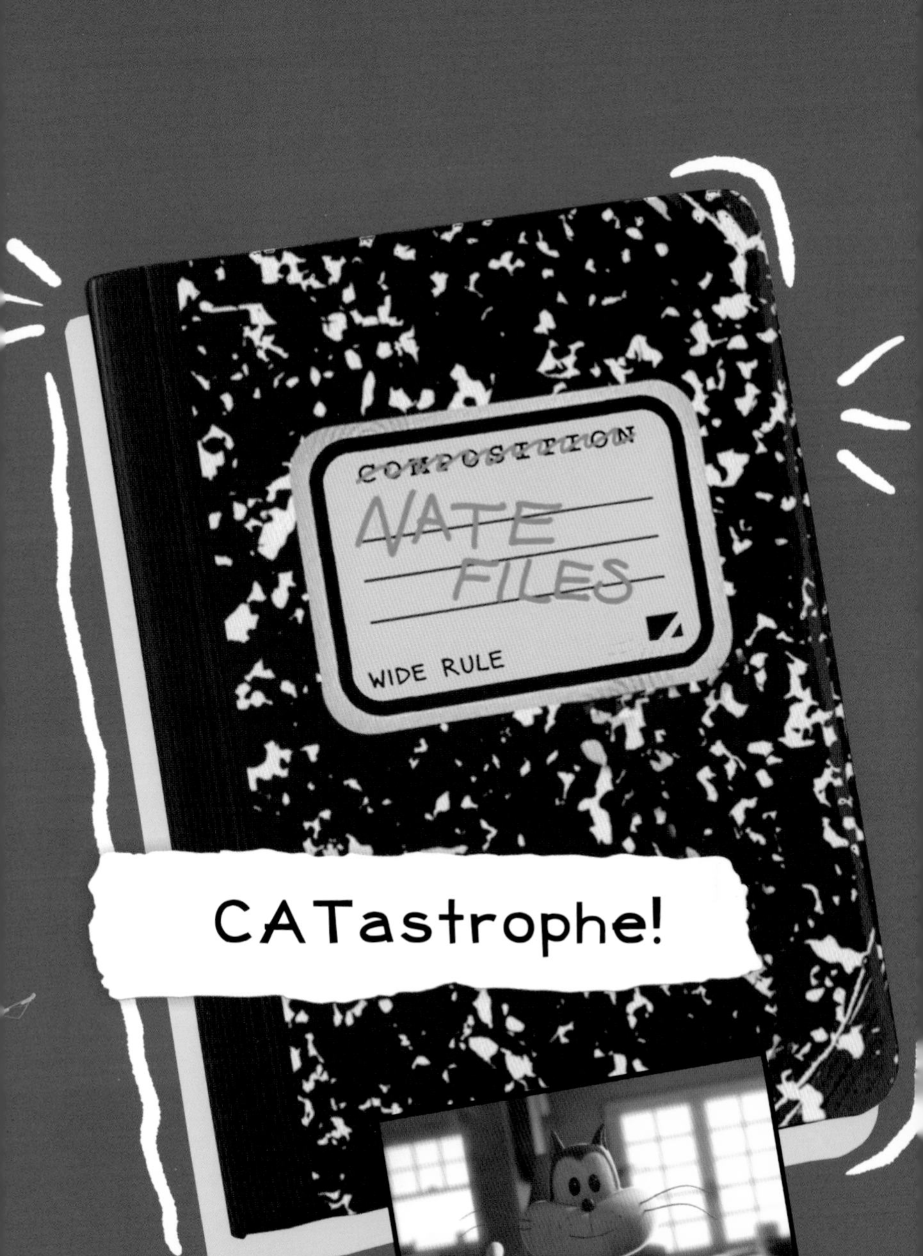
COMPOSITION
NATE FILES
WIDE RULE
CATastrophe!

Chapter 1
THE ASSIGNMENT

UHHH...BE RIGHT BACK, GANG.

WOOOSH!!!

DO YOU NOTICE DAD *ALWAYS* GOES BACK HOME WHEN IT'S TIME TO LEAVE?

HMM, NOW THAT YOU MENTION IT...

153

154

155

156

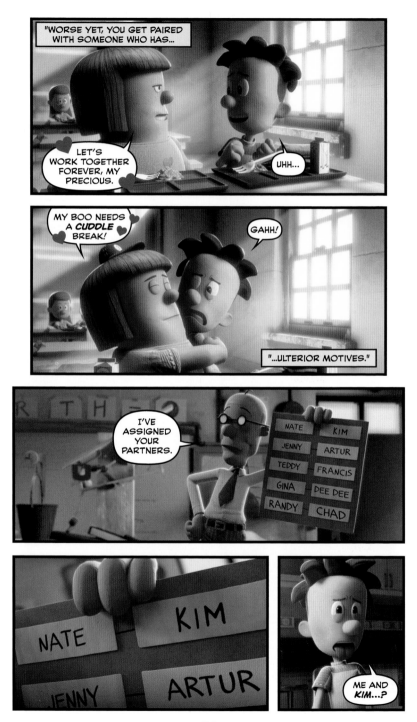

158

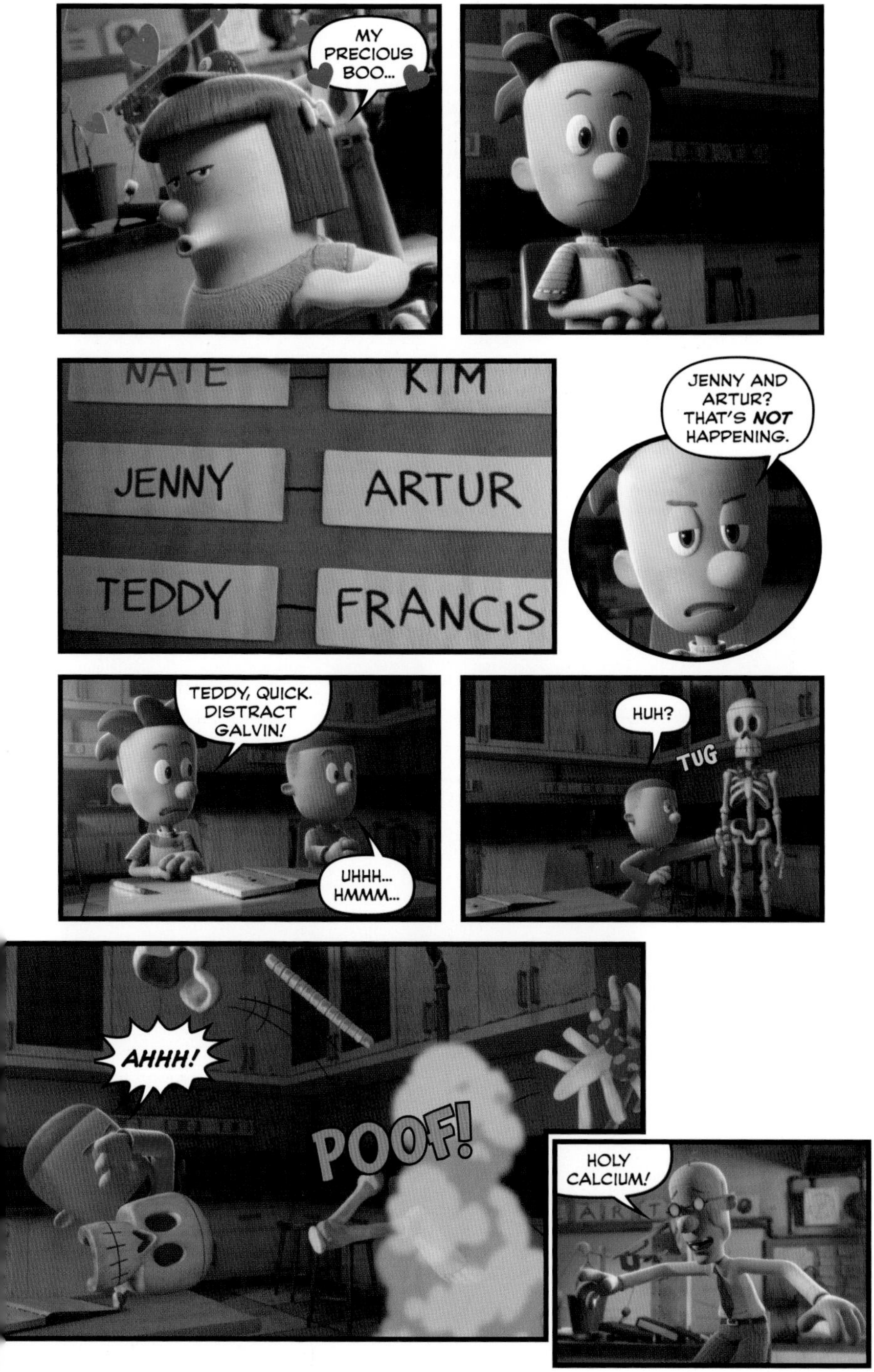
MY PRECIOUS BOO...
NATE
KIM
JENNY
ARTUR
TEDDY
FRANCIS
JENNY AND ARTUR? THAT'S *NOT* HAPPENING.
TEDDY, QUICK. DISTRACT GALVIN!
UHHH... HMMM...
HUH?
TUG
AHHH!
POOF!
HOLY CALCIUM!

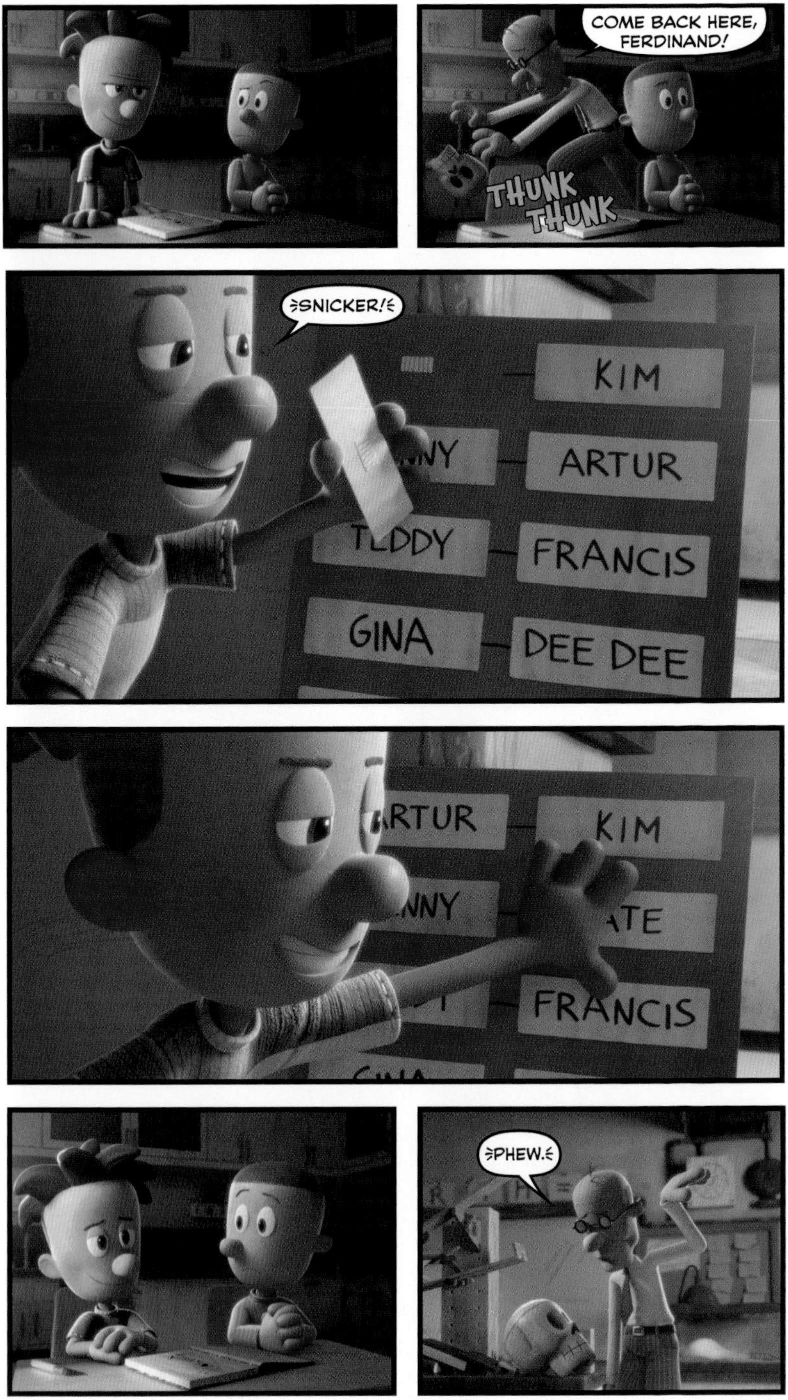
COME BACK HERE, FERDINAND!
THUNK
THUNK
SNICKER!
KIM
ARTUR
FRANCIS
GINA
DEE DEE
KIM
FRANCIS
PHEW.

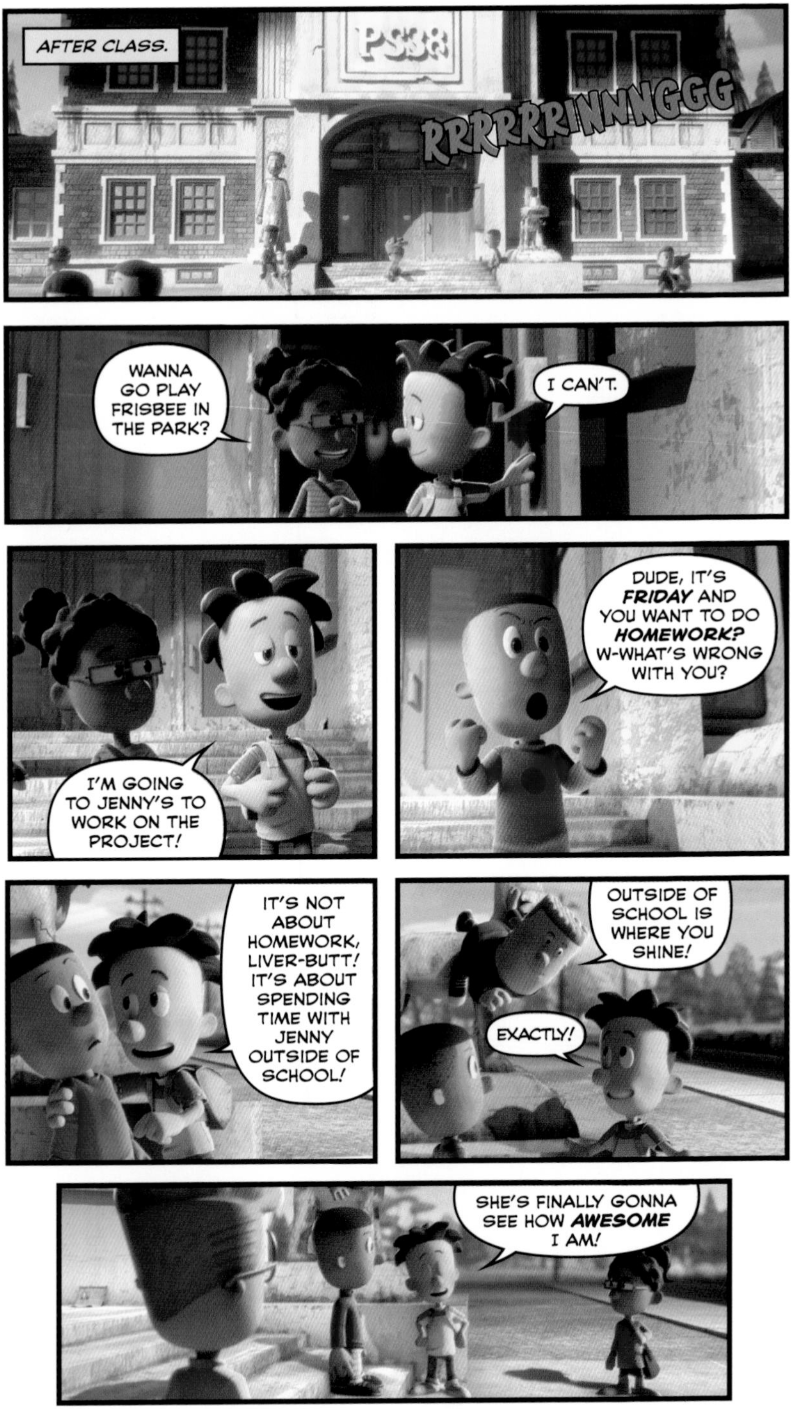
AFTER CLASS.
PS38
RRRRRRINNNGGG
WANNA GO PLAY FRISBEE IN THE PARK?
I CAN'T.
I'M GOING TO JENNY'S TO WORK ON THE PROJECT!
DUDE, IT'S FRIDAY AND YOU WANT TO DO HOMEWORK? W-WHAT'S WRONG WITH YOU?
IT'S NOT ABOUT HOMEWORK, LIVER-BUTT! IT'S ABOUT SPENDING TIME WITH JENNY OUTSIDE OF SCHOOL!
OUTSIDE OF SCHOOL IS WHERE YOU SHINE!
EXACTLY!
SHE'S FINALLY GONNA SEE HOW AWESOME I AM!

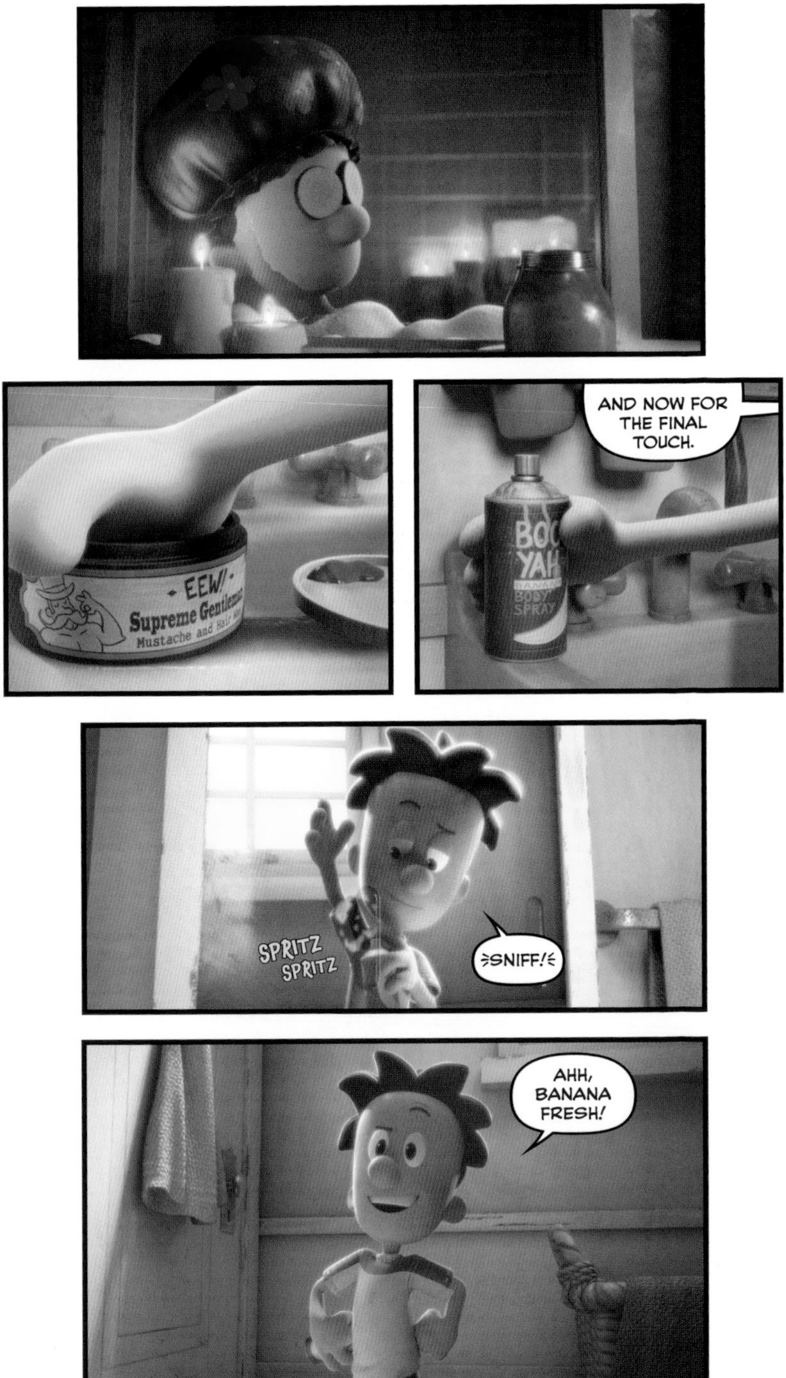
AND NOW FOR THE FINAL TOUCH.
SPRITZ SPRITZ
≷SNIFF!≶
AHH, BANANA FRESH!

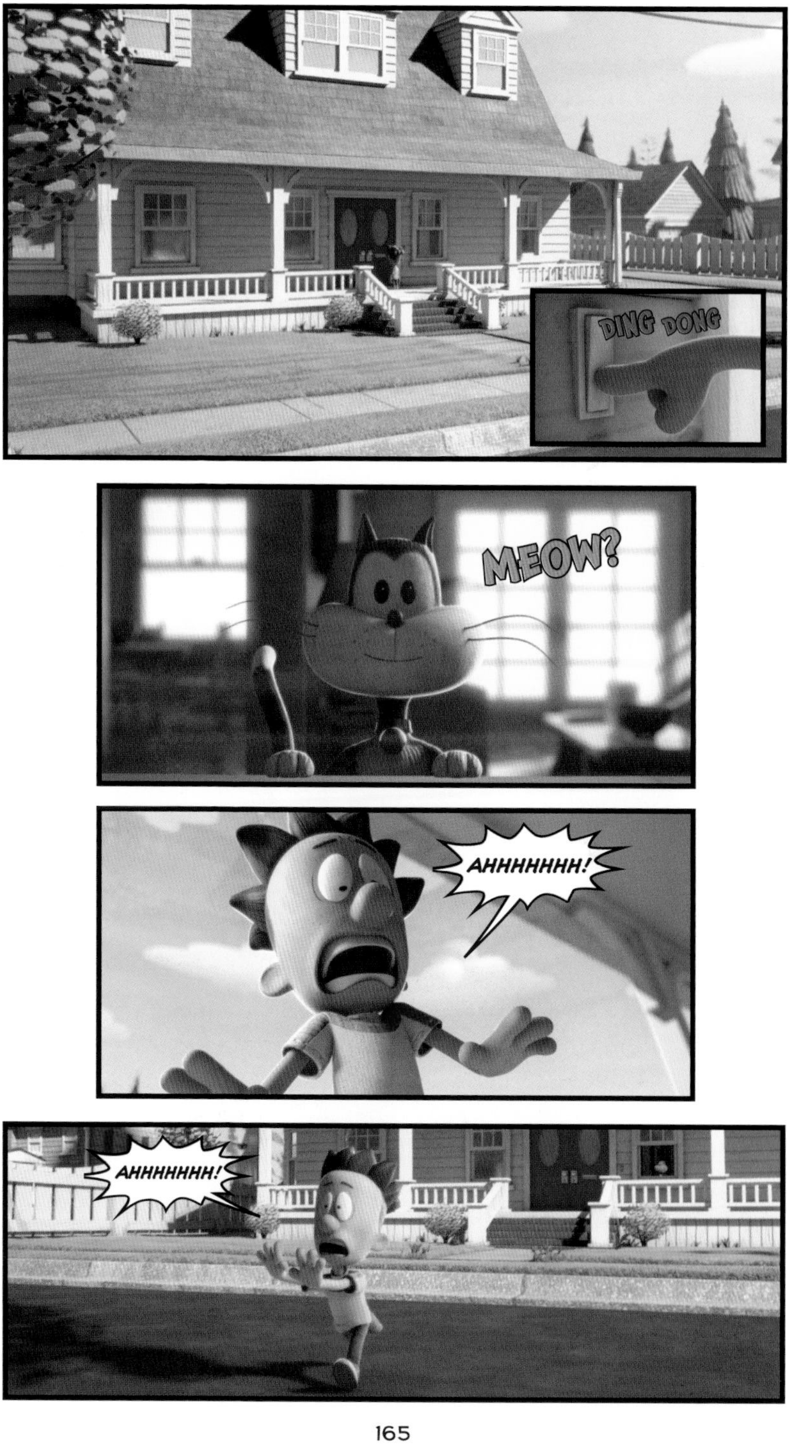
DING DONG
MEOW?
AHHHHHHH!
AHHHHHHH!

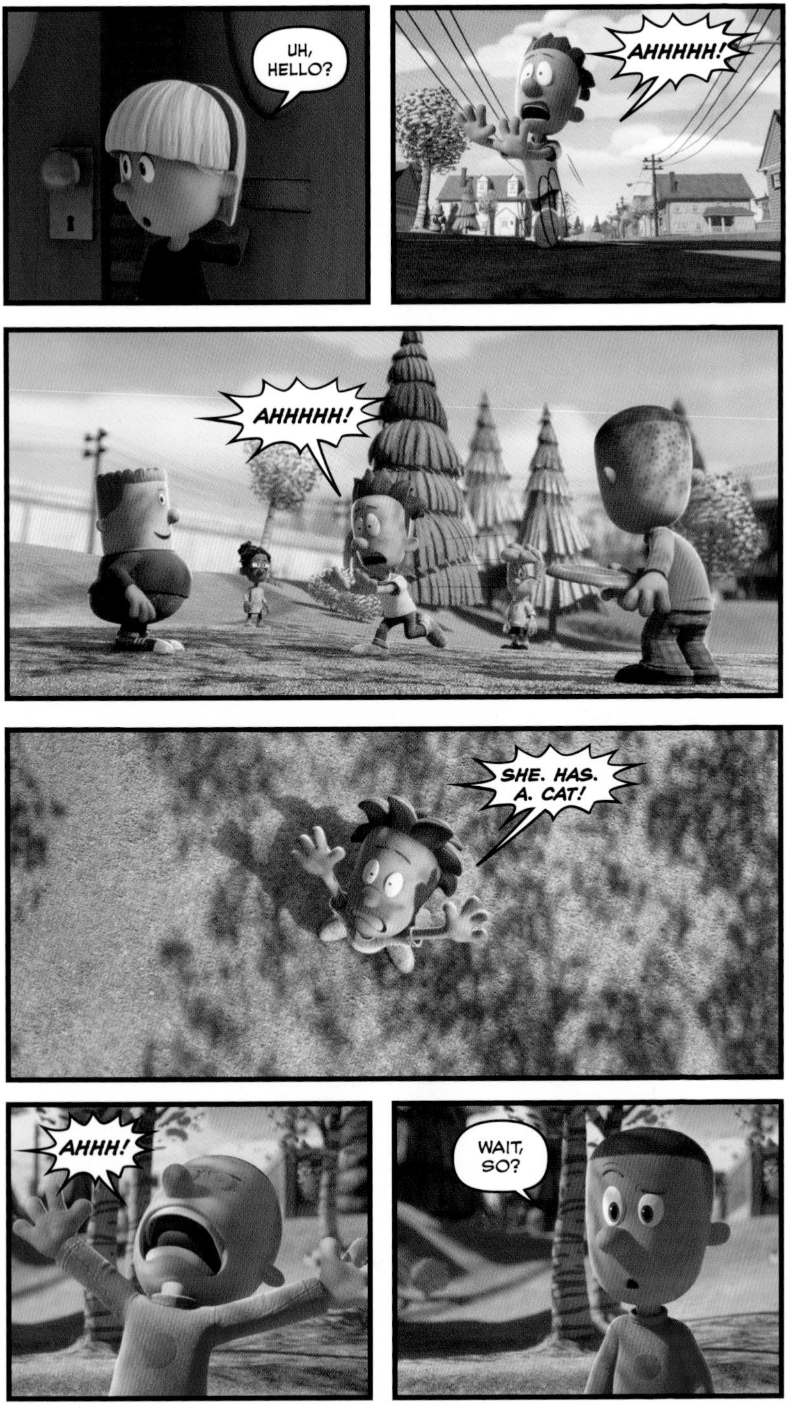
UH, HELLO?
AHHHHH!
AHHHHH!
SHE. HAS. A. CAT!
AHHH!
WAIT, SO?

Chapter 2
FACE YOUR
FEARS

HEY, UH, I'M GONNA GO RUN SOME ERRANDS.

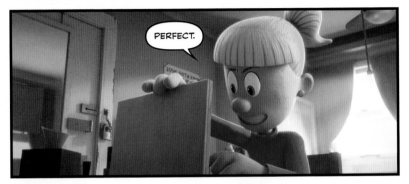

PERFECT.

C'MON, MARTY, THIS IS YOUR SAFE TOILET! GET ALL YOUR PEE OUT NOW!

YOU DON'T WANT TO USE A *STRANGE BATHROOM.*

≥GASP!≤ HE'S AFRAID OF RANDOM BATHROOMS?!

171

172

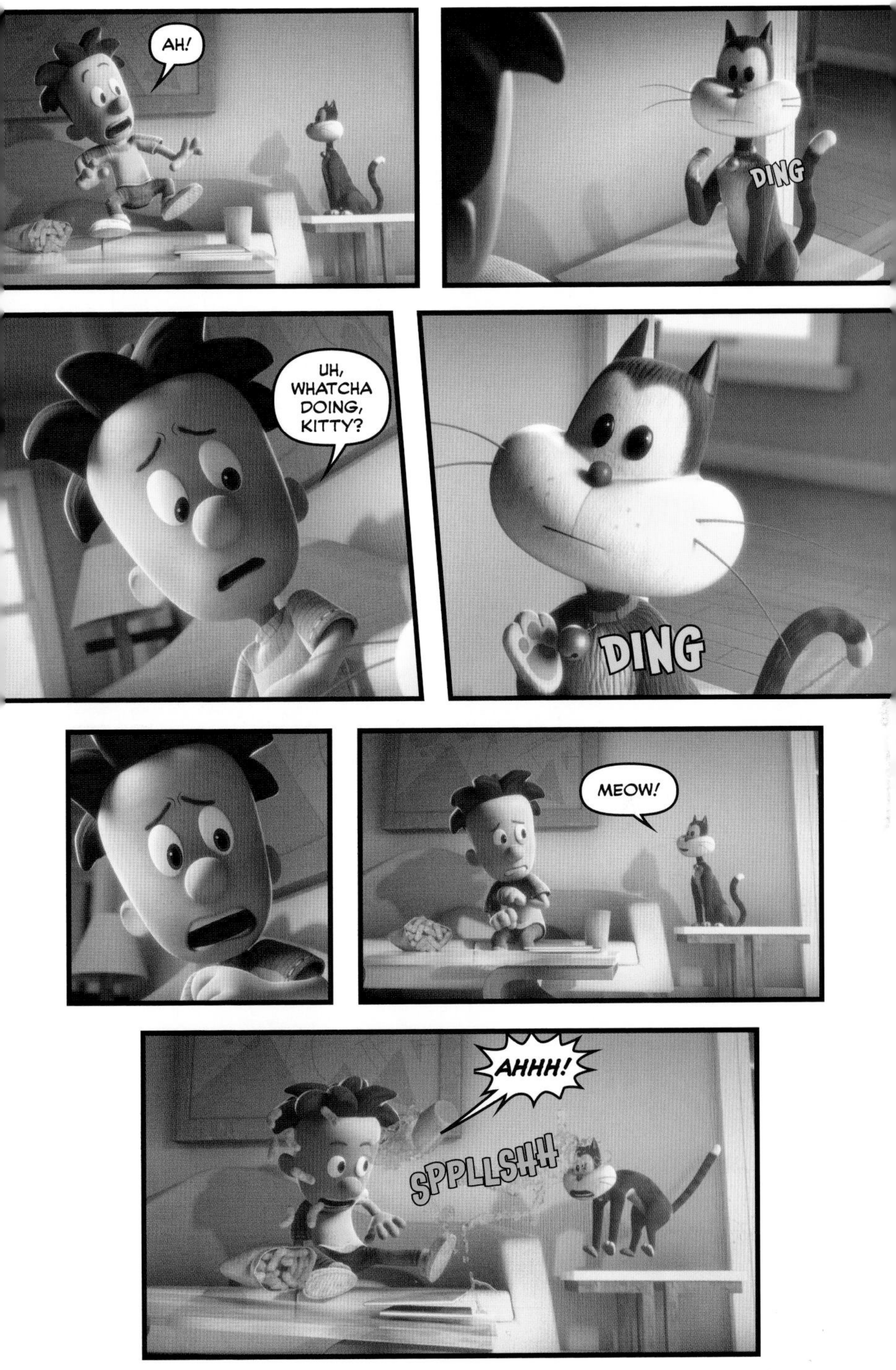
AH!
DING
UH, WHATCHA DOING, KITTY?
DING
MEOW!
AHHH!
SPPLLSHH

174

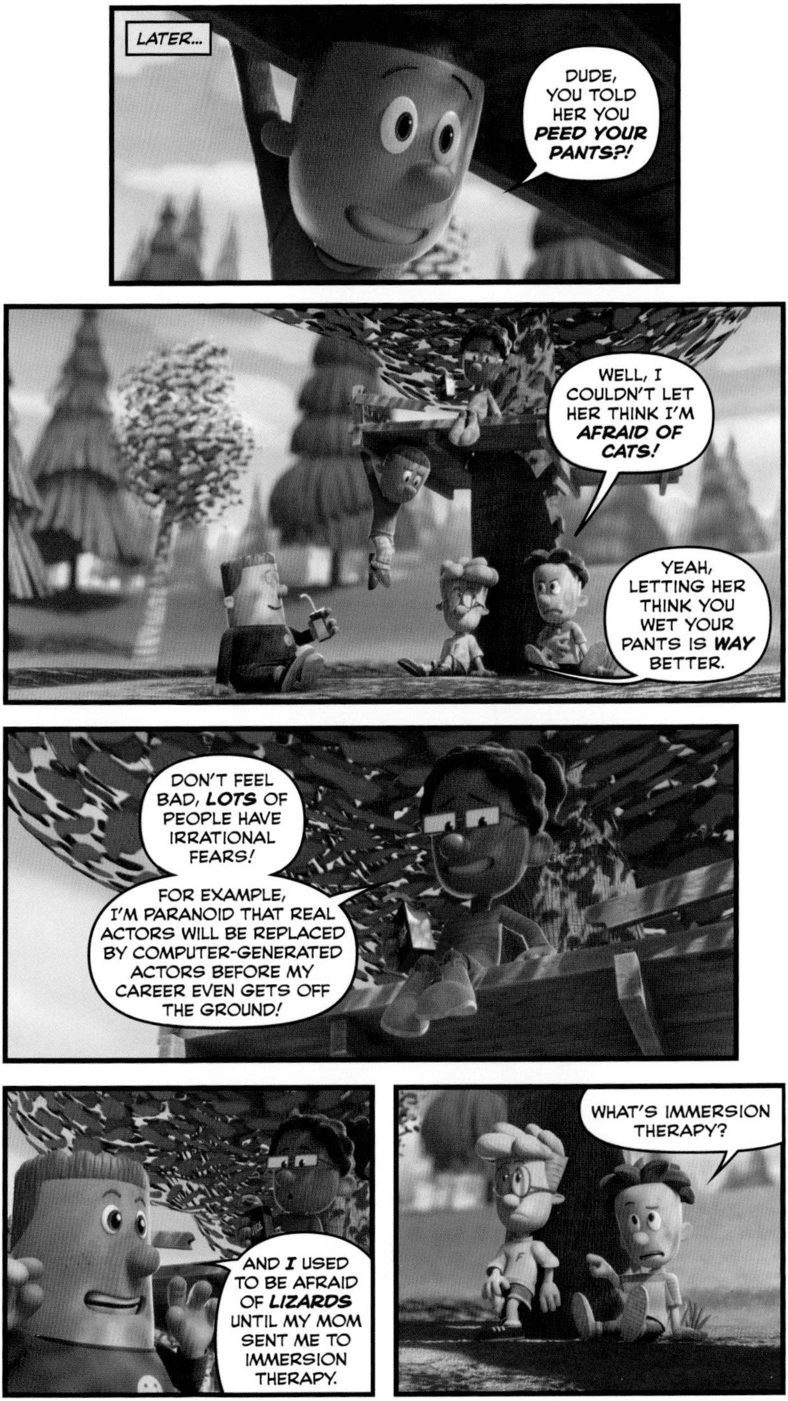
LATER...
DUDE, YOU TOLD HER YOU PEED YOUR PANTS?!
WELL, I COULDN'T LET HER THINK I'M AFRAID OF CATS!
YEAH, LETTING HER THINK YOU WET YOUR PANTS IS WAY BETTER.
DON'T FEEL BAD, LOTS OF PEOPLE HAVE IRRATIONAL FEARS!
FOR EXAMPLE, I'M PARANOID THAT REAL ACTORS WILL BE REPLACED BY COMPUTER-GENERATED ACTORS BEFORE MY CAREER EVEN GETS OFF THE GROUND!
AND I USED TO BE AFRAID OF LIZARDS UNTIL MY MOM SENT ME TO IMMERSION THERAPY.
WHAT'S IMMERSION THERAPY?

176

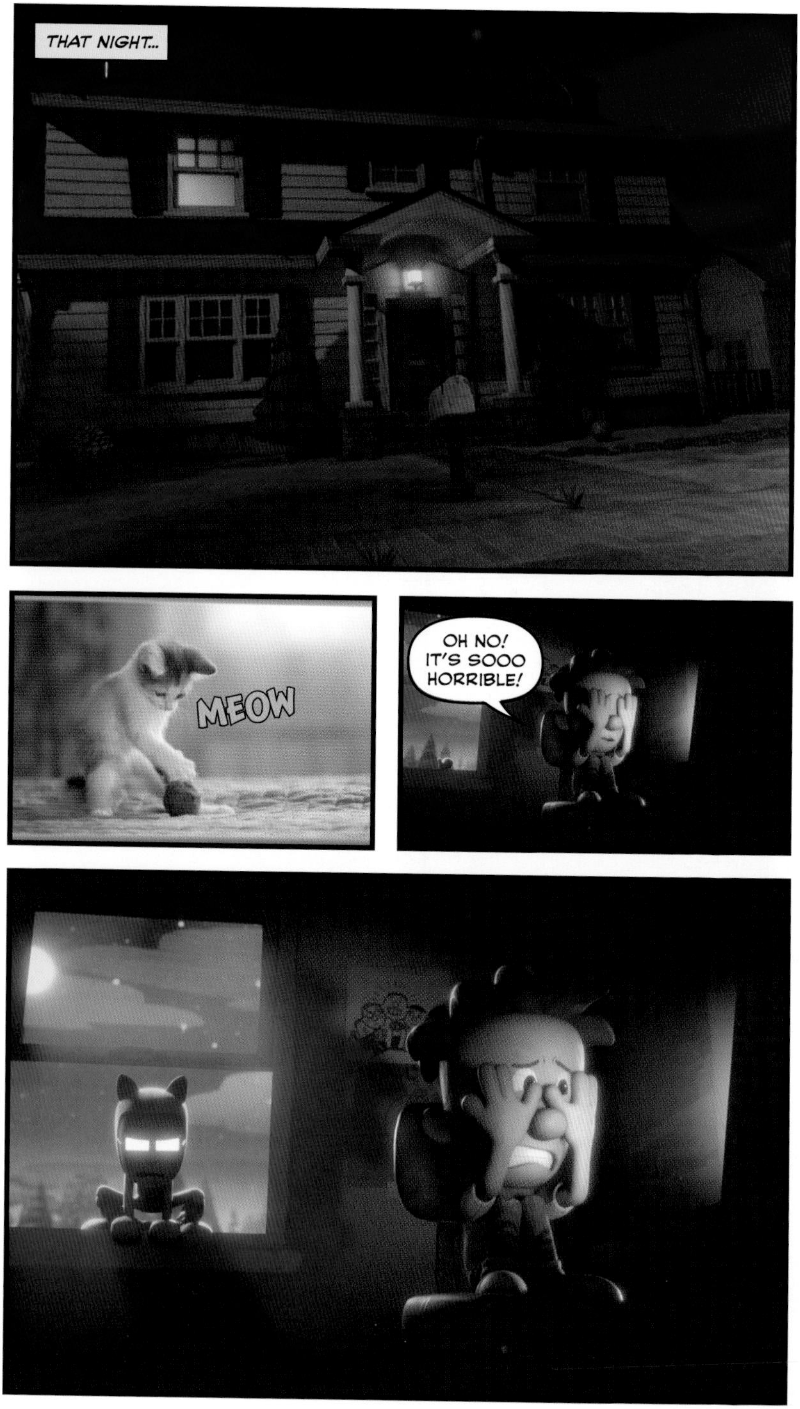
THAT NIGHT...
MEOW
OH NO! IT'S SOOO HORRIBLE!

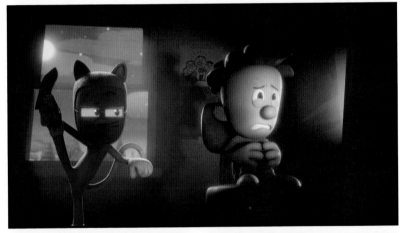

184

185

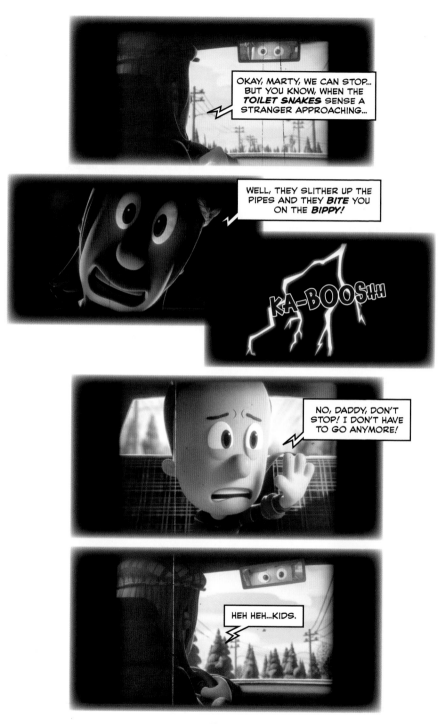

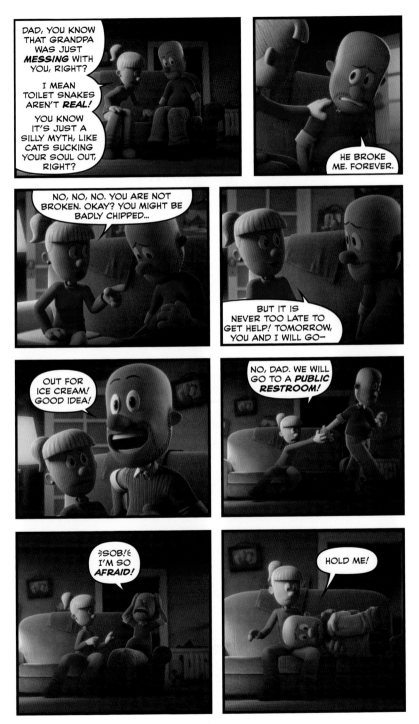

189

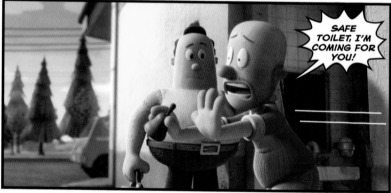

190

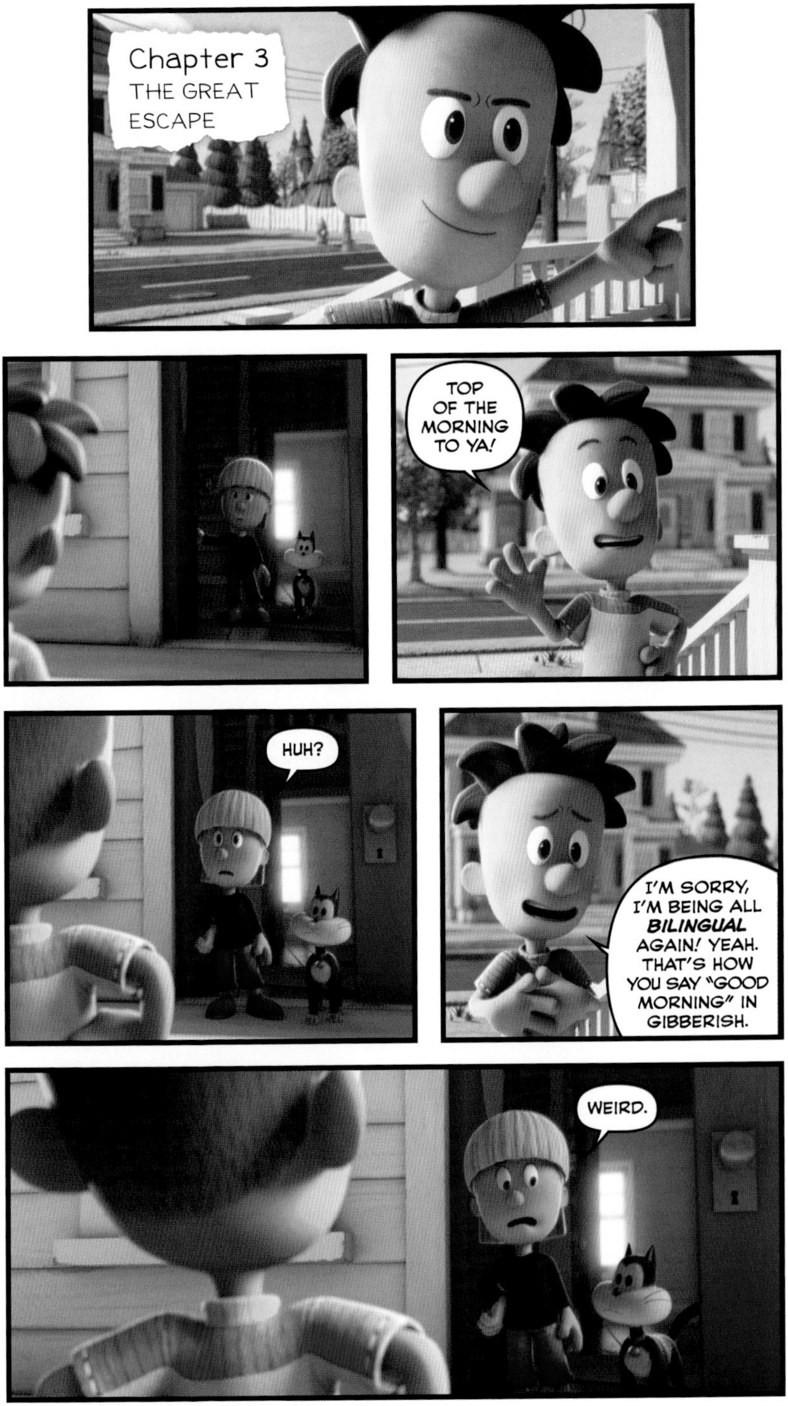
Chapter 3
THE GREAT ESCAPE
TOP OF THE MORNING TO YA!
HUH?
I'M SORRY, I'M BEING ALL BILINGUAL AGAIN! YEAH. THAT'S HOW YOU SAY "GOOD MORNING" IN GIBBERISH.
WEIRD.

192

194

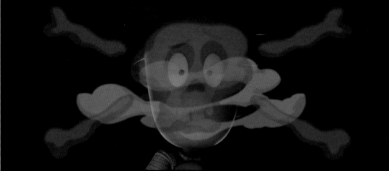

195

CREEEEEAK

≷GASP!≷ WHERE'S FELICIA? WAS SHE HERE WITH YOU WHEN I LEFT TO GET THE ROPE?

I-I-I...I DON'T THINK SO. I'M SURE SHE'S AROUND HERE SOMEWHERE THOUGH.

SHE'S BEEN TRYING TO GET OUT FOR YEARS! I CAN'T BELIEVE I LEFT THE DOOR OPEN!

DON'T WORRY, WE'LL FIND HER!

199

201

Chapter 4
THE EAGLE HAS LANDED

ALL RIGHT, EVERYBODY... *LET'S DO THIS!*

WOO-HOO!

THIS WILL WORK *PERFECTLY!*

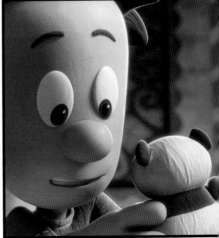

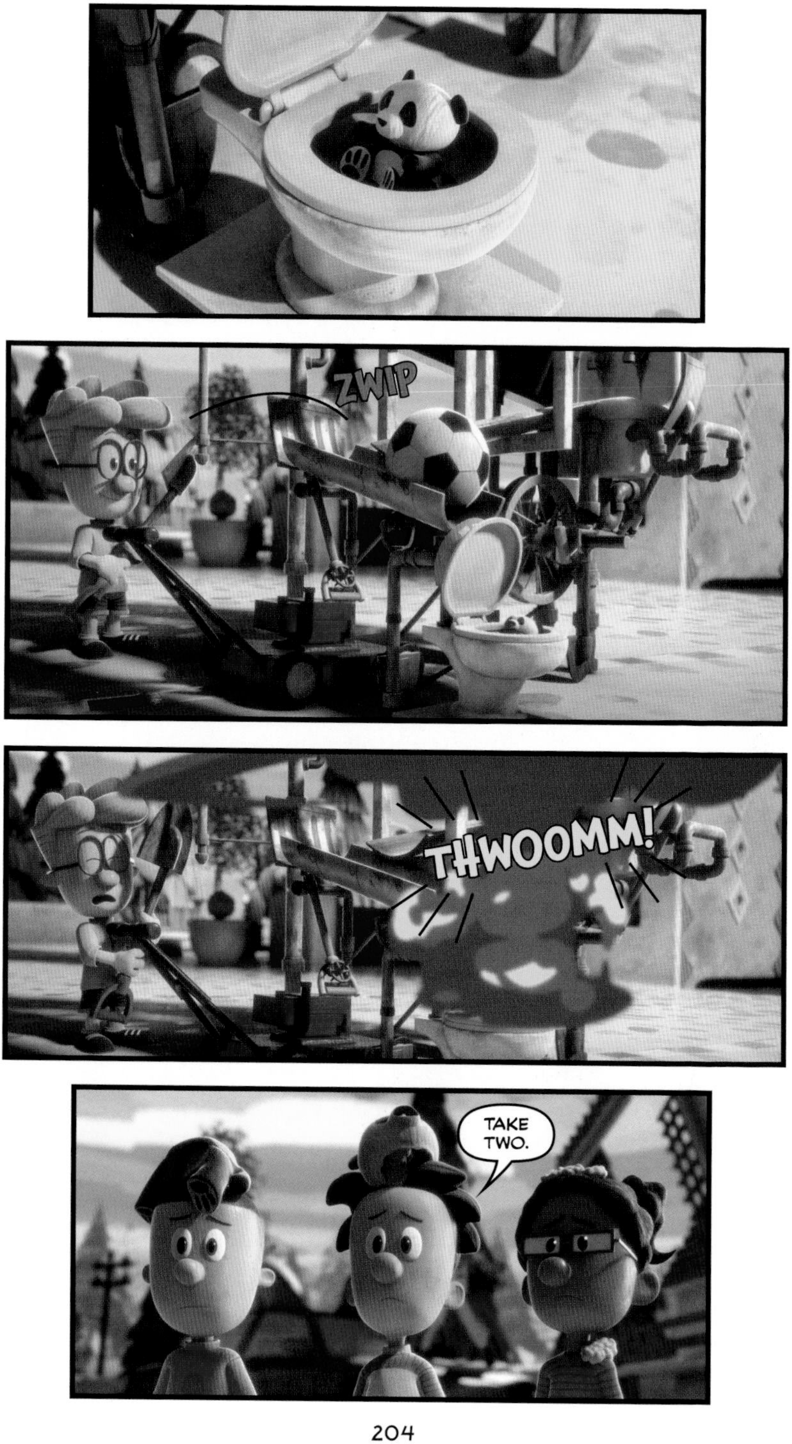
ZWIP
THWOOMM!
TAKE TWO.

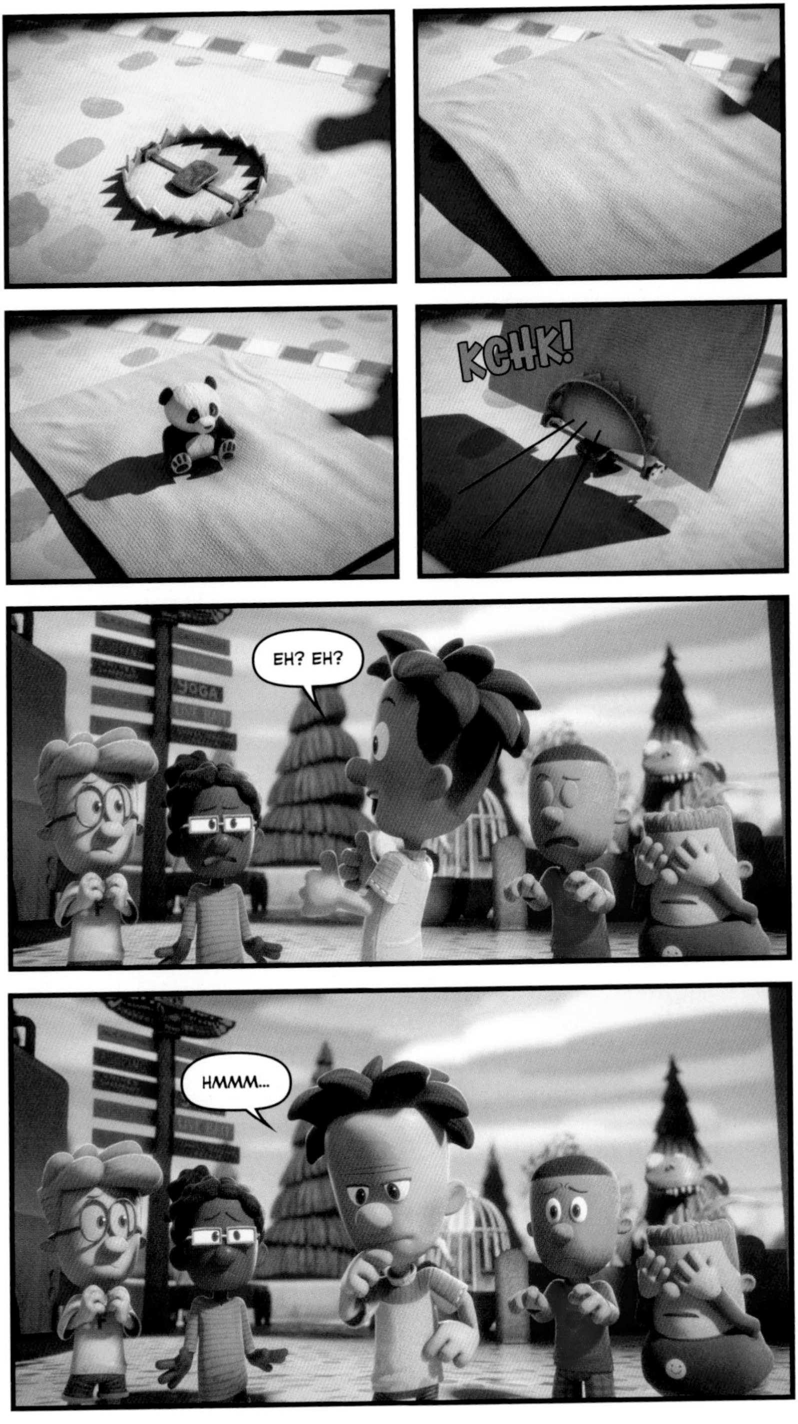
KCHK!
EH? EH?
HMMM...

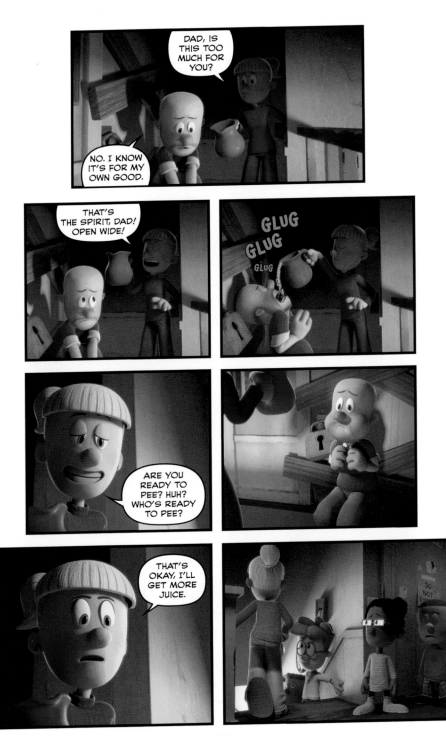

209

211

212

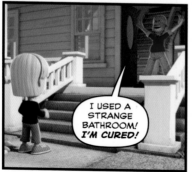

214

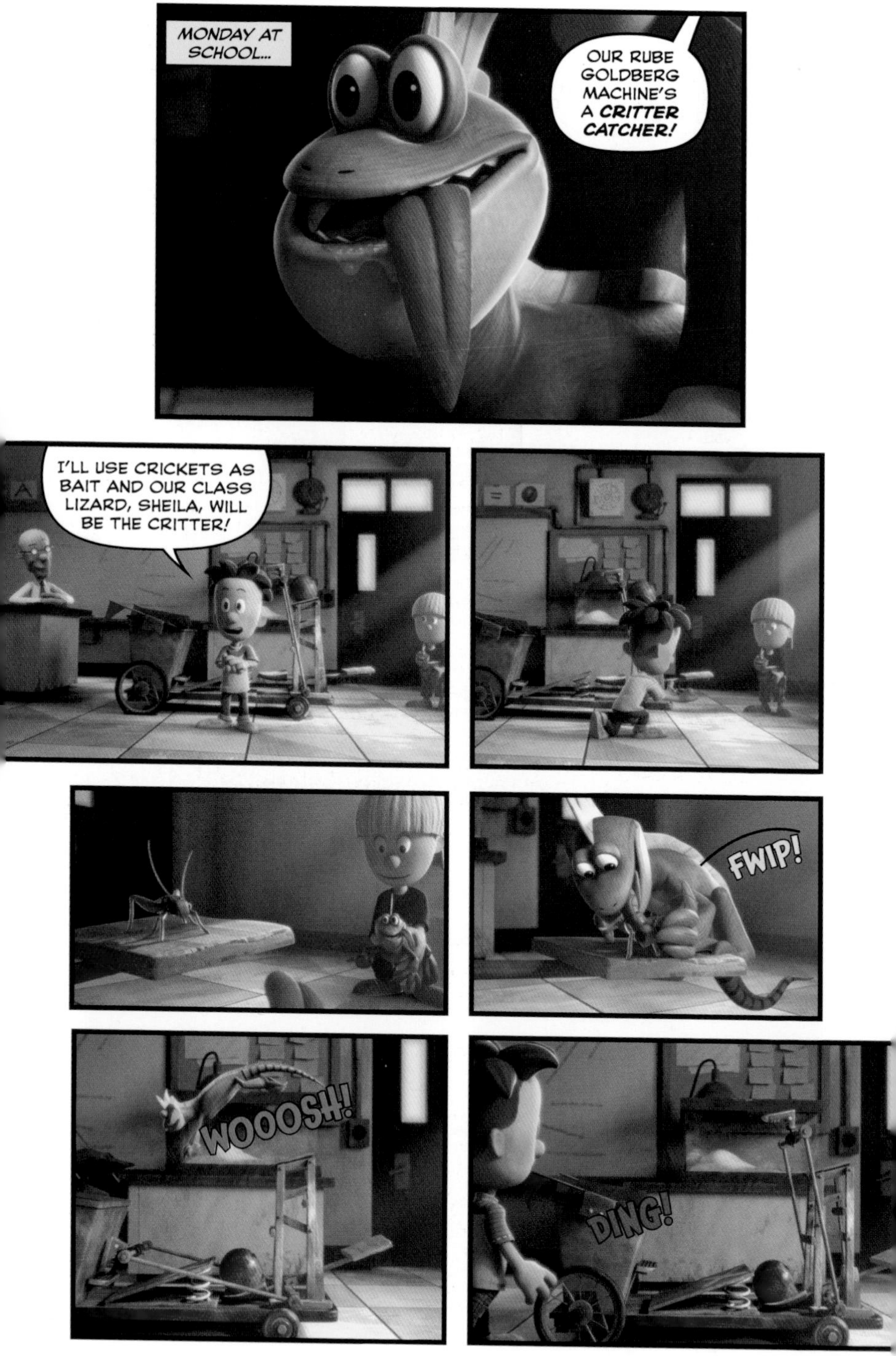
MONDAY AT SCHOOL...
OUR RUBE GOLDBERG MACHINE'S A CRITTER CATCHER!
I'LL USE CRICKETS AS BAIT AND OUR CLASS LIZARD, SHEILA, WILL BE THE CRITTER!
FWIP!
WOOOSH!
DING!

217

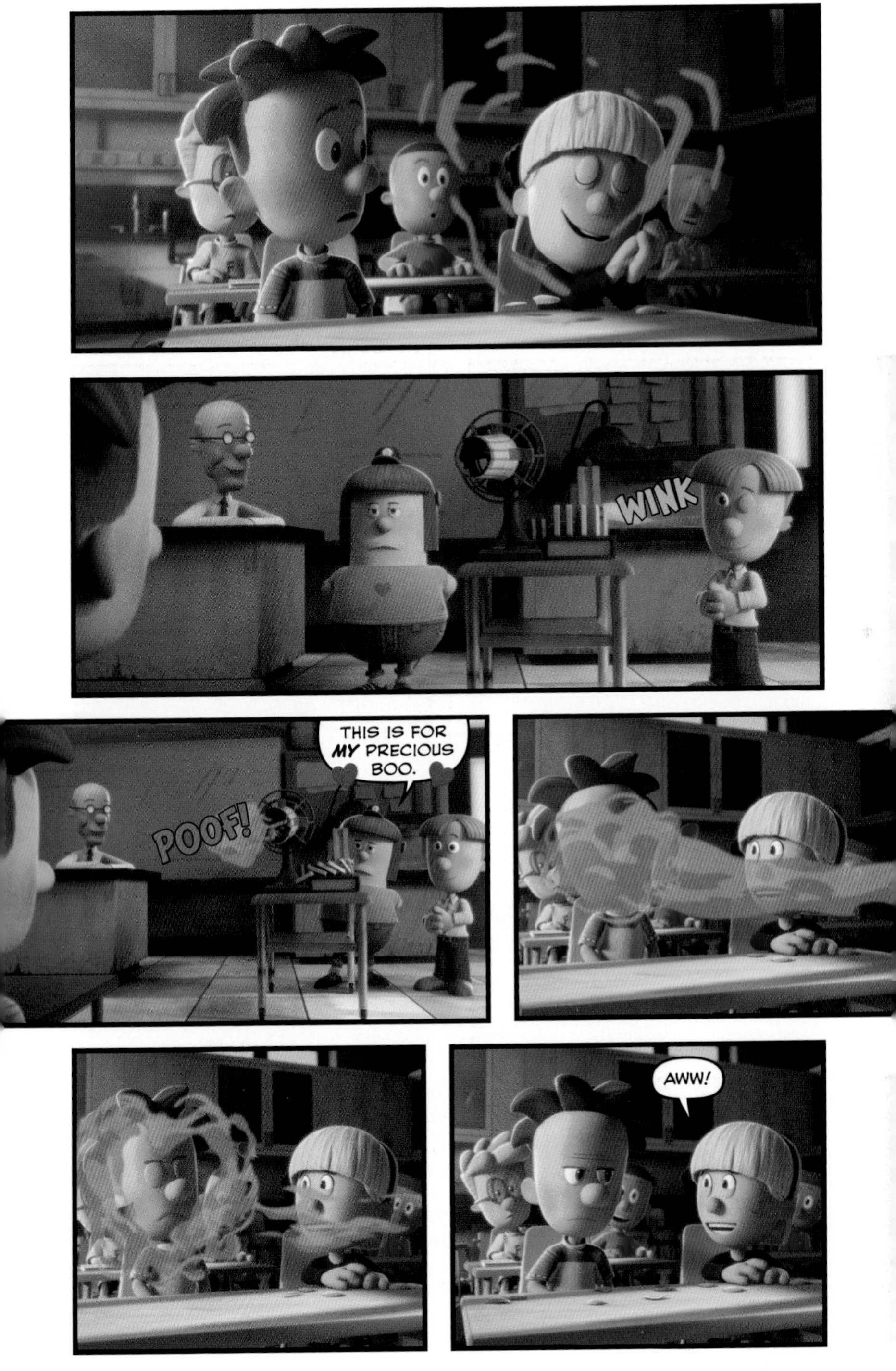
WINK
THIS IS FOR MY PRECIOUS BOO.
POOF!
AWW!

SHOW CREDITS

Complete Your *Big Nate* Collection